The Last Pier

Published by Hesperus Nova
Hesperus Press Limited
28 Mortimer Street, London W1W 7RD
www.hesperuspress.com

Copyright © Roma Tearne, 2015
First published by Hesperus Press Limited, 2015

Typeset by Sarah Newitt
Printed and bound by CPI Group (UK) Ltd, Croydon, CR0 4YY

ISBN: 978-1-84391-564-5

The Last Pier

Roma Tearne

Barrie

Nothing sorts out memories from ordinary moments.
Later on they claim remembrance when they show their scars.

La Jetée, by Chris Marker

'I have torn off the whole of May and June,' said Susan, 'and twenty days of July. I have torn them off and screwed them up so that they no longer exist, save as a weight in my side.'

The Waves, by Virginia Woolf

I

MONDAY AUGUST 14th 1939. It began in silence.

'Cecily!'

By midday the fields were stalked by a ferocious heat.

'Cecily!'

Silence.

'Oh for goodness' sake, C. Hurry up!'

Cecily Maudsley, rising with a start, threw off her bedclothes and flung open the bedroom door. Her mother Agnes stood waiting at the foot of the stairs with a box of strawberries and an exasperated expression on her upturned face as if she had been calling for an eternity. Behind her through the open door was the tunnelling green light of high summer.

How deep the summer had bitten into the land that last August, how cruelly it had burnt into earth and grass and air. What had started out as a pastel and water-faded spring became unexpectedly a splintering, shimmering thing. All it took was a spark to cause the fire. Why had no one noticed?

Their clothes became thinner and more transparent, their legs browner. Their mother Agnes, long hair swept up, slender neck in view, was worked off her feet. There was always so much work to be done in the orchard for every-thing seemed to ripen at once. Blackcurrants, raspberries, damsons and plums, all needing picking, not forgetting the season's first eating apples, the Scarlet Pimpernel. Their father Selwyn was kept busy in the top field or in the cowshed or mending the tractor. While Rose washed her dazzling blonde hair again and again or listened all day to the wireless playing jazz.

'Dancing's what's done it,' Aunt Kitty had declared, referring to a tear in Rose's stockings.

Disapproval was the constant ball Aunt Kitty used to bounce, hoping someone would bounce it back to her. But Agnes was far too busy getting ready for the tennis party and the harvest to bother.

And besides, Rose was *born* to dance.

Cecily and Rose were *still* sharing a bedroom because it was a good thing for sisters to do. But how cross it made Rose; and Cecily too for that matter.

The white dust-heat, thick with the scent of hay, hung in the air. And the flute-like sound of the kingfisher rushed across the land day after day with the regularity of a train.

Cecily hadn't been quite fourteen. Her sister Rose, not quite seventeen.

A band had played on the bandstand in Bly, its brass instruments flashing in the sunlight and what breeze there was sent the music all the way across the fields.

But although the war appeared stunted, it was growing like a beanstalk somewhere out of sight.

It had been the summer when Cecily discovered she had grown two small hard bumps on her chest like mosquito bites.

'Titties,' Rose informed her. 'Bet they itch!'

When Cecily asked her if they would become breasts Rose's reply was unsatisfactory.

'You'll just have to wait and see,' was all she said.

'How long?'

There was no answer.

Rose had nipples coloured like the inside of a bird's mouth, soft-pink and secret. Cecily couldn't help staring at them every time Rose stepped out of her nightdress.

So perhaps because of her own disappointing anatomy, Cecily began daily to search for other things. Pubic hair, for instance. She hoped to grow blonde tufts like Rose. But this too proved unsatisfactory. None appeared. Maybe I'm going to be like the freak-show lady, she decided.

'Please God,' she heard her sister whisper at night, 'let me get married and have sex.'

It's all right for her, Cecily thought, angrily watching her sister stroke the red pelt collar of an old coat with the same rhythm as a cat licking itself.

Meanwhile Selwyn could not stop the farmhands from singing

And when you get back to Old Blighty
And the war is over and done
Remember the poor Green Howard
Who was shot by an Eyetalian gun.

One by one those working on the land began signing up. But it only really hit them when Joe, their brother, came home one evening with his own announcement.

'Signing up before he needs to,' Agnes cried.

'He'll be fine,' Selwyn told her. 'You'll see.'

'He's just a boy. How can we let him go?'

'Thousands will be going,' Selwyn said. 'If it happens.'

He sounded odd, both sad and triumphant at the same time.

Joe began to get ready for that day, just in case.

'He'll turn strange,' Rose said, with satisfaction.

'What d'you mean?'

Startled out of other preoccupations, Cecily waited. Her sister didn't often talk to her. The three years' difference in their ages was the difference of foreign countries. Rose seemed to live in France, or wanted to. Cecily's life was in Palmyra Farm. Although it never stopped her trying, she doubted she would ever get to France. Not at the same time as Rose. Maybe never.

'He thinks he's special,' Rose said.

There was a hint of envy in her voice. A small box of invisible desire stood on Rose's bedside table. Cecily saw all sorts of unidentified jewels inside.

'Do you want to go, too?' she asked, feeling like a magpie, lifting the invisible lid with one finger.

'Of course not! I don't want to fight the Germans.'

Her sister's eyes were ablaze with lies as she prised Cecily's fingers off the lid and closed the box firmly.

'But I don't want to spend my life in this ghastly place, either.'

Selwyn was too old to go to war and would help the Government in other ways.

'What sort of ways?' asked Cecily.

Selwyn shook his head, smiling.

'Careless questions cause trouble,' he said closing his face like a cupboard door.

And then he disappeared up to London for an interview. When he returned he told his family he would be setting up the Air Raid Precautions in the town and their mother would have to take care of the milking as well as everything else she already did. Soon he was going to the ARP meetings twice a week, returning grim-faced and smelling of beer.

It was as if a secret game had started. Going To War, Cecily realised was like Going To School or Going To The Doctor. Something that was better done without too much fuss. The news on the wireless was boring. And rationing meant that everyone would have to write down everything they ate in a book. Which was also boring.

Except when her mother cried, Cecily was determined to close her ears to war-talk.

'Don't worry,' said bubbly Aunty Kitty with a giggle in her voice. 'Everything can wait, at least until after the harvest, when all is safely gathered in.'

Aunty Kitty lived most of the time in London in the smart flat she bought after her heart had been broken. But every so often, overcome by restlessness, she would take up residence at Palmyra House, bringing her stylish alligator purse that had a mirror and a red lipstick inside it. Cecily knew that Rose would have liked just such an object so, to annoy her, she would sing the old nursery rhyme.

'Dead said the doctor, dead said the nurse!' sang Cecily, making Rose scowl and annoying their mother at the same time.

Selwyn wouldn't take sides.

Meanwhile the land lay under a hazy golden silence. The river Ore with its lovely old pollarded willows still threaded its way behind the farm. The great elder bush still dropped its broad creamy flowers in profusion on the path between the farm and the fields. And beyond the deep-hedged footpaths, hidden behind a dip, there remained the faint blue mark that was the sea. Talk of war was just silly when you saw how wonderful the countryside looked.

Yes, that summer, when their world began shrinking the days were beautiful like Cecily's absurdly beautiful sister. Death watched them from amongst the froth of cow parsley, a panther with a saucy, sleepy look. While on a moonless night Bellamy stood on the soft grass of the roadside and waited, too. When he moved, his footsteps were so quiet that at times they eluded even the small animals waiting, listening tensely for any secret noise.

Bellamy walked like a black ghost through the shadows of the uncut fields, past the outhouses of Palmyra Farm until he reached the oak trees. Moving instinctively and rapidly into the deepest point of the darkness, soundlessly unrolling the nets, pegging them down by the mere pressure of his thumbs, he would, with one swift movement, set the ferrets free.

A vague whitish blur appeared and their bodies vanished into the earth. There followed a curious silence during which Bellamy crouched like a sprinter. A moment later there was a sudden madness of scuttling in the net as the first rabbit struggled wildly to escape.

He silenced it by seizing it in his hands, breaking its neck and striking the skull lightly. The rabbit gave a single great convulsion of pain and was dead.

It was as easy as throwing a ball. As always Bellamy felt a curious wave of lust and triumph as another rabbit began a wild struggle in the net.

Twenty minutes later he was unhooking the net pegs and folding it up across his shoulder, listening, his nerves taut, his hands sticky with rabbit blood. He walked on, following the distant surge of wind coming off the river. Then turning, slipping the ferrets into the tail pocket of his coat, he headed for the local public house, his work finished for the night. His father, the man they called Tinker, would get him a good price for his catch.

School of course had closed its doors for the long holiday in July. When they were opened again it would all be over.

'You only have one year left,' Cecily reminded Rose. 'Lucky!'

But Rose did nothing to avoid a confrontation.

'I want to leave *now*,' she told their mother. 'Why can't I? Indian girls get married at thirteen and have babies.'

'Perish the thought,' their mother said.

Cecily knew, she just *knew*, there was a connection between babies and sex.

'Every day the war is postponed,' Selwyn told them at supper, 'is good for building our defences.'

He helped himself to more rabbit pie.

The army let Joe come home for Rose's funeral that September. The war had not got going and Compassionate Leave were words Cecily would hear on several occasions without knowing their meaning. She heard other words too, used over and over again, but Compassionate Leave was what she remembered. There were officials in the church. Looking very sinister, they sat with the reporters in the congregation. There were lots of beautiful things in the church that day too. A jackdaw had dropped a piece of tin on a pew and a man stood holding a bunch of seven flowers.

'All Things Bright And Beautiful,' sang the man, trilby hat in hand. 'All creatures great and small.'

It was Rose's favourite hymn. Next, Cecily, getting the words muddled, sang 'Breath of Heaven'. And after that the vicar called Rose a 'Breath of Beauty', a young bud that hadn't opened. Not-yet-seventeen was on everyone's lips.

'Not given a chance to live, was she?' someone had cried, angrily.

Rose's coffin had already been slammed shut, closed, locked up. There was no point in keeping it open, no one would have recognised her.

'They had to fetch the dentist to identify her,' Cecily overheard Aunt Kitty telling someone.

Perhaps Rose had had a toothache when she died.

The undertaker's lilies were heavy with pollen.

'Tiger lilies are like turmeric,' an uncle she didn't know told Cecily, trying to sound friendly. 'They use it a lot in the East. Lovely colour!'

The uncle knew about the East, having served with the British army out there. Cecily ignored him.

'If you touch the stamens your fingers will stain,' the uncle added. 'And you'll look like the girls in India who draw patterns on their hands at weddings.'

'Horace!' said a great-aunt. 'This is *not* a wedding, in case you haven't noticed.'

The uncle tried to look repentant. He was going back out to India, shortly.

There were hundreds of candles in the church.

'Because,' the vicar said, 'this is the first sorrow that has come to our neighbourhood.'

Afterwards a man who came to the house, said, 'Never mind the neighbourhood, what about the Jews?'

'They are the cause of it all.'

'The Germans are the cause,' someone else said in a raised voice.

Someone said 'shush' and the guests turned like cattle all together and seemed to be staring in Cecily's direction. She stared back. This is my house, she thought. Rose is *my* sister.

But at the church everyone was still behaving well and Joe sang the loudest. He was very tall and important in his uniform, in amongst the crying women. He was the only one that Agnes would allow to put an arm around her, to comfort her. Selwyn, head bowed, jaw trembling with the effort of not crying, couldn't look at anyone. But then, suddenly, he did cry and Cecily found this a worse sight.

The two policemen sat close by, their eyes hard as marbles, their lips pinched.

Aunt Kitty pulled on Cecily's hand as though she was a pony trying to bolt. Agnes screamed once and the voices swelled like a flock of swallows trying and failing to hide her scream. The vicar closed his eyes while he sang, as if it were all too much for God. And the altar boys opened their throats like the swallows and sang, too. You could see the fillings inside their mouths. At that, everyone from the surrounding countryside and the other farms, everyone who knew the Maudsley family, held up their hymn books to shield their faces and sang with all their might. Cecily was certain they were thinking of something else entirely.

Overhead planes were scrambling from Minerhall. 'Work Is The Answer' was a phrase already being written deep inside Europe.

Rose's coffin was carried out by an uncle and her brother Joe, together with Partridge and the man called Robert Wilson. A neighbour held Agnes, helping her to walk down the aisle behind it. Bellamy had wanted to help carry the coffin but no one would let him. Which wasn't fair because he was Rose's true friend. So now Bellamy stood outside beating his head on a yew tree, ignored by everyone. The pallbearers held the coffin high above their shoulders and walked solemnly past him as if he didn't exist.

The word 'dead' tolled like a bell in Cecily's head. She looked around for her friends, Carlo and Franca and Anna Molinello.

She tried to see if Lucio or Mario were present in the church but they were nowhere in sight. And Tom, where was Tom? It was difficult to concentrate with Aunt Kitty holding her in a vice-like grip. Outside in the sunlight everything was still and watchful while in the distance and out of sight, the sea lay sedated.

Because she hadn't slept much, Cecily felt brittle-boned and unreal. She was wide awake and scratchy eyed. It wasn't often that she couldn't sleep. It wasn't often that her parents forgot to give her a goodnight kiss. It wasn't often that her father went off with the police to a government meeting and didn't come back for several nights. It wasn't often that Rose lay in a coffin. Wasn't Often was happening a lot lately.

Someone had placed sixteen red roses and a strand of honeysuckle on the coffin lid. The roses lay like a clot of blood from a wound. Someone else had put two cobra-headed, funeral lilies next to the puddle and the uncle from India was *staring* glazed-eyed at them.

When Aunt Kitty let go of her hand for a moment Cecily asked the man called Robert Wilson if they were his flowers but he started to shake and looked as if he might cry.

Cecily tried to imagine Rose-in-her-coffin dressed in the ivory dress covered in little pearls that looked like fishes' tears.

'I don't want to die a virgin,' she had told Franca, only a week before.

Cecily had overheard her. But *had* she died a virgin?

Rose-in-her-coffin laughing her head off at Cecily's questions as she always did, no longer cared. Staring hard, Cecily became aware of an area of darkness blacker than the hole in the ground.

'Ashes of Roses,' the vicar said, anointing the coffin with soil.

Covering up Rose, crushing her with the weight of his loud, too-solemn voice. Suddenly, Cecily hated the vicar.

'When my sister chose her engagement ring I told her opals would bring her bad luck one day,' Kitty said, moving her head in the direction of Agnes. 'But she didn't listen.'

But-she-didn't-listen whispered the breeze while overhead in the too-bright light, planes continued to mark the sky. Cecily wished she could close her eyes but they refused to shut.

Look, Rose whispered, pointing at the planes and making Cecily jump. Probably Robert Wilson is in one of them!

'No, Rose!' Cecily told her loudly, so that everyone, even her devastated mother, turned and looked at her. 'He's *here* in the churchyard!'

'It's too late for tears now,' Aunt Kitty said, pulling at her hand as though it were a bridle.

Cecily turned back into a pony.

Obedient for once.

Obedient too late.

Late, in the mysterious way Rose had now become.

The Late Rose Maudsley who had never been late for anything in her life.

Late, even though she was right here with everyone.

Cecily wanted to shout at them all.

'Shutting the door after the horse has bolted,' Aunt Kitty sniffed.

Inside her coffin Rose laughed and laughed and ate an ice-cream cone with the teeth the dentist had identified. The ice cream came from Mario's ice-cream parlour in the town, which now doubled as a funeral parlour because its owner, Mario, had vanished.

Too much ice cream killed her. Too much of a good thing killed her. On Rose's tombstone it would soon say, *To Our Darling Honeysuckle Rose*. Rest In Peace.

(No mention of ice cream, then.)

'Let us pray for peacetime,' the vicar murmured in a low voice.

He made peacetime sound like teatime. There would of course be strawberry scones after the funeral. Aunt Kitty had been making them since the early morning.

Cecily was still on the bus when she noticed the fire. It appeared as a vivid streak reflected on the windowpane. A moment later the sky turned a violet-blue and there followed an enormous explosion. Sparks flew upwards like gunshots. The bus turned directly onto the coast road. Horrified, she saw the crowd. The women in their faded print dresses, the men, many of them in shirt-sleeves and braces, moving with quickening footsteps. The whole town had its face turned towards the blaze in a collective gesture of amazement.

Watch out! she wanted to cry. Oh be careful! Please!

The flames whipped by the sea breeze began to billow high against the night sky and when another explosion occurred the crowd gasped. This one was an iridescent green.

The flames spoke to her in tongues from another age, sounding like a poisonous woman. Bitter, too, like a woman spurned.

She wanted to scream. But instead, bending low in her seat she stuffed her fingers into her mouth and crushed them hard between her teeth.

No, she wanted to shout. No! Please. Help me!

She felt she would faint.

Someone had once said it was the arsenic in the paint that produced the greenish colour. Cecily couldn't remember who; Aunt Kitty perhaps? No, not Aunt Kitty. Had they been talking about Dunkirk? No. They knew nothing of Dunkirk at the time. But after Dunkirk?

After Dunkirk there had been enough names to fill every side of the stone memorial, six, eight times over. Enough people to help forget one small death. You would have thought so anyway.

The bus was slowing down. Hers was the last stop, closest to the wild part of the sea marsh, furthest from the town centre, nearer to home.

'Goodnight,' the driver called but she didn't hear him.

A pinprick of light reflected in her eyes when she looked up. Like a bird it was, he thought, the way it glimmered. A moment later she was gone, and the light with her.

There were no other passengers.

'There isn't anywhere else to go,' muttered the driver.

Then he shrugged. This place had always attracted a certain type. The last he saw as he drove out of Bly in the direction of Eelburton, was Cecily's silhouette turned towards what the locals called the Last Pier.

There was no fire.

Now that she was standing on the grass verge she saw her mistake and shook her head, puzzled. So had she imagined it?

As she found the footpath the scent of late-flowering limes, exquisite and unexpected, confused her.

At the top of the path she stopped to get her breath back. The river curved to her right and she saw with surprise it had shrunk to a trickle, no bigger than a stream. There was a noise in her head like the scratching of a gramophone needle at the end of a record. Speak Rose. Speak!

'Sweet sixteen and never been kissed,' the boys used to say of Rose.

Only Cecily had known differently.

Somewhere here, she recalled vaguely, was the ford through which, when there were no adults in the car, Partridge their gardener used to drive the old Lancia with a fine splash dousing the windscreen and making her shriek.

She had been walking fast, running almost, until the sudden memory of Partridge's face, full of suppressed mischief, stopped her. The footpath further confused her and after that she lost her bearings. Many days of rain on the high coarse grass had made the path a marshy, muddy, yellow mess. The street light cast a dim glow across the ground and she heard, as through a fog, a curlew crying in pain.

Twenty-nine years after the war began.

And yes, she was home.

Bly was just a coastal backwater. It had no pier, only a promenade with a few broken amusement arcade machines and a street of shops. Most of the houses were clustered together facing the sea but they soon petered out into farmland and marshes. Having lived elsewhere for so long and only recently stepped off a plane from an exotic location Cecily was surprised at how small Bly was. Turning eastwards away from the town and crossing the causeway to the spit of land they used to call 'The Ness', she walked towards the beach. The rain stopped abruptly and twilight settled in the sulphurous sky. While the path that wound down to the sea was a shocked white, un-marked as a spilt bolt of bridal silk. Cecily hesitated. The Ness had always been cut off by the tides at certain times during each day. Walking on it could be dangerous.

But when she reached the water's edge, the sand was cool and the tide had clearly just left it. In the half-light she saw a flat, beaten world of shingle and broken shells. Ahead lay a darkly transparent sea and a sky filling up with fistfuls of stars.

Why had she imagined there had been a fire?

Turning, she retraced her steps back across the Ness following the smell of oilskins and rotting fish. She wasn't looking for the pier but as she approached the creek she saw it. And there on the waterline, a boat floated. Once long ago Cecily's older sister Rose, wearing a forget-me-not dress, had rowed across here at high tide on just such a boat.

Could it really be twenty-nine years and three days since Cecily had last walked this way?

Night hadn't quite fallen. As she regained the footpath and headed for the house she felt a sharp stab of memory. She saw herself, small suitcase, handle wobbling and with a voice trying not to cry, being marched firmly towards the station.

'I don't want to go.'

Then as now, only silence answered her.

'When can I come back?'

Still there had been no answer.

And it was then she had added, with something of the spirit of her sister Rose, something of the unresolved anger that had existed in Rose, 'I *hate* Aunt Kitty!'

But her mother Agnes Maudsley, holding her elbow with the same firmness as the line of her mouth, said nothing. And it had been this terrible look that had propelled Cecily onto the train on that day.

Twenty-nine years, three days and twelve hours ago.

The farmhouse, when she finally reached it, was not quite as she remembered although at the edge of the horizon to her left, she saw the woods were still there, stretched in a sash of fading blue. Almost instantly she saw that it was now dwarfed by the garden, which had gone on living, like a fingernail on a corpse while the house itself had almost disappeared under it. In the clarity of the twilight the shadow of the walnut tree darkened the ground. The sight of the tree reined Cecily in, pulling her back into watchfulness. She had dreamt about her return for so long, thinking she would recognise its every look. Now she saw this was not so and the beloved place she had believed so familiar was withholding essential things.

Opening the front gate she stopped. The house had shrunk or she had grown. Neglect had altered them both. She stood as though checking the place against a photograph.

The field-gate at the end where the lane began.

The cornerstone of the door where they had stood, all together.

Stilled on the threshold of the war.

Agnes and Kitty. Joe and Rose.

And Selwyn, of course. Her *family*!

Together again as though it were yesterday.

Six hundred years ago the house had begun its life as a farmhouse. Succeeding generations of occupants had added bits to it so that it was a jumble of gables and windows, with odd-shaped rooms, some no larger than walk-in cupboards. Now of course there was no farm; that was long gone. And the house had the air of existing in some other era. The front veranda was bare and the honeysuckle climber had been cut down. A cat flashed across the driveway and into the unkempt rhododendron bushes, its sprint reminding Cecily of the secretive behaviour of Rose's friend Bellamy. His sudden entrances and exits, the many parts he used to play. Aside from this small sign of life, nothing stirred. But the key was left by the agent under the flowerpot by the front door as promised. And the name, Palmyra House, was still nailed to the gate. Cecily stared at it. She felt colder than moonlight.

Palmyra, she murmured.

Palmyra; a distant country, blown away across the sands of time.

Returning to her at last.

The words of a song sung long ago,

a lighted window through which her childhood had fled,

a hand caressing her,

a kiss.

Why had she come back?

Her Aunt Kitty was no longer alive. After the war, when Cecily's mother Agnes had died, Aunt Kitty hadn't wanted anything more to do with Cecily. Her duty, she had said, had been done. And the Tragedy, buried for years under layers of mysterious things, became Cecily's responsibility, alone.

As she opened the front door on this August night, Cecily remembered certain things but not others. The ghost of her father Selwyn came out of the gloom, making her jump.

'Strawberry blonde!' his voice boomed.

'Oh Selwyn Maudsley!' Aunt Kitty had laughed.

There had been a field of strawberries on their fruit farm,

Cecily remembered. But as much as she searched, she never found a blonde one.

'Real life,' her mother Agnes had remarked, 'is persistently disappointing.'

Real life, then, was like a field of red strawberries.

This conversation had occurred just before war was declared. They had not really expected the war but after it was declared Cecily associated the moment with that field.

Other fragments of her childhood broke away from their anchor and floated effortlessly towards her. In the sullen light of her imagination she saw Bellamy, face closed and scowling, as he held the long grey prawn that he usually kept tucked in his trousers but was now sharing with Rose. She had wanted to ask Rose why it had got bigger and bigger but instinct had kept her silent. Rose would have been furious with her for spying on them.

Walking into the room they called the parlour, Cecily stopped. The silence that lived within it stirred and crawled under the door and the moth in her heart spread its wings. The room smelt just as before. Like an abandoned relic or a Christmas gift of crystallised fruit. Cecily gasped. Was that her brother Joe she was hearing? Whistling outside the window?

Ten bob a week, bugger all to eat, great big boots and blisters on your feet.

Another memory sprang out to startle her. It was Rose! In one of her bad moods of course, head bent, darning a stocking, swearing and sucking her finger.

A drop of blood spreading like an evil spell on her frock. Rose swore again.

'I'll tell,' Cecily had threatened.

'Tell then!'

'I shall. Unless you give me a penny!'

'What a joke, you outrageous child!'

And then Rose's laugh fading as suddenly as it began.

2.

AFTER THE FUNERAL was over, Selwyn and the policemen went away together in a car. There were two other men in the convoy of police cars. One of them was Robert Wilson in his trilby. He wouldn't look at Cecily even though she had tried to say hello.

People called him by another name. It sounded like Finch.

The police had been to Palmyra Farm several times earlier that week and one of them had talked to Cecily in a voice that couldn't make up its mind whether to be angry or sad. His voice had made Aunt Kitty very angry.

'Did you hear him?' she had shouted afterwards, glaring at Cecily. 'Anybody would think they felt sorry for the little wretch.'

'What is the point of shouting at her?' Cecily's mother had asked. '*She's* not the one to blame.'

'She might have kept her mouth shut!' Aunt Kitty snarled.

Cecily had heard the policeman tell her mother there would be no bail.

After Selwyn had gone Agnes cried harder. So, tactful for once, Cecily didn't ask why he needed to have a government meeting when they had just buried Rose. A small, invisible suitcase that no one knew existed as yet waited in Cecily's bedroom. Afterwards she would go to live with her Aunty Kitty.

But first, people had to stand around for ages eating cucumber sandwiches. It struck Cecily as funny that this gathering was called Awake when she herself felt as though she was dreaming. A girl from the village pub handed out plates. Normally Cecily's mother would have asked Cecily to be helpful but today wasn't normally, so Cecily was banished to the kitchen instead. To help Cook and the girl from the pub cut ham-into-thin-slices. The cook was slurring her speech. Ham-cut-into-thin-slices were what Cook was concentrating on.

No one talked about Rose. The absence of war was what they talked about. You would think it was the War that had died, the way they went on blaming it. The War, it seemed, was late like Cecily's sister.

Two children whom she knew by sight came up to the kitchen door and stared at her and the Eavesdropper became Eavesdropped-on, the Spy the Spied-on.

'There she is! That's her. She was talking to *herself* in the church!'

'The one who –'

'Shhh!'

The War's to blame, thought Cecily. Not me. And she went on cutting ham-into-thin-slices.

'That's enough, Cecily,' Cook said in her stern-slurry voice.

Cook had been crying for days.

'It's a great big machine,' Cecily heard someone else say. 'A killing machine for people.'

'Poor little mite,' Cook said to no one in particular. 'It were just a game that went wrong.'

'Pretty stupid game, eh?'

'They meant no harm and anyway it was the boy that started it!'

'And 'im that finished it. Don't forget the real culprit!'

Cecily heard that the boat Rose had used to row towards the Last Pier had probably sunk.

And still there was no Tom.

Or Carlo, or even Franca.

Only Bellamy, standing in the kitchen garden, by the black iron water pump scowling and refusing to come near the house. Cook took him out a cup of tea but he pushed her hand so the tea flew all over her and the cup smashed to the ground. The guests who were Awake stopped talking and looked outside.

'Land's sake!' Cook said and she started to cry, again. 'I can't be doing with you.'

And now, twenty-nine years, three days, twelve hours later, standing in the room that had things-brushed-under-the-carpet, Cecily was back once more. A prodigal daughter returning to an empty home, with a suitcase full of smart clothes. With ringless fingers and a divorce certificate. Thin and officially middle-aged. At long last! The letter she had received years ago was in the suitcase, too. The handwriting was still readable, the content still unbelievable. The letter said that her father, Selwyn Maudsley, had passed away and that Cecily Maudsley, next of kin, was being notified. It expressed deep sympathy and some regret. After she had read it Cecily calmly put the letter back in its envelope. Her father had joined all the other late people in the world.

Standing in the room in the soft twilight, she felt the house had developed a sly, stubborn air. So many people had stored secrets in it over the years – letters, journals, farm accounts, locks of hair, shreds of silk, sentimental rubbish of all sorts – that she felt certain some further revelations from that terrible day could leap out at her. Anything was possible.

A clock ticked.

She opened a window, let out a bee and saw the myrtle bush, grown from the cutting of some distant Maudsley bridal bouquet, still flourishing.

In the dining room a photograph hung damply over the mantelpiece like a holy picture in a disused chapel. She felt hand-cuffed to her childhood. So without turning on the electricity, she went upstairs hoping to unravel the golden questions that needed answering. The banister was wet. She could smell the dampness everywhere. It seemed to rise and follow her like an army of skeletons.

And because the moonlight flooded the house she failed to notice the silent figure moving with the wind across the road in full view of the window.

Upstairs her sister's bed lay phosphorescent in the stillness. The room itself was heavy with sleep; a place kept just so, for a dead child who was never coming back. It was tidily made up, forever. Rose's dresses, boxed up in the wardrobe, beautifully darned. Her name on a piece of paper pinned to one of them. The pin was rusty, the pierced paper discoloured. A loving hand had written the date on it.

Someone, somewhere in the centre of the town let off a firework, followed by another. One big bang followed by two others. One bright fountain of sherbet-coloured flowers followed by another rain of light. While all over Suffolk August funfairs were in full swing. The war had been dead for twenty-three years. Rose some time longer.

A week after Rose's funeral Joe went off to fight for England and a band played loudly in Cecily's head as he gave her a hug. Happy and Glorious, played the band.

'It's not your fault,' Joe said.

His words were light. As if he didn't want to acknowledge the weight they carried. Cecily looked at him. She badly wanted to ask him where Franca was but his eyes were so sad that she didn't dare. There was as yet no protective membrane stretched across her emotions, which Joe might, had he looked closely, seen. But that day Joe was in a hurry to catch his train and, giving his youngest sister a last hug, headed for the town of Bly instead. The band in Cecily's head carried on playing as she watched him go. It would still be playing long after she stopped crying.

'So you cry when your brother leaves but not when your sister dies,' someone, she couldn't remember who it was, said.

Cecily's mother had looked up angrily.

'There's no rule,' Agnes said sharply, 'to say when you should and shouldn't cry. Leave her alone!'

No one answered back. Cecily went up to her bedroom. She wanted her roommate back out of the ground but all she got was herself staring at herself in the mirror. White face, black hair. The same Cecily, nothing changed. She vomited. Then she picked up the silver-backed hairbrush and flung it at her reflection. This was the girl who had killed her sister Rose. Not Cecily. The mirror cracked from side to side. A trickle of blood coursed down Cecily's leg. The curse had come upon her at long last. She wanted to wreck the room but she did not, preferring to wreck the space in her head instead.

Good girl, said an approving voice she had never heard before.

Her mother coming in just then saw the trickle of blood running down Cecily's leg and went to fetch a towel.

Wicked, wicked child, said the voice.

Cecily's mother busied herself with this New Development, tears all gone for the moment. Concentrating hard.

'It's the shock,' Agnes said answering a question Cecily wasn't interested in asking.

However, soon after, Cecily felt a weakness had begun to follow Agnes around like a stray dog sniffing at her ankles. A weakness that would force Cecily's distraught mother to buckle under the weight of public dislike of her entire family. Cecily listened carefully to every word that was being said.

'What possessed her to play such a foolish game?'

'That child has always had a strange kind of imagination!'

'The truth would have come to light anyway.'

'Yes, but she set the ball rolling, didn't she?'

'She can't stay here, Agnes, are you mad?'

'She should leave for her own sake, you *all* should.'

'Agnes, you can't cope with the child. Not now! Not after such a great loss. And this latest disgrace.'

So that, perhaps in a desire to satisfy the world in some way with a public gesture, Agnes agreed; Cecily ought to go. But before she let her daughter leave Palmyra House Agnes consulted an expert on child behaviour.

All the man had were a few rumours and no real understanding of what had happened.

'Send her away to repent,' he said and Agnes, frowning,
asked him why he used the word repent.

'So that God will forgive her,' the doctor told her.

He was a Baptist lay preacher on the quiet, doing two jobs,
multi-tasking badly.

'She was far too old to be playing that sort of game,' he
said firmly. 'There's something evil about such an imagination.'

'Evil?'

'Yes, evil. An innocent girl died, didn't she?'

Cecily's mother hesitated. She was too confused, too upset.
Her world had been turned upside down. She made her decision on the advice given. Wondering, through a haze of grief
and betrayal, if she were making another mistake. But perhaps
Cecily *would* be better off away from Bly. For a while?

Out in the countryside the war, phoney though it was, kept
everyone busy. The wireless was full of unimaginable news:
dark fragments drifting through the September air.

After severe bombing and shelling Warsaw has been forced
too capitulate. It is the first epic event of the war.

Meanwhile overhead the planes were testing out a loose forma-
tion. Practice runs, the papers called it. The noise climbed
higher and then vanished above the barrage balloons.

'Just listen to our boys!'

'Prepared to sacrifice their lives for us.'

Ten thousand ready to die with more to come. Very soon.

'All right,' Aunt Kitty said grimly. 'It's my turn, I can see.
I'll take the little wretch. She's been nothing but a nuisance
since she was born!'

Aunt Kitty too would do her duty.

On the day Cecily was due to leave the heavens opened. She awoke to find a pair of voices locked in the room inside her head. They had arrived too late for Rose's funeral, they told her.

'I'm sorry I ignored you,' Cecily told them.

The voices grunted. They were here to stay, they said. And they demanded Cecily give them some sort of brief to follow. Cecily was still sleepy and confused, all she could think of was breakfast.

'Do whatever you like,' she told them.

'Good!' Agnes said, hearing her voice and coming in. 'Now that you're awake, can you help me pack your suitcase?'

Agnes spoke as if there were concrete slabs strapped to her chest. The voices in Cecily's head were clamouring for names. How about Coming and Going, thought Cecily, not really caring. And she smiled, startling her mother with the beauty of her violet eyes.

Agnes opened the suitcase. She began to pack up a childhood that was fast disappearing into the past.

'Come on, C,' she said. 'Help me. It won't hurt to go away for a bit.'

Cecily said nothing. There was something stuck in her throat.

'All this wretched gossip about what's happened,' her mother said. 'And what you did. Let it die down.'

Like the fire, thought Cecily.

'You can come back soon enough. After it's forgotten... after the war. Perhaps.'

Cecily was silent.

'It's for the best, you know. You'll get talked about unfairly at school. Best to start again. And you've always liked Aunt Kitty, haven't you?' her mother pleaded. 'Good to get to know her a little?'

Together the two of them packed some clothes for the winter.

'You'll be back in the spring,' her mother said turning her lovely, gentle face up towards Cecily's closed one. 'No point taking too many things.'

Cecily nodded.

They packed her notebook.

'You can write a story about the things you see, C.'

They packed a book of prayers.

'Don't forget to say them,' her mother said.

She never told Cecily to ask for forgiveness, she gave her a hug instead. Cecily loved her mother with a look.

They packed some envelopes and two ballpoint pens (one leaked), a rubber and a map of England. Cecily wondered if she should rub out Suffolk. If it would be better if it didn't exist any more?

'Promise me you will write?' Agnes asked, her green eyes like fields under water. 'You are going to be a writer, remember.'

But there were things you couldn't do, like write to parts of yourself. How do you write to your arm, or your leg, for instance? Or your heart? And what could you tell your heart that it didn't already know?

'Anything. Nothing. Just write. Tell me you are well.'

Cecily nodded. Might she be told when her father was coming home? Agnes shook her head, ready to cry again. She looked like a thundery cloud.

Better not ask, one of the voices in Cecily's head advised.

Cecily shook her head.

'Why are you shaking your head?' her mother asked. 'Does it hurt?'

And it was then, in that moment, that the miracle happened and her mother did the thing Cecily had been waiting for, for days and days.

She *kissed* her.

A small knot in Cecily's heart loosened. She tried to ignore the wanting-to-cry feeling.

'Can I take my tin?' she asked when she could breathe again. Really what she wanted was Rose's butterfly brooch.

'Of course,' Agnes said too eagerly, and packed it.

Good, good, said the voices in unison.

Steal the brooch when she leaves the room, added one.

Wicked child, admonished the other.

It was to be this way for years. No one noticed that Cecily was never lonely. She was always juggling many conversations in her head. Her quietness was not because she was shy or frightened – it was the only way to let the voices have their say.

A long time afterwards, years and years later, when she had hacked at her hair, cropping it in a way that inadvertently showed off her extraordinarily fine collarbones and her delicate lobed ears, she had tried, in a half-hearted way, to get rid of the voices. But they refused to go, saying this was no way to treat old friends. Fair enough, thought Cecily, giving up. And after that she left them to their own devices.

It was the way Greg, the man she was to marry, found her. Talking out loud to a night garden. He fell in love with her abstracted air. She was twenty-two by then. Older than Rose had been when she died.

The war being over, Greg had decided to become a pacifist. Remembering her Aunt Kitty (she no longer lived with her) Cecily thought: shutting the door after the horse had bolted.

Brava! cried the voices in her head, speaking Italian for the first time in years. Startling Cecily with the sound of it, for she had not yet made acquaintance with her addiction to Italian.

Associating the word with Greg (foolish girl) she married him but then grew restless when they made love. Grew impatient when he placed one hand on her breast and looked into her eyes. His own were a watery grey like the Suffolk sea. They didn't look a bit Italian. Why should they when he was English? Which was another disappointment. When he kissed her, it was a weak, socialist-without-passion kiss.

Aspetta! said the twin voices, in a taunting kind of voice. *Sei inglese! Sei un cretino*!

They were right.

In that first autumn of their marriage, in that very first year itself, long before mad-about-her Greg could begin talking about babies, Cecily left. Silently. Packing the bag that Agnes had given her (she still had it) and buying a train ticket to the continent. Greg when he came home to the empty house was broken-hearted for only a moment before relief set in. He had always felt as though he was living with three women.

As she crossed over to Europe Cecily noticed the voices were silent with approval, smirking at the way they had tricked her into getting rid of Greg. Shocking!

But tonight, here in Palmyra House, staring at the twenty-nine-years-ago impossible-to-forget furniture, a little shabbier, a little darker, but mostly unchanged, memories spun like Catherine wheels around Cecily. Guilt played upon her like a pair of hands on a washboard. Shame was hiding in the cupboard under the stairs, listening out for her footsteps. The war had flowed past her like a strong dark river taking everyone she knew along with it. Outside the stranger who had followed her all the way to the front door stood silent as starlight, watching the lights go on. One by one.

While in the pub in Bly one man talked to another over a pint of Adnams.

'Did you see who's returned?'

'No. Who?'

'It's her, that one... Palmyra Farm. You remember what happened at the pier, don't you?'

One man in a pub talking to another could so easily be multiplied across the town in other places. The local chip shop for instance. Owned now by a locally born and bred family.

'Must be getting on... what's her name? I forget.'

Mrs Moore, wrapping fish in Union Jack paper (anything fresher was still swimming in the sea) thought she had seen her too.

'Cecily,' she said. 'That's who it is. I could tell her a mile away. Same walk!'

'Thin-muscled, like a bird!'

'Getting on a bit, I'd say.'

'Quite likely so. Spitting image of her sister Rose, she is, now.'

'Fuss, was there?'

'I'll say.'

'Perhaps that's why 'e's back too.'

'Robert Wilson?'

'No, not 'im. The other one!'

'Anything else I can get you?' Mrs Moore asked.

'I'll have another cod. Looks good.'

Mrs Moore nodded.

'Did you see what happened?'

'No. I were a child too. Not much older, you know. Than Cecily. We were at school together.'

'Friends was ye?'

'No, no. They were from the big house. Outside Bly. Different from us.'

'Ah!'

'But I heard about it all right. There was more fuss made over it than the war itself. Blamed her, some kids did. Said she knew the truth of it. Which I swear she didn't. Nice child, really. Dreamy, like. Head in a book. Too much imagination, some said. The other one, 'im's the one that led her on. I'll be blowed! Never liked 'im. Foreign 'e was.'

'Left Suffolk, did she?'

'Never came back to school. Sent away with you-know-who!'

'And now she's back. I wonder why?'

'Who knows? People can't keep running away forever. There comes a time when you have to face the past.'

'Makes me shiver. How much is that?'

'One pound twenty, thank you.'

'Always eavesdropping wasn't she?'

'Seem to remember she was. One pound twenty, did you say?'

'Thank you.'

'Thank you.'

'Thank you.'

And all the thank yous over, it was time to talk about the street party, Cecily's shadow receding a little.

Inside Palmyra House Cecily was busy making sense of a silver-backed hairbrush and a cracked mirror. She was looking at a pair of pyjamas that she had outgrown before that summer had ended. And she was opening a box that had been shut for years. The landscape of her childhood was back, crying out to her. The soft rustle of the sea entered the house unnoticed and filled her ears and this, too, reminded her of that time. It was as if she had been swimming for years. She felt exhausted. Everything would remain, she thought. And perhaps another two thousand years would pass swiftly.

You couldn't see the Ness from the window anymore. Large chestnut trees that had once been only saplings blocked the view. Some of the stars had escaped from their bell jar and were now scattered across the sky. The night had become balmy, the wind had dropped its anchor as the man standing in the shadows lit another cigarette. Glancing out Cecily saw but didn't recognise him. He was leaning on a stick and his hair was completely white. The voices living inside Cecily's head stirred and yawned like sleepy birds. It had been a long journey.

Why are you bringing us back here? they asked Cecily, sleepily. *Perché?*

In answer to these insistent questions, which would be ceaseless now, Cecily knew she would have to go back to the beginning. To the summer when she was not yet fourteen, and Rose still sixteen. The summer when the last and only pier burnt down, and the sea was the colour of Agnes' eyes, and Selwyn Maudsley wasn't happy for reasons known only to him and Agnes, and Kitty.

That's why I'm here, she informed the voices in her head. To remember. To set you free. To get that time out of my blood.

3

THIS WAS ALL very well, but recalling that summer, Cecily had the impression that its beginning had been hidden in seven sweet williams. She had brought a bunch of roses back with her now, being unable to bear the sight of sweet williams. As a welcome gift to the house, a thank you for having survived the neglect of years. Seven old-fashioned flowers, two families; gone in a flash.

Finding a vase, she filled it with water and the scent from that long-ago-time returned, instantly.

Tuesday August 15th 1939, and in London the evacuation was already under way. In the orchard at Palmyra Farm Cecily, sitting under an apple tree, closed her book. It was hot and the afternoon was filled with a tender, straw-coloured light. Cook had sent her there to pick some fruit but instead Cecily had spent the afternoon reading *A Girl of the Limberlost*. The love story had left her feeling drowsy and she was reluctant to break its spell by returning to the house. Guiltily, picking up her empty basket, she became aware of a rustling in the hedge.

'Cecci!'

'Carlo! What are you doing here?'

'Why do you look so glum? Have you been punished?'

Cecily blushed and tried to hide her book.

'Let me guess. You were being a bookworm again? Am I right?'

'Oh Carlo, you *are*!'

'So now Cook will scold you. Shall I come and defend you?'

Cecily smiled, uncertain. Was he serious?

'What are you doing here, Carlo?'

'I was looking for Rose. She told me to meet her in the top field but I couldn't find her.'

The book's afterglow, the heroine's triumphant love, faded slightly.

'You are a dreamer, Cecci,' Carlo was saying, smiling down at her.

The sun was full on Cecily's face but still she could see the way Carlo's eyes crinkled when he smiled.

'Tell Rose I was looking for her,' he said. 'And that I'll see you both tomorrow.'

And then he was gone, with a splash of cotton whites amongst the golden wheat and the trees. Glimpses of bare sunburnt arms, as he ran along the dusty dirt track, seen through the trees. Taking with him all the myriad, unresolved hues of the afternoon, shimmering into the distance.

Turning towards home, Cecily saw a beetle-black Bentley parked smartly in the lane. She walked on. Cornflowers dotted the ground. A heavy fragrance of vanilla from some hidden blossom filled the air. Her mother, in a jaunty polka dot dress covered by a blue apron, was talking to a man in a hat.

Agnes was holding a bunch of flowers and when she saw Cecily coming up she smiled.

It was not a true smile.

'This is my younger daughter,' Cecily heard her say.

The green of the flower stalks exactly matched Agnes' eyes. Tendrils of unruly dark hair escaping from her French pleat. From the way she spoke Cecily suspected she was lying about something. The man lifted his trilby and put his hand out in a friendly way. Under the jacket of his suit he was wearing a pink shirt.

'Hello Cecily,' he said.

'Hello.'

'Good book?'

'Yes, thank you.'

'Robert Wilson is working on the agricultural survey for East Anglia,' Agnes said. 'He's here to map all the farms across the county and to help plan farming efforts in case of a war.'

The man looked at Cecily and nodded solemnly.

'The ploughing-up campaign,' he said. 'Did you hear about it at school, Cecily? The government will give your parents £2 for every acre of unused land that's put to good use. Should there be a war, I mean.'

And then he handed her an enormous box of chocolates tied with a pink ribbon.

'For both you girls,' he said.

'Pinky,' Rose remarked later, when they were in their shared bedroom. 'Everything about him is Pink!'

Cecily giggled and Rose wrinkled her nose. Helping herself to two chocolates, she bit into one without smudging her lipstick.

'He's renting Eel cottage,' Cecily said.

Originally Eel cottage had been built for an eel-catcher who used to set traps in the river. These days there weren't many eels. Now the cottage was mostly empty, rented occasionally to travelling salesmen. It sat on the edge of the Maudsleys' land, behind the orchard, out of sight of the house and hidden behind some trees. It was possible to walk from here along a bridle path into the town of Bly, about two miles away, without being seen by anyone.

'But he has to go all the way into the town to park his big car near the Martello,' Cecily added.

Rose yawned.

'I wouldn't say no to a ride in his car,' she said.

'He's already taken Mummy,' Cecily informed her, liking the idea of calling the man Pinky.

Rose bit into another chocolate. The centre oozed, dark, bitter, and thick as the marshland mud in the creek.

'How d'you know?' she asked lazily. 'I shall have to have a closer look at this Captain Pinky!'

She was shaking with silent laughter and would not share the joke. Cecily stared at her. There was something exceptionally wild about Rose today, she felt. Their mother's hope, that sharing a bedroom together would draw her girls closer together, hadn't worked. Rose's life, like her side of the room, remained a mystery, with its posters of John Gielgud playing Hamlet, and its starlet mirror decorated with lights which Cecily was forbidden to use. *She* had to brush her hair in the bathroom mirror, instead.

Rose ate another chocolate. Afterwards her curiosity about Captain Pinky moved like a moth in search of a different flame and she forgot this conversation.

The following day was Wednesday and Cecily woke to find time stretched like an old sock. She wondered why she felt so happy. The sun fell on her eyelids making them almost transparent as, with a hasty coltish movement, she leapt out of bed. Her long dark hair was all over her face and she pushed it back impatiently. The room was empty. Fearing she might be missing something interesting, she crashed downstairs where an argument was in full swing.

'Plenty to do,' Cook was saying in a loud belligerent voice.

'Plenty to do!' Rose was replying, throwing Cook's annoyance back at her as though it were a dirty old dishcloth, laughter like liquid bursting out of her.

'What?' asked Cecily, rushing in, arms flailing.

'You girls can help,' Agnes told them both, firmly.

She was recounting the strawberry punnets.

'Rose can take twelve punnets to Molinello's.' Cook said.

'Can she?' asked Rose, looking around for herself.

The Molinello ice-cream parlour was in the centre of Bly.

'Rose,' Agnes said in warning.

She looked hot. Small beads of perspiration strung abacus-like across her forehead. There was so much to do before the dance. Traditionally this annual charity dance to help orphaned children in Suffolk was always held at Palmyra Farm. But although Agnes had inherited the event many years before when she had married into the Maudsley family, its occurrence still flustered her.

'Cecily can help, can't you darling?'

'Can we go to the beach afterwards?' Cecily asked, pushing her luck around the uneven kitchen floor.

'*If* you deliver the strawberries, first,' Agnes said.

From Palmyra Farm it was two miles as the crow flies to the town of Bly, slightly longer by bicycle on the unmetalled road that cut across the fields.

'There are just seventeen days left before the tennis party,' Agnes said, 'and the Molinellos are very busy. If you don't take the fruit over today there won't be time for them to make the ice cream.'

'Are they making water ices, too?' asked Cecily.

Aunt Kitty, down for one of her long weekends, filling a glass jug with clear water from the old brass tap, looked up and narrowed her eyes. Reflections from the sky crept into them. The walnut tree outside in the yard had hard, green nuts hanging off it. Kitty plunged the seven flowers lying on the kitchen table into the jug.

Cecily frowned. Hadn't she seen those flowers before?

Kitty wiped her hands on her apron and a shutter clicked in Cecily's head.

Click-click.

Slow speed,

hand-held,

depth of field, very deep.

Seven for a secret never to be told.

Cecily blinked, amassing memories. Why this moment and not another? Who could tell?

'Let's finish breakfast,' their mother said peering down into the moment with her. 'And then you girls can go.'

Real time returned to the room.

'Ginny said the fair's here,' Cecily told them, toying with the morning, dunking her voice in it. 'Ginny's going, can I?'

'No you can't,' Agnes declared, unaware of stoking the desire burning in her younger daughter. 'There'll be gipsies there.'

She carried a rack of toast into the dining room where Selwyn sat reading the paper and listening to the wireless. Cecily, following behind, digested her mother's words in silence. Her desperation to visit the fair, taking wings, flapped dangerously around the room. She knew Rose had been the night before, slipping out in the usual way, through the open window. But what had happened there, or even what time Rose returned home was knowledge to which Cecily had no access.

'You're not old enough,' Rose had said when pressed. 'They wouldn't let *you* into the Freak House.'

'But what's there?' she had begged.

'Freakish things.'

'Like *what*?'

Never had her sister's cruel indifference pierced Cecily's heart as it did just then and in the end she had been forced to get her information in the old-fashioned way. By listening to Rose talking to Bellamy.

It had been how she heard of the Headless Girl and the Torturer with the Hook. And the black roses that turned into a bird of prey.

Cecily, leaning as far as she dared out of the window, had heard of the bearded woman who used her toes to knit, and the dog with the bird's face and the bird with a human one.

In this way fairy tales had crossed her path faster than gipsy silver. Magic spells now darted like swallows invading her mind. Rose's laughter in the bushes, always a little strange, was lately so excited as to be only a shade removed from hysteria.

It was all too much.

Returning to the present she helped herself to another egg. Perhaps she would write a story about all of it, she thought.

Selwyn, buttering his toast, let honey drip off his spoon onto his plate. Watching the golden stream, half in a dream, Cecily smiled. Kitty too, seated opposite, smiled for no reason. Time stood still.

'I heard there was a man with a lobster claw for a hand who had sex with a five-legged cow,' Cecily said, forgetting where she was.

'What?'

Both Agnes and Rose spoke sharply in unison. Too late Cecily wished she'd been more careful.

The wireless was droning on.

In the event of war, the Registrar-General has announced, everyone in Britain will have their own National Registration number and an identity card.

'You talk like a baby,' sneered Rose.

'Where did you get your information from, C?' Selwyn asked, turning the volume down.

The news had finished.

'From one of the farmhands,' Cecily lied.

'Bellamy, of course!' Agnes said. 'Where else?'

Triumph was Aunt Kitty making a noise like a grasshopper. Selwyn just turned the wireless back up. The Home Service was now playing light music.

'We should send her to Summerfield in the autumn,' Agnes said. 'Before things…'

'Maybe,' Selwyn spoke too quickly.

There was another silence into which the wireless played Music While You Work.

'You shouldn't listen to such nonsense, Cecily,' Aunt Kitty said.

'I'd like to go to the fair, anyway,' Cecily told her, correctly interpreting her aunt was on her side.

Aunty Kitty didn't look at Cecily's mother but instead put her hand gently on Selwyn's newspaper forcing him to look at her.

'*We* should let her go,' she said.

A piece of jigsaw floated in the air above their heads and did a jig. If she could just catch it, Cecily thought, she might complete the puzzle.

When after breakfast they went upstairs to clean their teeth she heard Agnes shouting at the other two.

'See what you've done, you stupid child,' Rose scolded, narrowing her eyes, as she painted her toenails. 'You were eavesdropping *as usual* when I was talking to Bellamy. Go on. Admit it!'

Two can play at the same game, decided Cecily, watching her sister wrap herself in her red fox pelt. The fur smelled rank.

'Will you wear it to the tennis party?' she asked.

Rose ignored her. Hot air floated in through the window. One of the farmhands was whistling *Run Rabbit Run*. So, thought Cecily, going out again, tonight, are we?

She had seen the red asterisk in Rose's diary.

'If you say anything about me...' Rose said.

Cecily stuck her tongue out. A spider's web of threats hung between them. Then Rose snapped shut her jewellery box as if a snake lived in it. There was a pause. Both sisters glared at each other. Neither wanted to look away.

'I'm coming with you, tonight,' Cecily said.

'No you're not!'

'I am! Carlo said I could!'

'Carlo? What a joke, Carlo won't want to play with a baby!'

Outside the orchard shivered with bloom and the doorbell rang but no one answered it. While all around, mockingly, was the sweet reek of something unknowable approaching. They heard their mother's voice, very clearly.

'She's just like you,' Agnes said bitterly.

'There are more important things to worry about,' said Selwyn.

4.

BUT IN SPITE of the endless talk of war, the sky over Bly on this August Wednesday remained blue enough to patch a sailor's trousers.

The town had a beach that could be reached by a set of stone steps from its promenade. It had a main road, some shops, a school, a church, a railway station and most importantly of all, on Union Street, Molinello's Hokey-Pokey Ice-Cream Parlour.

On this fine morning, as the sea breeze ruffled the soft sand dunes, the summer fair remained asleep on the green close by, its coloured lights still switched off, its helter-skelter mats out of sight. Two jolly fishermen returning with the catch lifted their lobster pots from their boat and struggled up towards the fishmonger's shop where a querulous seagull wrestled with a fish head discarded in the gutter.

While back on Union Street Molinello's was just opening its ice-cream coloured doors. For this was the Golden Era for all things Italian. And very foreign it looked too, with a blue and white striped awning flapping jauntily as Lucio Molinello began setting out the tables on the pavements. He was a tall, painfully thin man in his late thirties with black hair greying at the temples. The horn-rimmed spectacles he wore added to his serious, slightly melancholy air.

Polishing a new carmine-red roll-top Morris eight, was his older, portly brother Mario, the actual owner of the ice-cream parlour. Mario was in a happy mood today, a ready smile creasing his face, making it look like a walnut. Together the brothers were the butt of jokes amongst the locals, privately being referred to as Laurel and Hardy.

The reason for Mario's exceptionally good mood was the Morris eight, sparkling in the sun, a present to himself from himself. To celebrate the opening of yet another ice-cream stall on the promenade.

'Come on for God's sake!' Lucio grumbled. 'Playtime is over, you puppy. Your customers are waiting.'

'Let them wait,' grinned Mario. 'Where else can they get what I give them?'

Sunlight washed the ground with a broad brush. Two customers, both of them regulars, stood at the stainless steel counter waiting for their *brosca*, a soft brioche filled with ice cream.

It was a quarter to eight in the morning, too early for the English who frequented the shop, too early for the children from the neighbouring villages. Only the Neapolitan members of the community, the secretaries from the Italian Social Club, came on the early train from Ipswich at this hour. Tradition was tradition. Not even the threat of war could break the desire for *brosca*.

The Hokey-Pokey was the oldest ice-cream parlour in Britain. It stood in a prime spot in the town centre, close to the memorial of the Great War and was a magnet for the many Italians living in the region. Customers came from as far away as Felixstowe docks, Lowestoft and even, in the summer months, Great Yarmouth. From June to September Mario Molinello's ice cream sold almost as fast as it was made.

At the entrance was a notice.

Gelato Artigianale di Produzione Propria (Ice cream hand-made by the proprietor)

Mario finished polishing his car and spat on it. Then he gave it one last furious rub and went inside, calling to his children. There were five of them.

'Giorgio, Luigi, Beppe, Franca, Carlo, *venite qui!*' he bellowed.

Two Italian farmworkers entering the shop laughed. Most people in the town of Bly could not tell any of the Molinello children apart.

There was a movement of the beaded curtain and Mario's wife Anna emerged.

'We are not in Italy now, Mario,' she said. 'There is no need to shout. You will not get instant *servizio* here!'

Mario grinned.

'Mama!' said Franca.

Franca was a younger, thinner, nineteen-year-old version of her dark-haired, buxom mother. Franca, precious only daughter in a family of boys, good-natured like her mother, soft-hearted like her father but still inclined to fight with her youngest brother.

'Can you tell that *cretino* Carlo to leave my box of chocolates alone? They were my present, not his.'

'You see,' Anna told her husband. 'You are the one who has taught them to shout. Your daughter does not behave like a lady!'

'Franca!' cried Mario, feigning anger. 'Please, *cara*, mind your voice *and* your language! What will the British think of us?'

He finished serving his customer who grinned and left. Everyone knew Mario could deny his daughter nothing.

'*Cara,*' Anna said, 'let's not make a fuss. Your father does not like his British customers to see real life going on in this place.'

'He gave them to me!' cried Franca.

'Who?' asked Beppe, the middle child, coming in to enjoy the quarrel.

'Her boyfriend, Joe Maudsley, you idiot,' said Giorgio the eldest. At twenty-two he was a larger version of his brother Luigi.

'What's the crisis, Papi? Is it war, already!'

'He's not my boyfriend,' shouted Franca.

'It wasn't Joe,' said Lucio coming in, unamused.

'What's going on?' Anna asked. 'Who is giving my daughter presents?'

'Robert Wilson,' said Lucio.

Everyone turned to look at Franca.

'He's the man from the Ministry,' Lucio told them. 'He's renting Eel cottage at Palmyra Farm.'

'Oh him!' Mario threw his hands up in the air, losing interest. 'He wanted to speak to me, too. The Government has decided to look for any unused land around here. But as we don't have any...' he shrugged.

'That's what you think,' Lucio said.

There was a small silence.

'I know about this,' Anna said. 'Agnes told me. She said this man wanted them to plough up the tennis court.'

'To get rid of it?'

Beppe was shocked.

'No!'

'Where will we play tennis, then?'

'There may be a war coming,' Lucio told them. 'If that happens there won't be time for tennis.'

Again the uneasy silence. Mario glanced at his younger brother.

'Rubbish,' he said. 'It won't come to that.'

But he sounded uncertain.

'It probably will,' Lucio said flatly.

He was cleaning out the freezer and didn't look at anyone.

'What has this got to do with a present being given to my daughter,' Anna asked, 'from a man we don't know?'

She spoke half-jokingly for her daughter's face had gone suddenly white.

'He was looking for Papi and Uncle Lucio. And he gave me the present. He's given one to Rose, too. I'm sorry, Mama.'

'In that case,' Anna said, smoothly, 'it's fine. But you must share it with the others. Now, get Carlo because I too have some news.'

'What?' asked Carlo coming in, hoping the trouble had blown over.

Carlo was not yet seventeen, the youngest of the Molinello children. He had the same thick curly hair, the same dark eyes and the same easy-going manner that characterised the whole family. When he saw his mother he smiled sweetly and Mario groaned. Carlo was Anna's favourite and, in Mario's opinion, over-indulged. But then, Carlo was everyone's favourite, capable of getting away with most things.

'Mama –' began Franca.

Anna held up her hand.

'Now listen to me, all of you. The Maudsleys are going to have a big tennis party at the end of this harvest. The charity dance will take place as usual afterwards and we, of course will all be there for that. But the tennis party is just for a few close friends because of the selling of the land. So,' she paused, 'because Agnes does everything on her own, as usual, I thought it would be a good idea if you boys could help with getting the court ready for the match? Franca too?'

Beppe guffawed.

'Of course, Franca too! If Joe is there, certainly.'

'Shut *up*.'

Everyone laughed good-naturedly. Carlo winked at his sister but she only scowled back.

Straightening up, holding a stainless steel basin of ice cream, Lucio glanced briefly at his sister-in-law.

'I can help too,' he said, his face no longer severe.

The Molinellos had moved to England in 1920. Their story was that of so many Italian families. Mario and Lucio were the sons of a poor farmer living in a village called Bratto deep in a lovely chestnut valley of northern Tuscany. Beautiful waterfalls, poor soil, harsh winters, landslides and storms. Not a bit like Suffolk. Not flat and delicate and full of fragile seabirds beside the North Sea.

Long ago their mother, sensing her elder son's restlessness, knew he would leave. The little hamlet surrounded by its peaceful green hills would never be enough for Mario. Life for him existed elsewhere. The town of Pontremoli, which to everyone else was a metropolis, with its grand old cinema and its town square, was too small, too provincial for Mario. Not knowing what to do, his mother went to ask the priest for advice. After that she killed their only calf. Then she visited her neighbour to enquire about their daughter, Anna Varoli. Anna was exactly the sort of girl her son needed.

It had been a September wedding with grapes ripening on the vine and an accordion duo playing *Santa Lucia*. Even though he disapproved of his elder brother's frivolous ways, the more serious-minded and recently married Lucio was persuaded to be best man.

Outside the church, through the old stone archway overflowing with tubs of geraniums, the land appeared green and beautiful. The mountains of Lunigiana touched by a slant of Mediterranean light were at their best and for a brief moment winter was impossible to imagine.

That evening the groom and his bride had danced under a moon that shone full and low in the sky. Shooting stars rained down their blessings while all across the valley came the sweet haunting echoes of owls, calling to one another.

It was a night of wonder and promise. The sort to be taken out and remembered during the years of migration ahead. For, as he danced cheek-to-cheek with his new wife, Mario Molinello was already making plans. Overnight he had become a man of means. His wife's family owned a mill for making chestnut flour. Anna was their only child, her dowry had been large, and while nothing would alter the beauty of the mountains, Mario knew, if they were ever to make a success of their lives, they would have to leave.

'England is the place for us,' he said.

'And children?'

'We can have dozens!' Mario boasted joyously. 'Let's start tonight!'

With growing shrewdness, Anna saw her new husband was a dreamer. It would be her job to make those dreams come true.

In England, she began first to produce children at a daring rate and then to raise them with a fierce love that astonished the people who became her friends. One day, Anna informed her husband, their large boisterous family would grow up and become capable of many things. Capable of helping in the family business, capable of conversing in two languages, capable of straddling two worlds as they themselves never could. Mario was a little taken aback by Anna's determination but in less than three years she had found a place to settle.

'Italy has arrived in Suffolk,' she announced, smiling and nodding at the neighbours while conversing with her husband in Italian. 'This is where we will open our ice-cream parlour!'

Mario hesitated. Somehow, without his realising it, his wife had become the custodian of their joint plans. He had wanted a vegetable shop, selling fresh produce.

'Ice cream?' he asked. 'The ice cream here is disgusting, full of disease.'

'Not *English* ice cream,' his wife shrieked. 'Are you insane?'

Then reining in her voice because they were walking outside with the *bambini*, she whispered, '*gelato Italiano, caro*!'

'Really?'

'*Certo!* The English will love it. And there will be no diseases.'

Mario knew when he was beaten.

In the beginning the people in the town of Bly were wary of these strangers who breathed garlic as dragons breathed fire. But Anna, amused by her husband's cautiousness, was undeterred.

She set to work and found some premises. Then, two weeks before their third son Beppe was born, she bought a stainless steel counter (the first ever seen in England) and a huge refrigerator from London.

And with that, Molinello's Hokey-Pokey Ice-Cream Parlour was launched on Bly.

Mario was delighted. Observing his wife juggle the baby and their two older children he realised he had totally misjudged the little peasant girl whom he had first met, wearing clogs, and making *testaroli* over a charcoal fire.

The neighbourhood watched with interest, too. Suffolk, grey-green and beautiful, that most secretive of counties, stamped with ancient loyalty to the Crown, was notoriously difficult for newcomers to penetrate. But the sign-writer, taking a liking to this eccentric family, offered to write 'Molinello and Son' over the door.

'We haven't finished working on the family,' Anna told him firmly.

'My wife wants a dozen kids,' joked Mario.

The sign-writer offered to add the 's' but Anna was superstitious.

'Thank you, but we're calling it the Hokey-Pokey Parlour for now,' was all she said.

Then, a few days after the shop was fitted out, on Assumption night, Anna had a dream. In her dream the Virgin handed her a lily.

'You will have four sons,' the Virgin said. 'And a daughter.'

The children would be healthy and full of energy. The Molinello business would thrive and the family would become well-respected members of the Italian community. The Virgin spoke softly, smiling at the sleeping woman.

'You will grow to love this country,' she predicted. 'It will be as your own.'

'And my husband?' Anna mumbled.

'Yes, he too. Everyone who meets him will love him.'

Anna nodded, eyes closed.

'You will be prosperous,' the Virgin said. 'All your children will be Suffolk born and bred.'

There was a pause.

'You will want for nothing.'

'But...?'

The apparition shook her head placing a finger on Anna's lips.

'Be happy in your time of plenty. Many do not have as much.'

'Well?' Mario asked his wife when he heard of the dream the next morning. 'Why don't you sound happy, then?'

Anna didn't know. She could not understand why it was, when she woke with the scent of lilies pressed against her skin, she had felt so unutterably desolate.

The Virgin had asked one thing, only. The Molinellos must build a shrine facing the sea. Then, telling Anna to prepare herself for her new life, the apparition had faded away, leaving behind a sense of warning in the air, a sadness that did not shift for some time. It lay like wet sand, heavy against Anna's heart. As an untouchable, unreachable feeling of loss. In a country that had not been Catholic for so many centuries there was no one except Mario to tell.

They built the shrine in time for Assumption Day of the following year and a statue of the Lady Of The Sea arrived from Bratto. Anna collected scallop shells on Bly's white beach and with her two-year-old son Beppe began a lifelong hobby of decorating her sea-temple.

In later years this night-blue grotto would become something of a local attraction that had an undeniable fey charm. Seen from the water and helped by the rumour that it had saved two fishermen from drowning, it extended a calming effect on boats coming in out of a storm. Local men, buying a cone of ice cream at the parlour would often leave a lighted candle by the feet of the statue.

By the time the older Molinello boys were teenagers, the Hokey-Pokey Parlour had become an affectionate symbol in the area, its openness and friendly foreignness a talking point. The ice cream itself was of the best quality and the fruit used came from the oldest fruit farm in the area.

Palmyra Farm, famous for its strawberries, damsons and raspberries and its orchard of old-fashioned apples, was where the raw ingredients came from. Because of this, over time, both families, the Maudsleys and the Molinellos, became firm friends and very soon there emerged the Palmyra Water Ice, the Palmyra ice-cream cake and the Palmyra County Sorbet made from sun-ripened, locally grown quinces.

Four more years passed and the Molinello family was complete at last with the longed for daughter Franca followed by a youngest son Carlo. Then quite by chance Mario was offered some empty premises.

'No more ice cream!' he declared.

And he opened a fish and chip shop instead. He had noticed other Italians in London and Edinburgh were beginning to do so and didn't want to miss a chance. Anna, her hands full with their growing family, didn't argue with him as, in a triumphant moment, he acquired the ultimate symbol of prosperity. A telephone. Now orders began flooding in, deliveries stepped up and the Molinellos were rushed off their feet. The time had come for Mario to invite his younger brother Lucio to take over the management of the shop.

Some years before, Lucio Molinello's wife had died in a boating accident. Afterwards Lucio had changed, becoming silent and uncommunicative. Their mother, desperate to help him, consulted the tarot-card reader but the news wasn't encouraging.

'He must stay away from water,' the tarot reader had said. 'And not be so interested in politics, either.'

Lucio when he heard this laughed, carelessly. Water did not worry him and now that his life was finished, politics was all that interested him. At that their mother wrote to Mario.

'Can't you find him *something* to do?' she asked.

'He won't listen to me,' Mario replied. 'He's always been stubborn.'

In the end it was Anna who went back to Italy to convince him of his duty to his brother and his nephews. So that, reluctantly, towards the end of 1937, Lucio packed his bags and joined the lengthy chain of migrating Italians arriving at Liverpool docks.

He had two conditions.

One that he would stay only three years, until the business was established.

And secondly, on no account would he mix with the customers.

For a while the two brothers seemed to get along peacefully. Lucio worked hard, kept himself to himself, going up to London often to meet with other like-minded Italians and eventually editing a small underground publication that fought against the rise of Fascism in Italy. The Molinellos left him to his own devices, hoping this passion was just a passing phase. What harm could it do in any case now that Lucio had left Italy? Unobserved, Lucio continued to go to Communist party meetings where, in the smoke-filled and excitable atmosphere of the back rooms of pubs, he and his compatriots worried about the rumours coming from Europe.

Then, at the beginning of 1939, Mario came home one evening having made an important decision.

'I am joining the Association of Cafe Proprietors,' he told Anna.

And he paused, waiting for the reaction.

'Why?' she asked, puzzled. 'Isn't there a rumour that all Italian social clubs in England have come under Fascist control?'

'It's not a good idea,' Lucio told him.

'Nonsense! We are not Fascists.'

'So why join, then?'

Mario groaned. His brother was full of his usual conspiracy theories which only upset Anna. He had known all along it would not be a good thing to bring Lucio into the bosom of the family.

'Oh don't listen to him,' he said. 'You know he's a Communist.'

'*Senti*, Mario, don't be a fool,' Lucio said. 'One day your fool-ishness will get you into trouble. Let's hope it doesn't drag your family with you.'

'Why don't you go back home,' bellowed Mario, suddenly angry. 'Go and fight Mussolini, all by yourself! We can manage fine without you.'

'Papi,' Carlo cried, dismayed.

'It's true,' Mario said. 'Your uncle just wants to frighten everyone. There is nothing wrong with me joining the Association.'

He glared at Lucio. No one spoke. For all his good nature Mario had occasional bouts of rage and was best left alone when they occurred.

'I can tell you one or two things,' Lucio said at last. 'About this country that you think is your home. About Mussolini's party, too. If you're interested...'

Anna looked from one to the other anxiously.

'Don't fight,' she told her husband.

Mario shook his head. His brother's obsessions, his wife's fears, these were long-term issues. He, Mario, was interested in the here and now of life. Carlo and Franca were at the Italian school in Ipswich. By joining the Association they would be protected from any future discrimination by the Italian government.

'It's the long-term issues that we need to worry about,' Lucio said.

But Mario would not budge.

'If we join the Party it will simplify *everything* for us,' he argued. 'We can renew our passports without problems and our taxes will be easier to organise.'

'Don't,' warned Lucio. 'I'm telling you!'

'Well, get used to it. I've already joined.'

'You'll regret it.'

'Listen,' Mario said, temper flaring again, 'why don't you give up that stupid newspaper of yours, huh? Then we'll talk.'

Recently it had come to light that Lucio was himself the editor of a left-wing journal called *il Lotto*.

Anna was looking anxiously at them both but Mario had made his decision. There was nothing more to say. And in this way, all unsuspecting, the last spring of the decade passed slowly into radiant summer.

5.

THAT AUGUST PEACE hung on a thread like an acrobat, about to perform its last spectacular act. The future stretched above the hush of sleeping babies, ready to uncoil into a handstand; boneless, nerveless, recklessly on the brink of a disaster of its own making. On the marshes waterbirds came and went regardless. The sun shone as if its life depended on it and the river snaked its thinner, leaner, meaner silvery length between the flat white dry meadows. Beyond it stretched a row of pin-thin black poplars. And down by the empty part of the shore small breezes continued to eat at the sea. No one could imagine the lights going out in England. Or blackout blinds or ration books, or bombs.

And a ban on ice cream was simply unthinkable.

It was easy for those in the know to keep quiet and carry on in last-minute hope.

Meanwhile at the Hokey-Pokey Ice-Cream Parlour on that August morning Anna Molinello waited for her boxes of strawberries. Hand delivered, handlebar-balanced and arriving with a dash of bare brown legs, summer frocks, and laughter.

'Off to see those *Eytie* boys, I'll be bound,' said Partridge with a wink as he helped pack the boxes into the girls' baskets.

Bellamy, loading up the milk cart, out of sight and out of mind for the moment, stopped what he was doing and clenched his fists. And unclenched them, before moving the horse on.

'What's an *Eytie* boy?' Cecily asked.

Partridge chuckled.

'Never you mind,' Rose said, with a squeak of bicycle brakes. 'Partridge don't be so rude. They're Italians!'

The sea when it came into view at the bottom of the bridle path had a hint of aquamarine in it.

'*Ragazze!*' cried Mario, hearing their voices from afar. 'Girls, pretty girls!'

He called his daughter out from the back. Sea-light entered through the open door fluttering against Franca's dress as she hugged Cecily with her big smile.

'Is Carlo here?' Cecily asked.

The Italian brothers (some of them) came out from behind the bead curtain.

'Cecci!' cried Carlo, joyously.

Then he saw Rose.

'We are coming to your tennis party,' he said, his grin changing to a grown-up smile. 'And of course the dance. Will you dance with me, *la bella Rosa*? If I give a lot of money to the charity!'

Everyone wants to dance with Rose, thought Cecily.

'Who invited you?' Franca asked, rudely.

'Rosa's mama did,' her brother smirked.

'And I did, too,' Cecily said, reading some signs but not the others.

She felt terribly sad. Just for a moment the sea-light became dull green and distorted while the day itself appeared covered by a film.

Rose was busy examining the iced flowers on a wedding cake, pretending not to hear. She was wearing the defiant look usually reserved for their father Selwyn.

'*Ecco! la bella Rosa*,' cried Giorgio, entering. 'We will make iced flowers for *your* wedding, too.'

Rose blushed. But remained silent.

When they got there the sea presented itself in a series of glittering white lines that seemed fixed against the strip of sand. The night breeze having done its homework had smoothed out the whole of the beach and the fair had begun to set up for the day. Lucio Molinello stood beside his stall watching the waves break against the old sea wall. Business was already brisk.

Rose and Franca walked together, secrets and arms linked. Excluding Cecily.

'Come on!' called Carlo, grinning at Cecily. 'Catch me if you can!'

And at that, as if by magic, the day became a carpet, with all summer rolled up inside it. Cecily didn't want to unroll it; she didn't want to see what patterns it would make just in case they'd fade too quickly.

The Punch and Judy man, full of punch-drunk smiles, was waving his arms at them. His red-and-white booth looked as though it might collapse in the wind. Cecily wanted to stop but Rose wasn't interested.

'I got told off,' Franca was saying. 'For accepting the chocolates from that man.'

'Which man?' asked Cecily, her eye on the ball, ears flapping in the high sea breeze.

'Pinky!' Rose cried, carelessly, tossing her laugh in the air, watching it bounce around the peacetime sky. 'Who cares about Pinky!'

And she did a little dance.

'Are we or are we not going for a swim?' shouted Carlo.

So that Cecily, bathing costume at the ready, young girl's slim hips emerging unnoticed, chased after him.

'Got you, you wriggly worm,' cried a triumphant Carlo, wind-whipped arms around her.

Lifting her off the ground, threatening to throw her into the sea, while the war, playing its own game of hide-and-seek, kept conveniently out of sight.

'Look, there's Daddy,' Cecily cried, pointing further up the beach, in the direction of the Ness.

But it couldn't be because Selwyn was at the farm digging up a piece of unused land.

'Will there be lots of people at the dance?' Franca asked.

Rose whispering secrets, for Franca's ears alone, laughed again and again.

'Joe will be there, certainly!' she said.

'Catch me if you can!' shouted Carlo, letting go of Cecily and plunging into the warm-at-last North Sea.

And Cecily, getting it wrong as usual, chased after him laughing, laughing, singing, 'Breath of Heaven'.

She would sing it again at the end of summer but on that occasion the sun would have a different bite to it.

When they got home the black cat had been killed by the milk truck and Agnes their mother was crying, again. When questioned she told Cecily she'd burnt her hand taking the bread out of the oven but there were no signs of a burn. No one was saying anything, not even Selwyn who told them he'd been mending the digger all day. Which was how Cecily knew he had had a row with their mother.

'Nonsense,' Rose said, darkly. 'There are other things besides a row that puts *that man* in a mood.'

'I'm going to an ARP meeting tonight, don't forget,' Selwyn announced. 'Don't wait up for me. I'll have a snack while I'm out.'

'In the pub he means,' muttered Rose.

Aunt Kitty, whose long-weekend-visit had turned into a longer holiday, was nowhere in sight and Joe came home looking serious but then went out again almost immediately.

There were many unanswered questions in Cecily's head. So, in order to sort them out she made a Things-About-The-War list in her head.

Will they drop bombs on us, if there is a war?

How many people will be killed?

Will the schools still remain closed after the summer is over?

Will all the boys go to war?

If so, from which railway station?

Why do the grown-ups ask you questions but never answer yours?

'There is a boy coming to stay with us in a few days,' Agnes said.

No one commented.

'His name is Tom,' Agnes added, speaking to the silence. 'He'll be here on Saturday and he's the son of an old friend of your father.'

Rose yawned rudely but it was Cecily who had the most to lose.

'I'm not sharing anything,' she muttered under her breath.

Rose laughed and Agnes sighed.

'Please don't be difficult Cecily.'

Their mother's voice sounded weak.

'I'm so tired,' Rose told the room with another fake yawn that didn't fool Cecily.

That night after supper Agnes got out the special notebook she kept for Mass Observation. She liked the idea that one day all the things she wrote down about her life would be part of the social history of the time. She had become a volunteer for the MO research organisation after lovely King Edward VIII had abdicated.

On the Home Service the news was that the German ambassador was willing to fly to Moscow in order to make a German-Russian settlement. But Cecily coming in was more interested in giving her mother a slow goodnight kiss, squeezing the delicate, chiselled face in her hands, trying and failing to make the deep dimple in her cheek appear. Her mother looked lonely. Why didn't their father stay at home more often?

Rose, like Selwyn, couldn't stay in for long, either.

'Are you going out *again*?' Cecily asked when they were alone.

'Shhh!' Rose said. 'Go to sleep.'

Instantly Cecily was more awake than she had ever been in her life. The disappointing day looked set to develop into an interesting night.

'Are you going into Bly?'

Rose didn't answer.

'Mummy's still awake,' Cecily said.

There was a pause.

'You're not... going to the Ness, by any chance?'

And when there was still no reply, 'It's very, very dangerous there when the tide's coming in.'

The Ness was a narrow sea-thistle spit of land bordered by a bend in the River Ore on one side, and the sea on the other. When the tide was out it was possible to reach it by a short causeway. But both river and sea tides came in so fast that in the past several people had drowned crossing it. Although the Ness lay close to the boundary of Palmyra Farm, half a mile between the fields and the town of Bly, it did not, strictly speaking, belong to the Maudsleys. No one knew who owned it and no one cared much for its dank salty marshiness. Because of the silt it was impossible to cultivate and the tides made it a dangerous place to visit. During the Great War there had been a few coastguard huts put up. There was also an old landing structure the locals called the Last Pier, because the original pier on the seafront at Bly had been destroyed. Twice each day the river and sea tides collided to turn the Ness into an island. When that happened the Ness was entirely cut off.

Nobody went there except Selwyn when, many years before, he needed a quiet place to grieve over his brother's death.

And more recently, Cecily was certain, her sister Rose.

Cecily hated the place.

'Oh do shut up,' Rose said crossly. 'And learn to mind your own business!'

She rummaged in her special box of clothes handed down to her from Agnes, and brought out one wispy Liberty print after another. Soon her bed was a heap of summer-faded scraps. Watching her with sudden, sharp insight Cecily saw that really, whatever her sister wore made no difference. In the end, she would always look beautiful. Don't-care Rose was humming to herself.

'Physically, you have reached your peak,' Cecily observed.

'What?' Rose asked, startled.

Then she laughed.

'Who told you that?'

'No one,' Cecily said.

She herself had outgrown her pyjamas so that the legs came halfway up to her calves. Rose, dabbing on the last of some stolen perfume, seemed not to hear.

'Where did you get it?' Cecily asked without hope of an answer.

Her sister slipped on a satin skirt. Then she spent ages buttoning up her pink and white flowered blouse. The buttons were made of mother-of-pearl. Through the window a fresh green-scented night breeze blew in and stroked Cecily's neck. It stirred Rose's hair, making her frown. On the seafront the breeze would be much stronger.

'Why are you wearing that?'

'Sshh!'

'What if Daddy sees you coming back from the ARP?'

'He won't.'

'Why not?'

'Because!'

'Why, because?'

'Shut *up*, C!'

The clouds parted and in the moonlight the cast-up shimmer of the satin softened Rose's customary expression of irritation until it too vanished as suddenly as it had appeared. And Cecily was aware her sister's excitement had become more acute. When she next spoke Rose sounded less cross.

'When you're older,' she said, quite kindly, 'you'll go out too.'

It was the first time she had referred to Cecily ever doing similar things and Cecily felt an upsurge of warmth, an almost pyrotechnic explosion of love for Rose. They were both silent. And then it occurred to Cecily in another moment's clarity that her sister's interests would have moved on to something else entirely by the time she, Cecily, had reason to shimmy down the drainpipe.

'But what if there's a war, in the end?' she asked, suddenly.

Until she said the words she had not realised that she feared a war. There was a clicking sound in her head. Now all her eavesdropping came together and added up to a total.

Like a grocery bill or the pocket money owed to her.

There *was* going to be a war.

Joe *was* going to be in it.

She saw that her sister was young and free and angry about many things and that the war, and the waiting for it to happen, frightened her as much as it did the grown-ups. She understood that no one could see how it was that she, Cecily, wanted to be young, not young in the way she was now, which was just an extension of being a baby, but older-young, like Rose. To be old enough for Carlo to smile the smile for her that he reserved just for Rose.

Time was passing as swiftly as a swallow and everyone kept talking about changes ahead. But no one had stopped to think about what it would be like for *her* to grow up in this war. All of this Cecily saw in a single, clear moment. And then, like the gleam of moonlight in her sister's eyes, it was gone and she was just the youngest in the family again.

Rose pulled on some stockings.

'Can I come with you?'

'No, you fool.'

Cecily felt the urge to ask another question.

'Are you meeting someone?'

Silence. An owl hooted.

'When will you be back?'

Rose put on her shoes. Cecily caught another whiff of perfume. Or it might have been the honeysuckle growing under the window.

'Why can't I come?'

Again silence. Her sister's shape moved swiftly across the room. Cecily sighed. And closed her eyes. Danger was perhaps Rose's element. She thrived on it. Outside, the garden and the woods and the marshes beyond, all of it, seemed to merge together under the almost full moon. Nothing stirred. But what if their mother had been right, thought Cecily, and curiosity *had* killed the cat that morning? What of Rose?

She must have dropped off to sleep for she remembered nothing more and when she did wake it wasn't so much because she'd heard anything as such but rather it was the quality of the silence that woke her.

She climbed out of bed. There was just enough light to see the dew-damp grass. Their bedroom was at the back of the house, away from their parents, facing the apple orchard. Something was rustling beneath the honeysuckle creeper out of sight. Cecily saw a pair of arms, bare to the elbow, a satin sleeve, a foot in a sandal. Her sister's bent head came into view and there was a pause before it disappeared again. Cecily heard a slithering sound.

'Rose!'

A dark bird flew slowly across the horizon. For a second Cecily had a fleeting memory of the dead cat. Flattened into a perfect cat-shaped flatness.

Eyes closed,
whiskers intact,
tail curled,
dead.

'Rose!'

Cecily leaned so far out of the window that she nearly toppled over and had to grab the honeysuckle to steady herself. There was no sign of her sister but glancing up, she saw a figure between the trees. She blinked and then there was nothing. Instead the thin faint sound of the wind chimes in the vegetable garden drifted across. Then nothing. She stared into the distance, frowning, puzzled, wondering if she should creep downstairs, knowing that the creaking floorboards might wake everyone if she did. Her father was back she saw, his bicycle leaning against the shed. There it was again, that sound. And was that her aunt's skirt she had just glimpsed? Her Aunt *Kitty*, thought Cecily in astonishment. But then, in the bluish air, caught in the beam of a torch switched on and then off, was a man with the stub of his cigarette glowing and his trilby covering his eyes. Pinky Wilson, thought Cecily, distracted further. The darkness obscured some of the physical details but she recognised the way he stood with one hand in his trouser pocket, the tilt of his hat, the slowness of him. And she understood that he was watching her watching him. But then, moments later she saw it wasn't her but *Rose* he was stalking. Like the cat had stalked its prey. Before something bigger had finished it off, as Selwyn had said. This was how Robert Wilson, aka Pinky, was looking at Rose. Quietly, biding his time. And her sister, coming back into view, sandals off, skirt hitched up, climbing the honeysuckle wall with steady concentration, her back to the man, noticing nothing.

'Where've you been?' Cecily demanded, suddenly afraid.

She felt in one swift and bewildering transition that she was the older one. Rose must have thought so too because she laughed, softly.

'Never you mind, my girl.'

Her face was flushed and beautiful, and happy. There was a crumpled, held-close look that gave itself away in small tendrils of hair growing in different directions. It made Cecily feel excluded and sad.

'You should be asleep.'

'I woke, there was a noise...'

But when she glanced over towards the trees there was no one there. Mist from the river filled the ancient spaces. The trees were thick with leaves.

'Were you followed?'

There were fine particles of a darker sand clinging to Rose's leg. In a flash Cecily understood that Rose had actually been walking on the Ness and not the town beach two miles further on. But with whom? Turning to her sister, she was about to ask the question again but Rose, huddled under the covers, was fast asleep.

After Rose died Cecily grew beautiful. After Rose died Agnes had the honeysuckle cut down. After she died the man they had called Pinky disappeared and was never referred to again and the orchard where he had once stood was sold off. No one would need orchards like theirs ever again. After Rose died the leaves stayed on the trees for a long time and the war got bloodier and more brutal and Cecily became someone that people stared at from time to time. But then, after Rose died, that time passed too, and things got forgotten and lost and also altered in the way that things do. And Carlo's special smile and even his voice as he chased her on the beach became not a clear picture but an impression that blurred and receded. And afterwards something inexplicably precious was lost. Like a well-loved object stowed somewhere safe but not there when you looked for it again. That was how things changed after Rose died. Aunty Kitty went from being Aunty Kitty, best beloved aunty, pretty friend and prettier sister, someone who might once have had the world but now never would, to simply Kitty. That too was the way things changed.

Later, other, smaller changes occurred but Cecily noticed them without interest. The typeface on hoardings changed. The street signs changed. Women wore different clothes. The fifties came. And then the sixties. Bomb sites were covered over, Andersen shelters removed, wallpaper changed in design. And the Beatles brought sex Out-Into-The-Open in a way that had not been possible before. These changes though had no power to change Cecily. For the stillness that had always been in her, the watchfulness and the silence, had grown and blossomed into a large flowering tree since Rose's death. In her head, buried somewhere out of reach, a bell tolled, pulled by the twin voices, unalterable and here to stay. The bell never, ever stopped. Cecily had no idea what it was announcing, only that she had become sleepless.

As Cecily grew Aunt Kitty shrank and the figure of Rose grew even larger. Once Cecily's mother visited them in London. Cecily must have been about fifteen at the time. A full two years had passed since that summer. The delicate face was haggard, the deep dimple nowhere in sight. Her mother looked both achingly familiar and distant. The ribbon had been cut between them.

She's old, now, one voice said to the other.

Practically grey-haired at thirty-eight!

Cecily was surprised at how small her mother was. Now there seemed even less of her.

'Together,' Cecily heard her say to Aunt Kitty, 'we have destroyed something. Her world, perhaps. Mine, certainly. I miss her.'

There was a pause. I miss Rose too, thought Cecily.

'You are worn out,' Kitty was saying. 'The shock... I thought it would kill you. *That's* why I took... her. How could I let you go on, alone? In any case...'

Another silence followed.

'What?'

'She would have had to bear the brunt at school... can you imagine? The taunting... it wouldn't have been fair.'

'No.'

'I know I'm to blame too,' Kitty said.

She sounded kinder than Cecily ever remembered her being. And then a moment later, 'I'm sorry I let you carry the burden of it. You are a much better person than me.'

Then she said something else that Cecily, straining her ears to the point of bursting a blood vessel, could not make out. There was a silence.

What's that? the twin voices asked together.

'She's getting to look like her,' Kitty said.

'Yes.'

More silence followed. Pretending she had wings, Cecily glided towards the open door.

'Do you find that difficult?' Kitty was asking.

Her voice was silky but underneath, something nasty was feeling its way to the surface.

'Not surprising.'

'Don't!' Cecily's mother burst out.

She sounded like a tap being turned on with too much force. There would be water everywhere, now, Cecily thought.

'I shouldn't have let you take her away. But... I didn't know... I had no idea how much I would miss her. None of you saw. I lost two children.'

Agnes was weeping. Now the sound reminded Cecily of the hot-water pipes when air got into them. It sounded as if a small trickle of water had got much larger and was out of control, it sounded like the sea that Cecily could no longer live by and the Last Pier that was no longer part of her life. It sounded like her lost sister who would be twenty-two by now. It sounded as if the whole world was crying for something unspeakably sad. And the thought of the years ahead, of being the same age as Rose when she died, was intolerable and terrible.

6.

THERE HAD BEEN no one to ask the McNulty sisters, about their past.

No one was interested in what went on in the lives of Agnes and Kitty in the old days. No one wanted to know about 'before'.

Before Rose was born.

Before they grew old.

Before they wrecked their lives.

Before history was made.

The past was always a thing of little consequence.

But the facts were that Kitty was only eighteen months older than Agnes. When they were children people would often mistake them for twins, one more delicate, taller, and gentler than the other.

Kitty, whose smallness had always been a source of annoyance to herself, made up for it with a laugh that could be heard from a distance and a way of tossing her sleek black hair that excited men (Agnes thought).

Agnes, who wore any old hand-me-down clothes with ease, as though they came from Paris, had a deep, annoying dimple (Kitty thought).

Agnes' eyes were large and softly green. Kitty's heron-grey and somewhat smaller.

They had been brought up in a small town in Ireland. Years later they would both say (jokingly) that eighteen had been the age when they had grown up. First Kitty left for England when the boy she loved was ordained and then, eighteen months later, Agnes left on a scholarship to study at the Royal College of Music. But by the time Agnes arrived in London Kitty had completely reinvented herself. Now her story was that she had run away to England because a distant cousin had abused her at home. She told this story with eerie glibness, in public, and to total strangers, thus shocking the more conservative Agnes. Kitty refused to retract a single word. (Cecily was said to have the same stubborn streak.) Eventually, having heard her sister's fabrications so often, Agnes began to wonder if it had been true.

In London they saw each other rarely, at first. Agnes was busy studying the piano, learning composition and working as a student répétiteur. When she graduated from the Royal College it was with a distinction, but at her graduation performance (she played Liszt and nearly destroyed the piano) her parents were noted for their absence. Only Kitty was present.

Kitty, living in digs, working as a secretary at the government Board of Trade.

Kitty, mixing now in grand city circles, talking about export and bonds and taking trips abroad with her boss with whom she was on first name terms. He was a wealthy, important man, able to converse in several languages and able to introduce Kitty to people in the diplomatic service. Kitty talked so often and so highly of him that Agnes wondered if her sister was not a little in love. But any questions on her part were sharply dismissed. Then, the week after her graduation Agnes finally met the man himself.

Selwyn Maudsley, enigmatic loner, silent listener, slow to smile, up for the weekend expecting to meet Kitty for lunch, was surprised to find her sister Agnes present. Startled too, by the colour of Agnes' eyes. Green was a colour Selwyn associated with the land, not eyes, he told her, many weeks later. Over the course of these weeks he told Agnes other things.

That she reminded him of roses. (Later he would want to call his first daughter by this name).

That he would one day inherit his father's farm in Suffolk.

That he dreaded the very idea.

That the place reminded him of a childhood devoid of love with a father who had beaten both Selwyn and his older brother.

That although their father hated all Germans he still sent his oldest son, Selwyn's brother, to be killed by one.

That Selwyn had loved only that older brother.

That, were Agnes to marry him, he would buy her a grand piano.

That every little thing in life she might ever want was hers for the asking.

(How unrealistic, Kitty said, when she heard.)

That he would love her forever.

(Kitty had laughed until she almost cried when she heard *this*.)

The news that Kitty had decided to marry a diplomat was lost in what followed. What had also been lost on Agnes was Selwyn's momentary shocked silence after Kitty's announcement. Selwyn was twenty-one years older than Agnes and two days later he proposed to her. For a man so slow the speed with which he did this was astonishing. The die was cast. And, even though farms and rural life were what she, like Selwyn, was escaping from, Agnes developed certainty. Feeling fatally sorry for him, mistaking it for love, she agreed to marry him.

Selwyn Maudsley's family had lived at Palmyra House for three generations. The farm consisted of a twelve-acre orchard, a field of strawberries and three others of wheat. It was situated on a bend in the River Ore halfway between the town of Bly and that of Eelburton. Beyond the orchards and the fields belonging to the farm were the salt marshes. From the windows on the east side of the house it was possible to see the sea and on the west side there were the woods. In winter the Martello tower just outside Bly was clearly visible but in summer it was always screened by the trees. There hadn't been a wedding there for many years. The Maudsleys were a wealthy family known both for their charitable work and their aloofness so when Selwyn brought his new bride home the little town of Bly was suddenly abuzz with curiosity. Who would be invited?

In the event the church was packed and at the reception in Palmyra House the bride played Schubert on the piano her new husband had bought for her. Then she played a version of 'Honeysuckle Rose', setting the tone for the next decade.

But it was the even more brilliant and newly married Kitty who stole the show that day. Perhaps also, it was the presence of the girls' parents that gave Kitty her sense of triumph. Or it might have been the presence of Kitty's bored husband, adding a world-weary touch of glamour to a country event. Or it might have been the confusion in Selwyn's eyes, of course. Whatever the reason, it was Kitty the locals remembered.

After the wedding not a day passed without Selwyn seeing that he did not love his new wife. But the marriage set its own standards, unaided by anybody. They were neither happy nor sad together. Agnes quickly fell pregnant, and settled back into her old rural habits. The piano was still played but morning sickness moved uneasily into evening sickness and apathy took centre stage, supplanting Liszt. It was the best that could be expected although occasionally, when she heard a piece of piano music on the wireless, something a little dangerous would stir inside Agnes. Selwyn, about to be a father at forty-one, hardly noticed. It was left to Cecily to detect this unsafe edge in her mother in later years. Cecily wisely learnt to keep away from Agnes at such moments.

When the elderly Mr Maudsley died soon after his first grandchild, Joe Maudsley, was born it was obvious to Selwyn and Agnes, living temporarily in Eel cottage, that they would take over the running of the farm. They moved into Palmyra House. The year was 1920. Two years later Rosemary Maudsley was born and by the time Cecily appeared the strains of 'Honeysuckle Rose' were rarely heard in Palmyra House while the piano had fallen badly out of tune. But such was the business of the era that no one complained.

Staring at her wedding photograph, enveloped in yards of white tulle and Chantilly lace, Agnes would write in her notebook,

I am not unlike a pupa!

When one looked back several things happened in those last two weeks of August 1939 into which all time would be forever condensed. The first was that Cecily noticed her sister changing in an indefinable way. She had been listening to Partridge talking to Cook.

'That one is going to be a beauty,' he said.

Cook sniffed.

'D'you mean Rose?' Cecily asked coming out from behind the door.

'Curiosity killed the cat,' Cook said tartly.

'But do you mean Rose?'

'Ay,' Partridge said relighting his pipe.

'She doesn't think so,' Cecily told him.

Cook sniffed again and Partridge laughed.

'She will soon enough,' he said. 'I'll be bound!'

After that Cecily noticed that Rose's sleepy, slanty eyes had taken on a new indolence. She noticed her sister's languorous air, the way her mouth twisted into an ironic half-smile whenever the Italian boys stared at her, the way she held herself, still and watchful when Bellamy appeared at the kitchen door. The way she would scratch her throat with her left hand, once even to the point of drawing blood. The boys must have been aware of this too for they never ruffled Rose's hair, or offered her a piggy-back. It made Cecily look at her own face with dislike, longing for something just out of reach.

The second thing that happened was the appearance of air-raid shelters in Suffolk. Not that anyone really believed they would be needed.

Extracts of George VI's speech about the True Greatness of the Empire was printed in the paper although in Germany, Jews were not allowed in public gardens and *Picture Post* published an article about Britain preparing for war.

But the third thing that happened had nothing to do with war. Several posters appeared on the new pier announcing the arrival of the Sadler's Wells dance company. This was the real news!

Rose wanted to go with Franca.

Cecily wanted to go too but Rose didn't want a baby tagging behind.

Cecily knew her sister had plans for later on that involved the fair.

Agnes, knowing nothing of any of this, wanted Rose to take Cecily.

All was, therefore, chaos and rage.

A war developing right there around the farmhouse kitchen table.

'Generosity is an old-fashioned virtue that's getting lost in this talk of war,' Agnes observed.

'Like the scent of old roses,' Aunt Kitty added.

Aunt Kitty, long divorced, was by now nursing a Broken Heart as though it were a wounded soldier.

'Wounded enemy soldier,' Selwyn joked.

His voice was gruff and indistinct because he spoke with his pipe in his mouth.

There was an awkwardness around him that gave Cecily a puzzling feeling. Her father had changed somewhat of late and no longer played the I-spy games with her as he used to. These days he seemed preoccupied with the war, but once long ago it had been Selwyn who told Cecily that looking and listening were the most important skills for a writer. Her father no longer read or praised her stories. The war, it seemed, was destroying everything interesting.

The clouds at the far end of the garden were as big as ice-cream cones and the air was hot as though it was a hydrogen balloon about to burst.

Outside, behind the fields, the lanes had narrowed into a tangle of blackberry briar and pale pink dog roses. The sky was a silken blue. The larks, invisibly high up, threw down their eerie threads of song. It was the unforgettable summer voice of England calling out, a great humming bowl of activity, present in the murmur and buzz of uncut fields and the deep peaceful voices of the farmhands talking to each other. There could not possibly be a war.

Could there?

'I hate this waiting feeling,' Aunt Kitty admitted.

She made it sound like a song, Cecily thought. Aunt Kitty was what Cecily's father called exotic. Like tinned pineapples.

It was August the 16th, only two weeks before September arrived but still the summer squawked and hissed in the long grass. There had been no rain for ages. Agnes, head bent, was making strawberry jam.

'You children are getting as brown as cobnuts,' a farmhand observed.

Everyone should have been helping with clearing the tennis court and the meadow next to it. But not everyone did what they should, observed Partridge, jovial in spite of Rose's huffy manner, as he adjusted her bicycle brakes. And off Rose went, along the bridle path, somewhere on her own, calling out, toodle-pip.

'Now where has she gone?' Agnes asked, sighing out of sheer weariness.

'She's gone Out Of Sheer Weariness,' Cecily said.

'I'd like to get out of Sheer Weariness, occasionally,' Kitty said, hugging her, smiling away her Broken Heart. 'I've lived there too long already!'

Selwyn, on his way out to milk the cow, glanced at Aunt Kitty but she was counting sweet williams.

Sent by her unknown admirer.

Seven.

There were always seven, Cecily noticed. And every time Aunt Kitty received a bouquet of flowers she went out. Agnes saw Selwyn standing against the light in the doorway, smiling the smile that once had been her undoing but now only seemed to make her unhappy.

Naughty Rose, sailing past the window on her bicycle, hair streaming behind her, thin beautiful legs showing through the delicate fabric of her dress.

'Pinky's just gone out in his car!'

'Rose!' Agnes cried, shrilly, horrified. 'Come back immediately!'

'What on earth is she up to?' muttered Aunt Kitty, the laugh still in her voice, the Wounded Heart, in the recovery room.

'Oh she's just trying it on,' Selwyn said.

'Come back,' Agnes cried, again. 'You've forgotten to collect the eggs for me.'

'Black Swan, White Swan,' chanted Cecily.

The town would be the ballet company's hosts for only four nights before they moved on elsewhere. Four nights of B&Bs and resin and sweat and footlights and applause. Cecily, who had been reading her father's copy of *Murder in the Cathedral*, thought she might write a story about a murder in the theatre.

'Daddy says *Murder in the Cathedral* is really about the rise of fascism in central Europe,' she said out loud to no one in particular.

Robert Wilson, thin as a stick that could unblock a drain, had a face made for playing poker. Already it appeared as it would one day look, staring out from a hardback edition of history.

In a crowd he would be invisible.

In a crowd no one would notice the tortoiseshell spectacles he didn't need, but which made him look dependable.

And every single time Rose saw him dislike spread across her face like jam oozing from a scone.

'I wish you children would stop calling him Pinky,' complained Agnes again and again. 'It's very rude and ignorant especially now that he's going to be our long-term guest.'

'Why on earth does he have to stay in our cottage?' Cecily objected.

She liked going to Eel cottage, to tuck herself in its depths, out of sight and reading. Now she would have to move her den back to the hornbeam.

'We have to do the best we can in the current situation,' Agnes told her family.

She was using her I'm-not-having-an-argument-with-you voice.

'He's a nice man.'

'Who says?' asked Rose, returning through the back door grinning, unrepentant, Bellamy the tinker's lad hovering in her shadow.

There was menace in his raised fist. Now what's he angry about? wondered Cecily.

'Ah!' said Selwyn, amused by his elder daughter's flushed cheeks. 'Hello Bellamy. Come to give me a hand? Or to talk to Rose?'

He spoke with a kind of empty gentleness as if he were thinking of other things. Bellamy looked dumbly at Rose and Cecily couldn't help feeling sorry for him.

'Right, I'm off,' Selwyn said at last, bored, taking his hat down from the peg. Through the open kitchen door the fields were gold.

'Isn't that boy you told us about arriving soon? The *evacuee*,' Rose asked, looking at Cecily.

'Oh no! Not an evacuee, mummy?'

'Rose, stop teasing your sister,' snapped Agnes. 'He isn't an evacuee, Cecily. And I believe he's a nice boy.'

'Dear, dear,' said Kitty under her breath. 'What a lot of bother.'

And that was when Cecily saw her aunt pick up the jug full of sweet williams.

'I'll just put them in the cottage, for Pinky Wilson,' she said, smiling at Agnes. 'They will look nice there. And then I'm going into Ipswich.'

'For goodness' sake, don't you start,' cried Agnes. 'It's bad enough with the children. And anyway I'm sure he's not interested in flowers. Why don't you put them in the parlour instead?'

'I don't want any boys coming here,' muttered Cecily. 'I don't want to share my things with them. I'll kill them if they come.'

Years later on a crisply starched morning, when the Beatles were singing 'Yesterday', in quite a different place altogether, Cecily was reminded of the scent of flowers. It was different from any other scent. It was the scent of dew on sweet williams. A very slight fragrance that she had not realised she had caught and contained in her nose. Perhaps the dew had been different before the war? Purer, more innocent.

By the time she came to think this, the war had been long over, leaving only a few traces in their hastily rebuilt lives. One of them had been the scent that made her decide to return to her old home twenty-nine years, three days and twelve hours later.

However on that August day, now only three days before the evacuee arrived and sixteen before the tennis party, the war could not make up its mind whether to happen or not. The weather of course remained exceptional. For days now, the mornings had started in exactly the same way. There were deep white clouds on the horizon and the sun beat up against them, battling its way across the sky. Sometimes the clouds darkened and rolled slowly over the fields.

But there was no rain.

And the news on the wireless was so boring.

The Führer is jubilant because the Russians are prepared to sign a non-aggression pact.

The old charismatic Pope had died and some Italians were worried about the new Pope who hated Communists and preferred Fascists.

An article in *Picture Post* said: We want Peace. Britain Does Not Hate Germany. Everyone listened to the news on the wireless all the time. It drove Rose mad.

'But I hate them,' said Rose whose dress was almost ready for the charity dance.

'Me too,' agreed Cecily, ready to give the evacuee a terrible time when he arrived.

Although she no longer played with her childish toys, their presence reminded her of her past. If someone else played with them her memories would be destroyed. Then she remembered something else.

'I saw Pinky in the orchard, last night, again,' Cecily said.

'No you didn't,' Rose told her crossly, giving her a thump.

'Rose!' Agnes cried, aghast. 'Don't hit your little sister! And don't tell fibs either, Cecily!'

'But I *did* see him!' said Cecily.

'No you didn't. It's not true. It was Partridge, putting out the rat-traps,' Rose said.

Her sudden fierce anger pinned Cecily against the dining table. Confused, she stared at her sister. There must be a misunderstanding.

'You remember. It *was* him. You saw him too.'

'Shut up you stupid girl!'

Cecily saw Rose blush. Her eyes had turned an unexpectedly sharp blue. They looked like two ice picks. When Agnes put out the supper on the table Rose cut into her boiled beef as though she were Bellamy cutting grass with a scythe. Then she sunk her teeth into it as though it were Cecily's arm. Agnes didn't seem to notice and Selwyn was too busy reading his paper.

But when Cecily, leafing through her diary, recalled that particular evening two decades later, it was in a slightly different order. She realised it had been exactly like the first night of a play with everyone getting their lines muddled up. Rose, shifting in her chair, eating boiled beef, was smaller than she had seemed at the time. And were there really ice picks in her eyes? Selwyn's expression as he looked over the top of his newspaper at Agnes was hostile.

'You do know that chap Wilson used to work at the Ministry of Trade when I was there, don't you?' he had said and Aunt Kitty, sounding rather irritated, said, 'Oh yes!'

Cecily's mother's apparent indifference, in hindsight, had other emotions attached to it, but it was her father's look that had cowed them all. When the memory of that supper returned to Cecily with the clarity of hindsight she had been on a plane, arriving in another part of the world. She could not have been further from Suffolk. But as she came into land she looked down, seeing the marshy lines of a foreign lagoon flattened out and reedy and that was when she remembered the evening. In that moment she saw too how the colour of the sky and water were perfectly matched. Just like home.

In the old house, Maudsley's old house, as the townsfolk referred to it (they had forgotten the fancy name Palmyra), on this August night, twenty-nine years later, the recently returned Cecily stood looking at the old photographs on the walls. Her parents' wedding day, her fifth birthday, Joe in uniform (what had happened to his medals?). Sea sounds entered the rooms as she moved through them and pieces of the jigsaw floated like shipwrecked objects under the waves. Calling for help. The figure who had stood so patiently for hours hesitated and walked away. Like the words of a familiar song heard in a different context, Cecily felt as though another piece of the jigsaw joined up. Because of this she was glad to be back. Why then did she feel like crying?

7.

AS SHE GREW older Cecily had a recurring dream from which she would wake in a wave of sweat and terror. Bellamy was always in these nightmares. There were others there too but Bellamy's expression of horror dawning (long before anyone else's) was terrible to behold. It made Cecily feel like a war veteran, or a thief, or even, (a word she had been told by the therapist to wipe from her vocabulary), a murderess.

When she was fifteen, still living with doing-her-duty-Aunt Kitty, she began to study *Macbeth* at school.

'Why is Shakespeare still relevant to us today?' the teacher asked.

Everyone tried to find the answer. Cecily didn't even try.

'Oh Cecily,' the teacher sighed. 'Why don't you make an *effort*?'

There's a smell of blood everywhere, thought Cecily, keeping her face blank, going on to win the class prize for her essay on Shakespeare.

'With an imagination like yours,' the headmistress said, 'you should become a novelist.'

But despite all the encouragement she wrote nothing. And the dreams refused to go away for beneath the threshold of her mind the war years persisted.

The crying did not stop.

In her sleep she thought the sound was that of a child.

'I just ran away,' she told the shadowy therapist asking the questions.

Not 'just' Cecily. What made you?

'I heard a sound.'

What was it? asked the shadow.

'I don't know. I went to look… I suppose it was screaming, in a child's voice.'

So what happened next?

'I went into the barn but I was scared to look inside. But I had to...'

And? What did you see?

'The lambs were screaming. They were killing the spring lambs.'

'But it was September, Cecily,' the shadow said. 'Wasn't it?'

Cecily nodded.

The dream always stopped at this point and the shadow could not help her any more. Everything but the feeling of terror vanished. That, like the taste of medicine staying too long on the tongue, remained, curing nothing. Like the dampness of decay, it would persist in every place she lived. Following her around and penetrating every word she said, destroying the spontaneity she should have had. She felt stuck in the mud of it. The woman she saw every day for nearly five years asked her once if she ever woke up screaming. She found it difficult to explain she woke up with a silence that told her it was all over for her.

She forgot to mention the voices bickering in her head.

By Thursday August 17th 1939 Britain had already been building its defences for many months. On the wireless they said that Hitler had set the date for the invasion of Poland.

It will begin on Saturday, 26 August at 4.30 am.

While in the birdless high noon, stabbed by the heat, although no one spoke of it, everyone knew Joe would be involved.

And all the time, far away, in the dead of night, black cars glided to a standstill outside the houses of ordinary people, murdering their sleep.

Rose swept up her hair, copying her mother. Then she painted her lips a deep carmine like Aunt Kitty.

'All you need to do is eat some raspberries to make your lips red,' the watching Cecily suggested.

But Rose wanted more than that. That was the problem.

She wanted all the boys.

Rude Bellamy.

Luigi, Beppe and look-alike Giorgio.

And if that wasn't enough she wanted Carlo too.

Why did she want Carlo?

Whenever Rose was present Carlo treated Cecily like a baby.

Sometimes, Cecily wrote in her diary, *RM makes me feel really quite sick. She can be a maddening show-off. I believe she treats me in this way in order to make herself feel more grown up. What rot! (underlined) She's jolly lucky I don't tell Mummy about her night trips. But instead of being grateful to me she's just sarcastic. Example: When the clotted cream and scones arrived and we* all *laid into them, she said 'Aren't we being a bit greedy?' Meaning me, of course. And she wants to make them all laugh, not just Bellamy. Mummy says it's because of the political tension but what on earth does war have to do with RM showing off?*

The air was heavy with the buzzing of insects and the choking scent of cow parsley. Absolute stillness, absolute silence reigned.

Joe too had become very quiet. The war was offering him certain options. Whatever he had hoped for in the past was now irrelevant. The War appeared hell-bent on getting its own way with his life. Being so much older than Cecily he told her nothing, taking her instead for rides in the pony-trap whenever he was around. Late that Thursday afternoon with most of the work on the tennis court finished, he took her to Bly and bought her ice cream from Mario. The younger Molinello boys grinned and Joe grinned back, buying three gelati instead of one.

'Hello Cecci,' Carlo said. 'Would you like to go for a swim?'

But Cecily didn't have her bathing suit with her on this one occasion. She shook her head feeling a sudden strange shyness, a vice-like feeling, in her chest. Did she have consumption, she wondered, alarmed.

'Never mind,' said Carlo, as if he understood.

But then he spoilt it by asking eagerly where Rose was.

'Helping mother, for once,' Joe said with a wry smile, his eyes searching for and not finding Franca.

'You're very quiet, Cecci,' Carlo said, suddenly. 'Are you looking forward to your party?'

Cecily nodded. Belatedly and with a sinking feeling, she wished she wasn't wearing Rose's old cast-off dress that was really a little too short for her. She wished her knees weren't scratched from having fallen off her bicycle, and she wished her mother had let her put her hair up instead of insisting she wore it in pigtails. Of late, every time she saw Carlo she felt very awkward and childish. She no longer had anything of interest to say to him and the odd, dull pain in her chest made it difficult to breathe.

'How you've grown this summer, Cecci,' Lucio said, coming in and noticing her, his voice very gentle. 'Soon you will be taller than your older sister.'

But it wasn't that sort of growing that she wanted.

On the way home Joe was especially nice to a silent Cecily. He was, thought Cecily, the best brother in the world.

For Franca Molinello there were some things the war could never take from her. Joe was one of those things. For weeks she had been over at Palmyra Farm helping with any jobs Agnes could find her. Sometimes she collected eggs, sometimes she helped milk the cow and in the last few days she had been pulling up the weeds around the tennis court. Her other job was observing Joe as he walked towards the house across the field. His bare arms, summer-brown, tanned a paler shade under his bleached hair.

No, the war shall not have him, Franca promised herself. She would not allow it.

The sun was white beyond the blackberry hedges and the two main fields facing south were being burnished daily by this blinding light. In the distance a high hedge flung its blue-black shadow with careless abandon across the molten glow. All week

Partridge had been waiting for the dew to leave the wheat so the harvest could start.

'We have not had a summer like this in many a long year,' he told them.

Unknown to Franca, Joe had been watching her too. He thought her smile entrancing. Standing in the field he was fascinated by the way her body moved, by the colour of her hair, shining like rook's feathers in the hot, bright sun. He desperately wanted to walk along the creek with her but didn't know how to ask. So he gave Cecily a note to deliver instead. Did she mind going back into Bly?

Cecily got her bicycle out again. Then she looked at the white envelope solemnly. It was a long, tempting moment. She held it up to the light and turned it over, slowly. Inside was a white slip like a pair of knickers showing through a transparent dress. She hesitated but because she loved him she didn't open Joe's letter. Then, before her mother could call out to her she rode off towards the bridle path, head bent in concentration, into the town.

Mario was nailing a new sign over the door of the Hokey-Pokey Parlour. It was a candy pink and white.

I scream, you scream, we all scream for ice cream! it declared, luring more customers in. The only ban, he told Cecily, by way of welcome, was war-talk. After all, the war was a joke, wasn't it?

An Italian from the social club was talking in a loud voice praising Mussolini.

'You see what I mean,' Mario told Cecily, rolling his eyes.

The man's friend started shouting about the Jews.

'All our problems in Italy are because of them,' he shouted but Mario would not be drawn.

Instead he gave the man an extra, especially big helping of ice cream.

'Try this,' he said. 'It's my latest invention.'

Cecily left them alone and went off in search of Franca.

'Will you take one back for me?' whispered Franca.

Cecily nodded. She didn't altogether like being a postman, it did that dreadful thing of turning her into a small child again, she knew. But because of Joe she was prepared to make an exception.

Thankfully there was no sign of Carlo but as she was leaving she noticed that Mario and Lucio were having another quarrel.

'Mussolini is the problem, not the Jews,' Lucio was saying.

He sounded bitter.

'Of course, of course,' Mario agreed. 'But who cares about the Fascists, anyway?'

Lucio gave his brother a withering look and walked out. Cecily hesitated. Then she went over to say goodbye to Mario who gave her a hug and a scoop of ice cream as she had hoped. The door to the shop opened and a girl Cecily had never seen before walked in. From the way her feet were turned out Cecily knew she was something to do with the ballet.

'I'm looking for a room for two of our dancers,' the girl said.

'Then you must talk to this young lady,' Mario beamed, pointing at Cecily. 'Her mother is Agnes Maudsley and she has a wonderful farmhouse. I'm sure she can be persuaded to find you a room there. What do you say, Cecci?'

Cecily wasn't sure. Their house was getting awfully crowded but perhaps if this girl came to stay in the annexe there would be no room for the evacuee. The thought was cheering.

'And her breakfast is wonderful, too,' continued Mario closing his eyes and licking his lips. 'English, very *English*!'

The girl, who had been looking solemn, smiled at Cecily.

'We don't want breakfast, just a room,' the girl said so Cecily gave her directions to get to the farm.

'See,' Mario said, 'even the ballet is more important than this silly war.'

That night after the ice-cream parlour was closed, Mario got down his accordion from the shelf and began to sing, '*Com'è bello fa' l'amore quanno è sera!*' It was clear to the listening children, in spite of his brave denial, their father was missing his home. He had not sung this song for months. Because of the threat of war none of them would go to Italy this year.

Elsewhere, beyond the horizon, glass was being broken in large quantities. The sounds echoed faintly before being drowned by a distant sea. No one in the town of Bly recognised it as the starter gun it was. No one except Lucio.

Could an echo come before an event, he asked himself, feeling unutterably sad.

What has to be will be, thought Selwyn, walking home past the river after a day in the fields listening to the curlews call.

Cecily, turning over in her sleep, loved her father like a tight hug that had all the happy feelings of a goodnight kiss. And in the dream that followed, Carlo's face was close to her own.

'You have beautiful eyes,' the dream-Carlo said. 'Not a bit like Rose's.'

Outside the pale fluff of meadowsweet and the tarnished buttercups shimmered in the still-hot air and fireflies came out to dance the night away.

8.

SELWYN HAD NEVER wanted to own Palmyra Fruit Farm. Although there had been apple trees in these orchards since 1890, wonderful trees still producing twenty bushels of apples a year, there were other never-ending problems with pests.

While his father had been alive he had successfully and single-handedly managed the land. In those days it had simply been assumed Selwyn's older brother would take over the running of it. Then his brother had died during the First World War, killed, as it turned out, not by any German, but in an accidental shooting by someone from his own side.

Men mistaking friends for enemies.

It happened all the time but Selwyn had never got over it.

It served only to intensify his conviction that life was something that would always pass him by. A conviction born from an earlier event also impossible to forget.

He had been fifteen at the time and his parents had sent their two sons to stay with old friends in Germany. It had been as glorious a summer as this one of 1939 and Selwyn had fallen in love with a German girl living close by. She had been older than him and at first he had thought she was interested in the company of his elder, more dashing brother. But it was not so and soon they were spending most of their time together, laughing, teasing each other, swapping books, comparing the authors they both loved. They went boating on the lake and as the days turned warmer took to riding their bicycles along the linden avenues to other villages and other towns.

All through those long, delicious weeks the younger, shyer Selwyn blossomed. Never had he felt so alive. And then their parents, finding someone to mind Palmyra Farm for a short while, came to join their sons.

Within a few hours of arriving, Selwyn's father had beaten him to the point almost of unconsciousness. For his friendship with a German girl. He had beaten his older brother too, for allowing Selwyn to behave in this indecent way, although when questioned he would not say what was indecent about this innocent friendship. Throughout these beatings their mother had neither said nor done anything. The next day both boys were sent home, back to Palmyra Farm. Selwyn was not even allowed to say goodbye to the girl. He had little recollection of the journey back but he would never forget the incident and afterwards he hated his parents with a vengeance. Then the war came and his brother enlisted. When he died Selwyn left for Oxford.

At Oxford he read English and German, vaguely recalling the Wilson man there. After Oxford, he seemed to remember they had both begun working for the government. But they had gone their separate ways and he had never seen Wilson again. Until now.

A loner and a bachelor for many years, when Selwyn's boss sent him Kitty McNulty as his personal assistant he tried at first to have as little as possible to do with her. Grief over his brother's death had silenced him and conversation with Kitty was limited to matters of work. Eye contact was painfully uncomfortable.

Kitty, speaking French and German, efficient and vivacious, was not about to let this get in the way of a friendship. She liked Selwyn, finding him uncommonly handsome. Very soon she was managing his personal affairs as well as the office business. She would pay money into the bank for him, ghost letters to his mother and keep at bay all those people he did not want to meet. He began taking her on trips abroad, unaware of the gossip that followed them. Kitty was surprisingly good company.

When Selwyn's mother died his father wrote asking him to come back to manage the farm. He ignored the requests. For the first time in his life, in an odd sort of way, he was having a good time. But he did nothing about Kitty and it was only when she, fed up with waiting, startled him by announcing her engagement to some other man, that he became aware of disappointment quickly suppressed. Somewhere in the back of his mind was the knowledge, gleaned from the punishment meted out during his troubled childhood, that self-control was the answer. He congratulated Kitty.

Finding Agnes hadn't been part of any plan.

In the confusion of Kitty's news, with his slender grasp on his own emotions, Selwyn proposed to Agnes. He hoped Kitty would simply fade from his consciousness.

No one told him that marrying the younger sister was hardly the solution.

No one told him Agnes would have needs of her own.

Then his father died and Selwyn took Agnes back to the farm. Joe, born nine months later, was intended to be the cement needed in their marriage. Rose, following soon after, the reinforcement. Selwyn saw he *ought* to love his children but really, he wasn't up to the job. Duty was all he could manage. It was good but not good enough.

Thereafter a long gap followed when events settled uneasily on the topsoil of their lives. Kitty, living in Chicago with her new husband Danny, heard all her sister's news. How handsome Joe was, how like his father, how happy the Maudsleys were to have little Rose. In return Kitty sent them a photograph of Danny whose huge moustache Selwyn instantly distrusted.

'Didn't I tell you,' he told his startled wife, 'a cad, if ever I saw one!'

In the event Selwyn's distrust was to be proved right although it was several years before anyone put two and two together about the bruises on Kitty's face. And arms, and legs.

And that was just the start of things. When Kitty related the story that she had been forced to have an abortion Agnes burst into tears. When she claimed the backroom botched job had left her unable to have another child, Agnes was heartbroken for her.

The story prompted her to make her sister the godmother of her own third child.

Cecily, the godchild of Aunt Kitty, who would have predicted that!

Meanwhile Selwyn was making a discovery of his own. To his surprise he found that his feelings for his third child were altogether different from anything he had experienced before. It wasn't a subject he dwelt on but whenever his eyes lighted on little Cecily's dark head, hair straight like a Chinaman's, he felt an overwhelming, unaccountable tenderness towards her. He began to take her out for long walks and, as she grew older, taught her to read and write. When, at the age of five, Cecily developed a passion for writing stories, it was Selwyn who encouraged her. Agnes saw what was happening and made no comment. Joe saw and wasn't bothered, being so much older. Only Rose for some reason was furious and began to hate her father with a barely suppressed passion.

Eventually Kitty left her husband. Cecily was eight at the time and, remembering how her father had told her to listen, did so fiercely, hoping to hear something interesting about the divorce. In those days, eavesdropping was far more exciting than now.

'Perhaps Aunty Kitty has stopped loving him,' she suggested to Rose, in the privacy of their bedroom.

Rose shrugged. Her aunt's lily-livered lifestyle held no interest for her. So Cecily continued to chip her way through the puzzle alone until Rose gave in.

'No of course not, silly! She only married him to get her own back.'

Her Own Back over what, remained undisclosed information.

In school Cecily continued to go from strength to strength in English. She won two end-of-year prizes for her story about the girl who married a man she did not love.

In the end she got her Own Man Back, she wrote.

And when Agnes bumped into the teacher in Bly the woman took her hand eagerly.

'Mrs Maudsley, your daughter has great imagination,' she had smiled.

Cecily's eyes had sharpened. She had found a new daydream. It would last for many months and interfere with her ability to concentrate on the chores her mother gave her.

'If she goes on in this way I think she might become a writer some day,' the teacher enthused.

'She certainly is a compulsive eavesdropper,' Agnes said, exasperated.

'It's all part of the process, Mrs Maudsley,' the teacher beamed.

'Silly, earnest woman!' Agnes told Selwyn later. 'She was more or less giving Cecily permission to carry on poking her nose into other people's affairs.'

Selwyn laughed indulgently. He reminded Agnes how, long ago, he had been tied to a chair by his father, as part of the punishment for eavesdropping.

'There's nothing wrong with C,' he told his wife. 'It's all part of her vivid imagination, part of her creative spirit. We can't blame her if we say unsuitable things in her presence.'

Agnes was silent. It was useless to tell her husband that Cecily was hopelessly indulged, that her behaviour was immoral. Or that by refusing to punish her Selwyn was merely encouraging the child. Couldn't he see Cecily was far too headstrong?

'No wilder than Rose,' Selwyn said.

An edge had crept into his voice. Behind the door, still as a stork, Cecily was simply dying to scratch her leg.

'What's immoral about curiosity?' Selwyn asked. 'If we give her information she can use against us, that's not her fault, for heaven's sake! Don't be so old-fashioned.'

There was a silence.

'I'm going fishing,' Selwyn said.

Rose, on her way out on private business of her own, doubled up with laughter.

Standing in the kitchen all these many years later, Cecily remembered with an acute blinding pain her father's face. The love he had always had for her, the way he had encouraged her to write, to be curious. How had she forgotten these precious little things? There was a constriction in her chest. Memories were turning up like unwanted guests. Events from the past collided and buckled, making it hard for her to separate them out. She remembered the Ness and its dangerous tidal currents. And she recalled how she had always known that Rose had been there several times with Bellamy.

Yet, try as she might, staring at the sky on those last peaceful August days of 1939, Cecily failed to see the War Clouds everyone was talking about.

Perhaps they were hiding behind the Pole star?

By August, with her divorce long over and her ex-husband in North Africa, Aunt Kitty closed up her flat in London and came to stay on the farm. She had meant to stay for just a weekend but, because she was feeling bored, the visit went on for far longer. While in the sultry, sweet, hay-scented heat, Pinky Wilson's dark distorted shadow continued to survey the land belonging to Palmyra Farm. Aunt Kitty, meeting him for the first time on one of her walks along a country lane, told her sister she found him really rather nice. Especially when he gave her a bunch of lovely flowers.

Everyone in the town of Bly knew it was because of the impending crisis and the need to feed the troops that Pinky Wilson had to visit all the local farms. But in spite of this, many people distrusted him.

Bellamy was one, but for reasons that weren't clear.

Cook disliked him on principle. The man was a stranger to Suffolk, wasn't he? Well then!

And Anna Molinello disliked Pinky because he had not checked with her before giving chocolates to her daughter.

Lucio kept his thoughts to himself.

Selwyn remembered Robert Wilson as a nondescript man, now concerned only with national acreage.

Rose of course couldn't care less. She yawned rudely every time his name was mentioned. No one told her off because it would mean feeding her Attitude. Cecily wondered why, when there was only three years between them, it was *her* Attitude that needed feeding, whereas Rose's never did.

Every day they were saying it was the driest, hottest summer for fifty years. But some people, Partridge being one of them, shook his head because he felt there was something wrong about the sequence of dead dry days.

The tennis match and charity dance were to be held on Saturday September 2nd. Joe and Franca and Giorgio had been selling tickets for weeks and a lot of people were coming from Bly and Eelburton and even from Ipswich. Agnes grumbled that most of the locals were just coming out of curiosity but Selwyn didn't think that mattered so long as all the tickets were sold. He had grown up being host to such events. Both events were to be held the same day but the harvest would have to come first. Rose was only interested in the dance. Joe, it transpired, was looking forward to both. And Cecily, rereading *Wuthering Heights*, thought that Bellamy was very like Heathcliff. He would love Rose forever, no matter what. So why couldn't her sister be content with him? Rose is just greedy, decided Cecily, her anger rising like the bread Cook was baking.

'I'm staying up all night,' Rose said with a toss of her bright hair. 'I'm almost seventeen.'

'So shall I,' cried Cecily.

'Very well, then,' Agnes said cunning and quick. 'If you are all so grown up you should be helping your brother by collecting up the cut grass around the tennis court. He's been working there for days with very little help.'

Although Selwyn could not remember him, Robert Wilson remembered Selwyn well enough. He remembered the name Palmyra Farm and when the posting to Suffolk had come up he decided to look him up. He found they had an empty cottage on their land and curiosity made him rent it.

'Was it true,' he asked Agnes, 'Kitty used to work as Selwyn's personal assistant?'

Agnes laughed, nodding. It had all been so long ago.

'But our paths never crossed until now,' he told Agnes.

'Hmm,' said Rose, when Cecily conveyed this interesting information to her. 'Is Kitty McNulty after *him* now?'

Luckily Agnes didn't hear her say *that*.

Was he going to be Aunt Kitty's lover, Cecily wondered?

'How on earth do I know?' Rose asked crossly.

And she went out, again. The only thing that interested Rose these days was the dance after the tennis match.

Cecily could see her walking with Bellamy in the direction of the top field. It was one of the many stories she was following with some curiosity this summer. For research purposes. Rose and her friend Bellamy.

Cecily wondered if Bellamy would get his prawn out, again.

After the tennis party the court would be ploughed up, thanks to the wretched Pinky Wilson. Cecily thought of all the games Joe, and Carlo too, had played with her here when she had been small. How they had pushed her around the court in the old pram, while she screamed with delight. And she thought of the wind in her hair and Carlo's happy face and how he used to hug her in the way he no longer did. And thinking too how the court had been present her entire life and was now disappearing forever made her want to cry.

'The world is changing,' Agnes said in a voice that gave nothing away.

This match would be the very last one at Palmyra Farm and though August was almost gone, September still seemed a long way off.

9.

BUT SOMEONE WAS making lists in high places. There were lists of Fascists and lists of anti-Fascists in Britain. Italian names, jumbled together, reading like a cast list for an opera.

Alessandro Anzi from London,
Carlo Campolonghi from Edinburgh,
Giovanni Oresfi from Clerkenwell,
Francesco Cesar from Eastbourne and
Mario Molinello from Bly.

Who knew which list each belonged to?

Someone, a clerk with neat handwriting, wrote the names into a book. Then a fat man with a cigar dropped ash all over them and someone else with nimble fingers came along and filed them away. So that one day a man wearing a trilby would find the list.

No one except Cecily saw Pinky Wilson sitting in the apple orchard reading a newspaper in another language.

'It's in Italian, silly,' Rose said crossly when Cecily told her. 'Why don't you spy on someone else?'

The tennis party was on everyone's lips.

Franca talked about it all the time with Rose, their faces alight with anticipation. The Molinellos, when the shop was closed, came over to the farm to compare notes with Joe endlessly as to who was the best tennis player.

'Rose is,' said Franca.

'Yes,' admitted Joe smiling wryly. 'She is!'

'Papi thinks *he* is,' said Giorgio and Carlo laughed.

'Papi's hopeless,' he said. 'I'm the best in the family, you know.'

'Oh, Lucio is pretty good too,' Anna told them and at that, Agnes, who had just made her a cup of tea, looked up sharply.

Her deep dimple made a swift appearance. And disappeared again. There were just fourteen days left to the tennis match.

'Please God it doesn't rain,' prayed Franca.

Agnes was making a canary yellow satin dress that Rose would wear to the dance. They were giggling together, good friends for once. Cecily, hurrying along the corridor, heard Rose whispering to her mother and stopped to listen.

'But I *do* wish he wasn't my father,' Rose said.

Agnes spoke with her mouth full of pins so Cecily couldn't make out what she said. And then Rose said something else, her voice different now. She spoke in the same cold flat voice she used when upset. Finally she made an impatient sound, a slight 'oh' as though she had turned away.

'Keep still, darling,' Agnes said.

'Ah ha!' Aunty Kitty said, pouncing on Cecily.

Laughing.

'Caught you!'

And she propelled Cecily into the room with her.

'Look who was hiding outside!'

Rose scowled.

'Oh my! The Listening Queen! What a surprise!'

'Why can't I have a dress like Rose's?' demanded Cecily. 'Why do I always have to have her cast-offs?'

'Because you're not old enough,' Rose said.

'It's irreversibly damaging my character,' Cecily said.

And she stuck her tongue out at her sister. Kitty burst out laughing.

'I'm sorry, child,' Rose said glaring at Aunty Kitty. 'It's simply a matter of birth order.'

'Don't pull faces, Rose,' Aunt Kitty said, ready to start another argument.

Later Cecily learnt that birth order was an important kind of order, never spoken about but always present. Until you died.

'When I'm twenty you'll only be twenty-two,' murmured Cecily.

'You're not twenty yet.'

'But I will be!'

'Wait until then.'

'Oh for *goodness*' sake,' Agnes said, worn down like a step that had been walked on too often.

Like the step, she was becoming slippy and dangerous.

'What's the point?' wailed Cecily. 'There won't be a tennis dance when I'm twenty. Not if the war comes.'

Rose laughed.

'Wars don't last six years,' she said.

'I hate you,' Cecily said.

But she said it without heat. Carlo would be at the party and suddenly she hated him too. She had asked him again if he would dance with her and he had agreed. But he had answered in a way that made her feel she was begging.

Children aren't supposed to have feelings, she wrote in her diary.

Outside in the country lanes, along the cottage walls and in the tangled hedgerows, dog roses bloomed. Untended, wild, and beautiful. It was truly ferocious weather that made the scent of honeysuckles stronger than ever before. On the wireless the news was that Hitler had sent a personal message to Stalin. And life seemed hell-bent on passing Cecily by. Would the tennis party *never* come?

The two girls with feet turned out like Jemima Puddleduck's had moved into the small bedroom in the annexe at the back of the house. They were very thin and white.

'Pasty, city girls,' Partridge said, amused.

'Streamlined like soda fountains,' Selwyn agreed.

He seemed awfully jolly. Considering.

'Do you mean pretty?' Aunty Kitty asked with a trace of discord buried in her voice, annoyed at something no one else could see.

Selwyn grinned a young boyish grin, helplessly. Like a man carried along by sea currents.

'Yes,' agreed Joe, thinking of someone else, entirely. 'Very pretty.'

The others were dubious. A discussion on prettiness ensued; light-heartedly, innocently blowing away the cobwebs of past irritations.

But Cecily knew there was no one more beautiful than Rose.

At the ice-cream parlour one of the Italian boys began to practise *Honeysuckle Rose* on the violin. One of them (it was Carlo) had told Rose he would play it at the dance. By the way he blushed whenever he mentioned her name, everyone knew what he was thinking. The Molinellos smiled good-naturedly and Mario whistled, *Ain't Misbehavin'*. And when no one was around Lucio listened to the wireless to see how grim the news was getting.

By Friday the 18th the weather was scorching and there wasn't even a thread of a breeze. The thermometer stood at eighty-seven. The grand clear-up had taken four whole days because the heat made everyone stop for too many rests. Rose wore a large hat to keep the sun off her face but it soon got knocked off her head. Butterflies danced around her. Joe paused, straightening *his* hat. He didn't mind the sun on his face, he told Cecily when she arrived with the ice-cold lemonade. Bellamy, high on the tractor, glanced at Rose with heat-sapped, challenging eyes.

Rose looked away. Bellamy revved up the engine. He looks as hot as the devil himself, Cecily thought.

Across every field swallows flew low beneath the searing white clouds. The tractor, a lump of solidified oily heat, moved past Rose, leaving her with a curious air of being unsheltered in the shadeless field, under a naked sky. Bellamy was staring straight at the shadow between her legs and her white skirt. Rose stood up and wandered towards the trees. Her voice drifted towards them.

'This heat is something awful,' she said. 'If I sit too long in it I feel sick!'

'We've almost finished,' Joe called after her. 'Can't you get Bellamy to give us a bit more help?'

'Ask him yourself,' Rose said crossly over her shoulder.

The sweat was pouring down Bellamy's face as he moved the tractor towards the trees. Then it stopped and Cecily saw him get down. He raised his hand in the direction of Rose's head. She saw Rose turn her face towards him, her long white neck arching backwards. Then they both disappeared into the long grass and once again Cecily felt a ripple of some strange sensation rush across her own body. Carlo, who was walking towards them, must have seen it too because he stopped for a moment and looked towards the spot where Rose had stood. Feeling a sudden agony for him, Cecily ran across the field.

'Are you all right?' she asked a little out of breath.

Carlo turned towards her, startled. He frowned as though he didn't quite recognise who she was. Then he murmured something and raised his hand. And touched her hair, adjusting the silk ribbon that was falling off.

'Yes, yes,' he said, adding, 'you look different today.'

But then he laughed with delight, waved his hand and went to join Joe.

Inside the dark cool kitchen, Agnes held an ice-cold jug in her hands as Lucio Molinello, having loaded the trays of greengages onto his truck, backed out of the drive. When he saw Cecily running across the field he waved. But he did not smile.

'This war will change everything,' Agnes said. 'None of us will ever be the same.'

For once there was no one listening.

Cecily, sitting on the highest branch of the oak tree, was hugging herself.

10.

AND NOW, ALL these years later, back in Palmyra House, Cecily was daring to take out that summer from the drawer marked 'Interrupted' and place it in the one marked 'Remember'.

The summer of more strawberries than you could eat.

The summer of war clouds gathering over the streets.

The summer the tennis court was ploughed up.

The summer of the Last Pier.

She saw again the meadow beyond the bridle path where the huge oak grew. There had been a family living in Bly who rented it for their pony. With the distance of time, with so much exotic travel behind her now, she saw what she had never seen before; how like an eternal Constable it had looked.

She remembered laughter coming from behind the hedge. That had been Joe and Franca. And she remembered how, when Rose was nowhere in sight, Carlo had told her she was pretty. And how, sitting on a branch of the oak tree she had swung her legs in delight while the wind cooled her flushed face and Carlo's words went round and round her head until all the joy in the world came towards her. Carlo had spoken to her in the same voice he used for Rose.

Why were the days moving so slowly? It was still only August the 18th. Carlo had been marking out the tennis court with white paint and Cecily went over to talk to him. Twice in one day.

'I don't have a new dress like Rose,' she said. 'Mummy says I'm not old enough.'

'It doesn't matter,' Carlo told her. 'You must be patient.'

His head was bent in concentration. One false move and the line would come out wobbly.

'There might be a war,' she said.

'A war won't change anything, Cecci,' Carlo said. 'It won't stop you growing up. You'll do that anyway.'

She said nothing, staring down at his crouching figure, her body alight with the heat of the afternoon sun, trembling with an unaccountable desire to touch the back of his head. Knowing that, unlike last summer, she could not do so. Maybe I never will again, she thought sadly, remembering how she used to hang on to his curls as he gave her a piggy-back when she had been younger. All that, she dimly saw, was over. Carlo's upturned face was browner than the wheat itself.

'Rose will look beautiful,' she said, wanting but not knowing how to express what she felt.

The sun lay white on the ground. She could smell the sweet light fragrance of dry grass and late flowering limes. Carlo stopped what he was doing and straightened up. White paint dripped onto the ground. He looked sideways at Cecily. Then he smiled.

'You will too,' he said, adding as Cecily shook her head, 'but you *will*, Cecci. You look exactly like Rosa. Don't you know?'

His voice was so kind that for a moment she felt tears spring to her eyes.

'And you are going to be so tall and elegant. I can tell.'

Cecily stared at him, thinking how much older he was. She would never catch up with him, any more than she would with Rose. He must have sensed something of what she felt because he laughed and hugged her and she smelt the grass and the hot air and the dog roses spinning through the air. He went on hugging her and a moment later she saw her sister coming towards them. Rose was combing her fingers through her straw-laced hair and smoothening her dress. Bellamy was somewhere behind. Cecily saw him throw his head back and laugh, his usually sullen face relaxed.

'Why *does* she like him so much?' Carlo murmured, staring at the horizon where a line of heat pulsated under the deep blue sky. He shook his head, puzzled. They both stood watching as Rose walked away from the field, towards a patch of bright yellow buttercups. And as her sister disappeared through the white islands of rising clover, heading probably towards the river, Cecily saw Bellamy climb back onto the tractor. In the heat it appeared glowing like a huge ball of fire as he started it noisily up again.

In the annexe in Palmyra House, in the late afternoon, the dancers took their make-up bags and went away to be photographed. They had been rehearsing all morning and were exhausted.

'Glissade, plié, glissés, one, two, three. Rond de Jambe,' Madam shouted, banging her stick. 'And now the other side, please.'

When Cecily went back into Bly with the Molinello children she could hear them in the rehearsal studios next door.

'And one and two and three,' cried Madam.

Cecily heard a stick being banged in time with the music.

'All day,' said Anna Molinello, rolling her eyes heavenwards, 'those poor girls! What is she doing to them? They look as if they'll fade away.'

'Invite them in for an ice cream,' Mario said. 'Give them one on the house!'

Lucio shook his head at his brother's carefree attitude.

'Work is the answer,' he said.

He sounded bitter. Somewhere through an open window, music was playing on the wireless.

One day Cecily would see a photograph with his words on it and wonder why they appeared vaguely familiar.

In Whitehall no one had a clue about what might happen next. But, just in case, it was decided wise to continue making the list. Thereafter a smart alec took the matter a little further, deciding the lists needed to be colour coded. That was how the Black List came into being. When it became difficult to decipher the names on the other lists, the clerk in charge (he was a different fellow from the last List-Maker) stole from another list. Any old list, from any old file filled with the names of foreigners. *Forestieri* – that was the Italian word for foreigners. A nice-sounding word for a-not-so-nice meaning. The Black List had 1,500 Italians of 'dangerous character' on it.

Making lists was the new preoccupation all over Europe. Italy was no exception. In Italy, coincidentally, the word *forestiere* was being stamped on documents. Mostly these were secret documents kept by crazy Mussolini supporters. Meanwhile in Milan, at La Scala, Tito Gobi playing Leporello sang 'La Lista' from *Don Giovanni* to rave reviews.

While, unseen by any audience, Fear entered the arena. Underneath its cloak it wore the red and black stripes of Terror and its smile revealed a mouth of jagged glass. But *still* no one was taking much notice.

And now, to counteract this secret business, this gathering together of mutterings and rumours, a frantic happiness filled the cities and small towns of England's green and fragile land.

Artists hadn't started designing their classic posters yet. Patriotism hadn't quite grown into big business. And waiting-for-it-to-happen hadn't become a National Obsession. Not yet. So laughter and champers and ice cream with fresh strawberries were still possible. The weather, happily glorious, helped with the deception.

Most nights Rose climbed down the honeysuckle backwards, landing with a barely audible thump on the flowerbed. Agnes, complaining of stray cats flattening the plants under her daughter's window, wondered why no one ever caught them. No one ever saw Pinky Wilson standing with one hand in his pocket looking up at their window again. Perhaps Cecily had imagined it after all. Once down, Rose ran to the shed behind the tennis court and wheeled her bike away. Then in the darkness, keeping the sound of the sea beside her at all times, she headed for the funfair. Bright lights awaited her. And candyfloss. And someone, probably Carlo, took a photograph that still stands in its silver frame on the mantelpiece in the old house. Agnes must have found it among Rose's belongings and put it there as a reminder of the Secret Life of her Rose.

It was the same photograph Cecily would stare at on her return to the old home these twenty-nine years later, seeing it the moment she walked into the drawing room, her coat hanging limply from her shoulders. Rose, her sister, staring up at the lights, laughing, head thrown back with the distant horns of summer imprinted on her face.

Cecily remembered it as though it were yesterday.

There was the darn on the left shoulder of her sister's dress, the rip where the small posy of lily-of-the-valley had been pinned. There were Rose's pearly white teeth that the dentist knew about. Without those teeth there would have been no lovely smile, no pretty mouth, no body to bury underneath Rose's headstone. Agnes had had plenty to think of when she looked at those teeth made with the calcium from her own bones. Those teeth had outlived Rose and when Cecily returned they smiled at her from within their silver frame with a long-ago, life-is-full-of-promise smile.

The ballet people weren't the only visitors in Bly that August. A gipsy coming to the door told Cecily there was a circus there, too. It had camped just outside on the hill, with a proper magician's tent and a collapsible big top and a crow that was able to turn white when it saw that someone was going to die. But Agnes coming to see who Cecily was talking to, tried to shut the door. She feared the gipsy's sun-darkened skin and the bunches of rosemary they sold. So she banged the front door in their faces. Ignoring their curses.

'Yea'll be opening this door all right,' one of the women cried, before turning away. 'Yea'll be opening it for a coffin, yea'll see!'

And she grinned a toothless grin at Cecily so that Agnes, pulling the edges of *her* mouth together as though it were a purse string, pulled her daughter away.

'It was only a penny,' Aunty Kitty said.

She had been standing in the shadows, bare feet on uneven flagstones, unnoticed.

'You should have bought some rather than...'

Cecily's Aunt Kitty had the scent of flowers on her. As if she had been rolling in a field of them. Her clothes were crumpled and kissed by pollen.

'You had better wash your dress,' Agnes said, sharply.

Then she saw Cecily standing in the doorway, still listening, and got into a different kind of fury. Less understandable, more allowable, unrestrainable and all-of-a-sudden.

'Why *do* you keep eavesdropping, Cecily? Wherever I turn you're there. Haven't you got anything to do?'

'Let's go pod the peas,' Aunty Kitty said soothingly, pea-shooting looks at her sister. 'Let's do them together.' And then, when Cecily ran on ahead into the kitchen, 'Don't be so hard on her Agnes. Don't take it out on her.'

But Cecily, who loved her mother with a can't-get-close-enough-to-give-you-a-hug sort of love, didn't like the tone of Aunty Kitty's voice on this occasion.

'Do they hate each other?' she asked Rose that night.

Rose was doing her nails. She was clearly going out again tonight.

'No,' she said, her head bent in concentration. 'It's just that Daddy's in love with Aunt Kitty. That's all.'

II.

IN THE OLD room with its scrapyard of dead insects piled in corners (a leg here, a wing there), on a mattress dampened as though with water from the seabed, Cecily lay pinned back by thoughts. It was a new August morning in a new peacetime decade but old thoughts held her like pins driven through the heart of a butterfly. A 1939 life existing in a 1989 August.

The thoughts were so loud they almost excluded the voices that lived in her head. There were some good things about returning, then.

Summer was ending with a few soft apologetic wet days and the leaves of the walnut tree, getting the message, were beginning to fall. There were black edges on everything and suffocation seemed imminent. Outside the long brushes of rain brought the ghost of Rose wandering in. She was eating an orange and looked well kissed.

Perhaps I should not have come, thought Cecily, for the old home seemed to have forgotten her. She tried not to inhale the ghost of her sister clinging like spider's breath to her bed. Instead she began stocktaking, starting with the room itself. She counted the hours and the days and months and the years since she had last been here. In its way it was still a cared-for room, she decided. True, the moisture in the air had buckled and softened the Snakes and Ladders box. And the jigsaw puzzle (Genuine Lumar No.47 The Estuary) had lost most of its pieces. And the dress that once had seemed like a river of silky splendour was faded and moth-papery. But everything else, even the shoes made for dancing, the books about the girls from St Trinian's, the cut-out pictures from *Picture Post*, the stockings in their box, were still tidy in decay. The room was like a unit in an antique market where things were sold for a bob or two. Social history, Cecily imagined the stall-holders calling it.

'It's having quite a revival. Look how small their waists were, then!'

Yes, that was what they would say. Where had she been when her life was dissolving into history? Walking on a beach near Portofino? On the edge of Lake Trasimeno?

Taking herself across the decades that had passed, it must have been the late sixties by then, she remembered the man with a silk handkerchief who had approached her. He had breath that smelt of garlic but she had not minded. Nor had she minded when he had suggested they have dinner together. Candlelit, she remembered.

'You have extraordinary bones,' the man, she couldn't remember his name now, had told her. 'Do you know that?'

And he had run his finger across her cheek.

'Like a bird's,' he had said.

The waiter poured wine. Outside, obscured by the darkness, was the sea, or the lake. Some kind of water, anyway. Cecily hadn't cared which. She hadn't cared when the man had confessed his wife was dying of Alzheimer's.

'I am dealing with a different person, now,' he had said.

His voice had been very low and Cecily wondered if perhaps he sang bass in a choir or whether it was simply the voice of seduction.

'Every day,' he said, heavily, 'she forgets a little more.'

Cecily had wondered where the unknown forgetful woman was?

'I have a helper once a week. Tonight is my night off.'

He had looked deep into her eyes.

'If you like,' Cecily said eventually, having savoured for a moment the power of silence.

The shadows from the candles made soft little hollows under her cheeks. The voices in her head had gone to sleep just as though they were caged birds over whom a black cloth had been thrown. Maybe, thought Cecily, this is the one. She knew she was behaving like a woman searching for a pebble on a pebbly beach.

'What's wrong?' he asked her later in her hotel room. 'Didn't you?'

He sounded like Geoff. Cecily saw he was transparently interested in himself. She doubted she would be his preferred woman had he any choice in the matter.

'Don't you like me?' the man asked.

Oh not again! groaned one of the voices.

Cecily had a sudden glimpse of the beach at home. Floodlit by flames. And she saw, with awful clarity, Carlo Molinello laughing at a long-forgotten joke.

'We used to have fantastic sex,' the man told her a bit later on, trying again. 'My wife and I. Before…'

Cecily nodded quickly, hoping he couldn't hear the twin voices giggling.

Ask him if you can catch Alzheimer's, one of them said.

Useful for you if you could! said the other.

Yes, thought Cecily, wiping her thighs in the bathroom, knowing it was all over. In a moment he would get angry and call her frigid.

'Didn't you enjoy any of it?' he shouted on cue. 'Are you Catholic?'

Cecily was aware of the twins rolling around on the memory-strewn floor of her head, laughing.

'A young girl like you,' the man said. 'How weird!'

Cecily noticed how he checked to see if his shirt was creased.

There was unease in his voice. Here it comes, thought Cecily.

'Are you frigid? There are books, you know… you might consult a doctor…'

Time to get rid of him, the voices had said in unison. *Before it gets nasty.*

An hour after, with the water from the shower running in rivulets down her slim hips, she saw the hollows in her cheeks had deepened with the night. Outside through the open window, tangerine flowers scented the air. Her brief recall of Carlo Molinello had unnerved her. It was one of those moments when she might have thought of returning home but, as always happened, the thought was engulfed by an overwhelming desire for sleep. So that the next day and the day after that she would walk around as if drugged until the thought, expelled from her mind, would release its grip on her and she could let herself focus on the sunshine.

Outside Palmyra House, the rain stopped and Rose's ghost disappeared. It was morning. There were seven jars of honey on the windowsill with seven drops of hardened beeswax beside them. Opening the window, Cecily saw how the honeysuckle creeper had tried and failed to grow across the wall. She would have to go into the town for food. Last night she hadn't wanted anything, but looking at the grease-grimed shelves, the tacky dark walls, the crypt of old grief, she saw there wasn't even a slip of soap to wash her hands with. There would be a shop, she supposed vaguely. And what was there to be anxious about? No one would remember her. There was no one left to do so.

Grey clouds scudded across a sky that had lowered itself so far towards the ground that breathing itself was difficult. The front door would not open properly and the back door would not shut. Cecily observed the mildew in the bathroom and the crack across the frosted glass. There was a cut-throat razor blade and a blue bottle that had lost its stopper. There was a small transparent piece of alum stuck to the washbasin which itself was discoloured by water dripping from the leaking tap. And the floorboards were fretted with holes from a million termites.

What a mess! cried the voices in dismay.

Perhaps she should not have come.

'Look!' said the woman selling tampons to a customer at the chemist. 'Look who's just walked past.'

The pharmacist took a whole bunch of prescriptions and dispensed pills into a bottle. Red pills, yellow sugar-coated capsules, white, precisely shaped ones with daggers moulded across them. The bottles held several lifetimes of pills in them. The pharmacist handed out prescriptions to the waiting sick with a little shake and a rattle, as if he were a priest at communion.

'Take one three times a day,' he murmured.

Then he went to the back of the shop where he could get a better view. Word spread fast he knew and he had been the pharmacist in this town more or less forever. If anyone could spot a familiar face a mile away, it would be him.

'Yes,' he said. 'It's her.'

He sounded like a gamekeeper on safari who, having spotted the prey, was prepared to predict its movements to the crowd.

'Turned out pretty. But for the hair, she could be Rose herself!'

'They were a good-looking family,' said the tampon-seller, remembering.

'Hated her, the aunt did. God knows why. It weren't her fault.'

'Well I heard a different story…'

'Oh look, she's coming in here!'

Cecily entered the shop like a corps de ballet dancer coming on stage, wanting to stay in line and blend in with the others. Without expecting any applause, knowing she's just part of the whole. No one could see the elegant structure of her ribcage under her coat containing a heart fluttering like a bird. She skimmed around the edges of the shop floor now, thankfully, almost empty of noise. She picked up two bottles, shampoo and bubble bath, both green. And she walked over to the counter. It was then that all speech stopped and the pharmacist (grim-faced with the concentration of not being grim-faced) served her. Cecily's hair was damp from the spitting rain. Her small, lovely mouth was stretched shut in a slender line. But it was her eyes that astonished them. No one had remembered how vividly violet her eyes were.

'Well!' said the pharmacist after the door had clanged shut and Cecily's retreating figure hurried past. 'Whatever next!'

And he went back to his dispensing.

'I knew the father,' he added.

And he shook his head. That sort of memory doesn't go away in a hurry.

The high street was quiet. Changed but vaguely familiar in ways that could only disturb. Cecily felt it holding on to its secrets, refusing to give her the clue she needed most. An answer to the question, Why?

'*It's still early days,*' the voices told her, kindly. '*Wait a little.*'

But the thick, sluggish weight in her head, the slate-grey pain had become terrible.

It mingled with the sound of the sea, coming in from behind the houses.

Day-old flags dragged their pointed ends to the ground. A small pearl button rolled into a drain with a death rattle. The woman who had dressed up as Bly's answer to a Pearly Queen walked past.

'My God! Cecily,' she said.

Cecily did not reply. The silence in her head was blistering and she hurried past the woman. The woman looked as though she'd seen a ghost. The war had been dead for twenty-three years. Why was Rose still alive, then?

'Don't you remember me?' asked yesterday's pearly queen.

Cecily shook her head. Everything, she wanted to say, was distorted. But her mouth would not open. Time had closed it up like a damp pocket book.

'You were such a little girl,' the woman persisted. 'I went with your mother to get your train ticket. Remember?'

Cecily's memory refused to be kick-started into action.

'Ah well! You're back, that's the main thing. Staying up at the house, are you?'

In the absence of anyone coming to her rescue, Cecily nodded. Where were the twins when she needed them?

'If you need anyone to clean for you...?'

Concentrating hard, Cecily was forced to stare at the woman's face. Something moved in the locked room in her head.

'Are you Cook?' she asked.

Her voice, unused for so long, appeared reluctant to be squeezed out. There wasn't much of it in the tube.

'Oh no love. I worked at the pub. The one that was over there. It's gone now. We've only got the White Hart left but,' she hesitated.

Cecily had a blank look that frightened the woman. Perhaps she had gone too far but she'd started so she'd finish, she told her husband later.

'It used to be called The Golden Eagle. Remember it? I used to work there. I was quite young. Your sister's age.'

She stopped. Surely she *had* gone too far?

Cecily shook her head and moved on with a small, barely-heard murmur and a pair of delicate shoulders bent helplessly against the wind. The coat she was wearing was marsh-green, foreign-looking and fitted her like an old glove. Someone long ago had worn it once before.

She had wanted to ask the woman where the ice-cream parlour was but she couldn't remember its name. (In Italy she had stayed for a while in a village called Molinello simply because she had liked its name.) Perhaps her memory was finally going.

Nonsense, said her voices.

Glancing at a shop window, she caught sight of herself and jumped. What was her mother doing following her around? The thought of her mother living secretly inside her skin was scary. Cecily walked over to the window for a closer look. There were the high cheekbones, the dimple when she tightened her face. Only her eyes remained her own. Incontestably beautiful. Huge. Lustrous. A different colour from her mother's or her aunt's. *Irish* eyes, Geoff had said, in the heat of his passion. Smiling even when they weren't meant to. Seasick-making eyes, he had shouted at her, after the fires in him had been put out.

'Can I help you?' asked a youngish man, coming out of the shop.

It wasn't the shop it had once been, but an estate agent's now and the man hoped Cecily wanted to buy a house. Something about the man's face seemed familiar. She searched it for clues. In his hair, which was black and sprung straight up, perhaps? In the shape of his teeth? The man wore flared trousers and a thin shirt. When he smiled there was a puzzle in his smile that matched hers. Both of them shook their head.

'No, thank you,' Cecily said hurriedly and moved on.

Having come outside to sell a property, the youngish man felt thwarted. Disappointed, too. Who was this beautiful woman?

Cecily walked on. She was nearing the end of the high street before she remembered the name of the ice-cream parlour. There had been a chestnut village in Italy where she had lingered for a moment. Carlo's teasing voice had chased her through the dappled sunlit trees. Her bones had felt like small twigs snapping underfoot for Carlo too had deserted her.

'Molinello,' she murmured, now.

And she walked back up the High Street and turned left into Shingle Street.

BY AUGUST 1968 there had been so many changes in Shingle Street that it had unravelled like a woollen mitten. It had been reassembled after the war by a madman with little respect for history. The Molinellos' ice creams no longer existed of course and the house where the Italian family had lived was gone, replaced by lock-up garages and a warehouse. An old people's home with benches facing a melancholy sea occupied the space where Bunter's sweet shop once was.

Small traces of an elusive past confused Cecily, who pulled her coat closer. A beam of sealight dazzled her eyes and because of this she failed to see the silent figure on the street corner. Eyes hidden behind dark glasses, features shadowed by unknowable thoughts, sadness too ingrained to be discounted, statue-still the figure stood. Watching her.

Memories fell like rain on Cecily's thin frame. A billboard, advertising the ballet *Le Spectre de la Rose*, was one. A voice, so clearly heard, another.

'How on earth did you get tickets Papi?' Franca had asked.

'Your father,' Anna said, 'could get hold of Hitler's wallet, if he wanted to! Take Rose and Cecci with you. And give the other one to Agnes.'

'Or the aunt,' Mario added but Anna had shaken her head.

'No, Agnes.'

Even they had felt Agnes' aloneness.

'I'll take them over,' Lucio, off to pick up the morning's delivery, offered.

But his voice wasn't quite right.

'And what about your *fidanzato*?' Mario teased his daughter, *his* voice a happy echo on the now-deserted street.

'He's not my fiancé!' Franca replied crossly, eyes shining her denial. 'And anyway he doesn't like ballet.'

What was the past but a scrap of music, played on a piano? Cecily paused in mid-flight across the road and listened.

It was the very same tune that had long ago bothered Lucio, when, driving up to the back of Palmyra House, delivering ice cream to the Maudsleys, he had heard it for the first time.

Saturday August the 19th. Ah yes!

A waltz, floating effortlessly through the drawing-room window, as though it were a woman on a man's arm, was difficult to resist.

How many times had Agnes played that piece of music?

When the waltz came to an end on *that* day, he climbed down from the truck. His legs felt heavy.

Cecily watched with interest. Sometimes she thought her mother the most beautiful woman she had ever seen. This was one of those times.

The ballet tickets were in Lucio's pocket and Agnes, her face a flushed vibrato, shy as a nightingale caught singing, came to the door. She had no idea why it should be so, but the sight of Lucio always made her tongue-tied.

When she smiled the summer light shone straight into the green of her eyes and Lucio, staring at the dimple that came and went in her cheek, forgot what he was about to say.

'Won't you come in?' Agnes asked.

'What were you playing just then?' he asked, bending low under the beam of the door.

'The waltz from *Le Spectre*,' she told him, her slender hands making a gesture so lovely that he wanted to take them in his own large ones and hold them tightly and dance across the room into eternity. Wanted to hold her face close to his so that her dimple appeared once more.

'Will you play it at the dance?' he said instead with a smile not seen for many years.

Who was this man, Agnes wondered? The ache in her throat was choking her. Her face stung as if it had been slapped. She felt bewitched but where had the charm been hidden? Had the gipsy who had tried to sell her the bunch of rosemary done this?

'Not unless,' she said breathlessly, 'someone can find a piano.'

Lucio smiled. It shall be done, his smile promised. Why had he seldom heard her play, his eyes asked, again.

Because, well… because, you've never been here when I have, hers answered him.

But, oh dear, they were already saying far too much and hastily she retreated behind the ice cream and the ballet tickets.

'I'll pick the girls up afterwards,' he said while his eyes told her something altogether less mundane.

His voice cradled the day. It was warm and slow and full of promise. What could she do but nod?

Afterwards she stood in the cool, dark hall listening to the sound of his truck driving off, the tickets crushed in her hands; listening to the wild beating of her own heart.

Kitty coming in from the field, flushed from some private exertion of her own, heard the sound of the old out-of-tune piano, and frowned.

Cecily, letting out a breath in a mighty whoosh from behind the pantry door, listened, too. Lucio, she thought, looked so like Carlo.

Time stood still. So that now, when it was picked up again, here in desolate Shingle Street, with the seagulls' cries piercing her heart, Cecily remembered, they had been waiting for the evacuee that day. I hope he never comes, she had thought.

Her father had gone off to an ARP meeting. Again.

'But I'll be home in time for supper, to welcome the little chap,' he had said.

And the rest of them had gone, Cecily remembered, on that Saturday night, to the ballet. Agnes, wearing the emerald dress that had once, for a brief moment in the past, excited Selwyn, but later would barely raise an absent-minded smile from him.

'Go to the lavatory before it starts,' Agnes said.

Rose, with the cross look back on her face, was keeping an eye open for Franca.

'Go with her please, Rose,' Agnes said.

'I can go by myself,' Cecily muttered.

And she had made a dash for it down the stairs, an escapee from Home Rule, treading carefully on the red, plush carpet. In the ladies' powder room her face looked pretty after all, she thought, startled.

The lights in the auditorium were rose-coloured. So perhaps she had simply made a mistake and the mirror had lied. But her hair did shine and she appeared to have cheekbones rather like Rose's.

'Cecci,' Franca hissed, behind her in the queue. 'Can you give this letter to Joe, tonight?'

And then she vanished.

'Hello Cecily,' Robert Wilson had said as she went back to her seat. 'What's that you've got? A letter? From an admirer!'

Ah yes! Robert Wilson.

That name.

Again.

Playing another sort of game.

What had Pinky Wilson been doing at the ballet?

He liked the ballet very much, Pinky said, taking a seat just behind Rose. Cecily read the programme.

Triple Bill. Margot Fonteyn, Robert Helpman, Fredrick Ashton.

Agnes' pearls glowing against her skin. And Pinky Wilson leaning forward, handing them another box of chocolates.

But having left the opera glasses in the ladies' lavatory, Cecily arose with a long coltish movement, hair slipping out of its blue ribbon.

'Oh Cecily!' cried Agnes.

'Don't worry,' Robert Wilson said. 'I'll go with her.'

Cecily, taking no notice, rushed off.

'The child's a bloody nuisance,' Rose said, loudly.

She must have been bored.

'Really, Rose!' their mother said.

'There you are,' Robert Wilson cried, catching up.

He had smiled in his friendly way. So why hadn't she liked him one little bit?

Robert Wilson said something else as they returned to their seats. It sounded like, 'your secret's safe with me' but everyone was applauding the conductor.

Standing in Shingle Street, clutching her brown paper bag of shop-bought greengages, remembering how once their orchard had yielded heaps of them, Cecily worried over which moments had been significant and which not. She put her hand to her throat in a sweet, unconscious gesture that made the watcher watching, think first of her mother, and, when she bit her lip, of her sister Rose. As if it were too much for him, the watcher slunk deep into a doorway.

Cecily couldn't see she *was* the past.

Suddenly the light changed, draining to sepia.

Here we go, said one of the voices in her head.

She'll be like this for days, now, said the other.

Guarda là! Look over there!

But as usual Cecily was searching for what was no longer visible.

By the time the ballet was over Cecily wished she hadn't eaten so many chocolate violets. Or perhaps it was the fizzy ginger beer that was the problem. Clapping the loudest, she began to look for night-expedition-clues in Rose. Earlier her sister had folded a pair of stockings into her bag and she had stolen their mother's 'Evening in Paris' perfume. Why would you wear perfume when all you were going to do was sleep at Franca's house?

Robert Wilson planned to drive home in his motor car but first Agnes needed to hand the older girls over to Lucio.

'How long have you known the family?' Robert Wilson asked.

'Forever,' Agnes told him and old Pinky was taken aback by the radiance of her smile. But it was Lucio, waiting for them outside, who had been delighted by the sound of Agnes' laugh, travelling like a shooting star towards him. Cecily saw her mother bend her slender neck in greeting as she walked.

'Lucio!' Cecily cried, not to be outdone.

'*Ci vediamo presto*,' he said solemnly, talking to Cecily but looking at Agnes.

See you soon.

Agnes had been in danger from her own smile.

'See you girls tomorrow,' she called.

'*Sì, sì*. Don't worry, I'll deliver them to you in time!'

Franca stared pointedly at Cecily's pocket. Don't forget my letter the look said.

'I'll bring the boys, those that are free,' Lucio called. 'To help Joe.'

'Carlo, too?' asked Cecily.

'Yes, Carlo, too!'

'I had no idea,' Robert Wilson exclaimed, 'that you were on such good terms with the family.'

Agnes couldn't stop her unruly smile.

'Oh the children grew up together. They are a lovely family.'

She was silent.

'Bly wouldn't be what it is without the Molinellos.'

Pinky Wilson's hands on the steering wheel were lit by the light of the dashboard. Tomorrow, he told Agnes, he would help

Joe and the Italians. Even though there was hardly anything left to do.

'The sooner you get the tennis court ploughed up and ready for planting, the better,' he said. 'World events are moving faster than you realise.'

He spoke so softly that Cecily, staring out of the window, barely heard him. She must have been dreaming of something altogether more interesting. Her sister Rose, perhaps, or what was more likely, Carlo. They would be certain to be at the fair by now and Carlo would be buying candyfloss. Cecily loved candyfloss. And Rose was bound to have her fortune told by the parrot who picked out the cards of destiny. But she didn't need to bother, thought Cecily, angrily. *Her* destiny was just marvellous.

'I wonder if the evacuee's arrived,' Agnes said, her voice happier than it had sounded all day.

Cecily, thinking of Rose in love with Carlo, spoke absent-mindedly.

'Aunty Kitty loves Daddy,' she said.

What followed had been a stunned silence, so powerful that its echo remained with her, still.

Travelling through eternity, its dark tones lived on in Shingle Street, and Palmyra House, and other places in other corners of the world.

Still piercing Cecily's heart. *Still* burning a hole in her.

What on earth had made her say such a thing?

The car moved forward as though it was trying to escape the words.

'*Cecily*!' Agnes said, managing to say everything she wanted with that one, single word.

Cecily froze. Her words, arriving from nowhere, were now mixed with the stale taste of ginger beer, chocolate violets and undigested thoughts. Tangling with the evening, ruining it. Sorryness sticking to the roof of her mouth was what she tasted then, while desperation poked its vomity finger down her throat. Nothing came out.

Pinky Wilson laughed easily.

'Perhaps she'll be a comedian,' he said into the darkness, helping out, shifting gear so the car continued smoothly inland into the depths of the countryside and towards Palmyra House. But Agnes, looking over her shoulder at Cecily, spoke to her with Another Look that stated clearly, 'You're Old Enough To Know Better' and 'We'll Talk About This Later'.

Cecily, her voice torn into tissue-paper shreds, was silenced.

'I'm sorry, mummy,' she managed at last.

The back of her mother's head looked stiff and angry.

In the darkened countryside the headlights picked out certain things and missed others.

It shone its beam on a fox's green eye. Very soon a chicken would die.

The headlights moved on missing Bellamy, hands stained with blood, shirt torn from a back-room brawl in Bly from which Selwyn had rescued him.

Cecily swallowed. She longed to be elsewhere, walking the dunes in bare feet. Most of all she wanted to throw her indiscretion far into the wide night sky.

'You must be tired, Cecily,' Pinky Wilson said, keeping his voice friendly, making Cecily hate him all the more. 'It's been a long evening for you.'

'Yes, she is,' Agnes agreed, mouth snapping like a crocodile.

Some things come with their own punishment.

Cecily, leaning out of the car window, tried and failed to get the vomit to dislodge.

At the back of her mind was an image she half-remembered but couldn't get hold of.

Half-remembering was still the thing she was best at.

How hot it had been in the car. She clamped her teeth together and closed her eyes while a scrap of moon, no bigger than a cut fingernail, floated past. The direction of the wind had brought a

faint sound of fairground music and seawave sickness danced
before her eyes. She felt cold and clammy.

In the dimness of the car, Robert Wilson covered Cecily's
mother's clenched fist.

'Don't altogether trust them, Agnes,' he said.

What had he meant?

It was how they arrived home. Aunt Kitty sitting at the kitchen
table drinking a cup of tea, looked up with interest.

She was always the first to smell a rat, Rose used to say.

'Tea, anyone?' Kitty said, her voice golden as syrup.

'No thanks,' said Robert Wilson. 'I have an early start
tomorrow.'

'Are you going back up to London?' Agnes asked, the shine
all gone from her face.

''fraid so.'

'Did you have a nice time?' Aunt Kitty asked, still digging for
information with her invisible spade.

'It was a nice evening,' Robert Wilson said.

'Very nice,' agreed Agnes.

Niceness spread itself across the kitchen table.

'I feel sick,' Cecily had said.

Agnes wasn't interested. She simply wanted Cecily out
of the way so she could prepare for the arguments yet to
come.

'When's Daddy back?'

But Selwyn was with the ARP.

As usual.

'There are some jokes that are too rude to be made,' Agnes
continued gravely after Pinky Wilson had gone.

Cecily opened her mouth to say she hadn't been joking but
then closed it shut. For what was the point?

Surprisingly, her mother showed no signs of putting
any restrictions on the next day. So why did Cecily feel so
desolate?

'There's quite enough to think of with the war looming without having to deal with you as well,' said Agnes, clearly waiting for Cecily to go upstairs.

And then she turned her back and closed the kitchen door, her footsteps receding, tap, tap.

But, it was still a night of great beauty. That hadn't changed.

Tawny as the wings of a hunting owl in a forsaken corner of an English field.

With a trough of water from a tiny spring filled up with moonlight.

Meadowsweet clots of mist making the air ache with scent.

And Lucio, kneeling on a slab of stone, bathing hands and arms and then face in the delicious cool water.

All around lay the moon's lustrous sheen. It haunted Lucio terribly. Things had never looked so full of wonder. He watched the figure hurrying towards him, her breath against his skin even before she reached him. Threads of music from earlier that day followed behind. Scarves of phosphorescent light touched her hair. Lucio covered the distance between them but then stopped. They both hesitated for a moment longer before the last inevitable leap towards each other.

Neither heard the squeak of a bicycle for the night was full of many small noises, too numerous to bother with.

He saw her framed against the meadowsweet and she saw the distant lights of the town behind him. He was afraid to kiss her, so Agnes touched him first.

A piece of Italy in a forgotten corner of an English field. And a pair of Irish eyes.

They failed to see the figure of Cecily cycling furiously away.

Having waited awhile, Cecily had left the house. There were shadows in the folds of every object, imperceptible tremors in every glass of water. Something unnameable moved with the wind. So, after the house had settled and the footsteps belonging to her mother had hurried away past the walnut tree and the garden light had gone off, unable to wait any longer, Cecily sat up. If Rose could climb down the honeysuckle creeper why on earth couldn't she? The torch beside her sister's bed had gone so she would have to feel her way in the dark. Her bicycle was in the shed.

'I shall,' she muttered. 'I can do what I like.'

Carlo didn't belong to Rose no matter what she might think. She was positively bad for him. In *A Girl of the Limberlost* the heroine had fought for her love. Goose pimples of defiance played a wicked tune across Cecily's arms as she prepared to be a siren for the night and lure Carlo away from her sister.

With her sister's fishnet scarf around her hair, knees a little scratched from the climb, she sped towards the sea. On the way she saw the silhouette of her mother standing by a tree. It did not surprise her for she knew her mother had a different life by night. The breeze sang in the telegraph wires in a way it never would again. Faint fairground noise burst on the air as she approached. The ice-cream stall was still open and Cecily could see a girl she didn't recognise wiping down the counter. Behind the girl a small crowd was watching a man eating fire. Cecily stared. She leaned her bicycle against a fence. Away from the house the air was cooler and she felt it was easier to breathe. But now she was actually here she didn't know what to do next.

She wondered, as the tide was out, if she would at least walk down to the beach. It was cowardly not to and the whole escapade seemed a little pointless. There was no sign of Carlo and the constriction in her throat increased. Rose was like the tide. There was no stopping her. If she wanted Carlo then she would have him. Horrified by her treacherous thoughts, Cecily wondered if perhaps she should go back. Turning her bicycle around she was about to set off again when something made her look over her shoulder. Standing in the shadow, close by the ice-cream stall, facing the sea, was a trilby she recognised.

Pinky Wilson lighting a cigarette, hand cupped over the flame, head bent in concentration. Cecily frowned. Instinct made her move into the shadows. Suddenly a gust of wind lifted the trilby and sent it spinning along the pier with Pinky in pursuit. And as she stood, groping for information she knew of but had mislaid, she saw her Aunt Kitty.

Yes, thought Cecily, twenty-nine years too late the memory rang alarm bells.

Idiot! cried the voice in her head. *Why didn't you think about it, then? And didn't you think it odd to see Lucio kissing your mother?*

'I was too busy with other things,' Cecily mumbled, staring at the scraps of sea peeping out between two houses.

Why didn't you see the clues?

Cecily shook her head. She hadn't a clue.

The figure in the doorway fixed the adult Cecily with a long and thoughtful stare but she was busy with the seamlessly returning past.

Ah Mario! she thought, now.

She must have spoken aloud or else the slight breeze carried her voice towards the watching figure who straightened up, sharply.

'Mario!'

Cecily remembered how, when he had finished helping the girl, Mario had left. The girl had taken the broom and swept the floor. There had been no sign of either Franca or Rose. Perhaps Cecily had made a mistake and Rose had in fact been asleep in the Molinellos' house?

The night returned to her across the years.

Kitty moving in time to the music from the carousel, cigarette in hand. Cecily had never seen her aunt smoke before. Then, as she stood uncertainly, Cecily saw her aunt shrug her shoulders and throw her cigarette away before walking onto the darkened beach. Mounting her bicycle, Cecily rode off but in her haste she missed Pinky Wilson, hat back firmly on his head, coming up the steps from the beach. Had she looked back she would have seen him, lighting another cigarette. And watching her.

The moon vanished behind a cloud and as she cycled home Cecily remembered two things. She remembered that the evacuee must have arrived and now be asleep in Palmyra House. And she remembered that Pinky Wilson had told her mother he needed an early night because he was going to London in the morning.

And then, as she put her bicycle back in the shed (noticing with relief her father's was still absent) and began to climb up the honeysuckle creeper, she saw also that Pinky Wilson's car was parked in the driveway. Her window was just as she had left it, slightly ajar. The hump of clothes in the bed, left in case her mother walked in, looked suitably convincing and undisturbed. Taking off her sister's scarf, making sure she put it safely back in the hatbox, she realised she needed the bathroom. She opened the door and listened. Then, putting on the expression of a sleep-walker, she went towards the lavatory.

A floorboard creaked but she kept walking.

There was a small shuffling sound. Cecily kept going until she was back in her room. She shivered and shut the window. Pulling the covers over her shoulder, she closed her eyes. Tomorrow she would get up early to deal with the evacuee. Tomorrow she would be extra specially nice to her mother.

Somewhere in the distance the church clock in Shingle Street struck two and as she fell softly into sleep, the last thought Cecily had was that the sound she had heard on the landing was of someone crying.

By August 1968 the war memorial in Shingle Street had many more names dedicated to the fallen. It surprised Cecily her name wasn't on it.

Concentrate, admonished the voices in her head. *You've come back to remember, remember!*

The day after the ballet was a Sunday. August the 20th. By the time the morning penetrated her dream the sun was pouring its coins on the floor. The programme from the night before rested on her sister's bed. The house's faraway noises went on below with the wireless playing Hitler's silly voice over and over again. In the distance was the faint sound of the tractor. Leaping out of bed, Cecily dressed hastily and rushed downstairs.

Agnes was out. A strange boy with long grey socks sat at the kitchen table eating a boiled egg. There was no one else in sight. The boy looked up and stared hard at Cecily while chewing steadily. Then he nodded.

'Ah!' Aunt Kitty said, coming in. 'So you're up! I was beginning to think it was the Sleeping Beauty you saw last night.'

She looked normal.

The boy guffawed. He appeared perfectly at home in the kitchen.

'Is he the evacuee?' Cecily asked her aunt, ignoring him.

'Cecily this is Tom. Tom, meet Cecily. I think C is slightly older than you.'

Tom nodded and went back to his egg.

'Where's Mummy?'

'She's in the top field talking to your father and Partridge. Would you like an egg, Cecily?'

'Is Rose back?'

Aunt Kitty frowned. Then she switched off the wireless. The temperature on the thermometer was still at eighty-seven. Would it never get cooler?

'Not yet,' Kitty said. 'She and Franca and Partridge are going to help Joe with sorting out the barn now. Now do you want an egg? You can take Tom around the orchard after breakfast if you like.'

'I can go by myself, if you don't want to,' Tom said.

'You'll get lost,' said Cecily.

'No I won't. I have a compass.'

No one spoke. Tom finished his egg and reached for some toast.

Tom.

Why, after so long, was the sight of him buttering toast suddenly so clear?

'I think,' Aunt Kitty said, 'it would be good if Cecily takes you in this first instance.'

There was a flat tone to her voice but she was looking at Cecily and smiling. Cecily thought she looked exhausted.

'Now, C, for the last time. Egg or no egg?'

'Yes, please.'

'Can I have another one?' Tom asked. 'My mother said there would be plenty of eggs on a farm.'

'I don't know about that,' Aunt Kitty said.

Again Cecily heard the flat tone. It rang a clear warning. The boy didn't seem to notice and when he next spoke he simply said,

'Thank you.'

After Kitty left and they finished breakfast, Tom took two sugar lumps and put them in his pocket.

'That's stealing,' Cecily said in her best voice.

'No it's not. I'm going to give it to the horses.

Cecily was silent.

'C'mon then, let's go,' Tom said

'I have to go upstairs first.'

Instantly the boy was interested.

'Where's your room? Is it here in the main house?'

'Yes, of course.'

He pulled a face.

'I'm in the annexe next door,' he said. 'Next door to those *girls*! It's awfully hot in there.'

'They're dancers,' Cecily told him. 'They'll be gone next week, although Pinky says they might come back as Land Girls.'

'Who's Pinky?'

'Never mind.'

Her voice was beginning to sound a bit like Aunt Kitty's and her head felt confused and strange. Last night came back to her in fragments. Had she really gone to the beach or had she dreamt it?

'You've got a very funny look on your face,' Tom observed.

And he laughed, showing slightly crooked front teeth. For some reason this made Cecily like him a bit more.

'How many people are there in your family?'

'Rose and Joe,' said Cecily.

'So why can't I stay here in the main house?'

'Because there isn't room. We've got to keep the back bedroom free for Aunt Kitty for when she comes to stay.'

The boy digested this.

'Is Joe going to fight in the war?'

'There's not going to be a war.'

'Oh yes there is!'

'There might not be,' Cecily said, uncertainly. 'Aunt Kitty says if there is it will only last until October 25th.'

The boy laughed again. His laugh was older than the rest of him. It was remote and superior as though it was meant to put Cecily in her place.

'Is Kitty your aunt on your mother's side or your dad's?'

She was taken aback by his nosiness but Tom didn't seem to notice. 'She's pretty,' he added.

'You haven't seen Rose, yet,' Cecily said.

She wanted her sister back as reinforcement.

'She's still at the ice-cream parlour.'

'Ice cream,' Tom said, his face lighting up. 'Oh I say! I haven't had any for a year at least.'

It didn't seem possible.

'Can we go there? It would be a ripping thing to do!'

'I don't know,' Cecily said, doubtfully.

She wasn't going to share Carlo with him.

'How long are you staying for?'

'Oh a long time. At least until the war's over. Well... nearly over. Have you had your Anderson shelter yet?'

Cecily shook her head.

'You jolly well will,' the boy said and once again Cecily heard a kind of superior certainty in his voice.

There seemed nothing left to say after that. Tom took out the sugar lumps and put them absent-mindedly into his mouth and closed his eyes. Cecily watched him curiously. He seemed rather too confident for an evacuee. When Agnes had first talked about taking one in, Cecily had assumed it would be a much younger child.

This boy was only a year younger than her.

'I'm not strictly speaking an evacuee,' he said as though reading her mind. 'My father knows yours and he wanted me to have some fresh air after our horrendous trip back to England.'

'What trip?'

'Oh haven't you heard? We left Germany more or less overnight. Left all our things, our house, everything behind.'

Cecily swallowed. The question had to be asked.

'Are you *German*?'

'No, of course not!'

There was a further silence during which Tom looked at Cecily expectantly. When it was obvious she wasn't going to ask him anything else he sighed deeply.

'Your father and mine used to work together. My father owned a factory that did business with this country. But with Hitler in power we didn't want to stay in Germany. As I'm sure you can understand.'

'Oh yes,' Cecily said, quickly.

It was too soon to be giving him advantages.

'You don't have to worry,' he said, seeing her expression. 'I am *not* German. The government wouldn't have taken us in if we were! We used to own a factory in Germany and of course now there might be a war we decided to come home again.'

'All right,' Cecily said, making up her mind.

Perhaps they would be allowed to go to the fair together.

'I'll ask Mummy if we can go to Molinello's.'

'Wizard,' Tom said.

Clearly he believed it was settled. He smiled and she saw his crooked teeth. She saw that his chin, though stubborn, had become more relaxed and that he did in fact look a good deal younger than her. She noticed there was a hole in his sweater as if a large moth had attacked it.

'I'm going to change my shoes,' he said. 'See you down here in ten minutes.'

And he went.

Leaving a memory of himself that would outlast many things.

13.

I SHOULD NOT have come back, decided the adult Cecily, clutching her bag of translucent fruit. But hadn't she been told to do just that, when she had finally caved in, and begged for help?

'Go back to the beginning if you want to get rid of the voices. Find out what really happened.'

What nonsense, the voices themselves had protested at the time. *We will never leave you. Promise!*

'It's your only hope,' she'd been advised. 'Uncover that summer, peel your memory back.'

History isn't about facts, the voices had screamed.

But she was here now.

Continue, they commanded her. *What happened next?*

Tom, Tom! they added, beating an invisible drum.

Out in the meadow under the old oak where the pony grazed, Joe appeared to be talking to Franca. They stood very close to each other but when Cecily crept up they weren't talking, just smiling and looking. Then Joe leaned towards Franca and Franca swayed slightly as if she suddenly felt faint. But she didn't stop smiling. The light was wonderfully clear and liquid, making both of them appear sallow.

'Oh!' Cecily said, clasping her hand over her mouth, remembering the letter, not wanting to mention it in front of Tom who was watching them with interest. 'Oh, I forgot!'

'What?' asked Tom.

Franca laughed.

'Never mind. You won't lose the job, *cara* postie! As you see I'm here. Zio Lucio brought me.'

Franca hugged her so hard that it made Cecily wonder if it was really Joe she wanted to hug. And when Joe laughed and ruffled Cecily's hair she just *knew* he was thinking of something else.

But where was Rose?

'Over there, somewhere,' Joe said waving in the direction of the trees. 'Fooling around with Bellamy and hoping mother doesn't notice!'

Tom opened his mouth to ask another question.

'Hello, old chap,' Joe said, forestalling the question and shaking hands. 'Welcome to Palmyra Farm. I'm Joe and this is Franca!'

Wonderful Joe, suddenly looking, not ordinary old Joe, but someone grown-up and serious. And Franca, why, Franca looked wonderful, too. And Carlo? Where was he?

'On his way, Cecci,' Franca said.

Tom had changed into a pair of shorts and now wore a shirt of a grey flannel. Cecily thought he looked hot. Franca must have thought the same thing too because she asked him if he didn't have anything lighter to wear.

'It's one of the few things we brought with us,' Tom said.

Cecily tried not to stare and Franca and Joe exchanged amused looks but then the looks changed into something going on between them with laughter in the mix. There was a pause.

'And the rest of your family?' Franca asked. 'They're in London. But you were sent here because of possible raids?'

Tom shook his head.

'There won't be any daylight raids,' he said. 'Because of the expense. So they'll be safe.'

In spite of herself Cecily was impressed.

'Actually I would have stayed in London too but my parents wanted me to have fresh air after my illness.'

'What illness?' Cecily asked, interested.

'Appendicitis. Nearly developed into peritonitis,' he said importantly.

'Oh you poor thing. That could have been dangerous,' Franca said.

'Fatal,' Tom said, rather too loudly. 'Come on, let's go,' he added turning to Cecily. 'I'd like to eat some of that Italian ice cream you promised.'

'Eh…' Joe said warningly for Agnes was heading towards them. 'Just a minute… I think you'd better ask Mummy first, C.'

'May we?' Cecily asked cautiously.

'You must not be a nuisance when you get there,' Agnes said, picking something sharp from her shoe.

She sounded a little subdued. Had she stopped loving Cecily altogether?

'Perhaps Zio Lucio can take them,' Franca suggested.

'Oh, he's gone, Franca,' Agnes said, in a funny voice.

It was plum and wasp time.

With hindsight, Cecily saw that all summer had been contained within those few brief days. All summer, burning, blazing, turning in the bluest of skies, while the temperature hardly changed.

But you do understand Tom was the problem, insisted the voices in Cecily's head. *He was trouble from the start. You do see that?*

'No,' Cecily replied. 'That's too simple. I was the older one, I should have known better. And Rose was my sister.'

Tom's family had fled from Hitler's grasp. When the Nazi *putsch* came, their Jewish sympathy made it too dangerous to stay. They had left in the nick of time, via Switzerland. And when their visa arrived they were going to America.

Oh really! mocked the voices. *That's his story.*

On Sunday afternoon Joe began to scythe the rough grass in the meadow. Then Partridge got the old hand mower going. The stubble was coarse by the time he'd cut it and there were large patches of naked earth here and there, but everyone said it didn't matter. When the visitors arrived for the party they would park their cars in the meadow.

Bellamy had refused to join in, saying Sunday was his day off, but really it was because of Carlo's presence in the meadow. Carlo meanwhile, unaware of this, evened out the bumps on the tennis court with the roller. The net was up, the lines marked out. Now all they needed to do was find the old racquets in their wooden presses. Agnes had brought plates of ham and bread for them to eat.

Selwyn, present for once, smiled a welcome to Tom. Aunt Kitty, looking pretty as a picture, carried the blue enamel can of tea across the field. Selwyn's eyes followed her progress across the field for a fraction of a second before he turned away and lit his pipe. The sun was at its highest, the bees dipped in and out of the clover and in the distance, over the rattle of the lawn mower, Partridge's voice could be heard laughing at something Rose was saying.

Pigeons deep in the woods were calling out to each other, saying, 'I love you Lulu', before ending with a sudden abrupt, 'yes'.

Rose emerged through the trees, white dress a crumpled surrender flag.

'Have you been talking to that wretched boy again?' asked Agnes.

'Who?' asked Rose rudely and, seeing Carlo, smiled at him. 'You are going to be my tennis partner, Carlo, at the match. You're the only one worth playing with.'

'Charming, I must say,' said Aunt Kitty.

'Bellamy's gone to the ironmongers on an errand for me,' Selwyn said.

'Honestly, Selwyn,' Kitty said, 'you didn't trust him with money did you?'

'Who's Bellamy?' Tom asked.

'You'll see,' Rose said, looking at him for the first time.

'He's the tinker's son,' Agnes said. 'I don't really like him. There's something… something…'

'What?' Rose demanded, voice silky, eyes ready to cause a blaze.

'We've known him since he was a boy,' Selwyn said, not wanting to call the fire brigade. 'At least Rose has!'

'Rose most certainly has,' agreed Rose.

Cecily laughed but Selwyn held his hand up peaceably.

'Come now all of you, stop this prejudice. Bellamy is fine.'

'Better than any of you,' muttered Rose.

Like all grown-up rows this one was going nowhere. The heat made the air thick and heavy.

'My father is organising the Kagran Group,' Tom told them. 'I mean he's *advising* them.'

Cecily yawned and closed her eyes against the glare.

'Cover your mouth when you yawn, C,' Agnes said, but she too sounded half-hearted.

'An agricultural training school is a good idea,' Selwyn agreed.

'My parents are keen on rural crafts,' Tom continued. 'When this is all over they believe Germany's future will depend on it.'

Joe frowned.

Rose pulled a face. And Carlo laughed. The two of them were sharing a joke as though it were an egg and cress sandwich. There was none left for Cecily.

'Who knows how it will work out,' Joe said crunching down hard on a pickled onion, reaching for another bottle of ale.

'You'll fall asleep,' Aunt Kitty observed.

Joe ignored her.

No one said anything. There was a ladybird sitting motionless on Rose's yellow dress, pretending to be a brooch. Surely she would be too tired to go out again tonight?

Selwyn shook his head and the scent of his pipe smoke curled in the summer air, driving the bees away and filling the afternoon with an unexpected simple happiness.

The others must have thought so too because they stretched out on the rough-cut ground and Agnes said, in a happier voice,

'There won't be a war. I'm sure of it!'

And then Aunty Kitty, who had been silent, laughed again, a shimmering, light laugh like the lemonade bottle after it had been shaken up, and she squeezed her sister's hand so hard that Cecily, watching, decided that yes, she had finally stopped loving Selwyn and everything would now be all right.

But turning back the pages of those years, walking away from Shingle Street, Cecily thought, I can't go on with this. Surely it would just be easier to put up with the voices in her head?

That depends, said one voice, naughtily.

On how we behave! added the other.

A greengage, bright as a jewel, fell from Cecily's bag and rolled into the gutter. Passers-by stared hard at her before hurrying on and still she didn't notice the stranger tailing her.

She who had wanted to know everything now saw nothing.

It was time to return to Palmyra House and take an overdue pill. She needed to keep calm but the voices were pestering her.

What happened next?

After Sunday lunch, when Joe was piling up the cut grass in readiness for a bonfire and Selwyn was looking for his tools, and Rose had done her disappearing act, Cecily took Tom around the farm.

'How many days are there before the tennis match?' Tom asked.

'Twelve.'

'And who does your sister love?'

Cecily thought he sounded like a policeman. All he needed was a notebook and a licked pencil.

'Is it Carlo? Or the tinker's son?'

'He's called Bellamy,' Cecily told him.

Large blackberries, looking like shoe buttons, were scattered amongst the mauve pink and white flowers.

'A hard winter lies ahead,' Tom remarked.

He had begun to get on Cecily's nerves.

They crossed the field where flies settled in clusters on the horses' eyes. Unanswered questions swarmed around Cecily like the flies. One uppermost in her mind had to be asked first.

'Have you met Hitler?'

Tom looked at her sideways.

'Have *you* met the King?' he asked, sarcastically.

They reached the end of the field and the barn, when they went in, was dark. In the beam of light and the fly-clouded afternoon, the cows appeared restless. Sunlight came in hot spears through the cracks in the roof to lie on the straw and milk-sprinkled dung.

'Is this the barn you dream of?' the counsellor had asked her, years later when she had come to her, heavy with hopelessness. It was.

And there was Pinky Wilson's car parked in the damson lane.

'Hello Cecily,' he said, smiling. 'Is this your new friend?'

'I'm Tom,' the boy said and held out his hand.

'Yes. Nice for Cecily to have a friend, eh Cecily? Oh and don't worry... I meant to tell you, your secret is safe with me!'

Cecily stared at him. The damsons were getting ripe. Some of them had already fallen and dark purple skins, split golden by the wasps, lay scattered on the ground.

'What secret?' Tom asked.

'Oh nothing,' Robert Wilson said. 'Nothing a little cycle ride to the pier wouldn't cure!'

'You saw me!'

Robert Wilson laughed easily. Then he took out a packet of cigarettes and tapped one on the packet before putting it in his mouth.

'*You* saw *me*!' he said.

Cecily opened her mouth but then thought better of it.

'Have you taken Tom to the Hokey-Pokey Parlour yet?'

'I arrived last night,' Tom told him.

'Ah! Well you must get Cecily to take you there. You'll find the best ice cream in the whole of England there. In fact...' he reached into his pocket, 'here, buy yourself some on me.'

He handed Tom a sixpence.

Tom eyed him doubtfully.

'Do you have a spare bicycle?' he asked Cecily.

Cecily, still winded, could not answer. And then Robert-Pinky-Wilson did another unexpected thing. He gave Cecily a hug.

'Gosh! You're so like your older sister,' he said. 'Soon you'll have all the boys after you, just like your sister.'

Cecily swallowed. In the hard glitter of the August day, Pinky Wilson's face looked cruel and shadowless.

'Stop looking so worried,' Pinky Wilson said. 'I shan't breathe a word. Your mother has quite enough to think about! In any case you children ought to have a bit more freedom.'

All around, the wheat was rising heavy and dark in the sultry air. Soon it would be time for the harvest. Pinky Wilson told them he had to go into the town himself, on some important business. He drove his car across the rough track flanked by golden-crested stonecrop in flower. And apart from the low hum of the engine it was impossible to detect his big beetle from the house.

Maybe it was the sixpence or maybe it was his knowing her secret but to Cecily's surprise, she saw Tom distrusted Pinky, too.

'He spied on you?' he asked. 'And now he's blackmailing you? That's against the law.'

Impressed, Cecily nodded.

'You can tell from that,' Tom added with the same grown-up loftiness as Rose, 'the sort of man he is. He promised to keep your secret just so you'd trust him. He's being provocative.'

Under the weight of evidence she could not disagree and the subject was dropped.

At suppertime Kitty had another bunch of sweet williams. They had been delivered by a boy from the flower shop in Eelburton. Replacing the others that weren't even old yet.

'Lovely!' she said, and she hummed a little tune.

Aunt Kitty had so many admirers it was difficult to keep track of who sent what. How many had she invited to the dance? Agnes' laugh was like a bite into an unripe apple.

While Selwyn, of course, was marked like an absence chalked up on a blackboard.

'Another important meeting,' Agnes said, adding with a laugh, 'I'm going to write my Mass Observation notes, now.'

Agnes didn't sound as if she cared one way or the other about Selwyn's absence any more. So that staring at her beautiful mother a little slyly, a little puzzled, Cecily remembered her secret nightlife and thought how happy she looked in the dim glow of the lamp.

'Better get used to duller lights,' Joe told them.

'I can't say I'm looking forward to blackouts,' Aunt Kitty added, before letting herself out through the kitchen door.

Rose's eyes had a gleam in them that no one would blackout. Later in their shared bedroom she began to darn her stocking.

'It tore,' she said even before Cecily could ask the question.

But she didn't say how and Cecily couldn't ask. Couldn't-ask was like an itch on her arm. So Cecily asked another question instead. It was like scratching the wrong place, unsatisfactory but necessary in order to keep your mind off the Real Itch.

'Have you seen Pinky?' she asked, instead.

'Why should I?' Rose replied, head bent over her needle.

'I saw him today.'

'Good for you.'

'He was having a cigarette,' Cecily ventured, hoping to jog her sister's memory in some way.

Her sister looked up then. And the secret, soft look on her face was replaced first by irritation and then by slight amusement.

'Curiouser and curiouser,' Rose said.

Which meant nothing at all.

But,

Belatedly, now, on *this* August afternoon, the newly returned Cecily realised she had spent far too much time wandering the town. What had she hoped to discover all these years later? Any moment now she was in danger of being recognised. Crossing the road as quickly as she could, she hurried back to the house. It was almost four o'clock. Time had flown backwards without a glance. The voices were quiet. Cecily could tell they liked this part of the story, having heard it once before.

On Monday morning Kitty announced she was going up to Exeter to visit an old friend. She would be back for the harvest in a few days and if Agnes wanted to go to a concert in London she could use Kitty's flat.

'Not much of a broken heart, then,' Cecily overheard Cook tell The Help.

Agnes was bottling fruit.

The last time she had been to a concert in London had been before Rose was born. They had gone to a party afterwards and although Selwyn did not like that sort of thing he hadn't minded showing off his young wife on that occasion. Arthur Balfour, the Foreign Secretary, had praised Agnes' eyes.

'You wear them like jewels, m'dear,' he had said in his loud-enough-to-be-noticed boom.

A man at the piano began playing 'When Irish Eyes Are Smiling' and Selwyn had nodded, as though her eyes had been his doing. At the time Agnes had believed he loved her but that his feelings simply lagged a little behind hers. His emotions, she had believed, were merely folded like the wings of a nesting bird. He was simply a discreet man, she had thought.

Then.

These days she hardly went anywhere.

'Is it true?' asked Robert Wilson, popping his head in through the pantry door. 'That Selwyn has been asked to join the Anti-Aircraft Division?'

Agnes nodded.

'Yes,' she said.

It had happened the previous week.

Robert Wilson handed her a small bunch of violets.

'Kitty isn't here,' Agnes said.

'No these are for *you*!'

She smiled, inviting him in for a cup of tea.

'They're all out playing in the fields,' she said, meaning Cecily, believing it was so.

'Bit of a handful, eh!' Robert laughed and Agnes nodded ruefully.

There was an advertisement cut out from *Picture Post* on the table. 'Hints for a Happy Marriage', it said. Robert raised his eyebrows and Agnes laughed. She looked around for a small glass to put the violets in.

'No, don't do that, wear them!'

'It's an advertisement for ammonia,' she said, still laughing.

She liked Robert Wilson.

'*Do* you need ammonia for a happy marriage?'

Agnes looked for a pin to wear her violets but she was laughing so much that she almost pricked her finger.

'Here, let me,' Robert said.

They drank their tea sitting outside in the kitchen garden, out of Cook's way.

'You never stop working, do you?' Robert said.

'There's a lot to do on a farm this size.'

'What do you do for relaxation? Apart from the ballet?'

'I used to play the piano.'

'And…' he shook his head.

'Inquisitive fellow,' The Help, overhearing, remarked. 'What's he doing asking her all them questions?'

Cook sniffed but would not comment.

'What's Selwyn up to with the Anti-Aircraft Unit?'

Cecily, about to sneeze, stopped herself in the nick of time. Was Pinky Wilson trying to steal secrets from her father, now?

'I'm not really sure. It's all top secret, of course.'

'Of course.'

They both ignored the bitterness in Agnes' voice. Only Cecily, listening for all she was worth, heard it quite clearly.

'I wish it would come if it's going to.'

'The war?'

'Yes. I can't stand the tension. I wake up tense. I go to sleep tense. It's impossible to settle.'

There was a pause. In the background they could hear kitchen clatter; water being poured down the sink, bottles being sealed, footsteps. The war was a snake. Waiting, was what it was about. And air raids, of course.

'The British people don't want to be moles,' Agnes sighed. 'They don't want to go to ground.'

'You shouldn't worry. The air raids, if they happen, will only happen at night,' Robert said easily.

He hesitated.

'Oh by the way, I've got you that ticket I promised for the Wigmore Hall.'

Agnes smiled. Her hair had begun to curl slightly in the humidity. It framed her face, softening it, making her look younger than she was. In the bleached light, her eyes were startling. Their expression exactly like that of her younger daughter.

'What a kind man you are,' she said, solemnly.

Robert lit his cigarette. Agnes was a beautiful woman, he thought.

'So you'll go?'

Agnes laughed.

'There's a lot to be done to get this place ready for the dance.'

She didn't say she would get no help from Selwyn who was busy with more and more defence work of late.

'Might as well take advantage and go up when you can,' Robert said, encouragingly.

His eyes were very blue. She wondered if he were married.

'Once the blackouts start... well, it'll be hopeless.'

He smiled. There was something about him that reminded her of a coiled spring that seemed at odds with his deep blue eyes.

'Are you trying to get rid of me?' she laughed. 'As soon as I turn my back on them God knows what those girls will get up to!'

'They'll be fine,' Robert said easily. 'Go. Do you good to get away for a bit. Stay in your sister's flat. Come back in the morning.'

Inside the kitchen, looking out of the window, Cook sniffed and behind the scullery door, Cecily was still trying not to sneeze.

'Thank you,' said Agnes, faintly.

'How does he know about the flat?' Cook asked, puzzled, frowning, standing still for a brief moment.

'Maybe she told him?' The Help said.

Cook sniffed. Poking his nose about. Even the children disliked him.

'It'll end in tears, I'll be bound,' she said.

'What will?' asked The Help.

'Oh get on with it,' said Cook, cross about something invisible.

Having reached the safety of the house, Cecily poured herself a glass of water with shaking hands and swallowed her pill.

For it was Rose darning her stocking that she saw.

Now.

Clearly, as though it were yesterday.

'Why do you want to wear stockings in this heat?' Cecily asked.

'It isn't about the wearing,' Rose replied. 'It's about the taking off, as you will find out one day.'

'I'm having a discussion with Tom about Einstein,' Cecily said.

Rose raised one eyebrow.

'You two are mighty thick,' was all she said.

'*Amami di Più*,' sang Cecily and Rose laughed.

'Who taught you that? Carlo?'

Cecily had felt it was time to take stock of all her sister's unanswered questions.

'They embarked on a euthanasia programme in Germany and Austria,' she told her. 'That's why Tom's family left.'

'I shouldn't take too much notice of that one,' Rose said. 'He's trying too hard to impress.'

'Why?'

Rose put down her stocking and looked solemnly at Cecily.

'There are some things we don't ask Out Of Politeness To Others,' she said.

Then she began examining her long, sunburnt legs.

Tom had a cough and Out Of Politeness Cecily didn't like to ask if euthanasia was a cough medicine. There were several things she felt she couldn't ask. But she had been making a list of things both polite and impolite.

Why did their mother look suddenly happy?

Why was Captain Pinky buying her a ticket to a concert? ('Is he?' asked Rose, her expression thunderous. 'Where did you hear that, you pesky eavesdropper? I hope she's not following in the footsteps of that floozy, Kitty.')

How had Rose torn her dress?

Had she been with Carlo when it happened?

What had Captain Pinky been doing at the pier that night when he had told them he was having An Early Night?

Did Daddy *really* love Aunt Kitty?

There were many more questions but she couldn't remember them all.

The tennis racquets had been found and repaired. In her narrow bed that night, waiting for the party, Cecily thought that Rose was no fun any more. And the summer, she saw with a painful awareness never present before, was slipping away. She had spent it eavesdropping while all the while her sister Rose was becoming another person altogether. I'll never change, Cecily vowed. Never. It is part of the constitution of my character.

Afterwards she would remember that night as though it had been a dog-eared corner in a diary. The full moon pouring softly down somewhere above the roof of the house, washing away all the confusion of the day, leaving only a perfect stillness. Her mother's voice floating up from the garden through the open window, and Rose fast asleep for once, in a too-many-late-nights, exhausted sleep. Cecily had stretched under her thin covers thinking all these things. (She had heard somewhere that if you stretched a little bit every day you would grow taller). Thinking of Tom in his room over the stables, sleeping. And Joe across the landing, sleeping also. Soon he would be leaving them. Cecily had seen him standing in front of the mirror gazing at himself in the greatcoat his uncle had worn during the First World War. Cecily had watched through a crack in the door and seen that Joe's face was full of concentration as he did his buttons up and then blank again as he gazed at himself. Was he thinking of Franca? Cecily hoped so. She badly wanted him to marry Franca.

Selwyn was still at some meeting looking after National Security. He could not sleep very much because of this. As for Aunt Kitty, Cecily forgot to mention Kitty in her prayers that moonless summer night before finally dropping off to sleep.

No one heard the owl hoot.

No one heard the sea washing the pebbles.

No one heard the clock strike the hour or the squeak of a bicycle brake or the small breeze stirring a curtain.

From this distance no one could hear the music on the pier or the sound of tables being folded and put away at Molinellos'.

No one saw Lucio walk swiftly towards the river.

Not even me, thought Cecily, now, looking at her cold ringless hands in the light of a sixties day.

Nor had Cecily known that, after her mother had finished playing the 'Moonlight Sonata', with the soft pedal down so as not to wake the children, Agnes had closed the lid of the piano and sighed. She was sorry if she had been a little harsh with Cecily after the ballet. She was sorry about so many things that she had lost count of them. Creeping upstairs, she had looked in on them. Her girls.

Cecily and Rose.

Rose and Cecily.

She kissed them both. Equally, for they were equal in her mind.

She went into her room and turned down the covers of the large double bed. She would be sleeping in it alone later on for Selwyn was somewhere in London, she knew. She stood surveying the room for a moment longer. Then, taking a thin shawl out of a drawer, she slipped out of the sleeping house. Making for the river.

And when the owl that lived closest to the house had waited longer than usual he saw a small movement in the grass below. It wasn't an apple falling. So in one swift, graceful movement the bird spread his wings and swooped down. There was no sound. The animal was captured and airborne. Death came under the cover of a great wing.

White,
silent,
and instant.

14.

TO WAKE IN her old bed after so long was bad enough, but what was worse were the old scents that lay in wait in the hidden corners of the house. Cecily splashed the remnants of the awful night out of her eyes with cold water and went out again. Walking across to the Ness at low tide it shocked her to see the skeletal appearance of the burnt pier.

Death had left its footprints everywhere, corroding its posts and innards so that what remained was bent and buckled like rotten teeth in sea saliva. Neglect had grown its barnacles on the blackened planks while sightless carbuncles of mud from previous flooding had stuck to the rotten walls of its pavilion. There was nothing here for her except unresolved stories. What had made her love this place so much? What had drawn Rose to it? A curlew, wings outstretched, glided with strange slow-ness beyond all earthly anxieties. Once Cecily used to believe a water devil made its home in these marshy waters. The past was inscrutable and the story of the burnt-away pier remained an old, unsolvable story.

A white butterfly with black markings alighted on a stone at her feet, appearing to dry itself in the pale sunlight. When it didn't move she touched it but it remained motionless and she realised it was dead. Its wings were covered in ethereal dust. It rested like a shrouded corpse. Sorrow at its passing overcame Cecily in such a wave that turning, she set off towards Bly's seafront. Everything she had tried to love had gone.

But the seafront, when she reached it by the old route, the one taken long ago by Lucio and Agnes, had shifted and changed just as Shingle Street had altered. The wooden shacks were all gone. No Punch-and-Judy man, no helter-skelter and naturally, no ice-cream parlour awaited her. Instead there was the noise of a fast food cafe and a few fruit machines over whose flickering coloured light the unemployed dreamt. A puddle had grown in the road from the previous night's storm and a public toilet, abandoned years before, stood with a hole in its roof. Only the sea, impenetrable and unchanged, remained.

You see, said the voices in Cecily's head, *All Things Pass. No use crying. Okay?*

Was she meant to take comfort in this?

Had she asked the fishermen gathering their empty nets, some would have told Cecily how, on stormy nights there arose the sound of wailing from the ship called *The Arandora Star.* They would have told her of the bodies that had washed up on these shores. The fishermen would have, with some hesitation, told her that after a particularly bad storm there was *still* the chance of another corpse being spotted. It was not beyond the realm of possibility, they would have said. And then, had she pressed further, they might have told her it was always the gulls who picked them out first, passing on the news, hovering over the water like a great choir singing the dead to rest. But Cecily didn't ask and the fishermen were uncertain if it was really Cecily Maudsley, daughter of Selwyn Maudsley, younger sister of Rose Maudsley (and therefore tainted like all the Maudsleys in spite of their big house), who had finally returned.

On this warm day-after-the-street-party day, Bellamy Samuel Darby, seeing Cecily silhouetted against the light, paused in his work to take out his pipe. His hands were gnarled with over-knotting nylon netting. They were the same hands that once had twisted the necks of small rabbits. But Bellamy was a different sort of man.

Now.

'Time for a break,' he told his boatswain. 'Swift half down the pub?'

'Ever ready,' laughed the boatswain, puzzled by the figure too.

Then he remembered. Of course!

'I'm going to talk to her,' Bellamy said, chin pushed forward, determined.

The sun was in everyone's eyes and the pebbly beach wasn't easy to walk up but he went.

'Are you,' he asked, 'Cecily?'

Because there was water in the sky a rainbow formed. Somewhere over it was blueness but Cecily couldn't see it. Bellamy began to whistle the tune he used to whistle to her and then she remembered.

'I was thirteen, going on fourteen,' she said, without a trace of a smile.

It was the first real acknowledgement of past times and it rang clear as a bell within her. The sea shifted slightly but the tide remained out.

'You thought I had a prawn in my trouser pocket,' Bellamy said and he bent double with an old man's laughter.

Cecily stood very still; a butterfly, knowing the net will soon be pulled over its wings.

'We all thought you had gone for good,' Bellamy said, when he had done with laughing.

'No,' Cecily said. 'I'm here.'

'So I see.'

And he handed her a creased photo from inside his wallet.

'My missus,' he said. 'We've been married these eighteen years.'

There was defiance in his voice. Of a kind that needed an audience.

Once long ago, his look said, I loved a summer rose with thorns.

The breeze coming in from the sea hushed the thought. Cecily saw how great his hurt had been merely from looking at the creases in the photograph.

'You married, Cecily?' he asked when she made no move.

'No. Not any more.'

She felt someone breathing down her neck.

Shock him, shock him, the voices pleaded.

But Cecily was tired out. She was beginning to remember certain things about Bellamy.

'Ah!' Bellamy was saying, mockingly. 'Divorced, are you?'

She could not deny it, hoping her silence would do the trick. He took a step backwards. Awkwardness had got stuck to his foot. It clung like the damp sand and made his shoes heavy. The only way was to shake it off. Still, he thought, she's a stunner. Wonder if she knows? Different though. Quiet now. Never used to be quiet. My word, what a chatterbox she was.

Then.

'We've two kids,' he said. 'Two boys. Grand lads. Look.'

He held out another photograph, less creased, this one.

Small children,

young woman,

Bellamy.

Smiling up at the sunlight. Pride in his voice, brimming over like a net full of catch.

Things fell easily into place after that and Cecily remembered him with sharp clarity. Back-door begging, Cook had called it. She hadn't wanted him there. She didn't want caravan people working in Palmyra Farm, let alone coming up to the house.

'Gipsies!' she had said. 'Tinkers! They're all trouble, aren't they, Mrs Maudsley?'

Bellamy's face had darkened.

'I was her real love,' he said now, regret tucked discreetly out of sight.

'Touch of the tar brush there,' Cecily had heard Partridge say. 'Your sister's friend!'

Cecily hadn't known what he meant.

Then.

'Nonsense,' Selwyn had said coming in, holding his hand up against Cook's tirade.

Selwyn had been Bellamy's champion in those days. No one knew why and behind Selwyn's back Bellamy used to make rude gestures at Cook. He'd wink at Cecily before going in search of Rose.

'Ah Rose! Rose!' he said now.

Leaving what was best left unsaid.

'His mother's a good woman,' Selwyn used to say, 'She has a very hard time of it. And please stop calling them gipsies. They're nothing of the sort.'

Liberal, upright Selwyn. Always for the underdog.

What changed you, wondered the adult Cecily.

What confusion led you astray?

Was it anger over the way your brother died?

Was it Kitty?

Was it in the end just the old story of a misguided man led astray by a woman?

Was there nothing more to it than that?

Weak, desperate Selwyn, she thought.

Now.

'There's enough prejudice in the world, already,' she remembered her father had said. 'Besides which, we'll all be pulling against each other soon enough.'

'Your father is a socialist,' Agnes had told Cecily, after she had grown up. After it was all too late.

'He's before his time.'

Social List, thought Cecily, out of habit.

On August the 23rd the pact between Germany and Russia was agreed.

From Berlin, *The Times* correspondent noted that ordinary Germans felt that now at last they could do as they pleased and nobody would dare fight them.

'The war will make equals of us all,' Selwyn announced.

'Not during it,' Agnes said. '*After*, maybe.'

'Oh after,' Selwyn said carelessly, as though 'after' hadn't mattered.

'But there isn't going to be one,' Cecily reminded them.

'With any luck,' Selwyn agreed.

And then he had hired Bellamy, as he always did, to help with the harvest.

We all paid a price, Cecily thought, staring up at this thick set, middle-aged man. Bellamy had hated Tom from the very beginning.

'You're not his friend,' he had told her that day long ago. 'He's soft in the head.'

'He's not,' Cecily said and Bellamy had scowled.

'Know something I don't?'

There had been a fight in the orchard, she remembered. Captain Pinky had been present. What had he been talking about? It had been hot, of course. They had been watching a field mouse sitting on the stone wall, eating a grain of corn. It washed its face, and vanished and only the bees in clover remained.

That Monday they had planned to visit the ice-cream parlour again, not caring about Berlin. Apart from spying, Tom's other obsession was ice cream. On the way whom should they meet but Captain Pinky? Up to no good, they had felt. Wearing a straw boater and looking as though he was going to the beach.

'Here,' he said. 'Have one on me.'

And he had handed Tom that sixpence.

'Tell me how many Italians you see when you're there. Remember I'm doing a survey for the town census.'

'Thank you,' Tom said.

'Can I count the people too?' Cecily asked.

'Of course.'

But he hadn't given her anything and she had been miffed. But before she could question the unfairness, there had been a rustling in the bushes and Bellamy appeared. Hot, bothered, ready for a fight.

'Hello,' Captain Pinky said. 'Spying on us, are you?'

'*You're* the rotten spy,' Bellamy had said, coolly. 'As you well know.'

Had they been on different sides? Cecily wondered now, amazed.
Bit late to ask that! said the voices.

'Now look here, old chap,' Captain Pinky said, still smiling.

The smile, Cecily saw, was a little overstretched.

'*And* I saw you giving them money. Bribery, it is.'

For a moment Cecily felt a twinge of excitement.

'You silly boy,' Captain Pinky said, swinging his voice around. 'I'm working for the British Government to protect the British people.'

It would have all been fine if Tom hadn't laughed at Bellamy.

For a split second Bellamy looked confused. Then he turned slowly and with no warning, lunged out at Tom. Tom was caught off guard.

Legs flailing, moments later, both boys on the ground with Bellamy on top, and Cecily shouting at them to stop.

'Keep out of this,' Bellamy snarled and he punched Tom in the face.

Everyone was yelling.

Then Captain Pinky joined in the fray and tried to separate the villains but Cecily was in the way and a kick, aimed by Tom at the tinker's son, landed on her head, sending her flying over the boys' grunts into the dry abyss of thistles. And stones and cowpats. It was a rugger-mugger sort of scrum until Pinky Wilson saved the day with a swift, neat tackle, separating the boys while holding on to both.

Grimly.

Tom spat out blood.

Bellamy, saliva.

'Look what you've done,' he cried in fury. 'Cecily's bleeding.'

Captain Pinky grabbed hold of Bellamy, stopping him in mid-flight.

(Where d'you think you're going young man?)

Tom stood limply beside Cecily who, even though her face was cut, was enjoying it all very much.

'You've gashed your forehead,' Tom said, peering at her with horrified fascination.

They all looked at her.

'It's colossally deep. It's sort of white inside – I say! I think you've cut yourself to the bone!'

Cecily felt sick, but rather thrilled all the same. Who wouldn't? It was pretty important to have cut yourself to the bone. She could not feel any acute pain as yet, only the bruised ache where her whole face had hit the ground. It was gratifying to have something to show for it. Instantly Tom rose sublimely to the occasion, tearing a strip off the bottom of his shirt.

'No, no, wait,' Pinky said. 'I think we should take you back to the house, Cecily.'

But Tom was already binding the cloth untidily round her head.

'The blood's coming through…'

He sounded rather scared.

Captain P picked Cecily up easily and strode back to the house. Tom, a hero, trotting anxiously behind. They had forgotten about Bellamy, who disappeared as swiftly as one of his ferrets.

'Cecily's cut herself to the bone,' Tom announced before Captain P could stop him.

Cook and Agnes stared and Carlo, sitting at the kitchen table, waiting for Rose, stood up in alarm. The sight of Carlo had turned on the tap of tears behind Cecily's eyes. The cloth was blood-soaked and very gory. Everyone made a hell of a fuss. Carlo took her face in his hands and kissed it, gently. Sweetly. As if she were his little sister. And this made her cry more.

'Poor little Cecci,' Carlo said, wiping her eyes.

Cecily cried all the harder.

Bellamy's part in the events was discussed. Tom took his share of the blame manfully but Captain Pinky would have none of that. He explained everything first to Agnes and then to Cook and then later on once more to Kitty. He never once blamed either party more than the other, which was clever of him although Cook kept muttering about gipsies.

'Where's the wretched boy?' Agnes asked.

She would have to tell Selwyn that this would not do. But where was Selwyn when he was needed?

'I'll find him,' Tom said and ran out.

'I'll phone for the doctor,' Cook was putting water to boil. The doctor would want to sterilise the wound.

Doctor Denys, stitching stitches into Cecily's forehead as though he were a tailor, promised no more than a tiny scar.

'That's very important for you young ladies,' he said.

'What is?' asked Rose drifting in, interested in Cecily for a change, thus making it a very interesting day, all round.

But later it was Rose, quietly and alone, who defended Bellamy when a first-class row broke out between Agnes and Selwyn.

That had been Bellamy then. Now he had his own fishing fleet. And a wife and two grand lads.

He stood watching Cecily as she remembered. Perhaps he was remembering different things. How Rose's death had been made into quite a story by the newspapers, relieved to have something besides the war to write about. They had called it a Tragedy with Sex and Betrayal. Followed by Death. No one had asked his opinion. No one had asked if he had known the Victim. Or the Perpetrator. Or even if there had been any Collateral Damage. Staring down at Cecily's beautiful, empty face, these might have been the things Bellamy was remembering.

'The boys are doing well at school,' he said, using words to hide behind.

Standing with her feet sinking into the beach, Cecily listened without hearing.

'I don't want them to work the sea, or live in a caravan. I want them to be respected. To study, to get good jobs.'

Cecily wondered what his wife was like. As if he heard her thoughts, Bellamy smiled.

'You must come over,' he said. 'Meet the missus. She's like you!'

There was another heavy silence and Bellamy took a further step backwards.

'Tide's out,' he told her, uneasily. You staying up at the house?' Cecily nodded.

'Oh, okay,' he smiled, again. 'Come over.'

And he took something out of his pocket and pushed it into her hand.

'I heard you were about,' he said apologetically. 'So I fetched it.'

Cecily was silent. Then he turned and hurried off, his footsteps becoming fainter as he walked away. When he reached the pile of nets, he turned and shouted something, waving his hand. Cecily shook her head, not understanding, but he had turned away again. He was whistling. The sound of it threw itself backwards towards her.

A tune from long ago,
A rainbow that had vanished.

Walking quickly back towards Palmyra House (she was too shaken to stay out any longer) Cecily realised what it was he'd said.

'The quack was right,' Bellamy had said. 'It is only a tiny scar!'

Opening the front door with her right hand, she saw what he had put into her left hand. Her mind was a blank, her body trembling.

'Time for another pill, perhaps,' she said, aloud.

How many more years could she go on living in this way? I'll make a cup of tea, she thought, sitting down, confused, at the kitchen table. No one had sat here in years. The black and white photograph was of Rose. And Cecily. It wasn't large. There was nothing unusual about it. The black wasn't very black and the white was creased and unshiny. But Rose was smiling and so was Cecily. Someone had scratched away the face of the boy standing next to Cecily. She could tell from his legs and how he stood that the figure was that of Bellamy. The white scratches over his face had almost gone through to the other side. Hate marked the image with vigour and something inside Cecily shivered. It had not been what she had expected but then she saw, faintly in the background, the figure of Robert Pinky Wilson, one foot in front of the other, trying to walk out of shot. Cigarette-tapping Pinky Wilson, blurred features, still recognisable. While walking towards them from the spinney, a fleeting glimpse of polka-dotted Agnes, out of shot but for her hem. And was that Lucio behind her? What on earth had they all been doing on that day, twenty-nine years ago? With the sun so high that no one noticed these things, they could only be seen with hindsight.

That day, when Franca, wearing her pastel pink dress, could no longer hide her feelings for Joe, and when Joe (who wasn't even in the picture) plucked up the courage to tell her he loved her.

That day, or was it before, or even after the tennis court party, when Carlo told Cecily she was so tall now that she came up to his heart.

When the hoardings appearing all over England bore the slogan, 'What Price Churchill?' as though he was being auctioned off.

Going, going, gone, like the day itself.

Time running away like a shrew over a shoe.

Time running out like the tide.

Only three weeks before she died.

Rose Maudsley.

A Thing of Beauty.

Breaths of Heaven.

A living, breathing girl with a toothache smile.

Caused by eating too much ice cream.

15.

IN THE PANTRY in Palmyra House, there remained a solitary jar of Agnes' plum jam gathering dust on a shelf. The hand that bottled it was long gone. Cecily stared at the writing. August 23rd 1939. Was it edible?

For some reason the sight of the jar brought Carlo to mind, sleeves rolled up, eating a piece of freshly baked bread. Jam oozing out, warm butter from the churn, Cook cross with everyone as usual, except of course Carlo.

Agnes had agreed to go up to London but she needed to finish bottling the yellow plums first. She felt harassed and wondered if she could really spare the time. It was Wednesday now. Six days to harvest, ten to the party, how many to a war? The thermometer was a steady eighty-five and the wireless was on again.

World shocked by Berlin-Moscow pact.

Lucio had important business in London and had offered Agnes a lift.

'What sort of business?' Pinky Wilson asked, popping in for a cup of tea and his usual morning chat.

Oblivious to Cook's heavy sniffing.

Friendly gossip was what he called these chats.

Snooping was what Cook called it.

'Oh, he edits a small newspaper,' Agnes said. 'For homesick Italians.'

Agnes had developed a song in her heart and her dimple had come out of hibernation.

'Ah,' said Pinky Wilson in what Cecily felt was a significant way.

Captain P was being as nosy as Tom.

'Can I come?' Cecily asked, after *that man*, had gone.

Her mother ignored her and it occurred to Cecily that everyone was cross these days.

'When will you be back?' she asked. 'It will be a dismal day until you return.'

Agnes, who wasn't in the least bit cross, laughed and laughed.

'I'll be back tomorrow,' she said, 'and if you are good and don't fight with Rose I'll bring you a present.'

Cecily opened her mouth to speak but her sister's expression made her forget what she wanted to say.

'It isn't fair,' Rose said, in a *sotto voce* sulk. 'I want to go to London too. I hate this place. I shall die of boredom!'

Shocking liar, thought Cecily. From the way her hair was done, it was clear Rose had plenty of plans of her own for the evening.

Agnes was behaving like a dove released from a cage, and Tom was showing off again.

'Britain doesn't hate Germany,' he said.

Cecily wanted to hit him.

'True,' Joe agreed. 'All this talk of encirclement is nonsense. No one wants war with the Germans!'

'Then why are you going?' Cecily asked.

'I'm not, not really. Just preparing, as a precaution.'

Rose wasn't listening.

On the news it was announced that the Imperial War Museum was closing. Tomorrow all its works of art would be evacuated.

Lucio was feeling harassed too. Aware that the presence of Fascist Italians in Britain could become a big problem, he wanted to nose out the trouble in advance. He could not confide in anyone in his family. Only his nephew Carlo cared about what was going on behind the scenes. In Lucio's opinion, Carlo was the brightest Molinello of them all. He read all the Italian newspapers that Lucio brought home and helped distribute *il Lotto* amongst the Italian community. Sometimes he even attended events at the social club in Clerkenwell where, during innocent conversations with the children of friends, he gleaned pieces of information that might one day be important in ensuring the safety of the Italian community. So Lucio was proud of his nephew. Normally he would have taken Carlo with him on the trip but on this occasion he could not. This time he would have Agnes in the car with him.

'It isn't safe,' he told Carlo, 'something is bound to come out in conversation.'

Agnes was an innocent bystander, Lucio didn't want to endanger her in any way. If she accidentally repeated some small thing to Anna they could all be put in danger.

'In any case,' Lucio said, pulling a face, 'your father would have a fit if he knew what you got up to!'

Carlo had been ready to tail Robert Wilson. He had followed the man skilfully once before without being noticed. He was undoubtedly a natural. But now the plan, made many days before, would have to be abandoned. Carlo was bitterly disappointed.

Lucio had been keeping an eye on the Wilson man for some months, following him on his trips up to London. His presence at Palmyra House, his friendship with first Agnes and then Kitty, his gifts to the young girls, all these things worried Lucio for, through a network of contacts, he had found out that Robert Wilson was not the man he said he was. His boss was not Sir Dudley Stamp of the Land Utilisation Survey. His boss was Lord Halifax and possibly even the Prime Minister himself. These were rumours that Lucio desperately needed to investigate. He didn't want to alarm anyone but his unease was growing.

'Well,' he said, grimly, looking at his nephew's disappointed face. 'I'll do it myself this time. And, if my guess is right, there will be plenty more trips for you before this is over!'

'But I wanted to help *now*,' Carlo protested.

Lucio smiled wryly.

'Stay here and keep an eye on the place,' he murmured. 'You know what to do if I don't return!'

Carlo looked alarmed.

'I'm joking,' Lucio said. 'I'll tell you what happens tomorrow. Just don't tell your father, for God's sake!'

Then he drove off to Palmyra House to pick up Agnes and in spite of the world news he found himself whistling.

In London, just before she was dropped off at the Wigmore Hall, Agnes suddenly thought she saw her sister walking over Waterloo Bridge.

'How can this be?' Lucio asked, 'I thought you told me she'd gone to Exeter for a few days?'

For a second, the afternoon became shrouded in mystery. But it could not have been Kitty.

Lucio warned Agnes he would not be free to see her until much later. Was it okay? He had a meeting to attend.

'Take your time,' Agnes said. 'I've brought my diary with me. I'm writing for Mass Observation, you see.'

Her shy smile was at odds with the boldness in her eyes and Lucio's heart rose. Did he need to go to this meeting? Wouldn't he be happier picking her up after the concert, so they could have supper together?

'No, no! I'll make myself an omelette in Kitty's kitchen,' Agnes told him, adding softly, 'and then I'll wait for you.'

Lucio hesitated a moment longer. Her grave and tender look sent a strange fear over him. I am being superstitious, he told himself. We are safe. In the late summer light Agnes reminded him of a flower. When had his feelings for her become so intense? This was not what he had bargained for. He had a job of work to do. Agnes was not part of any plan.

'After this crisis is over,' he said, 'I would like to take you on a cruise ship. Across the Atlantic to America!'

He brushed her lips gently with his own, then reluctantly he drove on towards Wigmore Hall, dropping her off, watching her being swallowed up by the crowd, the image of her remaining before him, fixed and slightly disturbing. A moment later he crossed the river.

Robert Wilson, unaware he was being followed by Lucio Molinello, drove back up the Strand towards Chelsea. He had been dining with Lord Halifax. There had been several new faces at the meeting, including the editor of *The Telegraph*. Albert Einstein it seemed had written a letter to President Roosevelt that everyone in the Cabinet was talking about.

'Can one believe the claim,' asked the editor, 'that a single atomic bomb, if dropped on a port, might destroy everything, together with some surrounding territory? Can this be possible?'

No one had known what to say. Such destruction was impossible to imagine.

Was Germany bluffing? Should Britain go to war to defend Danzig? And what on earth was to be done about the growing number of foreigners in the country? Life was becoming a nightmare.

'Fascism is spreading unchecked in Britain,' one member of the cabinet remarked.

'Is this your own view?' Lord Halifax asked.

'No, sir, just what I heard.'

Everyone's sitting on the fence, thought Robert Wilson. In his opinion there was another more localised headache that had to be dealt with first. But when he finally got to speak privately to Halifax about his suspicions, the response had been predictable. Halifax was only interested in the main problem.

'I'm worried,' Robert admitted. 'Potentially this could be huge if it got out of control.

'How certain are you?' Lord Halifax asked.

'Not entirely, sir,' Robert said.

Halifax relit his cigar.

'Right. Well keep an eye on the situation,' he advised. 'No need to do anything yet. Things are changing daily. You know the drill, jump in your own time, old chap.'

Halifax trusted him. That was the main thing. Although, and here Robert Wilson paused, he knew that in the end he was on his own. Now, and probably forever. Not that he cared any more, he thought grimly.

An hour later Robert drove swiftly along Fleet Street, turned left into Shoe Lane, a narrow one-way overspill to all the news-paper offices in the area, and parked awkwardly outside number thirty-seven. He had a small, anonymous office here. Deciding to take the stairs, he went up to his office. Narrowly missing Kitty, who walked out of the lift and headed towards the river and the railway station.

It was a quarter to midnight.

He poured himself a glass of scotch.

Seven sweet williams stood in a glass of water on his desk. He looked thoughtfully at them. The sign they had agreed on.

So she had something to tell him, did she? Well...

Seven, not ten. Ten would have been serious.

Seven, not twelve. Which would have been catastrophic.

He continued to stare at the flowers. Then he broke off a head and threaded it absent-mindedly through his buttonhole. Something must have cropped up but obviously she couldn't stay. Damn, he thought. Looking around, he checked that nothing was amiss. He knew from past experience that Kitty often blew hot and cold, changed her mind, even became a little hysterical. As he had intimated to Halifax, he often had to have the informa-tion she gave him checked out. One could never be too careful. Kitty had uncertain allegiances. But nothing had been disturbed in the office and whatever it was it would have to wait.

He took a file from its usual hiding place. There were just two hours in which to finish his report.

Downstairs *Picture Post* was being put to bed, riding high on an editor's desire to embrace Germany. The sounds of machines in motion could be heard faintly through the floorboards. Robert Wilson, dog-tired and unhappy, could not leave until he had finished. A nagging thought, vague but persistent, kept returning to worry him. Sitting back in his chair, he tried to work out what it was. The boy Bellamy was a problem, too. Twice now Robert had met the boy on the footpath whilst going from his rented cottage across the field to Bly. Their exchanges had been guarded. Then yesterday he had caught Bellamy training a pair of binoculars on the Martello tower where he, Robert, kept his Bentley. Robert sighed. The sooner he could compile his list and leave Palmyra Farm, the better.

Soon, soon, the tempest would come. Of that he was certain. And the Maudsleys?

Selwyn,

Kitty,

Agnes?

Joe, soon to be conscripted.

Innocent Cecily.

And pretty Rose?

What of them all?

The collective problem he had not anticipated, that was what *they* were.

There were others who were a problem, too, but they were easily dealt with. When the time was right. For now, it was the Maudsleys who bothered him most. What could he do with them?

Feeding a fresh piece of paper into his typewriter, he was about to begin work when a small sound stopped him. He froze. Someone was outside on the landing. He was not expecting any visitors at this late hour.

There were only two other offices on this floor. One of them belonged to a literary agent and the other was a stockroom for the newspaper. Neither was used very much. Glancing down, he saw he'd forgotten to place the roll of felt against the door. Whoever was outside would see light seeping through.

Resisting the desire to cough, Robert took the phone off the hook. The receiver made a small click and he winced. There was nothing for it but to sit it out. The bottle of scotch was maddeningly out of reach. If he moved, the floorboards would creak. The revolver he possessed but did not wish to use was in the drawer of his desk.

He waited. In the silence his highly tuned ear detected a shoe being turned on a sole. The person outside didn't want to be heard, either. He saw the brass door handle turn slightly. Once to the left, and then back again. He had always made a point of oiling every door handle with which he came into contact and so it moved soundlessly.

Nothing between them, thought Robert, almost enjoying himself, *except the width of a door*. But then, wasn't that all there was between any of them? Part of his mind felt curiously relaxed, interested. The other part was ready. Except for the file, impossible to decipher, and impossible to find, there wasn't much to give him away. In the pause that followed, he heard receding footsteps and counted them. Then with one swift movement he lifted up a floorboard and deposited the file into the space below. The list he had been so carefully compiling was all in this file. There was no duplicate. He switched off the light and went over to the window.

But all he saw was a car pulling away with a dark-haired man in it. It was him all right. So they had become suspicious.

When it had gone, Robert waited for a moment longer. The Arab printers downstairs were still working furiously. He switched on the light, picked up the receiver, listening first for a tone before dialling.

'475321,' he said. 'Primrose.'

There was a pause during which he opened his cigarette case and took out another cigarette. He patted his pockets looking for his lighter and waited.

Yes,' he said, frowning. 'I think so, yes. The Italian, I think. No, nothing else. I'm back in the morning. Of course.'

The sounds downstairs were followed by muffled voices shouting instructions. A telephone rang in the depths and was answered.

'I shall need another place,' Robert said. 'Yes, yes. Of course.'

He hung up. Hesitating, he opened up the floorboards again and took out the file he had just hidden. Then he began to remove all the papers before stuffing them into his briefcase. He emptied the ashtray. Switching off the light once more, he made his way noiselessly downstairs and into the street, bypassing the newspaper's office. This time he did not lock the door.

Kitty's flat was empty as promised. A note in Kitty's handwriting instructed Agnes to use anything she needed. There was champagne in the fridge, cold salmon and brown bread and butter. The bed was freshly made up. There were clean towels and plenty of hot water. Some sweet williams stood in a vase by the bed, one small puddle of water freshly spilled on the bedside table.

When you leave just push the key back through the letterbox Kitty had written.

Lucio glanced at the note and hesitated. He had just arrived and Agnes was pouring him a drink. He was too tired for food, he told her. She saw his hands tremble as he held the glass.

'Are you sure?' he asked. 'I can leave, come back and pick you up in the morning? We can... wait...'

Agnes shook her head and presently she saw in his face, as he turned towards her in the soft glow of the lit lamp, a reflection of all that he was thinking. A shot of almost feverish desire seemed to leap up in him as, with the final decision reached, he cupped her face in his hands. All that had been growing in her, all the tender opening of her feelings, soaked into his fingers so that at last, turning, she led him towards the bed. She had forgotten, they both had, the tiny drops of fresh water, lying silently beside the vase.

Selwyn Maudsley wasn't at any anti-aircraft meeting. He wasn't with the ARPs, he wasn't reporting to headquarters in London. He was alone on the Ness, not very far from the Last Pier. He had been there since late afternoon, in the abandoned coastguard hut. It was his private space. From here he had a good view of the mainland and also of any sea landings, should they occur. He had been waiting off and on for days for the sight of Robert Wilson's black Bentley rolling along the marsh road at low tide. So far there had been no sign of it. So far Kitty, who had been delayed in Exeter, had got it wrong.

On the walls of the hut were pinned tidal maps of the area, marked at intervals with red rings. There was also a map of the Ness itself and the stretch of beach near Bly on which the Martello tower stood. It could be that the Bentley had been parked there already, of course. But if this was the case, he would have heard it or seen the low sweep of its headlight on the water.

Moonlight flooded the marshes and bleached the colour from the reed beds. In all the years he had been coming here Selwyn had never known the area look so dry and parched. There occurred the harsh cry of a waterbird fading into nothing. It was the same everywhere you looked, Selwyn thought, continuing to search the landscape. The world was red in tooth and claw. He would wait until the morning if need be and when the tide finally went out, he would cycle home via the causeway and across the fields. Taking out a hip flask, he poured himself another whisky and prepared to wait.

Waking, Cecily thought she was dreaming. Her sister was talking to herself.

'Oh shut up, shut up, you muff,' Rose breathed.

Abruptly Cecily was fully awake.

Rose, fully dressed, had gone into their parents' room and switched on the light. Cecily tiptoed out of bed and onto the landing. She was only doing this for research purposes, she told herself. Their parents' room looked curiously dead. On the dressing table was a silver framed photo of them on their wedding day. Agnes smiling up at Selwyn. Rose was staring at the image.

'I have to look my *very* best,' she said out aloud. 'I have to make him swoon at the dance. I *have* to!'

Cecily stared through a crack in the door as Rose swept up her hair, exposing her slender neck. Then with her other hand, she slowly unbuttoned her dress so she could see the entire length of herself naked in the glass.

Cecily swallowed. Their mother's jewellery box was half open. Inside were the emeralds their father had bought their mother. Rose picked out a tiny string of pearls. She turned, coming towards the door and, taking fright, Cecily fled.

But Rose did not come back to bed. Cecily heard her going downstairs. It was impossible to leave things as they stood. She would simply have to follow her sister. Rose walked out through the kitchen door to the shed where her bicycle was.

'Where are you going?' Bellamy asked, blocking her path.

Cecily jumped and almost knocked over a chair. She heard a scuffle and saw Rose push him fiercely and with force, both hands against his chest.

'Are you spying on me?'

In the dim moonlight Bellamy's face looked desperate. As if the recollection of a blistering earlier taunt was festering. Suddenly Cecily felt sorry for him. He was like a faithful hound. It wasn't fair that he should be kicked again and again. In a flash she saw, perhaps more clearly than before, that the complications about her sister, about Bellamy too, about everything to do with them both, were too vast for her to understand. And did Rose really love Carlo?

'I'm glad you came out,' Bellamy said, simply.

Cecily saw on her sister's face a look that seemed to be fighting with itself as, with a hopeless sound, Bellamy bent down and kissed Rose.

'Oh, do get away from me,' Rose said. 'I'm tired of you, don't you understand? I shall tell Daddy if you won't leave me alone and he'll sack you.'

There was a pause.

'Selwyn won't be back tonight,' Bellamy said.

Rose laughed.

'How d'you know?'

'I just do.'

'You do not! He's at an important meeting but he said he'd try to get back as soon as possible.'

There was a silence. Cecily could hear Bellamy's angry breathing.

'Look, Bell,' Rose said in a more conciliatory voice, 'I know I... I let you...'

'What?'

'It's over Bell. Can't you see? It's a very old story now.'

'Oh? So who's the new story, then?'

Rose made an impatient sound.

'I'm telling you, Bell, leave me alone or I shall have to tell Daddy you're being a nuisance. And then he'll be forced to get rid of you.'

'Tell Daddy, then,' Bellamy said and his voice suddenly coarsened. 'What will you tell him? He's busy knocking off Kitty.'

Rose slapped him. Bellamy stared at her, bitterness bubbling to the surface.

'Where are you going?' he asked again.

'I'm going to meet Joe at the corner. He's got a puncture and I'm going to meet him with the torch.'

She's lying, thought Cecily, shocked. She's going to meet Carlo. Suddenly, in spite of the balmy night she felt very cold and desolate. Bellamy continued to stare helplessly at Rose.

'You'd better stop loitering around here, you know!' she said at last. 'I'll simply have to tell Mummy and then you'll be in trouble.'

'So will you,' Bellamy said, but he turned and melted into the trees.

When she was satisfied he had really gone, Rose mounted her bicycle and rode off in the direction of the bright lights and the band music playing on the seafront.

Back in her bed, colder than she had ever been, Cecily saw a small piece of paper peeping out from under Rose's pillow.

Let's meet at the dance, it said. *But not raise suspicion with your parents.*

The handwriting was not Carlo's.

16.

ALL THE SCENTS from the orchard were in that old pot of plum jam. Sitting where Carlo once had, right there at the kitchen table, Cecily broke off a piece of the bread she had bought. Surrounding her were seven ghosts. They reminded her that although peace had been taking its last breath and the newspapers had been spewing out one terrible story after another, she hadn't felt the agony of waiting for war in the same way as the adults.

On those last days of peace all along the riverbank, there appeared sudden sightings of kingfishers, blue and incomparable, rare and ominous. Reminding the country of what was passing.

And still the waiting had continued.

> *From the White House, President Roosevelt sends a personal appeal to Hitler.*

By now the world's oracle was undeniably the wireless, its sound impossible to escape, its news carrying across the open sun-soaked fields of England. The whole country had been living in such a state of anticipation for so long that it almost passed for ordinary living. London transformed itself in the minds of busy Londoners. Until this moment it had been taken for granted. The idea that it might soon be in mortal danger was unthinkable. Overnight the city became infinitely precious. Never in the history of British conflict had so many understood what might well be lost.

And all the time the question *when?*, *when?*, cried out from every sweltering street corner while the desire to carry on calmly still remained the order of the day. It was part of the terror of having to wait. Part of the blindness.

At the National Gallery, at the very moment the city became bloated with protective sandbags, Kenneth Clark was making plans for part of the collection to travel to Aberystwyth.

'World Shocked!' cried the news vendors.

For now there was a new word on every pair of lips.

Poland!

The colour green in a school atlas.

There came across the towns and villages of England the oddest of hushes, as though the very trees and streams, the green-hinged country lanes, the orchards, heavy now with fruit, were bracing against an unknowable horror. Loyalty flowed gently in its ancient rivers, love for home, fierce and invincible, was stamped on every face. If the Germans came, would any of this remain in a thousand years? Would it look different, were it to belong to others? Would the foxgloves bloom again on some other lovely summer's day?

All over England excited children ran amok, their gas masks thumping against their backs, singing songs not sung since 1914.

'Be prepared,' Brown Owl warned.

And now at last everyone had heard the name Mussolini.

In Suffolk there were those who laughed at the mountain of sandbags in London. Here, everyone had a sandbag or two, in case of flooding. In Bly, the Molinellos were disappointed with their Pope. His broadcasted appeal for peace, in terms so general and trite, had almost passed unnoticed by the world. But the people in the town, not knowing about the Molinellos' disappointment, began to look strangely at them. *Were* they related to that chap called Mussolini?

Parliament has been recalled. The British government, the Prime Minister has announced, will not go back on their obligations to Poland. All railway stations will now have their blue anti-glare lights fixed.

'Blacker and blacker,' said Selwyn, but how much blacker could the news really get?

> *This is a special announcement. From Friday, August 25th, the BBC will begin broadcasting news bulletins from 10.30 a.m.*

Kitty, back from Exeter and listening to one of the news bulletins over supper, turned away to clatter plates in the scullery. Then she came back with the summer pudding.

'People are collecting tinned food in the cities,' she said, pouring custard made from fresh cream.

Nobody made summer pudding like Cook.

No one had seen Robert Wilson for some days.

'He's gone to see his boss in London,' Kitty told them.

'He'll be back in time for the match, won't he?' Agnes asked.

'Why does he have to come?' Cecily asked. 'He's boring.'

'Because,' said Rose with an odd gleam in her eyes, 'he *likes* Aunt Kitty.'

No one spoke. Agnes went to put the kettle on.

'You haven't finished your pudding, Rose,' she said, finally. 'Robert Wilson likes us *all*, not just Aunt Kitty.'

'You can have mine,' Rose told Tom, holding out her plate.

She looked pale and angry. Perhaps she was sickening.

'As a matter of interest, what's our friend Mr Wilson up to?' Selwyn asked, lighting his pipe.

No one was interested but Aunt Kitty stared hard at him with a look that she usually reserved for Rose.

'Tom, dear,' Agnes said, with a crack in her voice. 'Eat a little more.'

Tom grinned. Don't worry about me, his grin said. I'm rather excited.

'Don't you have a meeting tonight?' Agnes asked.

Selwyn shook his head and helped himself to seconds. Not tonight.

Cecily watched Tom slurping up raspberry juice at the bottom of his cut-glass bowl. There was no need for anyone to eat out of tins when the orchard was bursting with fruit. The orchard always reminded her of Carlo. Of late, since the accident, when she had had to have stitches, he had been very solicitous towards her. Thinking of him made Cecily blush.

'I say,' Tom was saying, 'did you know that Bly fire station has got its anti-glares already? And is it true that the old school will be used for Top Secret missions?'

'It's a Top Secret!' Selwyn joked.

But it wasn't a joking matter.

'My nerves are in shreds,' Agnes confessed.

Mussolini has informed Hitler that Italy is in no position to render Germany any military assistance.

'Captain Pinky's done a bunk. Hurrah!' Rose said out of the blue, forgetting what could and could not be said.

She was sounding a little hysterical, Cecily felt. Tom kicked her under the table but if Rose saw, she didn't care. She had on a Black Look over her summer dress that made Kitty laugh in an oddly bitter way.

'Thank you, Rose,' Agnes told her. 'Robert Wilson has been very supportive of this family.'

'Yes,' agreed Selwyn, non-committal.

He looked as if he could say more. On the table there were seven fresh flowers. Aunt Kitty was going out later.

'Off out to see her admirer, I bet,' Rose said, adding, in a nastily under-breath voice that only Cecily heard, 'but who it is this time is anyone's guess!'

In fact Aunt Kitty was only going to play bridge over in Bly.

On the news there were the usual stories of 'incidents' on the frontiers between Poland and Germany.

'Just a minute,' Selwyn said, raising his hand. 'I want to hear the latest news bulletin.'

'I bet you do,' muttered Rose.

What in the world was the matter with Rose?

'Shush!' Aunt Kitty said crossly.

This is the BBC. Hitler has sent orders to halt the attack on Poland scheduled to start at 4.30 tomorrow morning.

'Who *does* she think she is?' muttered Rose, glaring at their aunt.

Luckily only Cecily knew of her sister's own undercover plans.

'Our ambassador has gone back to talk to Hitler.'

'Well, the next three days will be important,' Selwyn agreed. 'Let's stay hopeful until then.'

'I'd like to have a word with Mister Hitler!' Kitty said.

'And me!' agreed Cecily.

Everyone was amused, even Agnes, and all at once the atmosphere changed and became happy and glorious again.

'What would you say, C?' Tom asked, joining in.

Cecily hesitated. On the one hand she would have liked to fool around and make them laugh but on the other, she knew if she did, everyone would continue to treat her as though she was a child.

'She'd vomit on him,' Rose cried.

She had found a Don't-Care straw hat and wore it rakishly over her Black Look.

'Be quiet,' Selwyn admonished, turning the radio up and they were all silent, listening to the boring voice.

President Roosevelt was urging peace. Great efforts were being made to preserve it by all the Scandinavian countries, too.

When supper was finally over Agnes went off to complete her Mass Observation entries. Then she promised Rose she would finish her dress. Rose's dance dress was straight out of a fairy tale. Cecily's a mere cast off.

Then, in spite of what he had said earlier, Selwyn put on his bicycle clips and went out into the lovely evening, disappearing amongst the dusky dog roses. He had so much to do before the harvest began on Monday.

'Let's meet in the den tomorrow,' Tom hissed.

Cecily nodded.

Afterwards, in no time at all, the harvest arrived and for a whole week the farmhands worked furiously to finish the job. Bellamy was paid extra by Selwyn to join in, simply because he was such a good strong worker. Always the first to arrive in the coolness of dawn, he was also the last to leave, working steadily, wasting no time and speaking to no one. The helpers, aware of his unpredictable moods and made uneasy by his brute strength, gave him a wide berth. Often he would be found standing stock-still, as if in a dream, staring across the waves of softly undulating white oats in the blaze of sunshine. In contrast to the gentleness of the abundant countryside, Bellamy's scythe sounded harsh against the wheat stalks. There seemed always to be a glint of anger in his eyes.

Soon the swathes lay yellow and beautiful on the stubble. The local girls began making the bonds, the mothers binding the sheaves. And except for the noon rest and the mid-morning break and the pauses for the drinking of tea, the work went on all day until darkness fell.

One afternoon during that week, Rose came out into the field where Bellamy was working. She was carrying the tin pot of tea.

'Hello, gipsy,' she called, her voice rising like a lark over the translucent light.

She had not seen him since their row.

Bellamy took the pot from her. He wiped his forehead with the back of his hand. Then he threw the tea in a wide glittering arc across the stubble. Cecily, hurrying across to the secret hiding place she now shared with Tom, saw them and stopped. Bellamy and Rose were fighting.

'Still in your silly mood?' asked Rose.

She didn't sound as if she cared much.

'If that's what it pleases you to say,' Bellamy answered.

The threat in his voice threw itself across the field.

Until this summer Bellamy had always gone to Bly fair with Rose. They went after dark because Rose thought fairs were more fun if you sneaked up on them. When it arrived, she used to climb down through the bedroom window and the two of them raced off to the seafront. Then with no warning she withdrew her friendship and developed another interest.

'It wasn't Joe you saw,' Bellamy said.

'Shut up!' Rose whispered savagely.

In the stillness of the air, her voice carried all the way to Cecily.

'You *like* that idiot? You really *like* him?'

'What if I do?' asked Rose. 'What will you do?'

'I'll... I'll...' Bellamy grabbed her wrist, leaning towards her.

Cecily heard Rose's careless laugh as it skirted his threat.

'It's nothing to do with you, you fool.'

'Yes it is. Everything about you is my business. If I find it's true...'

Rose laughed again. Then she pushed him away with surprising force.

'If you *want* to kiss me, kiss me, then,' she said. 'Don't creep all over me.'

But Bellamy's attempt to kiss her was not successful, either.

'Why don't you wash?' Rose snapped, suddenly. 'You smell something terrible.'

Bellamy experienced a moment of confusion. He had been drinking beer and the strangely repetitive taste of the hops began to rise and quarrel with another sensation just above his heart.

'I have,' he lied.

'No you haven't,' she said furiously. 'You've been here all day. And I've already told you I don't want to go on the rides with you any more.'

Bellamy was silent.

'You can't go on your own,' he said mildly, adding, 'I've nearly finished for the day and I'll wash in the stream if you like.'

'If I *like*! You smell like a pig, like… like the poacher you are. I'm sick of it.'

They had moved away from the stocks and the sun was full and harsh on them. Bellamy looked at her upturned face. The expression on her face was one of supreme indifference. The flat, faint impression of her voice carried sharply across to Cecily. Her sister's sudden rage, which Cecily had been well used to since childhood, seemed to have on this occasion come from nowhere. It wasn't Bellamy who usually angered Rose.

'But you know I poach,' he said, frowning. 'You've always known. What's wrong?'

'Well I'm tired of the way you are. I'm tired of doing the same things with you, tired of your stupid habits.'

He seemed to digest this.

But they had been friends forever, thought Cecily in dismay. Been inseparable since they had been children, since Selwyn had first employed Bellamy on the farm. No one, not even Agnes, had been able to break that. Palmyra Farm and all of the surrounding countryside that they had roamed together *was* Bellamy. Cecily could not imagine a life in which he did not exist.

'Don't be silly,' he was saying.

'I'm not being silly,' Rose cried. 'I've already made up my mind. The time has come for me to go to the fair on my own this year.'

'What?'

'Yes. I shall meet the Molinello boys, they'll bring me back. I don't need you.'

Her cruelty winded Cecily. It seemed to render Bellamy speechless too.

'So that's it,' he said, dully. 'The Eyties? Those fools?'

'Don't you dare call them fools!'

There was a silence. Cecily shivered.

'Go then,' Bellamy said at last with a sudden flash of anger. 'Bugger off.'

And he pushed her so hard that she almost fell. Turning, Rose marched swiftly in the direction of the house.

Bellamy hesitated. He seemed uncertain as to what to do next. As he dropped his beer bottle into his jacket, a young rabbit started out of the shadow of a stock and came towards him, running in blind terror. He had stopped poaching for some time, being afraid of getting caught by Pinky Wilson, but seeing the rabbit so close was clearly more than he could resist. *Oh no!* thought Cecily, knowing what he was about to do. She saw him drop flat onto his stomach and in one swift movement pin the rabbit to the earth, cracking its neck with his hands in a sound that echoed through the air. Then, getting up, he swung the soft body over his shoulders. There was a look of strange elation on his face until something made him look belatedly across the field where Cecily stood. She froze, but with an indifferent shake of his head, Bellamy picked up his scythe and spat on it. Then with slow deliberation he disappeared in the opposite direction.

Tom was waiting in the den. The den was really the hollow of the old hornbeam. Since Cecily had decided to share the place with him, he had turned it into a boy's hideout of his own. It no longer felt like Cecily's secret place where she came to escape from Rose or their mother, to read or dream of things beyond her reach. The den had turned into the sort of play area she might have liked a year ago but in truth had now outgrown. There was an overturned crate doubling as a table and two broken footstools Tom had found in the barn. He had discarded the rag rug Cook had given Cecily, saying it was just for sissies. Tom was beginning to bore Cecily. But in the absence of any other company what else was she to do?

'Who's there?' Tom asked as she approached.

Cecily sighed. She had forgotten his password and she knew this would prolong the agony.

'Woodstock,' she said.

'Wrong,' Tom cried.

'Harris?'

'No!'

'Hannibal?'

'Nope!'

'Well what is it?'

'You tell me,' Tom said.

'Well I'll go home then,' Cecily said crossly.

'Rabbits,' he allowed, reluctantly. 'But we'll have to change it now.'

On one of the footstools was the book he was reading. *Uncommon Danger,* a crackerjack of a spy story. Tom was going to be a spy himself one day.

'Were you talking to Bellamy?'

Cecily shook her head. When she sat down on the floor of the den she was now so tall that she had to fold her knees right up to her chin. Tom frowned. He was considerably smaller than she was.

'Have you been growing since Sunday?' he asked.

Cecily didn't answer. Her height embarrassed her.

'Bellamy's had a fight with Rose,' she said at last.

She was still upset and couldn't simply put it down to the rabbit that had been killed.

'It isn't Bellamy you should be worrying about,' Tom told her. He spoke with portentous deliberation.

'I think,' Cecily said, slowly, half to herself, 'Rose doesn't like Bellamy any more. I think she prefers Carlo.'

There! She had said it. But the lump in her chest seemed to have grown heavier. Tom was busy whittling his pencil to a sharp point. Then he held out his hand.

'Give me your finger,' he said sternly.

'What for?'

'We have to swear a solemn oath. That's what spies do.'

'I'm not a spy,' Cecily said.

She felt suddenly utterly weary of this game. Tom reminded her of a small bluebottle, impossible to swat and constantly buzzing in her ear. Perhaps, she thought, there was going to be a thunderstorm, after all.

'Because,' Tom was saying, 'I have something important to tell you about *your* sister.'

He took her hand in his and with a sudden, quick movement ran the blade of the knife across first her little finger and then his. Cecily gasped but Tom put a finger to his lips. Then he touched the bead of blood that was on Cecily's finger with the one on his own.

'Right,' he said, triumphantly, 'now we are blood brothers. And what I have to tell you, as a result of my research, is that Pinky Wilson is trying to turn your sister into a traitor!'

It was perfectly clear, wasn't it, from all the evidence he had gathered?

Pinky Wilson was following Rose.

Everywhere!

Tailing her,

stalking her

talking to her,

biding his time as though she was prey.

Momentarily startled out of her own preoccupations, Cecily stared at Tom who nodded triumphantly.

Could he be right?

'Of course I am,' Tom said, his triumph maturing into a quiet, magnificent thing.

Again Cecily sighed. He was really irritating her. What was worse, Tom's research tied in with her own earlier suspicions. Hadn't Captain Pinky been watching Rose when she climbed down from the window at night?

'There, you see? I'm right! He's following her. He's simply up to no good.'

Cecily felt the lump in her chest shift and disperse. So Rose didn't prefer Carlo to Bellamy, after all?

'She's being groomed to become a spy!'

Tom's triumph was now threatening to rise into the hot air like a balloon.

It hardly seemed possible. Her sister? Rose? But spying on *whom*? Tom shrugged impatiently. It hardly mattered, what was important was the fact of it. Pinky Wilson, the traitor!

'Stranger things have happened,' Tom told her with studied casualness, eyes shining like marbles.

And he pointed to Chapter Seven in his well-thumbed book.

'You should read this chapter,' he said.

Then he stood up and turned west so he could see across the field and towards the house.

'Look!' he said. 'There he is.'

Walking slowly across the field, head bent, was the familiar stick-thin figure of a man. Shadowed face, preoccupied, all unawares. Both children shrank into the hollow of the tree.

'It's him,' Tom hissed.

'I haven't seen him for days,' Cecily said, sitting up with reluctant interest. 'I wonder if he still goes to the beach to meet Aunt Kitty.'

'*What*? How do you know? Why haven't you mentioned this before?'

Cecily chewed the inside of her cheek. There was only so much that she was prepared to reveal. Tom was writing furiously in his notebook.

'Right,' he said, when he had finished. 'Now for The Plan.'

He sucked the end of his pencil, frowning.

'Just to recap. You say you overheard your sister say she's going to the beach after the dance? Correct?'

Cecily nodded half-heartedly. The heat was rising something awful. She was unaware that Tom's stern look was meant to emulate an officer talking to the troops. He picked up a stick and pointed it at her.

'I don't know if it's Captain Pinky or Carlo she's meeting,' Cecily said forlornly.

She blinked. She felt as though she might cry.

'Forget about the Eytie. We're not interested in him.'

Cecily said nothing.

'Action stations,' Tom added encouragingly. 'Buck up, do!'

Cecily nodded.

The plan, it seemed, was to follow Rose, and therefore Captain Pinky, to the beach. They would do this under cover of the dance. Cecily, who was thinking of something else, agreed.

'Should we take our gas masks?' she asked. 'I mean we're supposed to carry them everywhere.'

Tom ignored her. There followed a short silence. Would children have to fight too? Cecily wondered.

'We are going to unearth all the Evidence and find out if Captain Pinky is a spy and a murderer,' Tom said.

Cecily looked confused. Her finger and her head were hurting and she had momentarily forgotten what the Evidence actually was. But then she remembered her sister's life was in danger. Was Pinky really planning to murder her?

'He is a spy, I'm telling you,' Tom insisted. 'He can speak German, you know.'

Doubt entered the courtroom.

'Well,' Cecily said, 'so can Daddy. And your family.'

'But that was because we've lived there, silly!'

Still Cecily hesitated.

'I only *thought* I saw him spying on Rose,' she said, wishing she hadn't mentioned anything.

Actually she was feeling a little sick.

'Don't worry,' Tom reassured her, 'we'll denounce him soon enough. All we need is the vital piece of evidence...' He waited for her reaction and when none came, added, '...that he's following your sister. I say, you are looking a little green.'

For a moment Cecily wondered if it might not be simpler to tell her parents what she herself had seen. Rose was going to be furious with her when she saw them tailing her. And what if it was Carlo she was meeting? Cecily wasn't at all sure she wanted to see them together.

'Perhaps we shouldn't do anything just yet,' she said uneasily.

'Nonsense! All we're doing is fact-finding.'

He pointed his stick at her accusingly.

'Are you getting cold feet, old bean?'

Cecily shook her head until her hair was in her eyes. The ache in her heart continued, regardless of Tom.

'Capital!' Tom said, satisfied.

He continued to glare at her in the way he had seen his father once outstare a worker in his factory. Then suddenly he grinned. In just a few days it was the tennis party.

By now they had found a bike for Tom and all that was needed was:

1. a night when Rose would stay out all night (tomorrow's dance was the ideal moment)

2. a night when Pinky Wilson was around (luck was on their side, he would be here tomorrow)

3. a night when Agnes and everyone else was preoccupied with silly things (like kissing)

It was all decided, then.

'We need just one last meeting, if this is to go ahead tomorrow,' Tom said. 'And let's hope for a night without a moon.'

Now he sounded like Selwyn organising the harvest, thought Cecily, struggling not to laugh.

'Think how everyone will thank us when we uncover the truth about Captain P!'

Cecily stared out at the shimmering field. What if Agnes had made *her* a new dress for the dance.

Tom was having his own daydream.

'Well done, Tom,' Selwyn Maudsley was saying in his dream, driving him to meet Neville Chamberlain. 'The Maudsleys of course are very grateful, for all you've done. Particularly Rose. She's half in love with you already, you know, old chap.'

'Goodness!' a voice said. 'A penny for them?'

Both children started.

'You two are looking very pleased with yourselves!'

It was Captain Pinky Wilson. He had walked all the way round the field and they hadn't heard him.

And he was laughing.

Cecily blinked, her smile fading into goosebumps on her arms and legs.

Tom stood woodenly.

'You're looking very serious,' Captain P said, his face wobbling.

Then he too grew serious.

'I say, you don't happen to know where that Bellamy has gone?' he asked.

They shook their heads truthfully. Pinky was frowning slightly. There were small beads of perspiration on his brow and his white shirt looked a little sticky. He held out his hand to help Cecily down. Jutting out of his coat pocket was a small handkerchief with a strawberry embroidered on it. Cecily frowned. Good gracious! she thought. What was he doing with Rose's handkerchief? Suddenly she was fully alert.

'Keep an eye on him, will you? For me?'

Cecily was speechless. But Tom, the first to recover, grinned at Captain Pinky Wilson.

'Of course we will,' he said in his friendliest manner.

'Good!' said Pinky. 'Oh and Cecily, your Aunt Kitty was looking for you. Something about a dress for the party?'

Turning, he waved cheerily and carried on walking away from Palmyra House, saying something as he went. It sounded like 'I'm looking forward to seeing Rose's new dress.'

'Murderer,' muttered Cecily, both shocked and certain at last.

In Palmyra House, in their parents' bedroom, the wireless droned boringly on.

...hospitals are being cleared, sandbags continue to be heaped up in front of buildings, all ARP people are being called up or told to be ready to go to their posts with forty-eight hours' supply of food.

'Either you stand still,' Agnes said in mock irritation, 'or I'll stick pins in you!'

Whenever Rose moved the almost-finished dress shimmered like the heat outside. Cecily stared open-mouthed at her sister.

Rose looked stunning.

The sunlight was full on her face and made her large eyes even larger. They were an intense, pure blue, wet and shining. Rose stared out of the window, casually. She seemed unaware of the impression she created and it occurred to Cecily that her sister was almost sick with some sort of secret unhappiness she was trying to hide. Which was puzzling as she had been longing for the dance to arrive.

'Can't you lower the neckline a little more?' she asked.

Aunt Kitty, walking past, stopped and frowned. Envy swept in through the doorway with her.

'You don't want to look like a tart,' was all Aunt Kitty said.

'Tart, yourself,' Rose said, tossing her head.

'Rose!' Agnes sighed. 'And Kitty! For God's sake, you're the older one!'

Agnes had made a timeless dress for her impossibly rude and lovely daughter.

Cecily, momentarily filled with dissatisfaction, stared Envy in the face. Rose, a sly look over her smooth shoulder, laughed her daredevil laugh. Outside a kingfisher whistled shrilly.

'Now look what you've done!' Agnes said, exasperated.

Pins scattered like bad thoughts across the polished wooden floor.

'You let her get away with murder, Agnes,' Kitty said.

'You and me, both,' mocked Rose.

'What d'you mean by that?' Kitty asked threateningly.

'Don't you know?' taunted Rose.

'No, tell me!' dared Kitty.

'Oh for heaven's sake!' Agnes shouted.

Cecily sucked her breath like a boiled sweet. Their mother never shouted.

'Well I'm sick of her veiled abuse,' Kitty said, but she spoke uncertainly and Rose, standing poised against the light, had an unwipable smile of triumph on her face. Then as though unaware of the poetry of her appearance, she pulled off the dress with a small, elegant gesture and threw it on a chair. They all stared.

'Rose!' Agnes cried aghast. 'You've no brassiere on! What in the world are you thinking of?'

But Rose, morose for days, interested only in the tennis dance, laughed with sudden delight.

A discordant laugh that later, only two weeks later, Cecily would remember.

'You'll get a name as a floozy, Rose, if you go on this way. What will your father say?'

There was the smallest of pauses, barely discernable, but enough for Cecily to see the look of hatred in her sister's eyes at the mention of Selwyn. A look that even then was frightening to behold in so lovely a face. Agnes must have thought so too because she hurried over to Rose with her clothes.

'Put your dress back on, there's a good girl,' she said with unexpected gentleness, adding, 'and there's no need for such language, Kitty.'

By such straws as these was Cecily able to gauge the tide of Rose's feelings flowing towards their Aunt Kitty.

Remembering that moment on a darker day, Cecily had wondered what Rose actually wore in her coffin. Did she have her brassiere on? She remembered her Aunt Kitty's sniff of disapproval. The slight sneer in her eyes. She remembered staring at Rose's blonde muff.

By August the 31st the harvest was over and the two large fields facing south were cleared. The farmhands built a massive stack that rose dishevelled and radiant above the glare of the field. In this last magnificent burst of heat came the voice on the wireless.

Herr Hitler has sent a reply to the Duke of Windsor. 'You may rest assured that my attitude towards Britain and my desire to avoid another war between our two people remain unchanged.'

A little further back was another finished stack where the haymakers moved slowly; white dots amongst the stubble.

Cecily and Tom climbed it until they were high above the hedge-tops. There was absolutely nothing in the world up there, except the shallow ramparts of the stack, the blazing sky and the hot, sweet-scented hay, suffocating in the heat.

And then at last, the dance dress was ready. Agnes cut the last loose thread and ironed the hem so it looked shop bought.

'You look lovely, darling,' she said in the sweet voice she sometimes reserved for Rose alone.

Cecily noted Agnes' smile and in that fleeting moment, when her mother's features lost their habitual severity of cast, saw how they revealed one of the chief sources from which Rose got her great beauty.

Upstream and several miles away from the farm, as evening began to fall, silence swooped like a night-bird in the gloaming. A thread of wind ruffled the river. Lucio lay on its banks and watched Agnes. Tomorrow was the party and they would be in full view of everyone. These snatched moments were the only privacy they would have for days. Blackberries smothered the hedges, and the empty wheat field was filled with dark birds.

'Your brother is bound to guess!' Agnes said.

Lucio looked at her gravely. There were flecks of light reflected in his eyes.

'My nephew already does,' he said solemnly.

Agnes blushed.

'No! Which one?'

'Carlo,' Lucio said.

'Oh God! Has he been playing with Cecily? Have they been spying on us?'

She was laughing.

'I am very close to Carlo,' he said finally. 'The boy is like me. He believes in social justice.'

She didn't speak and when he had waited a moment longer he turned and ran a finger across her lips. In the sparkle of light he thought she looked alert and assured, not nervous as he had first thought. The reflected ripple of the water made a bright mark on her throat. The Irish are wonderful, he decided, amazed. The image of her strengthened the resolve growing in him. The last of the sun's rays poured across it as his tenderness for her grew.

'Well?' she asked, a hint of laughter in her voice. 'So you told him?'

He shook his head bemused and began to touch her wide clear forehead under the thick black hair and then the smooth sun-sallow skin of her face and arms. He felt his heart rise at the sight of her and he felt, also, a sudden sick despair at the complications in their lives.

'There's probably a war coming,' he murmured, burying his face in her hair. 'I wanted... I wanted Carlo to know about us because...' he shrugged.

He wanted to tell her that he was an Italian and that his country might call him back at any moment, that things could change in a day, that the war might go on for years. But he said none of these things, continuing instead to stroke her face, thinking how like a young girl she still was. Did she know? She could have been Rose's sister.

'Even if there is a war we will find a way.'

She lifted her face towards his and he turned to put his lips against her throat. When he kissed her he felt the summer turn slowly, mocking him. Wood pigeons were cooing huskily above their heads. And he was certain, more certain than ever, that he wanted to marry her.

Afterwards they swam in the river and he watched the rise and fall of her bare arms and listened to the calm confidence of her voice as the light played on her wet hair. Thinking of the ways in which, starved of affection for so long, believing herself to be unlovable, she now loved him so wholeheartedly. How, confident as an acrobat on a high wire, she had launched herself on him, again and again. It stunned him, this trust. He would never betray it.

She pulled her dress on and towelled her hair. The sunburn on her face was very warm, first against his face and then his hands. She let her face remain lightly against him and he put his hand on her neck and the whole day spun on its axis when he kissed her, again. Staring at the furthest reaches of the clean blue river, Lucio made his decision. Tonight he would talk to Mauro. Once made, the decision overwhelmed him. Agnes continued to rest her head against his.

'I can't believe it will actually happen,' she said.

He closed his eyes and the sun beat down on his lids. It burnt his face for a few moments longer.

'I fear so,' he said, at last.

He did not tell her he would almost certainly be called back to Italy. They had promised each other only honesty but how could he tell her this?

'We could... all move to Italy,' she said. 'I mean the girls and I.'

A heron, grave as an abbot, attended to his fishing amongst the drooping branches of the willow. Lucio stared at it without moving, marvelling at its quiet elegance. Lately they had discovered they could read each other's thoughts. Did love do that? Or war? All the dustiness of the afternoon was suspended in the air with the fineness of powdered sulphur. He shook his head and at last Agnes understood what he was trying so hard to hide from her.

'If there *is* a war,' he said, 'none of this will matter.'

He reached up and wordlessly gathered her to him before she could start crying. Theirs was a marriage already, he thought. In some sense he had known her all her life.

'But what if you get killed?' she asked suddenly, voicing what, he suspected, she had kept to herself for many weeks.

'I won't,' he promised.

Death, on this glittering, white-hot afternoon seemed impossible. They heard the kingfisher's bullet-like whistle as it came upstream. It repeated the same fluid, fine-drawn sound that faded instantly. Lying with his arms around her, Lucio thought the sound was like this moment itself. Gone in an instant. When he opened his eyes again he was struck by the brutal sharpness of black leaves against blue sky. His eyes felt shocked into fresh alertness. And as he began to brush his hand against her naked shoulder, carefully beginning to make love to her again, he was aware of the unbearably sweet scent of late summer in the limes.

Much later they heard children's voices and he pulled her gently to her feet and began removing the leaves from her crumpled dress. She looked at him with sleepy, trusting eyes, making the blood beat up into his throat.

'I don't want you to go,' he mumbled at last.

'I must,' she said. 'The children will be out looking for me and there is so much to do before tomorrow.'

He loved all three of her children, he told her. She pulled a face.

'They would spy on me, given a chance!'

They had been meeting when they could, remaining patient when it wasn't possible. But did Rose suspect?

'No,' Agnes said. She hesitated. 'But she isn't happy.'

He wondered how much Rose really knew but didn't like to ask.

'We are made for each other,' he said instead.

What was on the surface a quiet thing was deep and certain, now.

They went together along the footpath and parted at the stile and he watched as she hurried away from him, back towards the house, her blue dress swinging as she walked. Then, turning towards the town and the ice-cream parlour he met up with Robert Wilson who was on his way there too and they walked the half a mile back together.

Carlo watched his mother as she broke the last of the egg yolks into a mountain of white flour.

'Cecci was here earlier asking about the cakes I'm making for the tennis party,' she said.

'I'll take them over later if you like,' Carlo offered. 'Then that's one job done.'

Carlo put the bag of flour away for his mother. Then he washed his hands. Of all the children, he was the closest to Anna.

'There's no hurry, she said, shaking her head. Lucio can take the van because I've got lots of other things for you to take too.'

She looked at her youngest son and hesitated. He had a loving heart but sometimes he missed certain things.

'Cecci was really looking for you,' she said.

She kneaded the eggs into the flour to make a soft dough and shook off the excess from her elbow. Then she rolled the dough into a long, straight finger. Carlo got out the kitchen knife for her. She could tell by the way he was hovering around her that he was hungry.

'It won't be long,' she smiled. 'Put the water on to boil, will you, *caro*.'

She began cutting up the finger of dough into small sections. Carlo started stirring the tomato *sugo* on the stove and instantly the scent of basil and garlic filled the kitchen.

'Oi,' his mother said. 'No tasting yet! Now then, at the dance I want you to be very nice to Cecci.'

'I always am,' Carlo said.

He dipped his finger quickly into the *sugo* and licked it.

'I can see what you're doing,' Anna warned. 'And I mean be really nice to her.'

'*Perché*?' Carlo said. 'I'm very nice to Cecci, as you know. This *sugo* needs a little salt, by the way.'

'Well make sure you notice her,' Anna said.

She handed him the tub of salt.

'That little one is in the shadow of Rosa. You should dance with her on Saturday. Rosa has plenty of admirers and Cecci loves you.'

'I love her too, Mama,' Carlo said.

And he helped himself to a spoonful of grated Parmesan behind his mother's back.

Anna sighed.

'If this war really were to happen,' she said, 'we can offer to supply the troops with ice cream I suppose. But I hope there will be no war!'

Carlo wanted to disagree but he could not shatter her illusions. He could not tell her what he knew, what his Uncle had told him. That if war came *all* the men in the Molinello family would be forced to return to Italy. Nobody in his family, none of his brothers or his father was prepared to face reality. The rubbish they believed in, the foolish certainty that peace would prevail, frightened Carlo. Mario still joked with his customers even though he had just bought blackout blinds. Their lives were being ruined by this shadow and no one cared. Rose, he knew, thought this way too but with her, perhaps because she was English, it was less complicated.

'Ah, lunch,' Mario cried, coming in.

Then he saw Carlo.

'So, where is your uncle?'

Anna turned away to check her oven and Mario glanced uneasily in her direction.

'I need to talk to Lucio,' he muttered and went out.

Later on, before the dance, he wanted to take a photograph with his Brownie, of his family, all together.

'Lunch is at one,' Anna called. 'Tell them, Carlo.'

Lucio returned at twelve. Behind him were Giorgio, Beppe, Mario.

Robert Wilson, arriving at the parlour, found himself invited to stay for lunch, too. He was a friend of the Maudsleys and that was good enough for Anna. Lucio went over to the sink to wash his hands. He looked hot and a little dazed as though he had been staring at the sun for too long. Wiping her hands, Anna gave Robert Wilson a kiss on both cheeks, Italian style, and invited him to sit down.

'Come, have a little gnocchi.'

She placed a small carafe of red wine on the table, brought back by Lucio on the last trip home. Lucio was looking rather solemn. Mario gave his wife a warning look.

Don't say anything, his look said. I will tell you everything later.

It better be a good story, Anna looked back. Your brother is very sulky today!

Beppe had forgotten to wash his hands because he was too busy watching his parents communicate through their eyes.

'Wash your hands, *caro*,' his mother told him. '*Before* you help yourself to the antipasti!'

The bell to the ice-cream parlour clanged again and the door into their private quarters was opened. Franca came in looking flushed. *Madonna*! thought Anna.

'*Cara, vieni, vieni*, come. Hello Joe, come in, just in time.'

'Wash your hands, children.'

Beppe fetched the water glasses. Giorgio poured the wine. Franca got an extra chair for Joe, who smiled shyly. Robert Wilson sat down at Mario's request. Anna put a platter of ham on the table with some salted olives. Everyone smiled. Even Lucio, who knew his sister-in-law's eagle eyes were on him.

And they held up their glasses. The moment froze.

'*Salute*, Mama!'

'*Salute!*' Mario said, loudly.

'Cheers,' said Robert Wilson. 'Down the hatch!'

'*Salute*,' said Joe, who was secretly learning Italian.

Franca giggled. And blushed.

'Will you be there?'

'At the tennis match? Of course, of course. Wouldn't miss it for the world!'

It would be a day of Anglo-Italian celebrations. Anna was making a surprise cake for the event. No, she couldn't say what sort. Only that they made it at *Peck's* in Milano.

'Ah well!' Robert teased. 'If it's good enough for Milan!'

The chef who worked for il Duce had given her the secret recipe.

'You know il Duce?'

'No, no, Roberto. Only his cook! He comes from the same village as us.'

'What village is that?'

'It's called Bratto,' Mauro told him.

Then he mopped up the rest of his tomato *sugo* with a small piece of bread.

'Mmm,' he said, miming a corkscrew boring into his cheek with one finger.

'*Buono!*' repeated his sons, making the same gesture.

I wish I were like this family, thought Joe, too shy to copy them.

Funny gesture, thought Robert, nodding, amazed at how good the food was.

17.

THE DAWN WAS what they remembered, arriving slowly, brimming with promise. Suffolk oaks loomed darkly through the low-lying mist where in a few hours the gauzy light would blaze into heat. There was the scent of woodsmoke everywhere, touched by the beginnings of autumn. For it was September now.

A calm, sad, gentlemanly voice on the wireless was talking about Germany invading Poland and as she stood, with her basket, picking peas, Agnes thought, *I'll remember this day.* She hurried through the orchard in a dress so pale it appeared white, humming to herself. Selwyn was nowhere in sight. And Partridge's voice, reassuring as it came up the path, saying yes, the gipsies were moving on.

'That Wilson fellow got rid of them,' he said, accepting a mug of tea from Cook who was busy frying bacon and eggs.

'Oh, he's back, is he?' said Agnes. 'Good!'

'Were they roasting hedgehogs?' Cecily asked, creeping up.

'Good gracious, C! You're up early.'

'Up with the lark,' said Partridge. 'But unfortunately with the owl too!'

'What d'you mean?' Cecily asked, suspiciously.

But Partridge only grinned and handed her a small colander. She could help him pick raspberries.

'Rose will look very pretty, today,' Cecily told him.

Partridge disappeared into the bushes. His voice coming through the raspberry canes was muffled.

'You'll look exactly like her one day,' he said eventually. When he emerged Partridge had drops of dew all over his shirt. 'You'll see,' he said.

All the tickets for the charity dance had sold. Local people would not have missed it for the world and this year, with the anxiety of what might lie ahead there would be many Italians from all over Suffolk, invited by the Molinellos.

Cook had made the lemonade the night before and the jugs were cooling in the scullery with beaded cloths covering them. There was a man from the Aga shop bending over the open oven door and Cook was lamenting the delay of the scones. Ever since electricity had come to Palmyra Farm a year ago, baking had become easier. So why, today of all days, had something gone wrong?

'Don't just stand there,' she told the children, crossly. 'Here, you can stone the cherries.'

And she handed them each a bowl.

'Does anyone know where there is a spare racquet?' Rose asked.

A shadow fell against the whitewashed farmhouse wall. Bellamy, incandescent with rage, made Cecily shiver. But Rose didn't give a toss.

'Oh dear,' she sighed. '*Now* what d'you want?'

And off she went, humming to herself. Cook made a tck-tch sound at the back of her throat.

Joe had cleared a place in the shrubbery beside the tennis court and was building a fire to boil kettles of water for the tea. Cecily, carrying cutlery and a tablecloth, saw that buttercups had come out in their hundreds on the uncut parts of the grass.

'*Mia bella sorella*!' Joe said, seeing her, speaking Italian a little self-consciously. 'Where is the queen of the day?'

He was happy for secret reasons of his own, even though his call-up papers were for Monday and Russia had ordered the mobilisation of two million men.

'I hate that gypo, Bellamy,' Tom said, staring after Rose.

Passers-by have noticed that the parks in London are quieter than usual. Because of the evacuation there are no children playing there.

The milk had been poured into bottles and placed in the scullery.

There were sandwiches made with fresh sardines and egg-and-cress and roast beef and horseradish and turnip pickle.

Cecily helped slice the ham.

She would do so again very soon, but on that day the radio would not be playing a waltz.

And Rose would not be laughing at what Franca and Carlo were saying.

And Bellamy would have an altogether different sort of expression on his face.

The Molinello boys were getting the barn ready for the evening.

Beppe was testing the microphone.

Lucio had arranged for the piano to be brought out from the drawing room. Agnes had promised, a little reluctantly, to play it.

'Wait,' Mario bellowed. 'I need a little more practice, first.'

His family groaned.

'You've practiced enough Papi,' they cried all together.

But Mario was adamant.

Giorgio was tuning his sax. Snatches of old songs mixed with laughter.

'Where are my tennis whites?' Mario shouted.

'*O Dio!*' said Carlo, 'Mama! You must stop him, please, I beg you. He thinks he's going to beat everyone. Papi, don't play with Rose, whatever you do.'

Lucio, rushing backwards and forwards with boxes of ice cream and equipment, grinned happily every time he bumped into Agnes. His sister-in-law's eyes were on him. *Ah!* he thought, wanting to laugh out loud. *Our family policeman.*

'Carlo!' Cecily cried. 'You're early. Are you staying for elevenses?'

Carlo grinned. He looked very handsome in a blue shirt that complemented his eyes.

'*Carissima Cecci*,' he said, vaguely remembering something his mother had said.

But then Rose came up, ruining everything.

'There you are, Carlo. I've decided you will be my partner in the first game.'

Carlo hesitated. He had thought Rose was starting the afternoon with Bellamy.

'He is much better than me,' he said. 'I will make you lose!'

'Don't be silly, besides it's only a mouldy old game,' Rose said.

Bellamy looked as though someone had slapped him. Lucio had brought four different types of ice cream. Chocolate marshmallow sundae, chocolate and damson ice cream, strawberry-chocolate creams and a *sorbetto* called Purple Cow that no one had heard of before.

Lucio shut the refrigerator door, turned round and saw Agnes. Cecily, peering through a crack in the doorway, had never heard her mother giggle in such a way before. She watched the deep dimple in Agnes' cheek come and go and with no warning she thought, *I Am Alone*. The words reverberated in her head and a chasm appeared to have opened up in her life. Peering down into it she wondered what she might do. For it seemed to her on this morning that all the talk of war was nothing compared to her own confused desires. Going out into the sunlight, seeing Bellamy, she thought, we are both of no consequence.

'Shall we go and help Joe?' she asked.

But Bellamy shook his head dumbly and turned away.

The first match was well underway by the time Robert Wilson arrived.

'Hello, Selwyn,' he said softly, lighting a cigarette. 'We appear to be at the point of no return.'

His tone made Mario, who was watching the game, turn sharply. Lucio had been leaning against a tree but now he too strolled over to Selwyn. There was a round of applause, fragmented and hollow in the sunshine. Tomorrow Chamberlain would have his answer.

'Rose is the tennis queen of Bly,' Beppe shouted and Pinky Wilson looked up.

Rose had won again and everyone wanted to play alongside her. But she was having none of it. Carlo was her partner for the afternoon. Bellamy, standing at the corner of the field, looked awfully hot. Kitty, holding another bunch of flowers, smiled.

'I'll just put them in water,' she said.

Mussolini has proposed a five-power conference to try and settle the current crisis. The British attitude is that there must be a withdrawal of German forces from Polish soil before any such conference can take place.

The game stopped. They were all ravenous as rats. Especially Tom. Beppe, who had been keeping the score, vowed when they continued he would beat Rose and Carlo. But for the moment it was the food they fell on and after that they all sat round talking and smacking at the midges.

'No one will play after this!' predicted Kitty.

She had cut Selwyn a piece of Cook's huge chicken pie and some cheese.

'Lucio,' Agnes said softly, 'would you like to try the ham?'

'Please,' he said, looking at her and not the ham.

'The waiting will soon be over,' the vicar said, nodding like a dog without a collar.

The Cabinet has decided that the time limit for the ultimatum to the Germans to withdraw their troops from Poland should expire at midnight tonight.

Rose looked very cool and unruffled. Out of the corner of her eye, Cecily saw Bellamy staring at her. He looked terrible.

'Are you all right?' she asked.

'Why are there foreigners here, today?' he said, disdainfully. 'We're almost at war and they invite these Fascists.'

'*Bellamy*!' Joe said, outraged. 'Apologise at once! Or go home. The Molinellos are our friends. I won't have you insult them.'

'He didn't mean it,' Cecily said.

'Go on,' Joe said, grimly. 'Apologise.'

Bellamy scowled.

He was the only blemish on the day.

There was always one, Cook would have said, had she heard.

But Franca, laughter wiped off her happy face, shivered. A goose was walking over her grave.

'Why does your mother let that boy play with Cecily?' she asked.

Joe shook his head, too angry to speak.

'What d'you expect from a gipsy,' Tom said later, without heat.

Cecily felt as if she were carrying a jelly that was melting. Any moment it would lose its shape and it would be all her fault.

'He's not a gipsy,' she retorted. 'He's just not got any manners, that's all. His mother is very poor and we mustn't forget the unemployment in Britain.'

She was aware of sounding like her father. Tom laughed.

'Well, Hitler will see to that,' he said in a grown-up voice. 'This war will take care of all the unemployed in this country.'

The afternoon moved on but the heat did not let up. Soon the tennis players had had enough to eat and were ready to start up again. Cook and The Help went back to the house to prepare the cream tea. They could hear Agnes' voice calling everyone to take their seats. Selwyn, too, hurried towards the court with his racquet. He had changed into his whites. He and Aunt Kitty were playing against Mario and Agnes. Rose didn't look as if she were going to play any more.

'What, not playing, Rose?' Robert Wilson asked in a friendly way.

But Rose scowled ferociously at him.

'How about a game with me?'

Cecily didn't hear her sister's answer but she saw Carlo walk up to Rose and take hold of her hand. There was no doubt, she thought, he does love her. Sadness was making a hole through her heart. Carlo had hardly spoken to her. In spite of his promise, she knew he would not dance with her either.

All that long, hot afternoon the balls continued to zip to and fro across the net, pinging off the strings and throwing up dust into the Suffolk air. The news bulletins were forgotten in the score-keeping as voices called out in exasperation at the missed shots or the possibility of cheating. Laughter came and went. Would there ever be another party like this again?

The sun moved around the sky and the players wiped their foreheads with increasing frequency. Cecily and Tom collected the balls and threw them back to the servers who smiled their thanks and sometimes shouted, 'Oh well done, C!' Or 'Neatly fielded, Tom!'

There was no sign of Bellamy but once or twice Carlo, running across the court, called out and waved at Cecily.

Tom discovered he was better at tennis than he had first thought so that finally he was roped in to play with Franca and another girl called Bella. No one dared suggest he played with Rose. She had beaten all the others. Only Carlo was anywhere near a match for her. Lucio watched the players while he smoked, his eyes half-closed against the glare. When Rose won he clapped loudly, the cigarette dangling from his lips. Now and then his eyes would stray in the direction of the spectators sitting under the oak. After a while he went to fetch the ice cream. It was the moment they had all been waiting for. A shutter opened and closed, preserving forever an image in Cecily's head.

Rose, laughing, bad mood all gone.

Carlo handing her a huge strawberry and chocolate Melba.

Rose's laughter running around the garden like wildfire, touching everyone so they turned and looked at her and began to laugh too, without quite knowing why. Spontaneously combusting.

'Bet you can't eat it!' Carlo said.

'Bet you I can!'

Rose, hair tied in a hasty knot because she was so hot, wisps escaping.

Like honeysuckle.

Carlo tucking a strand into the knot with quick fingers as Rose kept on spooning ice cream into her mouth.

'Oh!' giggled Rose. 'Oh! Oh!'

And then she was kissing and kissing him right up against the lilac bush.

Oh! Oh!

Rose, made for loving, meant for dancing.

Honeysuckle Rose.

Tennis-dressed.

Laughter rambling all over her face.

Rambling not-dead-yet.

When she had finished all of the ice cream, she wiped her mouth on a handkerchief embroidered with strawberries and tied in a knot. Then she went with him to find Franca and Joe.

Forget-me-nots?

Who ever would?

18.

BY SIX O'CLOCK the field had cleared and the band was warming up in the barn. Nothing would begin for another hour. Partridge was on his way to the station to pick up the last of the guests. Lucio had placed two barrels under a tarpaulin to keep them cool and there were two wooden butter-boxes with glasses in them borrowed from the White Hart pub. Next Lucio drove the car around the walnut tree and backed it up by the barn. Then he and Joe set up the tables with Anna's white starched cloths. Agnes caught sight of Cecily and Tom as they raced into the house.

'You children will be wrecked by this evening,' she said, disapprovingly.

'They should lie down on their beds,' Cook said 'and cogitate for a bit.'

Thankfully it was too late for that. But then, clamping his hand over his mouth, Tom remembered The Plan.

'We must pack,' he whispered.

'Must we?' asked Cecily.

'Ssh! Not so loud. Remember, careless talk costs lives. You'll give the game away at this rate.'

'Cecily! Cecily! C!' called Agnes.

But Cecily was escaping.

'Coming!' she lied.

'Cecily!' Rose shouted. 'You took it. Who else would have? I'm going to tell unless you give it back.'

They were dressing for the dance. Cecily glared at her sister. Envy, disguised as a pair of Bakelite earrings, unclipped itself and was hurled into the air. Rose made an exasperated sound, trying and failing to catch them.

'You little minx,' she shouted.

Cecily put out her tongue.

'You're a rude little thief,' Rose declared.

'I'm not!'

'Yes you are. You stole them, don't deny it.'

'I didn't. I didn't. They were on the *stairs*! I found them.'

'You found them? *Whose* did you think they were?'

'Stop showing off,' Cecily cried at last. 'You just want to show off to the Molinellos,' she added with unusual bitterness.

Agnes groaned. And turned the iron off.

'What's going on?' she asked, raising her head. Then with a rustle of tulle under smooth tissue she picked up the dress she had been ironing and followed the noise.

Both girls stared sullenly at her.

'Really!' Aunt Kitty said, 'you are too old to fight with your sister, Rose.'

Rose opened her mouth to speak and closed it again. The look she gave her aunt was the old scary one but she remained silent and Cecily, feeling a strange allegiance to her sister admitted, quietly, 'It was my fault.'

Her sister had looked just for a moment as though she needed help.

'Here's your dress, Rose,' Agnes said, handing over the long perfectly pressed satin sheath.

The satin gave off a faint scent of gardenias. As the door closed both girls heard Aunt Kitty's voice, still grumbling.

'At least she had her petticoat on this time.'

'Well of course,' Agnes replied. 'What d'you expect?'

Rose and Cecily looked at each other. And then Rose burst out laughing. Cecily joined in. Her sister would look beautiful tonight. Suddenly, no longer jealous, she remembered the danger Rose was in. It was Cecily's job to save her. And expose the traitorous Pinky Wilson. Cecily would do her duty and take care of all of it. Rose was looking at her in a funny way.

'What are you muttering to yourself, now?' she asked, amused.

Agnes had put her hair up, Mrs Simpson-style. She looked better than the wretched Simpson woman, Cook remarked. Selwyn was wearing black tie.

'What for?' scowled Rose. 'It's only the charity dance.'

Cecily was wearing a ballerina dress that had belonged to Rose, years before. It floated whenever she moved.

'You look very nice indeed,' Agnes told her, tugging at her long hair until it shone, her smile going all the way up to her eyes. 'This dress is appropriate for someone of your age.'

Everyone stared at the impossibly beautiful Rose as if they were seeing her for the very first time. Where had the old Rose gone? Years of nursery talk, of giggling, of midnight feasts and brown legs in sandals running across the beach, vanished in that moment, whisked away on a piece of buttercup-coloured satin. With sudden clarity Cecily saw her sister had left their joint childhood forever, leaving her, Cecily, to fend for herself.

Luckily Tom was on hand with the Mission Ahead.

'Have you brought something to write with?' he whispered.

'So, why d'you need a pen?' Rose asked in her new, amused voice.

Aunt Kitty became an unexpected ally.

'I expect all would-be writers write things down,' she said.

Aunt Kitty hadn't got dressed up. It was just a mouldy old barn dance. It wasn't *London*. Aunt Kitty was sulking and no one knew why.

Bellamy watched them walk towards to the barn. Then he slunk away. Captain Pinky was driving his car through the gloaming. He was going in the opposite direction, away from Palmyra Farm, but no one, except Lucio, saw him.

The Italian foreign minister has been told that Britain cannot agree to the five-power conference unless German forces withdraw completely from Poland. To which he is reported as saying, 'the last glimmer of hope has died.'

It was a proper dance. Not just Mario playing his accordion. Cecily and Tom sat drinking lemonade out of tall glasses. There were lots of other children from Bly but Cecily didn't want to join in with their games. At one point Carlo Molinello had come over. He was dressed formally and wore a jacket in spite of the heat. Cecily thought he was quite the smartest person present. He was the waiter for the evening.

'Have some cider, Cecci,' he said, and he handed her a tall glass with bits of fruit floating in it.

Then he tilted his head and gave her a considered look.

'You look perfect!' he said.

Cecily controlled the desire to ask him what he thought of Rose.

'In fact,' he whispered, as though he could read her mind, 'one day you are going to look prettier than *even* your sister!'

He rolled his eyes and made a gesture suggesting despair.

'You will forget all about us, then,' he cried.

Then Mario called him.

'Wait,' he told Cecily. 'I'll be back.'

But he wasn't.

Franca, her dress tied with a red satin sash, danced with Joe. They danced the foxtrot. She had strung a daisy chain in her hair and every time Joe swung her around it threatened to fall and make them both laugh. It was hard to believe that Joe would be gone in a day. Agnes and Anna were organising mountains more food.

'Your mother always liked to dirty her hands,' Kitty said, coming over to a vacant seat beside Cecily. She lit a cigarette.

Even though they were now allies, Cecily didn't like the slight sneer in her aunt's voice. Kitty tapped her foot in time to the music, flicking it like a cat's tail.

She finished her cigarette. Her mouth had a thin, sour twist to it that she was trying to hide but Cecily saw it anyway.

'I'm going out for some fresh air,' she said.

The music changed and Joe and Franca now tried to dance the tango but failed because they were laughing too much. Their audience shouted encouraging words and whistled.

'Is your brother going to marry her?' Tom asked.

Cecily nodded. She hadn't delivered much post of late but maybe she didn't need to any more.

'What about the war? He'll be leaving to fight in it, won't he?'

Cecily pretended she hadn't heard him. There was still no sign of Captain Pinky. It seemed several people could fall into the No-Sign-Of category.

Selwyn was one. Kitty had become another.

More cars were turning into the makeshift car park beside the tennis court. Lucio, standing with one foot against a wall, was smoking.

'I wanted some fresh air,' he said, smiling at Cecily.

'Have you seen Pinky Wilson?' Tom asked.

'No!' Cecily hissed.

She turned to Lucio.

'He means Robert Wilson.'

Lucio looked surprised. Then he smiled.

'Pinky?'

'We're not meant to call him that,' Cecily said.

Lucio looked at her. Then he burst out laughing. He laughed so loud and for so long that they looked at him bewildered. When he had finished, he threw away his cigarette and kissed the top of Cecily's head.

'One day you'll look like... your sister,' he said.

Cecily shook her head, crossly. Why did grown-ups tell so many lies?

'I won't.'

'Oh you will,' Lucio said. 'Rose looks just like Agnes. And you do too.'

He sounded both certain and sad.

'Oh never mind that,' Tom said impatiently. 'We've got to go, Cecily.'

'What's the hurry?' Lucio asked.

Cecily looked uncertainly at them both.

'We think there is someone here up to No Good!' she said.

'What sort of No Good?' Lucio asked, whispering too.

'We've a hunch…'

Lucio waited.

'No we haven't,' Tom said.

'No we haven't,' she agreed.

There was a long silence during which Lucio looked thoughtfully at Cecily.

'What d'you think of your friend, Pinky?' he asked.

Cecily was taken aback.

'Why do you ask?' Tom, the first to recover, demanded.

'We don't… like him,' Cecily admitted.

Lucio said nothing.

'C'mon Cecily,' Tom said impatiently.

Agnes, hovering in the doorway, faint music escaping behind her, saw Cecily looking up at Lucio and felt the same unfettered delight mirrored in her own heart.

She saw Cecily hanging on Lucio's arm and the grave manner in which he listened to her, his face lit by something other than the twilight. And she felt her own body tighten with desire. All around in the summery scented skies were darting swallows.

Anna coming quietly up, seeing it too, placed an arm around Agnes' waist and kissed the back of her head.

The music inside the hall changed. Mario was playing his accordion with the trio now.

'How old are you, Lucio?' Cecily asked above it, ignoring Tom for a moment longer.

'*Quanti anni hai*?' Lucio said. 'You must learn a little Italian, Cecci!'

'*Quanta anni hai*, then?'

'*Quanti*,' Lucio corrected her. '*Alora*! You are slaughtering the Italian language.'

'But how old *are* you?'

If I could speak Italian, thought Cecily, *would it help?*

'Your father is back,' Tom said.

Lucio glanced up. And saw Agnes standing against the doorway cradled by an old Italian song. The music had thrown up all sorts of flowers around her. He looked on for a moment longer, drinking her in. Then he closed his eyes briefly. When he opened them again Agnes was no longer there.

The photograph that Mario would take that night was full of people who would not have cause for any future reunion. Most of those in the picture were untraceable after the war but for the purpose of the evening stared clear-eyed and smiling into a pensionable future, dressed in their September best. Oblivious to how, from memory's frame, they would appear to a grown-up Cecily many years later.

No one smiling at that moment would know how time would blur their faces, for on that last evening of peace, no one wanted to think about the future. So after the tango (badly danced) and a couple of waltzes (executed now to perfection by Joe and Franca) the Italians settled into a comfortable stream of songs. And as the starry September night descended everyone danced with everyone else. A full harvest moon swung above them and the party spilled out onto the grass outside.

Rose danced with Carlo. And then with Giorgio. And after that, with Mario, who shouted to everyone to watch the pair of them.

'See how this beautiful young woman is prepared to dance with me!' he shouted.

Beppe, who had the beginnings of a fine crooner's voice, grabbed the microphone and, slightly mockingly, addressing his father, began to sing. Anna rolled her eyes and handed around cake to those sitting on the edge of the room.

Franca came to find her mother. She had Joe in tow. Ah! thought Anna. So here we have it! The music changed. Beppe began an old love song as suddenly, in full view of them all, Lucio walked across to Agnes, took the tea towel out of her hand and led her out to the dance floor. But all eyes were on Joe and Franca.

'Well,' Anna said. 'So when are you going to announce it?'

In answer Mario reached for Joe, pulling him towards him in a bear hug. A second later Franca was in his arms. Joe grinned. He looked around for his father but his father was nowhere in sight. Only his mother, turning in Lucio's arms, with an expression Joe had never seen on her face, came hurrying towards him.

'We make an announcement,' Mario said. 'Where is Selwyn?'

No one knew.

'He was here a moment ago,' Agnes said. 'C, have you seen your father?'

'I have, Mrs Maudsley,' Tom said. 'He's in the car.'

'Can you children fetch him?' Mario said. 'Tell him it is important! Hurry, hurry!'

Beppe was still singing. Anna would remember the song for the rest of her life, remember the look on her second son's face, the sparkling lights, her husband standing with his arm around their daughter.

Anna would remember all of this in the years ahead. And she would remember Agnes in the emerald frock that matched her eyes dancing with her brother-in-law. But she would not recall where little Cecci was.

Selwyn was outside talking to Aunt Kitty.

'You know they have invaded Poland,' Kitty said in a peculiar voice.

They came in then, to hear the announcement of the engagement between English Joe and Italian Franca. Mario, grabbing the microphone, made it all official, after which everyone clapped and clapped and some, chiefly Anna, cried. And Lucio, switching the radio off, wiping tables, squeezed water savagely out of his dishcloth as if it were an unwanted thought, trying not to look at Agnes.

Tomorrow was Sunday. Tomorrow would bring news of the future.

The spotlight followed Franca and her fiancé around the dance floor with everyone clapping in time to the music as madness escaped and attached itself to history in the making. Cecily was going to be the bridesmaid. And Rose too.

'Where's Rose?' Cecily asked.

'She's got a headache,' Agnes said.

'Damn,' whispered Tom. 'There go all our carefully laid plans!'

Fools, thought Lucio. And he poured himself a grappa with a savage movement.

The air cooled.

'Go and check,' Tom demanded, so Cecily went obediently back to the house.

'What are you up to, child?' Cook asked, catching her just as she was sneaking across the doorway. And she caught Cecily's skinny arm. Cook had a way of reading everyone's mind.

'Nothing,' Cecily said.

And she relaxed her hand, cunning as a cat, so that Cook immediately stopped being suspicious and let go of her. Cook was looking for lamps to take into the field.

'Can you look in the cupboard, there's a good girl,' she asked. 'I think there are at least three more there.'

Cecily heard her remove the glass from one of the lamps and a match was struck. Then she turned up the wick and put the glass back over the flame and turned round. In the orange glow of the light thrown across the kitchen Cook looked enormous, like a hobgoblin in a fairy tale.

'There's two more, somewhere,' she muttered. 'Ah yes, I've got 'em.'

'They're heavy and too unstable when lit.'

'Don't worry,' Cook said and she gave one of the lamps to Partridge.

Going upstairs Cecily paused by the landing window. She could see the woods ahead.

One grown-up voice was talking to another outside in soft mumbly murmurs.

'It's been a happy day.'

'But now it's all over.'

'We said it would never happen again but we were wrong!'

'There's still a slight chance.'

Cecily tip-toeing distracted, hearing other murmurs, soft rustlings inside the house itself, which, like an itch, needed investigating.

'Give me a little hope... don't you see?'

The voices were drifting away into the trees. In the distance a huge bird, an owl perhaps, hung suspended by an invisible thread. The moon was rising as the stars appeared one by one, like candles being lit.

Now, with the hindsight of twenty-three years, Cecily thought, *but everything was different after that*.

Now, her body was shaking.

'You've been a long time,' Tom told her when she got back.

But it was Bellamy, still standing stock-still, shocked, white-faced, staring at them all, that Cecily would remember in later years. His expression that night, reflecting so perfectly her own.

'We'll start making the blackout curtains tomorrow,' Agnes was saying.

Were German planes *really* going to bother with them? Here in Suffolk?

'Not Suffolk,' Joe said and Franca looked and looked at him as if she wanted to learn his face off by heart.

Like a song.

Or the words of a new language.

'Will you have to go back to Italy, Aunty Anna?' Cecily asked, at last.

'No, no of course not! We have been citizens here for too long. We work here. No one will send us back.'

'Now,' Tom hissed, pulling at Cecily's arm, dragging her out of earshot of the adults.

'So? Where is she?' he asked, 'In bed?'

But Cecily had forgotten to check.

'You nincompoop,' Tom said. 'She could have been abducted by Pinky for all we know!'

'Don't be silly,' Cecily said.

But even to her own ears the words rang hollow. Tom was looking intently at her.

'Well, where *is* she, then?'

Cecily wasn't sure. Tom made an exasperated sound.

'He's following her. He's following *all* of you, even your mother. Even me. You have to see if she's gone out!' Tom said, angrily.

Cecily shook her head. She didn't want to go back to the house. Tom shrugged. Because of a stupid girl their plans for tonight were ruined.

'Would you like a smoke?' he asked, abruptly.

'No thank you.'

'Please yourself,' he said indifferently. 'I'm going to have one.'

In the distance the Italians were still singing *o bella ciao, bella ciao, bella ciao, ciao, ciao.*

In the field small lights flickered like fireflies. It was as if the whole of Italy stood united in that field. Waiting for tomorrow. Then the sky was filled with an explosion of fiery flowers and everyone looked heavenwards and gasped.

'We won't be able to light up the fields like this any more.'

We Won't Be Able To Any More surrounded them in an ever decreasing circle.

'Tomorrow,' Tom said, coming back, his good mood restored. 'We will follow him. You will do as I say.'

Cecily was beginning to hate all Germans.

When her mother came to kiss her goodnight (and yes Rose was in bed), Cecily remembered something she had overheard Lucio say. She asked Agnes what it meant.

'Cruelty is natural,' he had said.

But Agnes would not answer Cecily's question.

'Think of something nice,' she said, instead.

And then she blew out the lamp in order not to break the spell of the night.

Bella ciao, bella ciao, bella ciao, ciao, ciao.

The song was still playing in her head when Cecily woke a few hours later to see her sister's hands disappearing through the window. Instantly wide awake, she listened. Someone was talking in a fierce whisper. Cecily frowned, trying to place the voice.

'You don't understand,' Rose was saying, her voice agitated.

Bella ciao, ciao, ciao. The song went on and on in Cecily's head. If she moved Rose might hear her. The window was wide open. There was the squeak of a bicycle and then Rose's urgent voice.

'Oh look! There he goes again.'

Who? thought Cecily. And then Rose again, puzzled, upset.

'I don't know.'

There was another silence below the window that went on for so long that Cecily almost dropped off to sleep again. But then there was the sound of someone struggling up the honeysuckle and a pair of hands appeared again.

'Goodnight,' Rose whispered, hoarsely, leaning back out.

She glanced quickly in the direction of Cecily and then, turning back to the window, blew a hasty kiss. Cecily lay rigid, thinking furiously. Something didn't add up. Rose was taking her clothes off as quickly as she could. When she was completely naked she slipped under the covers and sighed. In the faint light from outside Cecily saw her sister's face mysteriously watchful and filled with some secret, terrific pleasure. Was it possible, Cecily wondered, to be watchful and asleep?

The next morning they heard the news that Bellamy's father had killed himself. Bellamy had found him with his boots unlaced. The buttons of his trousers were undone showing the thickness of congealed blood on his shirt where the shot had entered the groin. Bellamy's father's head hung stiffly on his chest. The note beside him stated he was the son of an Irish Republican and the thought of another war frightened him.

19

NOW WITH A new dawn rising over Palmyra House Cecily awoke from another dream. An old dream in an old location, with the same cast of actors playing the same unfinished roles. Rose's suitcase, lined with a honeysuckle print, had featured in it.

The roof of Cecily's mouth felt dry. The returning past, rising like floodwater, threatened to drown her. Terrified, she saw that what she had finally started could not be stopped. When she went downstairs to the kitchen she found the back door open, letting in the day. Perhaps she had forgotten to shut it the night before. She made herself a pot of tea. And finding a piece of paper, drew two columns on it. Just like long-ago Tom.

She would write down *everything* she could remember. Every little thing.

When the police found Rose's suitcase on the night of September the 4th the war was only one day old.

The case was singed but still intact.

Full of future memories.

Full of things a young girl might pack when planning an elopement.

Full of dreams, hopes and other nonsense.

For instance there were two pearly-buttoned cardigans, needed for a cold climate in a neutral country. Ice-cream colours, strawberry pink and minty green from a lazy, hazy summertime. Two dresses, one of soft autumn colours and another one for the winter ahead. Gloves, of course. Kid-soft and belonging to Agnes.

Stolen well in advance. (Now that the war was upon them gloves were bound to be hard to come by.)

One small yellow suitcase; packed. Carried boldly out through the back door of Palmyra House.

One yellow suitcase leaving home with Rose. Under the circumstances she needed no suitcase where she was going.

There had been flames of happiness in her heart as she rode off down the country road towards freedom. Love being in the air meant she could have managed without a torch. There had been nothing tentative about her exit. Nothing she regretted leaving behind. But I did nothing, thought Cecily dully, her tea going cold in her hands. I knew and I didn't stop her.

'Oh Rose, don't rock the boat!' Agnes had said.

When had she said that?

'Don't hate your father. There's a war coming. Everything will change and what happened long ago will not matter as it once did.'

Why had she said that?

Rose shouting,

'I won't be like *you!* Your life is never going to be *my* future. I won't have a sham of a marriage. I must have love! I won't stay at home working on the farm when there is a war on. I won't, I won't!'

Cecily shook her head, defeated. The threads refused to knit.

That September night the spectacle of fireworks rising in fountains of light marked the last of the Last Pier. Later Cecily would hear how all kinds of things were thrown up.

An arm, raised in surprise, fingers young and ringless.

A shoe. Flung towards a moored boat.

A scrap of cloth that later would be identified as part of a summer dress.

Inappropriately worn, for the cold was already beginning to drift inland from the North Sea.

Cecily had run in. Dropping the jar of dying glow-worms, forgetting about Tom. Searching for Rose. Just in case, just in case. Coming to an abrupt halt when she saw Agnes, hands folded motionless in her lap like a dove's wings, waiting for news of the whereabouts of her eldest daughter. All around were reflections of Cecily's worst fears dancing to a macabre tune. As slowly, like a cast taking a bow, Selwyn and Kitty and Cook and Partridge and the Chief of Police and finally Robert Wilson himself, came in. To stand, heads bowed, silent amidst their horrific discovery.

'Get out of my life,' Agnes had screamed.

Crazed by grief. Demented by it.

And Selwyn?

'Fetch the child,' he had whispered, his bullying powers all gone, the enormity of his own terrible crime unfolding.

'*What have I done?*' cried Selwyn.

'Get out, get out, all of you!' Agnes screamed, unstoppable. 'I want my daughter back!'

And Robert Wilson, too, as if in a trance, walked over to the window to check the blackout blinds were secured. For there was, in spite of everything, a war going on outside.

Robert Wilson, unaware of the white and stricken face of the young girl they called C standing in the doorway listening to adult sobs.

Cecily.

Cecci.

Coming in, un-fetched, of her own accord. Handing herself over. Looking suddenly exactly like her dead sister.

Saying,

'It's All My Fault.'

Even though no one was blaming her,

'My Fault! My Fault!' she would go on saying, forever.

'How many were guilty that night?' cried the adult Cecily, now.

At last, arms wrapped around her own waist, rocking herself.

But on that night, as the house emptied and Selwyn was led away by the police, in the shocked silence, Robert Wilson watched as Agnes held on to Cecily, trying and failing to stop herself from shaking. For most of all, the thing that made Agnes weep bewildered tears, and Cecily stare unblinkingly, was a small spotted purse. Escaping the explosion somehow. With fifty pounds and three photographs. Intact. Like Rose's teeth.

Cecily was not going anywhere.

Not yet. Not ever, not in her head.

And after that, as if it wasn't enough, the all-clear had sounded its flute-like note (no one had heard the siren in the first place but of course there was a war on), and Cook turned her back on everyone and went off to make a pot of tea.

'I will always love you,' Agnes had whispered. Cecily had wondered who she was talking to. Her? Or Rose?

For once Aunt Kitty had nothing to say. Numb. Oh yes, they were all numb.

Meet your new sister Numb, Cecily. She will empty you of life.

Looking back across the years Cecily saw how, at the time when it had happened there had been only disconnection. Incoherent things, too terrible to examine. Things that gave up their heart-ache only slowly and with time's magic.

Perfumes.

Body scents.

Room scents.

Love.

Invisible feelings that didn't mean anything after that moment.

You need a code-breaker to break the hidden patterns, the voices in her head told her quietly.

They sounded shocked.

But who had caused the fire? Tell us!

Nor was it possible to explain how, throughout the lonely years of the war, while Cecily fought her own war and Agnes discovered the Drink, and Kitty lost those things she had never truly had, *still*, certain fragments remained. Preserved in amber.

How, on that September night, Agnes had sat, refusing to move.

How nothing Robert Wilson said, on that night, or any other occasion, made the least bit of difference to anyone.

How, on that night, even when Robert Wilson took hold of Agnes' cold hand she did not look up, did not recognise him.

How her voice calling out for her newly discovered love would reverberate down the years. Echoing terribly in Cecily's mind.

And how Agnes, just one day after war had been declared, broken without any help from Mister Hitler, sitting in the very same room, being advised by experts, could only utter the words, 'Where's Lucio?'

Lucio?

And then came the chorus of voices Cecily remembered so well.

'Send her away!'

Who had they meant?

'Find Lucio!'

'She can't stay *here*, Agnes, are you mad?'

Why not? The whole world had gone mad, why couldn't she?

'Lucio,' cried Agnes in a waterfall of grief.

And thereafter began the rigmarole of lists of a different sort. Socks. Uniform shirts Shoes (One pair because you'll be home soon.) School bag. (This war won't go on for much longer.) Ration Book.

On and on.

Don't forget to clean your teeth every night. Don't forget to wash your hands before you eat. Don't forget to look before you cross the road. Don't forget that even though I forgot to say the words, they exist in the ether. I love you.

'Don't forget, C.'

'I won't,' Cecily had said, even though she had no idea what it was she shouldn't forget.

Her new school uniform had added to her confusion, although it would not be long before she found other distractions to help her pass the time from waking to sleeping. From one year to the next. Then as now, she saw the diminutive pile of clothes that had been laid out, waiting to be packed into a suitcase with Rose's name on it. A suitcase lying in state, in this very house to which Cecily had now returned in order to understand the true heritage of her violet eyes.

Violet, like the violets Agnes had once worn.

Violets like those Selwyn had sent Cecily on her twenty-first birthday.

From prison.

We'll gather violets in the spring again, he had written on the card.

'I still have it,' she told the voices in her head, scribbling across the columns on her piece of paper. 'It's here with me, with all his letters.'

20.

BELLAMY'S FATHER HAD been only the first to die that summer, Cecily thought. Taking down another photograph from the wall, wiping the dust off, the adult Cecily gazed intently at it.

'How odd,' she murmured. 'It's Robert Wilson standing on the steps of Broadcasting House.'

She remembered something her father had said in one of his scantily read letters.

Saturday September 2nd 1939 and the bar of history had finally been reached.

Some felt the violent storm that burst over England was Nature's way of putting the finishing touches to the whole affair.

'God reminding us that our little wars are nothing in the scheme of things!' the Prime Minister said.

They had been drinking cold beer; the humidity had demanded it. The final decision, the agreement to go to war, had required some sort of closure, some ceremony, after all these months of waiting.

Walking back to his car, rain pelted down on Robert, soaking him.

'Can I give you a lift anywhere?' he asked, seeing Lord Halifax behind him.

'Thank you, no. I think I'll walk.'

Robert nodded.

'Let's hope I live to see the end of it. Good luck, by the way.'

'Thank you, sir,' Robert said, raising his hand.

The city was in darkness. He turned his car around and headed back to Suffolk. Fragments of conversation floated across his tired mind.

'It must be war, "Chips" old boy.'

'There's no other way out.'

'Nerves are getting frayed.'

The violence of the storm meant he had to drive more slowly. The tempest appeared to seal the whole ghastly situation, while all over England, in market towns and quiet country lanes, people slept the last sleep of innocence. As he turned towards the east he wondered what would now happen to the beautiful Maudsley women. Agnes, Rose, the child. What future was there for them in this sorry mess? He shook his head. Something was rotten at the very core of the apple, he thought. A melancholy darkness seemed to cloak the fields speeding past. *No one talked of the beauty of darkness*, Robert thought as with a heavy heart he drove towards the old Ipswich Road. Lightning tore at the sky. Sleep was what he craved most of all. Sleep and a forgetting of all that lay ahead. A line of poetry, learnt long ago, in his university days, came back to him.

Many deaths lay ahead. How sleep the brave, he thought. Suddenly he wanted to weep.

'The real work is about to begin,' the Prime Minister had told them. And as the meeting ended every man around the table had been left wondering if they would be alive at the end of it. Will I, wondered Robert? He was not afraid. Fear was too definite, too dramatic. No, it was sadness he felt. Unaccountable, helpless, elusive, sadness at what he had done. At what he had yet to do.

The rain hadn't quite reached Palmyra House and a watery moon still shone.

Tomorrow I shall leave for Salisbury, thought Joe, turning in his last peacetime bed. His bags were packed. Tomorrow he would listen to Chamberlain's speech at Franca's house. They were going to spend the day together.

A nightingale was singing somewhere in the woods.

Agnes heard it and was filled with sadness. My only son will fight in this war, she thought. And Lucio, too. There is only pain ahead.

Cecily heard it and, forgetting about her foiled adventure, thought of something Carlo had said to her, instead.

Joe heard it and hoped Franca heard it too. From now on everything he did would be with Franca in mind.

By some fluke Franca heard the bird singing too. She was a little psychic, everyone said. She heard things others could not.

Rose heard nothing. She lay deep in a leaden sleep that helped her keep a secret disappointment at bay.

Selwyn may have heard it but if he did, he didn't care. It was just a nightingale, for God's sake. There were bigger things at stake!

And strangely it was Kitty who heard the nightingale and decided, if there were no war, she would turn over a new leaf. It was a promise made only to herself and if broken, nobody would be any the wiser.

While all the time the pale moon kept steady watch over Palmyra House.

In Germany, Lucio told Carlo, there were terrible atrocities being done to the Jews. Unheard of things, unspeakable acts.

'The anti-Fascist movement is our only hope,' Lucio said.

Carlo shivered. Like his uncle, Carlo had no doubt that war would come. Lucio had told him that war, like death, was nature's way of pruning. Thousands were being killed in Poland already, millions more would go.

Somewhere in the interior of Palmyra House one door banged and then another, letting in the sea breeze and clearing the air.

The house had closed down on its secrets and fell into a final pre-war silence as Agnes hurried across the sodden garden one last time.

'It's over between them,' Lucio would tell Carlo, later, with relief. 'She will leave him when the war is declared.'

'But uncle,' Carlo said 'what about your work? Does she know what you do?'

Lucio had shaken his head. Not yet.

'Selwyn wants her back but thank God it's too late. Selwyn is a fool.'

Carlo would remember his words.

In his worst moments Lucio peered down the road to the future and saw only shadows. Whichever way he went, they followed him.

'I will remove it from your path,' Agnes had promised. 'I will make your life free of stones.'

But Lucio had less certainty than she did. He was frightened of the future. He had held Agnes tightly, kissing the fingers of her hands one by one. He had massaged her back by the light of the oil lamp. Then he turned her over and lay on top of her. Slender, fragile Agnes, in her last hours of beauty. The orchard was full of fruit. Eyes looked their last as with one hand on her small breast, Lucio saw again the deep dimple with its tendency to appear at the slightest provocation. During laughter, but also during tears.

He had pressed a flower from the white tobacco plant into her navel and held it down with his tongue until it was fixed on her skin. From now on, he told her, she would have the impression of a tobacco flower on her body.

Forever.

Even when she was old and close to death the impression of it would remain with her, he promised. Like a kiss. Or a wish. Or a vow of faithfulness.

After she had left him, and later that night in her sleep, Agnes smiled a smile she seldom used in her waking hours. Cecily could vouch for that. She had seen the smile when she crept into her parent's room and stood staring down at her mother's face and because of that stolen moment, remembering it many years later,

Cecily would understand, dreams were like that. They gave you chances that were impossible by day.

'Lucio,' Agnes murmured on that last happy night.

And yet something was not right, Lucio told his nephew. Selwyn was one problem, but the man Robert Wilson – he was something far more deadly. Wily as a stoat. He was something to do with the future and Lucio was afraid of him.

In their young girls' beds the sisters, together for a short while longer, moved restlessly. At the first roll of thunder Cecily turned over.

'I think we should tell the grown-ups about Pinky,' she mumbled.

Rose slept the sleep of the newly disappointed while the lightning slashed its cold knife-like streaks across the room, revealing what should and should not be seen. Those things that would, and would not, be lost.

A counterpane with roses embroidered on it.

A countenance of great promise.

A childhood story.

A crumpled, fairy-tale dress.

A crimson flower.

A way of life that was vanishing.

There was no one to stand guard over what would be lost; those small things, those young things, those tender, fragile things with no name.

The noise of a door closing woke Cecily and quietly, she left the room, wanting to know more. Wanting-to-know was the itch she could not be rid of.

And now the whole world was flooded in wet, black ink. In her parent's room Cecily tried to see into her own misty future but saw instead her mother, waiting at a crossroads for Lucio. Her mother's Difficult Decision was nothing to do with Poland, or Germany, Cecily saw. But it was still, technically speaking, a war. Was it possible to have two world wars going on simultaneously?

The skin of Agnes' dream hadn't quite peeled away. There were bits still sticking to her eyelids as she murmured Lucio's name.

Again.

That night too, Bellamy standing under a tree saw a light go on in Palmyra House and stood waiting. The bar of history might have decimated Poland but another tendril on the honeysuckle climber grew three more flowers. More would blossom for Rose in a week's time.

And at the same moment the local dentist awoke with a headache caused by a feeling of foreboding. *He* noticed it had begun to rain.

And the undertaker in Dunsburgh, having quarrelled with his wife over a remark about job opportunities ahead, began to snore.

And Cecily, the inquisitive, listened.

List-ened.

As she would never listen again.

While in Whitehall, an army of workers, with sweaty not-altogether-white collars, poor people with marching feet, listened, too. For those laws that governed the land, deciding between what was a fact and what was not, had begun to turn their wheels.

A fact is true, the law said.

Fiction is a lie.

Propaganda is a derogatory word for a fact.

There can be no mistake.

Carelessness *did* costs lives.

And a true patriot lives in the country where he was born.

Armed with these flashcards the army of Whitehall War Workers set to work.

They opened unopened files and read the names on the lists made at least a year before, by one Robert Wilson: Alessandro

Anzi from London, Carlo Campolonghi from Edinburgh, Giovanni Oresfi from Clerkenwell, Francesco Cesar from Eastbourne and Mario Molinello from Bly were just some of the names on it.

'Collar the lot!' said the man with the big cigar. 'Don't take any chances.'

Through the slightly open window of Robert Wilson's car, the fragrance of the parched earth rose in spite of the rain, reminding him of a love that would soon be lost. He had been hot. Now he shivered slightly. Tension drained out of him like water out of sand. What had started could not be stopped and all he could do was begin to do his job.

Ahead was the house he would remember forever. A place he had come to call home in spite of all he had uncovered, all he would have to implement.

Sunrise came. It was the first Sunday of September and the official end to the night's blackout. Agnes woke and tried to recall her dream. Selwyn lay asleep beside her. She hadn't woken when he had come in. She lay without moving for a few moments longer, thinking of the day ahead.

She longed for peace, no announcement by the Prime Minister, no war, no difficulty in leaving Selwyn. Pulling back the bedcovers, she went downstairs.

The newspaper boy had just delivered the paper and, pouring out her first cup of tea, Agnes read of the eye-witness accounts of Germany's invasion of Poland. What good was it reading of bombed and burning villages? She could not help the civilians at the roadside or the fair-haired girl weeping beside her murdered siblings. She couldn't even help herself. Here she was contemplating tearing her family apart, breaking what she had held together for so long, beginning again. Shuddering, she poured more tea and stared at the mist still lying heavily on the ground outside. The sun was up and warming the chill. It would, in the end, be a fine day.

There was a knock on the window and Robert Wilson's face came into view. She had not known he was back.

'Turn the wireless on,' he said.

Chamberlain was going to speak to the nation at 11.15.

'Good that it's Sunday, at least,' Agnes said.

They drank tea together.

'Everyone asleep? Selwyn away?'

Robert Wilson, clipped like a well-kept hedge, distant as a cloud, would be leaving soon, he told her. The tennis court would be ploughed up this week and soon there would be crops. In spite of what all the others said, Agnes liked him. She wondered if he had a wife. Or a love of any sort.

'No,' she said, speaking of Selwyn. 'He's back. He'll be down in a minute I expect.'

But in fact it was Cecily clattering downstairs, book in hand, some sort of complicated tall story to tell.

In the end they were all there. Tom and Robert, Selwyn and Joe and Rose (with Bellamy scowling in the doorway), Cook and The Help from the village, Partridge and three of the farm-hands too.

The day was beautiful like all the days had been this whole long summer. But then, with a harsh cry a hurricane of crows rose from the hedgerows and a dandelion clock, detaching and then drifting on the slight breeze, entered the room.

Click, click, went the shutter in Cecily's head. Chamberlain's words and the dandelion joined up, like dots in the picture she was drawing. All together, around the wireless, they would stay joined up forever.

'*I have to tell you now that no such undertaking has been received and that consequently this country is at war with Germany,*' Chamberlain said and Cecily caught and held a dandelion wisp.

Tom was giving her meaningful looks. Tonight there would be no moon which meant they would have another chance to catch that rat, Captain Pinky. Perfect timing, Tom's look said. Red-handed, wartime traitor. Caught! Cecily suppressed a giggle.

Rose, hovering at the back, was scowling.

Tom edged towards Cecily. Careless laughter gave games away.

But then Cook burst into tears, shocking them all.

Nobody spoke. Only the wood pigeons cooing outside, the smell of smoke from Partridge's bonfire and Cook's crying interrupted the silence. Kitty turned towards the back door as the speech about right prevailing, ended. She lit a cigarette and stared outside. Cecily saw her shrug her shoulders.

'Well, that's that,' Selwyn said.

Cook, her hands shaking, her eyes wiped, went off to get lunch.

'Make sure you're down in half an hour, Rose,' she called after the closing door. 'With your face and hands washed.'

Cecily had crushed the dandelion clock in her hand by mistake. Dandelion bits fell to the ground.

'Don't make a mess,' Agnes said, absent-mindedly. 'Go and wash your hands.'

'Come on, C,' Tom said but the hideous wailing of the air raid siren made them all jump. No one could find their gas masks.

It's the end of everything as we know it, Cecily thought.

She was thinking of the fields, the woods, the church with its lovely spire and the marshes with all the birds that lived in it. And of Joe, who was leaving tonight.

And of Carlo who wasn't old enough to be called up. He was angry that his brothers could. It made him feel useless, he had said, a serious look on his face.

Agnes had tears in her eyes. She could not even mention Lucio's name to herself.

There was no air raid. It had been a false alarm and a moment later the notes of the all-clear sounded. Perhaps, thought Agnes, that's a good omen. Kitty announced she would perhaps need to travel to London, to join the Wrens.

'I don't want to be a Land Girl,' she said, wrinkling her nose. 'I'm not interested in taking a step backwards!'

'After lunch,' Selwyn said, 'I shall have to call a meeting with the ARPs. And after that I may need to go up to London, too. I could give you a lift, Kitty, if you wanted? Petrol rationing will start immediately, you know.'

But Kitty wasn't quite ready.

'Thank you, but I won't stay for lunch, if you don't mind,' Robert Wilson said, smiling politely. 'I still haven't finished writing my report on the land management in this area.'

No one minded.

'Good,' muttered Tom.

It would make it easier to watch him. But it was a long time until the evening and what if he drove off to London, now?

'What on earth are you children plotting, now?' Kitty asked, making them jump.

'This evening,' Tom said loudly, 'C and I are going to look for glow-worms. We're going to use them as torches from now on.'

It was a very long and tiring day with unaccountable tensions. At five, Joe left. It was much worse for Franca, Agnes reminded them. Agnes did not make a fuss, although Cecily saw that the fuss was going on inside her mother. Joe was stopping off in town to say goodbye to Franca and the Molinellos. When he returned in two weeks (he hoped) he would buy a ring.

'That's nice,' Rose said in a voice that didn't quite match her words.

Only Cecily noticed. Everyone else was too subdued. Everyone except Kitty, of course, who went outside to read a book. Rose just wanted to sleep and sleep.

'Are you going out tonight?' Cecily asked her, not really expecting a reply and not getting one, either.

Lethargy hung around Palmyra Farm like a dying wasp. While Anger followed Bellamy into the bushes. He too was making plans.

Night came slowly. Starless and moonless and all that Tom had hoped for. It was still damp from last night's rain. Joe would be at his camp by now, listening to the King's speech from his mess.

'There may be dark days ahead, and war can no longer be confined to the battlefields,' the King said.

Afterwards as they stood for the National Anthem, Cecily saw Captain Pinky hurrying across the lawn. But he had missed the King. Agnes in heightened mood, tears not far off, looked around at those members of her family that were present. What was Lucio thinking? It was not his National Anthem. The lights were going out all over Europe. In the Molinellos' little village in Italy, too. What were they feeling at this moment?

'I'm going to post a letter,' Kitty said, abruptly.

That evening Robert Wilson brought round a bottle of champagne to toast a speedy end to the war.

'You see,' Tom hissed. 'He's always here.'

'He's waiting to see if Rose goes out.'

'I'm going to bed,' Tom said.

'We're tired,' Cecily told her mother, ignoring Pinky.

A preoccupied Agnes accepted this flawed story.

'Did you see his black file?' Tom asked as they parted on the stairs. 'He's trying to recruit your mother, make her a spy, like him.'

'Tonight's the night,' Cecily agreed. 'When the fish will bite!'

They synchronised their watches and went their separate ways.

September the 3rd, 1939; it might as well have been etched on her own headstone in gold letters.

Afterwards Agnes blamed herself for drinking too much champagne. But hindsight was still some hours away as Robert Wilson poured her another glass of fizzing, bubbling trouble.

'He had salt and pepper hair,' she said of Selwyn.

And he had remarked on her eyes.

For a love-starved girl who had only lived for Liszt, this was a thrill like no other.

'And Kitty?'

'Oh she was always prettier than me,' Agnes said, misunderstanding.

Robert Wilson refrained from comment.

'I don't want you to think it was all bad,' Agnes said.

'No.'

'We got on very well to start with.'

She paused, thinking through the jungle of missed opportunities.

'He used to make me laugh...'

Ah! thought Robert. Yes!

'And he loved my music.'

She remembered how in the early days they had had little concerts. How Joe in his pram had grown up listening to Beethoven and Mozart and Schubert. Getting his musical education from the cradle, Selwyn had said. As indeed Rose had, too.

'Until it all changed.'

'How?' Robert asked, his voice gentle.

Agnes hesitated. When had she realised?

'What?' asked Robert Wilson.

'His bitterness.'

'Bitterness?'

Again Agnes hesitated. How could a man like Robert Wilson understand?

'It hasn't been easy for me either,' Robert said, slowly.

There was a pause.

'His father was a terrible man,' Agnes said at last. 'Selwyn never forgave him for what he did to him.'

Something to do with a German girl he had been friendly with.

'Yes…'

'And of course there was also his brother's death…'

'Yes.'

'He closed his mind to everything except C. He loves her with a passion that makes Rose resent him.'

'Why have favourites?' asked Robert Wilson, surprised.

Agnes shrugged.

'When Selwyn has an obsession, he doesn't give it up easily,' she said. 'When the job offer came he could not refuse. So I took over the running of the farm. Bit by bit, you know.'

Bit by bit Selwyn staying away, going up to London early, returning late.

'In the end we thought it sensible to buy a small flat. So he wouldn't have to keep driving back at all sorts of unearthly hours.'

'Did you stay there too?'

'Oh goodness, no. There was no room and besides I had the farm and the children to take care of. We thought it a good investment.'

'Where did the money come from?'

'His work at the Ministry,' she shrugged. 'It was well paid. He was an advisor to the Minister of Trade.'

Robert Wilson nodded. This wasn't news, he said. Then he held the empty bottle up to the light. And opened a new bottle.

'My word!' laughed Agnes, uneasily. 'We shall be drunk.'

But the day had been terrible enough, she supposed. She thought with longing about Lucio. He would come only under cover of the blackout. She was certain. Crossing the fields, the long way round. Bubbles of happiness rose in her.

'Agnes,' Robert Wilson said, at last.

And he stopped. They sipped their champagne in silence.

'Have you any idea what work Selwyn is doing now?'

'Well of course not, it's top secret,' she giggled.

She was beginning to sound like Tom, she thought. Robert Wilson was looking at her gravely.

'He doesn't talk to you about it?'

Agnes shook her head.

'Oh you needn't worry, Robert. Selwyn isn't in any special danger I promise you.'

There was a pause.

'How well d'you know the Italians?' Robert asked, gently.

'The Molinellos? They're wonderful people. Why?'

'No reason, but now we are at war and...'

'They won't be able to visit their relatives, poor things.'

It would hit Mario hard, she told him. He was often home-sick.

'I'll visit them in the morning. After all, we're going to be related, soon!'

Robert nodded.

'I'm worried about them,' he said, slowly. 'We have to be careful of careless talk. From now on.'

'Oh I know,' Agnes told him, giggling again.

'I think you should keep an eye open,' he said, vaguely.

Then he rose.

'I should go to bed. Tomorrow all hell will be let loose. In all probability, I'll have to return to London.'

Picking up the file he had brought with him, he opened it, and then changed his mind and shut it again, noticing how Agnes glanced at her watch. She had looked at it several times during the evening. He wondered if she was expecting someone, later. He wished her goodnight. And stepped outside. He did not see Tom with a jam jar, slipping across to the orchard in search of glow-worms. He did not see, and neither did Agnes, Rose climbing down the honeysuckle wearing her best satin shoes.

With a torch covered with two layers of black crepe paper, making for the bicycle shed.

But Cecily could see it now. Every bit of it. She could not stop seeing the image of Agnes crying out that she would take to her grave the x-ray of her daughter's teeth. Small, pearly, even, white teeth, held up to the light by the dentist.

Oh yes, it was Rose's all right.

Rose's teeth without its smile.

Teeth without the mouth that ranted at the world at large.

And a dress burnt to a cinder.

Cinders? (Cecily would murmur out of habit later on, ensuring a slap) Like Cinderella?

Without the glass slipper.

Someone (it was forgotten in the cacophony of sounds whether it had been Kitty) would be unable to stop slapping Cecily.

Shut up! Shut Up! Haven't you done enough damage already? With your stupid games, your foolish imagination? Will you never learn to shut up?

Stop, stop, stop! someone would cry, pulling Kitty's hands apart as though they were a bunch of cut flowers. Reminding everyone of the seven flowers Robert Wilson sent as a sign every time he wanted a secret word with Kitty.

Cecily had heard them tell Agnes it would not be advisable for her to see the rest of her daughter, Rose. Cecily had no idea who the devil *they* were. Even now, years later, she could not remember their faces, or their names; those people who lined up to hold her mother upright.

And Agnes Maudsley never forgave herself for listening with horror to the news of the first British ship to go down in the middle of the Atlantic at the same moment that her own daughter was going up in flames.

Twenty-nine years later, draining her cold tea into the dark-stained sink, Cecily washed up her mug. She realised she did not want to visit the grave.

21

ON HER LAST visit, when Cecily was almost nineteen, Agnes broke a silence of a different sort.

'At least she never knew what was to follow,' she said.

Sick, sad, quietly mad Agnes who visited Cecily for one last time, climbing up the steps to the front door, ringing the bell marked *Maudsley*. Out of breath, with a rattle in her chest and years of neglect imprinted on her eyes, bursting in on Cecily with random thoughts that were beyond comprehension.

'We've breached the ordered peace we once had,' she announced and Cecily, tired of her mother's evasive lies, her refusal to tell her what had really gone on, the guilt of all she herself was carrying, closed her eyes and sighed.

Leave me alone, she wanted to cry. None of this is relevant.

But although on the edge of extinction, Agnes was unable to stop sifting the stones of confusion that would fill her life until it reached its bitter end.

So on that last visit she had thrust a small cutting from *The Times* into Cecily's hand, insisting she read of the boat the Italians had sailed on. Before the war it had been a luxury cruise liner floating across the Mediterranean.

The British liner Arandora Star, with about 1,500 Germans and Italian subjects on board, has been torpedoed and sunk by a German U-boat in the Atlantic. Germans and Italians, men interned at the outbreak of war, were being taken to Canada. It is feared that all Italian lives have been lost. British survivors state that as the ship was rapidly sinking there was panic amongst the aliens, and especially amongst the Germans, who thrust aside Italians in their efforts to reach the lifeboats first.

'He loved me, you know,' Agnes burst out. 'Lucio! And now he's gone.'

'And the other Molinellos?' Cecily had asked, unable to ask more.

'All of them,' Agnes said, pressing her lips tightly together.

There had been only silence after that. Agnes sat, eyes closed, still as a bird, her tea untouched. On the table was a paper bag with some fresh brown eggs. All Agnes had these days were a few chickens. The orchard had gone, as had the top field where one magical night they had sung 'Bella Ciao'.

Her mother, Cecily saw, had painted pink hearts on the eggs as though they were for a child.

On that last visit Agnes spent the morning with Cecily in her room at the top of a house on the Old Kent Road. The room was Cecily's first completely Maudsley-free space. It was paid for by the grant she got from the County Council for her teacher-training course in Avery Hill.

'Do you still write stories?' Agnes asked.

Cecily shook her head.

'You used to write all the time, when you weren't reading. And when you weren't eavesdropping!'

Neither of them laughed. The silence that had been growing between them stepped out of its shoes and pushed against the room.

'I brought you Rose's rug,' Agnes said, finally.

It had been an ordinary morning without pain.

Until Cecily saw that rug.

Why was her mother doing this? Did she want Rose to follow her everywhere?

The voices in Cecily's head, knowing silence was more powerful than words, were quiet.

'See how nice it looks beside your bed,' Agnes said.

Her face, in the wake of her chemotherapy treatment, was yellow, her lovely piano-playing fingers swollen by steroids. The long slender neck truncated somehow. The sadness surrounding

Agnes tainted the air like escaping gas, making Cecily want to cry.

'It suits you, doesn't it?' Agnes asked. 'Living here.'

Not really a question, more of a distress flare. Cecily nodded. Agnes began to cough. Cecily prepared to wait. The spasm, she knew, would go on for longer than was socially polite.

'Have you registered with a doctor, Cecci?'

The old name slipping out made Cecily angry. She resented her mother using a nickname that wasn't hers to use. Agnes continued to cough. Was she still smoking as much as before, Cecily wondered?

'Not yet.'

'Well you should, you know. Health is wealth.'

They paused as though they were boxers taking a break. Too many unsaid things made it impossible to move the slagheaps of regret. Truth remained trapped under them.

'What are your flatmates like? D'you like them?'

Agnes smiled a ghastly smile through a volume of sagging flesh. The tiny, lovely mother whose dimples had so delighted Cecily, where had she gone? Had the green eyes darkened through loss?

'I want you to be happy.' Agnes said. 'I mean *really* happy.'

In the silence that followed, the dead were not named.

'Shall we go out for lunch?' Cecily asked.

The room had become stuffy. She needed to get out into the open.

'I would like a steak,' her mother said and proceeded to lead the way to Leicester Square.

Cecily wondered whether she had been drinking.

Over lunch (Agnes insisted that she would pay, 'Of course you're not paying. This is my treat!') the silence between the two of them was broken only by the sound of Agnes chewing her steak. Her mother had lost one of her bottom teeth and when she ate it sounded as if she were swallowing phlegm. Cecily felt sick. It was all she could do to eat her salad without retching.

Agnes ordered a gin and slurped it in great glugs. She cut into another piece of meat. Blood oozed out. Cecily saw white sinewy bits.

'It's very fatty,' Agnes said, her mouth open as she chewed.

The waiter hovered and then went away again. Agnes dropped first her fork and then her napkin. When the waiter tried to give her a new fork she waved him away, then changed her mind and asked for another gin instead.

'We must do this again,' she said squeezing Cecily's hand.

Despair took Cecily's voice hostage.

The waiter returned with Agnes' drink. This time there were two ice cubes in the glass and a piece of lemon. Agnes pushed her plate away.

'You should come home,' she ventured.

She lit a cigarette. In spite of what cigarettes had done to her, she still loved them. *An abusive relationship if ever there was one*, Cecily thought.

Carlo was dead. What was there to come home for now?

Agnes shrugged.

'I don't know. To see the sea, maybe?'

Speechless, Cecily thought of all the years when she had fallen asleep in her attic room in Kitty's house, listening to the sound of the trains rumbling along the railway line towards Vauxhall Bridge. Wishing it were the sound of the sea. Wishing she were lying in her bed in Palmyra House. And she thought of the years she had spent wishing her mother would invite her back. Just once. Just to collect those things she had left behind in the unseemly haste of her departure from paradise.

'I wonder if I could have another drink?' Agnes asked.

'You've had enough,' Cecily told her.

Hopelessness melted in Agnes' glass. Cecily felt the obstruction in her chest was growing.

'I have to go to the library,' she lied.

'Do you need money?' Agnes asked, peering anxiously at her.

Cecily shook her head. Outside it had begun to rain. Red London buses were passing noiselessly by. Agnes sighed. I don't know what you want, her sigh said. She gathered up her shopping bag, a string one that Cecily remembered from years before.

'I suppose I had better be getting back then,' she said. 'It's a bit of a journey.'

Cecily stood up and went to the lavatory. When she returned, Agnes was sitting at the empty table hugging her bag and staring out of the window, her eyes bewildered.

'Let's go,' she said.

It was the last time Cecily saw her mother alive.

Agnes died in her bedroom in Palmyra House twenty-five years after she had arrived there as a young bride. She died alone. With a sackful of green walnuts ready to be pickled standing in the grimy kitchen. She was fifty-one. No age at all, the people in the town would say. Pity, they would say, there had never been another man to warm her bed.

All the staff working at the farm before the war had left, even Partridge. The orchard had gone. Cook took retirement when her arthritis had made it impossible to lift the chicken feed into the yard. Agnes had tried to get a girl from the town but most of them, having heard the rumours that circulated about the Maudsleys, were reluctant to come. In any case, after the farm had been sold, what was the point of having any help when no help was needed? Agnes had no friends in the town. The war had swept a lot away. Things that were unnecessary in this new after-the-war life had gone, like ice-cream parlours and digging-for-victory kitchen gardens. Only the walnut tree remained, still producing two sackfuls of nuts.

For years she hadn't bothered to pickle any but on the day before she died she went into the yard and stared up at the tree. Then she found the ladder. The cat, seeing this unusual activity, wandered out with a kitten in its mouth, alarmed. Agnes took no notice of it. She began to collect the unripe walnuts. They were particularly large this year. She would send Cecily some, she decided. Frowning, she continued with her task until the sun had travelled across the yard. Then she dragged her sack in towards the kitchen door to deal with later. Later she would go into the town to buy vinegar. Later she would sterilise some of the hundreds of bottles in the scullery and warm them ready for the walnuts. Later. Smoking her thirtieth cigarette of the day, she brushed ash off her cardigan. There was comfort in the notion of Later. It gave shape to the rest of her life.

'Taste me,' she had said, once long ago, in some other life, 'I'm real!'

Where are you, now, she wanted to cry.

'You will be with me wherever I go,' he had told her. 'What I hand over to you is yourself; yourself loved in every part.'

Oh the things he had said! She had trusted him, never doubting he would remain with her throughout the war. But he had vanished, leaving only the sound of his name. To be remembered by her.

'Lucio!' she cried, helplessly.

That night she was awoken by a recurring dream. In the dream she was making a list just as Cecily used to. Agnes' list was about the things she once Had Not Known.

She had not known about what was about to happen.

Or that she was having her last unsullied memories.

That the sound of the fire engines would stay with her for the rest of her life.

That the knives and forks she was setting out on the table for tomorrow's breakfast were merely decorative.

That the kidney pie in the oven would go to waste.

That she would never have an appetite again.

That the war when it came would be of no importance for her.

That the car slowing down outside the house on the night the pier burnt down would not belong to Selwyn.

Or that the man driving the car would take from her all that mattered.

Sitting up in her large bed she pushed away the cover. It was the eiderdown that had once, long ago, belonged on Cecily's bed but which, after she had banished Cecily, Agnes had taken to keep her company and staunch her grief.

'Why,' she asked herself now, as she had done a thousand times before, 'why did I send her away? We could have weathered it together.'

Outside a thin, cloud-veiled moon shone on the rooftops of the houses built where the tennis court had once been. Agnes sat up, puzzled. Where had the tennis court gone?

The room was suddenly full of other people's whispered voices contradicting each other.

'Love,' she cried, 'where are you?'

She put her hand over her ears trying to blot out the noise but the sounds got louder. She tried to call out to her daughter Rose but the name wouldn't form in her throat. She thought of her sister but couldn't remember what *her* name was.

'Cecci,' she said, out of habit.

And that was all she remembered.

Outside in the early autumn sky, the paper-thin moon had had enough of spreading itself over Palmyra Farm and moved off silently in another direction.

She wasn't found for two days and then it was by chance that the postman, delivering a gas bill to the house, noticed the side light still switched on and walked round to the kitchen. There he saw the open sack of walnuts and the ladder leaning against the tree.

He knew Mrs Maudsley from many years before. He knew all about her hard life, in fact he had been a young boy when she had first come to live at Palmyra House. He remembered her as a tall, slender beauty with vivid green eyes who didn't take care of herself. Others had thought her sister prettier but the postman knew better. Besides, he had seen how quickly the older sister went to seed after trouble came to Palmyra Farm. Whereas poor

Mrs Maudsley, for what it was worth, had kept her looks for much longer. The postman had taken it upon himself to keep an eye on her whenever he came up this way. Seeing the light on, he followed it to its source and saw the scullery door ajar.

She had fallen off the bed holding the eiderdown and now lay on the cold floor clutching a photograph. One of those Eytie men who used to work in the ice-cream parlour, thought Postie, puzzled. He saw that poor Mrs Maudsley's face had darkened and her lips parted. Only her deep green eyes, wide open and unseeing, remained as iridescent as ever. Like a finch's wing, the postman thought sadly, much later after he had called the ambulance.

Outside in the corpse-free air he saw with relief that the autumn mist was clearing. He stared up at the big house where, for the first time in years, no smoke rose from the chimney, remembering the day, many decades before, when he had come here to play in a tennis match.

'Ah, yes,' he said later when recounting the story. 'The fellow was called Lucio.'

Kitty did not come to the funeral. She was abroad and had no forwarding address. Selwyn didn't come either because he was already dead. So it was left to Cecily to organise everything. It was the undoing of her teacher-training course. Afterwards she was unable to concentrate on anything and had to go to the continent. But first she had the funeral to organise. She did not visit the house. She did not inform any of the relatives in Ireland. She had had quite enough of them at the last funeral. She didn't tell anyone in the town either, although the postman found out afterwards. And she decided not to inform the church. So Agnes wasn't buried. She was cremated.

Cecily sat alone on a bench at the front of the altar at the chapel of rest. She sat with her eyes closed. Agnes with her eyes closed (presumably) lay in her coffin. Resting also. When asked by the undertaker what her preferences were, Cecily had asked if the hymn 'Breath of Heaven' could be played. They agreed, giving her a strange look.

The priest asked her if there were any others attending and she shook her head.

'They've gone on ahead,' she said, but she said it so softly that the priest didn't catch her words.

He felt a little sorry for this lovely girl but then he looked at his watch, and sorrow was replaced by passing time.

'Let us begin,' he said, changing his voice and his glasses.

Cecily sat quietly. There was nothing more for her to do. The steel rollers on which Agnes' coffin rested made a tiny sound. Like a biker revving up a very small engine. They were getting ready to take Agnes through the door to eternity. Her green eyes were going with her. And her hair. And the hands that had combed Cecily's hair and sewed the dress that Rose had worn to the tennis dance. The same hands that had baked the cream heart-shaped sponge cakes for Cecily's birthdays, all thirteen of them, seven of which Cecily remembered quite clearly. They were about to take Agnes' lips, the ones that used to kiss Cecily goodnight. And the arms that had given her all the hugs of her life. Including the important one at the railway station when Cecily had gone on her Long Journey. And Agnes' voice saying, 'I don't care what you write. Just say if you are all right.'

That voice was going through the door marked eternity, too.

The canned music stopped and a man in a black suit came over and whispered to her that the next funeral was waiting to come in. When Cecily said nothing, he took her by the elbow and steered her out. It would seem the money for Agnes' funeral had run out.

Like a slot machine, or a candle lit inside a shrine running out. Finished. Over.

There was no one to talk to. The voices in Cecily's head refused to engage with the subject. In their view everything that had happened was (partly, at least) Agnes' fault.

Months later when she went back to Avery Hill to sit her first exam and saw the word 'discuss' written on the page, she wrote about Agnes' funeral. Her tutor called her into the office and told her to take a bit of time off.

'Give yourself some space to grieve,' the tutor said.

How much time had the tutor in mind?

'As long as it takes.'

Cecily packed up her room. She returned her library books. Then she booked a ticket on Interrail Europe. She was a rich woman now. She owned a house and a small fortune. She didn't need Kitty any more. She thought she would revisit the land of Guilt. She knew she had a lifetime's visa.

Some time after the solicitor had found her and read out her mother's will, Kitty finally contacted Cecily. The last occasion she had been in touch was just before Cecily left London. Kitty did not even know her sister had died until Cecily told her. There was a small pause when Cecily told her about the inheritance.

'Sell it,' she had said of Palmyra House. 'There's nothing but grief waiting for you there.'

Kitty's voice had come from some faraway place that she wished to keep to herself.

'You'd be a fool to go back,' she said.

It sounded like a threat. Or a dare. Cecily didn't care what it was. She had lived in Guilt for years. Perhaps after all it was time to visit Grief, instead?

And now, staring in the mirror, all these years later Cecily thought she saw Rose looking at her, with a watchful expression in her eyes.

So, you're back, are you? Outrageous child! Come to visit the dead?

Rose appeared to be wearing Cecily's dress. Smart, shiftless, black. A 1960s dress worn with Rose's effortless ease. Rose's face on Cecily's body.

Palmyra House, full of its heavy dusty furniture, its hunting pictures, its old books on land cultivation and horse doctoring, was silent, reluctant to give anything away. Two green-striped spiders, very small and compact, sixteen legs between them, walked the windowsill as if it were a plank.

Cecily dabbed stale perfume on her slender wrist and instantly opened another bottleful of memories. Going downstairs she found what she had been unconsciously looking for. A hardcover notebook marked *Mass Observation* and two padded photograph albums. Someone, Agnes probably, certainly not Kitty, had hidden them in a drawer. Cecily could scrutinise them at leisure. She felt there was a shape to her investigations at last. Well... shape was too definite a word. The hope of a shape, perhaps? Once again the voices in her head were silent. Anticipation being a quiet thing.

Both books were dusty. Silver fish had left fine silvery shavings on the puffed out, swollen covers. River damp and marsh air had tried to wreck their chances of survival. But Cecily was here now, ready to rescue them. Ready to pick up the clues as though they were daisies for a daisy chain.

On Your Marks, Get Set, Go! the voices in her head yelled, screaming with laughter.

She took a cloth and wiped the covers. Then she cleaned the little occasional table by the window and drew up a chair. Ignoring the fact that the leather binding disintegrated at her touch, some memories were like that, she opened the notebook first. Inside was a bundle tied in black ribbon.

Selwyn Maudsley's letters, she read. *1939–1945.* She had forgotten her mother had received letters from him too. None of them seemed to have been opened except for the first one. Cecily put the bundle to one side for a moment.

Time moved smoothly.

She found other things behind the books in the cupboard.

A Prayer Card of 'The Lady Of The Sea'. (Bellamy the Skipper had told her the statue was headless now)

A Ration Book (a prayer card of a different kind)

Selwyn's Anti-Aircraft Division badge (ripped off his uniform in anger)

A brittle piece of a 78 record. ('Goodnight Sweetheart')

Cecily put everything in a line on the table and stared greedily. The room was suddenly full of forgotten faces jostling for attention. A pouting pair of lips. An eyebrow raised a fraction, attached to some mysterious and long-dead thoughts.

When a shadow fell across the garden Cecily didn't even notice. Something was falling into place, bringing with it a terrible sense of inevitability. There was a small piece of paper, folded neatly between the unopened letters.

Don't trust him, was what it said. *Don't trust him, cara.*

'Who?' asked Cecily aloud.

Her fingers moved restlessly. Disappointment. What had she hoped for?

Turning to the albums she opened first one and then the other and found herself imprinted on every face. She felt a small powerful wave swim up her throat. The terrible ghosts of her impossible-to-forget family were everywhere. She felt her voice being lifted upwards towards her mouth, carrying with it some old, hideous sound. Her eyes were ready to overflow. She looked like Rose. Had others seen this, too?

Hands shaking, she gathered up the photographs, holding onto large chunks of precious time. The past appeared out of cold storage.

Selwyn, driving the tractor in his shirt sleeves.

Partridge digging furrows with two horses, straighter than anyone else could.

Kitty in the garden.

Rose, tendrils of laughter entwining Carlo and Lucio, and Franca. And Bellamy, of course.

Cecily's brother Joe. Ah!

Unable to go on, unable to bear Joe's anticipation of the years he would never have, Cecily closed both albums. But then she opened one of them again, for something was bothering her. Something she couldn't put her finger on. Carlo and all the other Molinellos smiled, laughed as Rose laughed. And all of them, as far as she knew, were dead.

Kitty had told her it would have been better if she had not been born. And Cecily had simply blamed herself for all those deaths.

But she couldn't think what it was about the photograph album that niggled her.

Was it the images from their tennis party?

Or the newly cut grass, telling tales of who kissed whom long ago?

Old things, buried under whispering trees?

Cecily paused. Then she opened Selwyn's opened letter and a pressed dandelion clock fell out. In pieces.

> *Agnes,* Cecily read,
> *Oh Agnes! I cannot bear C finding out. It is all I can think of. Promise me you never will tell her? I cannot bear to hurt her. Not since my brother died have I been loved so unconditionally. You know this, don't you? We, Agnes, made our mistakes, you, I... the others... but C is still a child. Once long ago I asked something of you, which in your generosity you gave me. Now I have another request. I do not deserve or expect it of you but still, I will ask. For Cecily's sake.*
>
> *Please. Do not tell her it was I who sent the message, that I was on Foulness that night, that I had an office there. Please, Agnes.*

The writing was smudged and indistinct.

> *If, as I hope, you send her away she will not hear any of the rumours, or be taunted by children from the local school.*

*She will not be called the daughter of a spy. She will not
know her father is being tried for 'betraying' his country.*

*I don't expect you to forgive me, Agnes, or even to under-
stand my motives. What you or anyone thinks of me now
hardly matters. Although I do not feel guilt in helping plan
an invasion, the truth is I am finished. When the children
told me Rose had gone to the Martello tower to find Robert
Wilson I panicked. All the evidence was in the hut on the pier
and I wanted to destroy it.*

It is my fault that Rose died. No one else's.

Cecily stared at the words.

Selwyn Maudsley?

Father, husband, traitor; mastermind, information-leaker?
Sneaking over the airways into enemy lines. Double-dealer,
hoping for a German invasion, covering his tracks for fear of
discovery, hiding his secrets by setting fire to the Last Pier. Killing
his own daughter, unaware that she was in there. Was it true?

No! No!

Please Agnes, I beg you, don't tell her!

'No!' Cecily cried. Was *that* why I was sent away?

*For what it's worth, Germany is a country I loved long ago.
Do you remember the girl I knew? And how my father beat
me for my association with her? How he destroyed the career
of her family? She will be in this war, Agnes. I couldn't bear
that thought. This was, for me, a war that had a human face.*

Disbelief silenced Cecily. She could not think, reading was hard
enough.

*That day, I went out, don't you remember, after Chamber-
lain's speech? You thought I was at an ARP meeting but in*

fact I was typing out a warning. And now they will splash it across the paper.

A yellowing newspaper cutting opened out in Cecily's hand.

IT HAS BEGUN. STOP. I AM READY TO RECEIVE THEM. STOP. WOTAN CONFIRMED. STOP.
This was the message sent to a sixteen-strong German crew planning a landing on Foulness beach. It was written by the double agent Selwyn Maudsley, codenamed Wotan.

Wotan?

That night, after I had sent the message to Berlin, I sat without expectations. Waiting for the rain to reach the coast, not knowing who else might be out on the marshes. Then, after a while, packing away the equipment, I headed for home along the causeway. I had fulfilled my obligation, done what I had so foolishly promised to do. I understood that possibly it was too late to change directions again. You were asleep and I stared at you, my heart filled with regret. What you didn't know was that I no longer wanted Kitty. I had told her finally that when the war was over I wanted to try again with you. Have a new beginning. We quarrelled; her anger was frightening. I did not know then how I would soon pay a heavy price.

Selwyn, her father. Protecting her.
Cecily was motionless. Listening down the tunnel of years to the rustle of long-felled voices once heard but never, until now, understood.

She had been watching a beetle and waiting for Tom in the den.

They were going to make the Plan but he had gone back to the house to get his wretched logbook and his magnifying glass. Cecily yawned. It was late afternoon and the sun had bleached the empty stubble. She could smell the sweet fragrance of grass and from somewhere in the distance the sound of voices drifted towards her. The beetle opened its blue-tinged wings, rising clumsily, and flew away. Cecily closed her eyes against the glare. It was almost teatime. She wished Tom would hurry up. The voices grew louder and instantly she was wide awake, again. It was Aunt Kitty shouting. Instinctively Cecily drew her legs far back into the hollow of the den.

'I loved you first!' Aunt Kitty said, voice anguished, head thrown back. 'Everything I've done, I've done for you. And you tell me *now*, you love *her?*'

'Kitty...'

'Oh you bastard, Selwyn, you'll pay for this.'

'Keep your voice down for God's sake, there might be children about.'

'D'you think I care? You've ruined my life. We all know...'

'Kitty... we strayed along a path too far, we lost our way...'

'You're frightened now, aren't you? Go on admit it, I could... I could do a lot of damage...'

'Kitty, Kitty, please, it was a joint mistake. It's over. Please don't do anything silly about the other business. You are as involved as I am. Things change, people too. We've both moved on. Don't let's wreck more lives.'

'You vile bastard!' Kitty said, again. 'You think I'm not capable of telling your friend, Mister Wilson? How do you know I haven't told him already? Do you know what the penalty is? For what you've done?'

There was a long silence. Mister Wilson, thought Cecily, ears pricked, alert. Pinky?

'Yes. But you are in it too.'

'Oh no I'm not! I'll see you rot in hell,' screamed Kitty.

They were only a few feet away from the den. Selwyn lowered his voice. Cecily thought her father sounded frightened. She strained to catch his words but they were moving off. So, she thought with satisfaction, she had been right all along. Her father didn't love Kitty any more. And Kitty sounded as if she was crying. Was she going to tell Pinky that Selwyn didn't love her any more? This would please Rose.

I slipped under the covers, Cecily read, returning to the present.

Lightning flashed in the room, showing me your sleeping face. I wanted to touch you Agnes, to feel some human connection in my terrible loneliness. I remember thinking, maybe there was still a chance. But while I hesitated you sighed, and turned away from me and I knew all that remained was an illusion.

Cecily folded her father's letter and slid it into its envelope. She closed the photograph album. Their purpose it seemed had been simply to remind her of those things she had forgotten, like the expression on Agnes' face when she was counting punnets of strawberries. If she stared hard at the photo she could still see the stains on her fingers. How a stain could last longer than the finger itself was one of the mysteries of photography, she presumed.

Outside a tentative sun had come out. She wanted to walk on the marshes but that could wait until her shock subsided. She knew there was one thing that had to be done. She knew but kept putting it off. At some point, she would have to visit the churchyard. To see Rose. And Joe. And Selwyn. And the rosebush that stood in for Agnes.

A curlew cried out and was answered by another.

Two echoes of a tennis ball, against a racquet. Four-love.

She was like an invalid dreaming about her first outing. Maybe she would be strong enough, maybe not.

She closed the albums and put them back in the cupboard. Then, because the door didn't shut properly, she took them out again. She reached into the back of the cupboard. Someone else's fingers had been there before her and finding what they had hidden was easy. Like a prospector finding treasure, like a fisherman, she fished out her catch. It was impossible to know a significant moment from an ordinary one. So Cecily opened the plastic folder and took out its contents. Three faded envelopes, all from Joe. She put them aside to read later. A lock of hair. Blonde like Rose's. A ring small enough for a magpie's beak. A piece of pink string tied in a small circle and half a child's smocked dress. There was a small tag on the string that said Cecily Catherine Maudsley. Six pounds, one ounce.

There was also a long, cream envelope different from the thin army ones that Joe had used. Cecily turned it over and opened it. It was a document and what looked like a birth certificate. Cecily Catherine Maudsley, Cecily read.

Date of Birth: June 3rd 1926.

Place of Birth: Connemara, Ireland.

Father's name: Selwyn Maudsley.

Cecily eyes refused to look.

Look! Look! urged the voices in her head.

Mother's name: Kitty Stella McNulty.

22.

THE JULY SKY changed slowly and the light seeped out, draining it of colour. It rained. The gloom over the marshes made everything seem on the point of vanishing. Sea birds appeared out of the grey air and disappeared again like props left over from a magic trick. In spite of the wideness of the sky, Cecily felt there wasn't enough air. It was the end of summer. The wet, squelching land was full of drips and splashes. She had fled outside without thinking and she was not dressed for walking in such weather and her shoes sank deep into the sodden grass. She clutched at an invisible scarf around her throat, wanting to get to the south side of the river. She wanted to look at the half-sunken boat that had greeted her on her arrival. As she walked towards the meadow she saw only remnants and ruins, relics of other efforts from other lives. It was the chaos of dereliction. The wild heaps of iron, broken bedsteads, harrows and binders, cumbersome pieces of farm machinery, rusting everywhere along the edges of the marshes.

She passed an old hayrick with bales of hay stacked into a cone-shaped structure and covered with old black plastic sheeting standing up against the horizon. The hay had grown old like everything else. Green shoots sprouted out of the black sheets that covered it. She could imagine how it had been cut one summer, baled and stored. But those who had worked here had died or moved on so that now the hay was rotting. And the new farm stored its hay in a modern open shed, a pre-fabricated building carrying the printed name of a company just below the apex of the roof. Cecily walked on, head bowed. Shadows from a blue remembered past pressed like a stranger's overcoat in a crowd, right up against her mouth.

She was no one. She was flotsam. Nobody wanted her. This hostile landscape had nothing to do with her memory. In the confusion of her cut-short youth she had missed the reality. And the war had come and created a further complication. It had created another country, a shanty-town of the mind, a temporary residence not meant to last. And what traces of the past remained were too fragmented to be of use.

Shivering with the shock, she walked on. The boat was there and she stood for a moment, looking at it with the wind in her hair. The rain increased and she lifted her face to greet it. Wanting to wash away everything, the past, the present and what future there might be. Silence broke down in the falling water. At last tear ducts released the tension she had held so tightly. In the long years of exile, what had kept her going had been the belief she knew this place like a piece of loved music. But even this was not so.

Kitty! The name rose unbidden. Why hadn't she realised? The truth, discarded for years, floated towards her. Aunts don't keep coming to visit.

One down, Cecily thought, filling in the puzzle.

Kitty to Agnes: 'It isn't her fault. Why are you always hardest on her?' (There, it was spoken.)

Selwyn to Kitty and Cecily: 'My two little girls.' (How true.)

Rose: 'Oh quite!' (Had she known?)

Resentful Rose.

And then, much later after the betrayal, Agnes: 'I lost two children. You forget.'

Yes!

There were other clues, thought Cecily, raising her cry to the skies. She heard her voice returning across the sodden meadow, like the wild song of a captured bird.

'Daddy loves Kitty.'

'Daddy's *in* love with Kitty,' Rose had said, head bent, darning a tear in her favourite dress.

'Don't be cruel, C.' Agnes had said. 'Don't be cruel.'

Cruel, replied the echo, reproachfully. There was a boat bobbing on the water. On closer inspection, its base was smashed and how it floated was a mystery.

Rose had rowed across to her rendezvous on just such a boat. And then Cecily remembered something else. Yes! *Yes*!

'Where are you going?' she had asked, waking, making Rose jump.

Rose had thought she was asleep. Fooled you, Rose. I spy with my little eye. Rose had been busy with packing.

'You can have my things.'

Cecily had thought she would say more but her sister had clammed up.

'I don't want you to go,' Cecily had said.

'I'm going anyway,' Rose had said but she hadn't sounded sure.

Cecily had seen her sister was almost crying. Sisterly feelings, undetected until now, surfaced and swam towards each other. They would go on swimming lengths forever more.

'I'm coming with you.'

'Don't be silly. You're too young.'

Neither had known what to say after that, the cold hand of the inevitable being upon them. A hand that had never left Cecily in twenty-nine years.

'Are you meeting Carlo?' she had asked.

And Rose laughing her last laugh had replied,

'Why would I be meeting Carlo?'

'Because he loves you.'

'No he doesn't!'

'He does!'

'Carlo,' Rose had said, heavily, 'is just a game.'

And she had continued packing. A small cardboard suitcase. Coat slung over her arm. How was she going to climb down the honeysuckle?

'I'm not,' Rose said, chin up, defiant.

The old Rose was suddenly in charge.

'I'm going out through the back door.'

And she had gone. While the house slept and the air was cooler and the blackout blinds were in place in preparation for what was to come. She too had had a handful of glow-worms and a wobbly bicycle. A smile that would be remembered forever afterwards. Teeth that would survive her last adventure.

Cecily had strained her ears and heard the squeak of brakes and then nothing. So she had *told* Tom.

'Of course,' Tom had said. 'I told you so, didn't I?'

Excited Tom. There had been no one about. What else could she do?

You were *not* the sinner, thought Cecily, eyes wide against the rain. You were sinned against. You were just a little girl. A victim that no one counted in the census.

There had been just four hours of life left. How could either of them have known?

The rain had softened the cry of the curlew.

Thinking hard, Cecily realised she had missed the biggest clue of all on that Saturday afternoon.

Where had the others been at the time?

It had been during the tennis-court party. Everyone had their eye on the ball, of course.

Or had it been at night?

Speak memory, speak!

Cecily frowned, dredging up the past from the marshy waters. Using only the frayed threads she carried in her pocket and her bare hands.

When had it happened?

It must have been night. Or maybe the shutters had been closed because she remembered the blueness of the light. A white curtain moving like a flag at half-mast and a sound striking the surface of Cecily's consciousness, sinking like a stone into mud, very, very slowly. It was why she had investigated further.

From the distance of years Agnes' voice came to her.

'Curiosity killed the cat, Cecily.'

Her *mother!* Kitty's voice singing,

Why tell them all the old things
Who kissed there long ago?

There was blue-and-white wallpaper. Or maybe it was Agnes' dress that was blue and white. Distance had slyly changed the view. So had she imagined it? But now she remembered how, for days after, she had rerun the scene in slow motion.

'Oh Selwyn,' a woman's voice had gasped. 'Say you still love me. Tell me there's still a chance...'

Cecily had opened the door a fraction and seen two people lying completely naked, one on top of the other on the bed. She had stood perfectly still. The crack in the door was not wide enough for her to see faces. The blue, liquid light flowed into the tall room and she saw a naked piece of flesh, a prawn just like the one Bellamy had, stabbing away. On and on it went, as Cecily stood puzzled, one eye in the crack of the door. She had heard shouting far away.

'Four-love!'

Applause, the faint sound of a ball being struck. It must have been during the tennis match after all. But then she had been distracted by a new development on the bed.

'Selwyn,' the voice said, again. Then more urgently, with a gasp, 'Selwyn.'

There was a noise as if the bed was being rocked by poltergeists. Cecily opened the door a fraction wider but she still couldn't see any faces.

Two body parts were what she saw.

Two pairs of legs, stretched out.

But only one prawn.

Moving slightly into the room she watched, fascinated, as the people on the bed seemed to tear at each other. Dismayed she wondered if she should break up the fight before something terrible happened. There was a shuffling and gasping. And as she watched, uncertain, witnessing what she should not, the terrible thing that had lurked in the room, waiting to happen, happened. Like an explosion, thought Cecily. Or a grenade going off. Like the way they must have killed people in the Great War. Was this how it would be if war came again?

'Out, out!' someone shouted over by the tennis court and there followed laughter.

But in the blue, backlit room, now that it was all over there was only the soft sound of two people kissing. Making up, thought Cecily. The man on the bed moved and Cecily saw he no longer had his prawn. Perhaps it had broken off, she thought. And suddenly she was no longer interested but angry. Only she couldn't say what about. And in that moment while she hesitated, wanting to leave, not knowing how she could do so without being seen, the man turned his head. And saw her.

'What are you doing here, Cecily?' he asked.

He pulled himself up on his knees and Cecily saw that he hadn't in fact lost the prawn-thing but that it just was smaller. And she saw too, with something close to dismay, that the voice questioning her was that of her father. The figure on the bed had turned her face away and was pulling a sheet over herself.

'I told you to knock whenever you wanted to come into our bedroom,' Selwyn said, sternly. 'What are you doing here? You should be watching the match.'

'I...' Cecily said.

For once she had nothing to say.

'Now go downstairs and leave your mother and me alone. We were feeling tired and we came upstairs for a rest.'

Her father sounded out of breath. Cecily swallowed. Her eyes felt prickly and she was shivery. Perhaps she was coming down with a fever and she would have to go to bed too. She nodded.

'Go on, C. Scram. Get Rose to give you some ice cream. It's very hot. We'll be down in a minute. All right?'

Again Cecily nodded. She tried to look at the figure on the bed but her father was blocking her view. She looked up into his face because she didn't know where to look. Nowhere else seemed safe. Selwyn bent his head and kissed her forehead and although she didn't make a sound she felt herself shrink into her shell like a small animal. Smaller than her father's prawn. And then, without a sound, she turned and scurried downstairs. It was only on her way towards the tennis court that she remembered her father had called the person on the bed Kitty.

Stopping beside the lilac bush, (there was no sign of her sister) Cecily convulsed. But nothing came out except thoughts. And sounds. In and out, between her father's gasps.

'Kitty, Kitty!'

But then thankfully, everything in her had contracted and she vomited. It was how, first Bellamy, and then Tom, found her.

'Are you sick?'

'No.'

'Yes you are.'

She had everything she wanted.

A long summer holiday.

As much ice cream as possible.

No worries.

Two parents.

People who loved her.

'It must be the ice cream,' she said. 'Maybe I ate too much.'

'Maybe,' Bellamy said, laughing, 'you've eaten a prawn.'

Cecily vomited again and a second later Tom, hurrying around the corner, saw Bellamy standing like an exhibitionist bat with his batwings open like a mackintosh. Tom saw the things he'd been wanting to see for days.

'I'm telling,' he said, absolutely certain.

Both boys rolled together in a ground fight, narrowly avoiding the vomit. Only they, Cecily saw, had their clothes on.

'Don't tell,' she whispered.

She was alarmed although, what was there to tell, anyway?

A bluish room,

An open window,

Her father forgetting her mother's name.

There wasn't anything to tell.

'Cecci, Cecci,' Carlo has cried coming up. 'What's wrong, *cara*?'

And he had *hugged* her.

'I think it's bed for you, my girl,' Agnes said, her clothes back on, her normal self in place by the tennis court.

'Too much ice cream, I should think,' smiled Anna in her comforting way.

Their faces swam before Cecily and she thought what sad smiles they all had. The singing was still going on in the field. There were lanterns of light like night buttercups.

There would never be another party like this again, everyone said.

Now she stood, twenty-nine years too late, in the rain, hearing the sound of an imaginary piano. The day had taken on a whitish blur. It wasn't the sort of day that could be withdrawn. Like the vomit from long ago, it had to come out. Useless asking more questions or hunting for clues. Most had been washed away with buckets of passing years. Cecily lifted her wet face to the sky and made a list.

Her last list but one.

Well it's why you came, wasn't it, the voices in her head said, in unison.

Twin voices that were like two little girls in a Gilbert and Sullivan operetta.

More things happened at the tennis-court party than Cecily had realised.

Bellamy had been punished by Selwyn for making her sick. But Bellamy hadn't made her sick. Tom had only *thought* he had done so.

A water vole scurried past on its way to its reed-bed home and the wind whipped up the rain so that it now fell in slants against her. She was soaking wet. Turning, she ran back to the house, head bent, mind screaming. She had hated Kitty for so long that she had convinced herself she had been born with her hatred. In Palmyra House the rain saturated the air and she realised that she would have to light the stove. There was wood in the shed she knew. She took off her wet things, thin legs on the damp linoleum floor, and stared at herself in the mirror, looking for changes when there were none to be seen. Two eyes still stared back at her. Raven-black hair, pale, delicate face, good cheekbones. Rose, uncovered, and with a different mother.

Exchanged; like people taking clothes back to the shop.

Please can I have my life back?

In a different colour?

This one doesn't suit me.

A car drove past. And then another. Two cars on a side road were unusual in this part of the world. Cecily marvelled at the way her mind could hold so many thoughts. When a cock crowed in the distance, the sound separated into two parts, like a document clipped to another document.

In spite of the wetness, the man who had been watching the house was back standing patiently next to the lamp post. In spite of the gloom he was wearing dark glasses. He was eating chips and seemed to be waiting for an imaginary bus. Cecily both did, and did not, notice. The file in her head marked 'irrelevant' was only half-open. The man looked hard at the tall hollyhocks growing over the wall. As if he were studying rare flowering biennials.

Cecily ate two oat crackers with some cottage cheese. And then drank some tea. She picked up the two-part document that she had discarded in her flight and stared at it. Did it matter, after so long, who her mother really was? Was her real mother going to make her dresses? Kiss her? Comb her hair a hundred times a night for years and years? And did it matter if her aunt knitted her a cardigan instead? The questions puzzled her, as did the small shift in her upper chest, somewhere in the region where her heart was. It was not raining in the house, yet her face remained wet.

Agnes holding her tight, kissing her in that last moment, voice muffled, before Cecily boarded the train. It was only now that she saw the sweetness in the gesture. Agnes, the family dress-maker, making Rose's made-to-dance-in dress. Agnes' gentle hand on first Rose's waist, and then Cecily's, pinning a skirt, breathing down her neck, her calloused, nimble fingers caressing a leg as she measured it.

An aunt loving like a mother.

An aunt breathing like a mother.

It would have been easier to shatter the illusion, to refuse to care.

To ruin a small life.

To refuse to be party to a crime.

What Agnes did was much harder. Cecily saw. She didn't deserve to be punished for her crime.

All it took was two clipped-together sheets of paper for years of good work to be undone.

23.

SO WHO ELSE had known these terrible secrets?

'Oh Daddy!' cried Cecily, switching on a light that had no bulb in it.

Identity was everything.

The house had darkened; rain clouds hid the sun. Lighting a candle, she poured herself a drink. Then she opened the book marked *Mass Observation*. It was as if she was determined to look for other shocks.

He does not need to tell me to protect C, Agnes had written in an angry scrawl.

When? When had she written it?

Agnes had taken in her niece Cecily out of love for her sister, knowing Selwyn was the father. Was it possible? She had wanted to save Kitty from ruin. But when she held the scrap of life (three days old and unwanted already) in her arms she had discovered love of a different kind.

After Rose was born Agnes had wanted another child but nothing happened. Selwyn was too busy sowing his oats elsewhere and Agnes, unaware of what was going on under her nose, blamed herself for her secondary childlessness. Kitty, wandering in and out of Palmyra House, breezing through the high wheat fields in unsuitable shoes, was no different from the restless girl she used to be. If Agnes had occasionally caught her husband looking at her sister with a deep oblique pulse of feeling, she had assumed it had been because they had once been close.

But one summer she was forced to admit what she had ignored. It was during one of Kitty's brief visits to the farm, which Rose so hated. Agnes, hurrying through her chores, collecting eggs before meeting the school bus, glanced up and saw her sister by the open window, looking out over the harvest fields. Kitty looked as though she had just woken from a nap. Her skin, even from this distance, was as oily as a pear hidden in a drawer for too long.

It was hot. The heat swept across the field carrying the faint sound of the tractor. In the shimmering waves of light Agnes saw her sister turn and look towards it. Presently the tractor drew towards the very edge of the field and Agnes saw that it wasn't Bellamy but Selwyn who was driving. The reflection of the sun on Selwyn's face was green and flame-like. There was a smear of oil where he had wiped his hand across his cheek.

As Agnes walked slowly back to the house with her basket of eggs, Kitty appeared in a white dress, hair fastened, wearing white flat-heeled shoes. She was walking towards the half-harvested field. It occurred to Agnes that the field held the last of what she considered to belong to her. And Kitty was walking towards it.

Later when she went out with the can of tea, the tractor had moved away on a half-circuit and Kitty was nowhere in sight. There wasn't a sound except that of a yellow hammer bleating its song in a patch of burnt hedgerow. She walked past the burnt stubble where some corn had caught fire a few days before. Suddenly they emerged, Selwyn, head thrown back, laughing. To Agnes they were two parts of the same story and she was struck by how much was carelessly written across their faces.

July 3rd 1926, Cecily read.
I feel like a woman drowning, Agnes wrote.

She had, Cecily read, been handed to Agnes by a nun. Asleep. While her mother Kitty stood in a loose white cotton dress, hair scrubbed back, frightened eyes saying no to everything. No, she didn't want to see Selwyn, not now, not ever. What lies!

And after that, night after night, alone with only the scent of tobacco flowers coming in through the window, Agnes had watched over her two little girls. Alone.

June 28th 1927, read Cecily. She had only been a year old.
Rose suffers most, Agnes had written.

'She's not my sister,' Rose said.

'You will grow to love her,' Agnes told her.

'Rubbish,' Rose said.

She shook her head so hard her teeth almost rattled. No one had taken account of Rose in the plans.

'You spoilt little bitch!' Kitty said.

And she slapped Rose before Agnes could stop her. Rose raised her hand and then let it fall but they saw the look she gave her aunt. After that Kitty was careful to keep her distance.

July 5th 1928, Cecily read.
Still, Kitty is unable to keep her hands off Selwyn, Agnes had written.

Blaming herself, for she had begged her sister to at least be an aunt to Cecily, Agnes understood that she had made her own bed. Her husband was disturbed to have them both under the same roof, occupying the bed with one sister while desiring the other.

Time passed and Rose began taking life with a sprinkling of salt. Nothing was believable any more. Her father's cool hand on her head made her shiver. She never called Aunt Kitty 'Aunt', any more. And it pleased her that Selwyn was hurt by such coldness. Joe of course was at boarding school. He didn't care much.

And in the fairy tales Rose now began telling Cecily, Joe was always a bystander. The pair of boots that Puss wore, the servant at the Beast's palace, the footman who carried the glass slipper. That, Cecily remembered, was Joe's role.

A few pages were torn out here.

January 21st 1936, Cecily read.
The King died last night.

January 22nd 1936, Agnes had written.
The people in America are mourning, as if for their own King & the Japanese are in tears. We are only allowed official announcements on the BBC. If you turn the wireless on you only hear the ticking of a vast clock. The shops are all black.

September 12th 1938.

Ah! thought Cecily. Here it was.

I think Rose told Bellamy today that C is Kitty's daughter. He's been scowling at me. Perhaps that's why I dislike him so much. Poor, ugly Bellamy!

And then…

October 20th 1938.
Rose asked me, 'Is she my cousin?'

Cecily swallowed. She could imagine Rose's voice all right. Full of disdain.

'She's your half-sister.'
   'Half?' Rose demanded, and she went out.
   Bellamy must have caught her crying. He was in the top field unblocking the dyke. A corncrake flew across the bleached sky. Bellamy must have been twelve but already he was more than a head taller than Rose. He watched over her daily after that, never prying, teaching her, after a fashion, the ways of the

countryside. It was because of him that Rose still loved Palmyra Farm. Inseparable for that brief moment in time.

Sometimes, when she thought no one was watching, Agnes wrote, she noticed Rose display a curious tenderness for this child with only half of everything and no knowledge of who her real mother was.

'Are you going to tell her?' she had asked once.

'One day, perhaps,' Agnes had replied. 'When she's your age.'

And then she asked the question Agnes had been dreading.

'Doesn't Kitty care?'

Reading, Cecily felt her eyes blur over the answer.

> *April 20th 1939.*
> *Hitler's birthday. I hope he enjoyed himself!*

> *May 5th 1939,* Agnes had written.
> *I overheard someone say at the butcher's that Chamberlain looks like a turkey who's missed Christmas!*

Cecily skipped a page.

> *June 3rd 1939.*
> *In Picture Post they say we will be safe from war until perhaps after the harvest. This is what K believes too. I think K gets her information from elsewhere, though.*

Kitty! Had Agnes ever understood how her own sister had betrayed Selwyn?

> *August 4th 1939.*
> *I no longer care about what Selwyn does or doesn't do. The truth is he only loves C and K is jealous of this! News as bad as ever. I am sure there will be a war.*

Cecily turned a few more pages.

August 27th 1939.
Robert Wilson says the Cabinet met this evening and our
ambassador flies back to report to Hitler. RW seems to
always get the news before anyone else.

Lucio says this war will be different and will change
everything. England will change irreversibly. People will die
in their thousands. L said of course people will die but he
means something else, entirely. I asked him what he meant
and he looked at me with those deep eyes of his. Then he
made a gesture with his hands and I thought how foreign
the movement was. No one else could have said so much in
a gesture. Then instead of answering me directly he told me
he had wanted to sleep with me from the very beginning.
I was silenced by his love.

Lucio saw the fruit hanging under the moon.
This entry was undated.

'A kind of innocence is about to vanish,' Lucio said. 'A sort
of magic.'

'But I thought magic was just for children,' Agnes
replied.

'No, no, that isn't what I mean,' he insisted. 'There's a kind
of pagan enchantment in existence, here in England; still.
Something untamed, left over from another era.'

It was going to be lost he had said, pointing upwards
towards the sheltering sky. Fish-shaped spots of moonlight had
swum in the darkness; a bat moved its cloak, about to perform
a burlesque, making them both laugh.

'Perhaps,' Lucio had told Agnes, holding her close. 'I'm
simply in love and talking nonsense!'

Further on, Agnes had written,

August 30th 1939.
I am frightened for Cecily. And in an odd way, for the house,
too. What the war might do to it. Palmyra House is grand in
a way that is unusual for Suffolk. The architect who built it
believed houses were created with their own personalities
and took very little from those who owned them. Nature
rather than nurture was the architect's theory. We could offer
the house very little by way of addition to its character. Three
generations have lived here already and barely skimmed the
surface of its aloofness.

I brought Bach to its rooms but it was already too late
to disprove the architect's views. There was moss on its roof,
wisteria growing across its brow and honeysuckle climbing
on its back. And I noticed the front door opened into the
hallway so that if you stood by the door you could see from
front to back. My mother told me that was bad luck, room
for an ill wind to blow straight through.

The diary stopped. There were pages missing but a photograph
was stuck to a page, it showed Cecily in Agnes' arms, waving her
blurry hands. She had a baby expression on her face.

24.

DRUNK NOW, CECILY closed Agnes' notebook knowing that while some things were a little clearer, others were still obscured. Shock had slowed her down but finding another piece of paper she wrote:

Matters Outstanding.

Visit the grave. If I must.

Whose fault was it? Mine.

Would it have changed anything if we hadn't met Daddy that night?

She shook her head.

The pyrotechnics of that night, the high-wire acts of heart-breaking daring were far worse than any detonated bomb. Worse than a war brought on by an enemy.

When the news of a fire on the pier and the discovery of the charred remains of a female who could well be her daughter reached her, Agnes' first confused thought was that Cecily had gone to the seafront in the middle of the night. But then she saw, on her mad dash up to the girls' bedroom (which someone had locked from the inside) that neither of them were there. It was at this point she broke down. It was how Robert Wilson found her. Robert Wilson on his way *back* to Palmyra House, following a police car that carried Selwyn Maudsley. Robert Wilson grim-faced, but still not in full possession of all the terrible facts, colliding with a soaking wet and white-faced Cecily. Other feet would soon follow, traipsing over the house, turning on lights, forgetting about the blackouts in their eagerness to be distracted by something more immediate than this wretched war with its darkness and its unknown dangers.

While over by the pier the fire was lighting up the sky. It didn't seem to care about Mr Hitler, the Prime Minister or the rules of the Home Office. The fire had its own rules.

Imagine the scene.

September 3rd. At midnight (or thereabouts) Rose left. Tom, waving a jar of glow-worms, and Cecily hell-bent on saving her sister from Captain Pinky the traitor, had followed soon after.

Children copying adult games.

Tom had caught twenty-seven glow-worms, he would tell Agnes afterwards.

Outside a star crossed the sky like a useless wish. Cecily caught its flight with the corner of her eye but failed to make one. A shock like cold electricity darted up her arm and into her heart for Selwyn was standing on the spot where the star had fallen. He had just lit a cigar.

'Well, well,' he said, but he didn't sound all that angry. 'So what are you two up to?'

In the town a little earlier, the Molinellos had eaten their evening meal in silence. All day the ice-cream parlour had filled up with worried Italians desperate to listen to talk about news bulletins so that Mario decided to close the shop. He did not wish to be seen as being frivolous and besides, his daughter Franca was inconsolable at Joe's departure.

There was also another issue on Mario's mind, one a little difficult to discuss with Anna. He ate his excellent *risotto ai funghi* in silent abstraction, slurping a little for the food was hot and he was hungry. Anna watched him. It was in this unusually subdued atmosphere that, in the end, Lucio raised the subject.

'Mussolini is going to cause trouble for us,' he said.

'Rubbish!' Mario said quickly, his mouth full of food.

He wished Anna would stop staring at him.

'It's true,' Lucio said.

Mario looked hard at his brother who pushed his plate of almost untouched risotto away.

'I've already told you,' Lucio told him.

'What's wrong with the risotto?' Anna asked. 'Why is no one eating?'

No one answered.

'Just because war's been announced,' Anna said with exceptional forcefulness, 'it doesn't mean we don't need to eat.'

She was looking at Franca's bent head.

'I'm not hungry,' Lucio said. 'And I've got to go out soon.'

'I am!' Carlo said, helping himself.

'Perhaps we should leave the social club,' Giorgio suggested.

'Good idea,' Carlo said.

'Don't talk with your mouth full,' Anna told him, switching to Italian.

'That's a ridiculous idea. Why should we leave the club? It's for Italians. We are Italians.'

'It's a good idea,' Lucio said. 'I mean, because of the rumours.'

Instantly everyone jumped on him.

'What rumours?'

'Is there something you know that we don't, Lucio?'

'You'd better tell us.'

Lucio looked at his brother. Tell them, his look said.

'It's all nonsense,' Mario cried. 'It's only that old fear about the Fascists.'

'Ah!' Anna said, triumph in her eyes. 'I knew it!'

She looked like someone who had been digging for a splinter in a piece of flesh and had finally found it. Mario tried another tactic.

'It's a stupid rumour. And it doesn't affect us.'

'So why are you worried?' Anna asked.

In answer her husband reached for the carafe and poured himself more wine.

'I'm not. I'm just concerned about supplies now that the war is definite. You know our stock of wine will diminish.'

'Oh Papi, this war isn't going to last that long!' Beppe told him. 'We couldn't possibly drink our cellar dry before it finishes!'

Carlo laughed, uneasily.

'What is it, Papi?' Franca asked.

Mario drained his glass and turned to his daughter.

'*Cara*, you must not worry about Joe,' he told her, softly. 'He will be safe. But… Lucio is right, this rumour is a different matter.'

They heard a seagull's plaintive cry. Mario looked around the table. Everyone he loved was in this room.

'It is about the arrest of some Jewish people I know,' he said, heavily and at last.

The silence lengthened.

'In Germany?'

'No.'

'Where then?'

'In London,' Mario said, reluctantly.

'One of the tribunals that decide the fate of aliens,' Lucio told them, taking up the story, 'has interned a group of Jews. Guido Murucchi is one of them. He's one of our suppliers.'

'How d'you mean, interned? Where?'

'I don't know,' Lucio said.

Without looking at his wife, Mario lit a cigarette. Normally Anna did not allow smoking at the dinner table but now she said nothing. If they could intern Jews…

'Exactly,' Lucio told her.

'Does it mean they're prisoners, Papi?' Franca asked.

'Yes. It's a prison camp.'

'It can't be true,' Beppe said.

Disbelief spread on the tablecloth, staining it with fear. The smoke from Mario's cigarette rose above their heads like incense. Anna wouldn't look at him. She desperately wanted to go to her grotto and light a candle. The last of the *sugo* lay congealed in its dish.

'Oh my God,' Franca murmured.

Her eyes were magnified by unshed tears. She stared at her uncle. He had not talked to her but Anna had told her that Lucio loved Joe's mother. Their families were intertwined like trees in an orchard. Suddenly Franca was desperately afraid.

'We have to be careful,' Lucio told them. 'We must get out of the social club, immediately.'

'But *Zio*, we are not Jews.'

'We are Italian,' Lucio told his nephews sternly. 'We are not English. I told your father this a year ago. The social club is not a good thing.'

A chill went around the warm, homely room.

'Rubbish,' Mario bellowed, galvanised, outraged, ready for a fight.

He began speaking in dialect.

'That would amount to closing the door to our home. What about our relatives in Bratto? What about our passports? What if we *can't* get our passports renewed? What then?'

'Papi, I don't want to go back to Italy,' Franca cried.

Lucio drained his wine.

'Mussolini is Mr Hitler's friend.'

'Italy is neutral.'

Anna rose from the table. There was no use in any further speculation. She indicated to Franca to help clear the table. Her daughter needed to keep busy. Joe would be back in a fortnight. As if on cue the telephone rang and everyone looked weakly at it. It was Joe.

But later, after the rosary, after her prayers, when they were alone in bed, Anna asked Mario what was really going on.

'Nothing's going on. Britain is at war, that's all.'

'So what has the social club got to do with that?'

'We're Italian.'

'So you keep saying.'

He was in two minds, uncertain how to go on.

'But we might not always be neutral. Have you heard people talk of the fifth column, at the club?'

Of course she had heard the expression. But why would it affect them?

'Fascists. The British are worried about enemy aliens.'

Anna was puzzled. Mario was talking in a strange way as though he was repeating something he had heard.

'Who is saying this?'

Again he hesitated.

'Lucio found out. But you must not repeat a word of this. Understand?'

She nodded in the darkness. But how did Lucio know?

'*Senti*, Anna, listen to me. Lucio is involved in certain dangerous things, things he can't talk about. He knows that sooner or later all foreigners in England will be in danger. That includes Italians.'

Still she didn't understand.

'There is a feeling amongst some people in the British government, that the fifth column is growing. That Mussolini has Italian spies here. We are Italian. Now do you understand?'

'But how does he know all this?'

Mario hesitated.

'I don't know. Obviously he is involved in certain – how shall I say – certain kinds of *work*. And... he's been tailing that Wilson man... for some time. He's uncovered something.'

Mario paused.

'Is Selwyn Maudsley involved in this, too? Are all the English people suspicious of us?' Anna asked, alarmed.

'Selwyn, no. Why? He's just a farmer.'

'Why hasn't Lucio said anything, before... about the Wilson man?'

'He has. We've talked about it. But there was no point in worrying you before the war was announced.'

Night-time sea-light rode into the room on the back of a pale moon.

'There are more than twenty thousand Italians in Great Britain. There is a file with names in it in Whitehall. Lucio's got copies of it.'

'How?'

'He stole them,' Mario said, abruptly. 'Don't ask me who from, but he knows what he's talking about.'

Anna was silent. She did not dare ask if the Molinellos were in this file too.

'So?' Selwyn asked, them. 'What were your plans?'

Cecily thought he was laughing. Tom held up the jar of worms.

'Collecting glow-worms, Tom?'

'No,' Cecily said firmly, deciding. 'We're going to go and warn Rose.'

'Warn her? Of what? And more to the point, where is she?'

There was a silence. Now they were all in trouble.

'Not in her bed, obviously,' murmured Selwyn.

Later, when she was much older, rerunning the moment, Cecily would think her father had sounded abstracted. Or perhaps it was simply disinterest on his part. They had been caught climbing out of the window when they should have been asleep and he had felt it was his duty to reprimand them. It was Cecily who had been too quick, too ready with information.

'We want to warn her,' she said again, stalling for time.

'*Warn* her? That she will be in trouble if mother finds out? I should think so. Where's she gone?'

'She's in danger,' Tom told Selwyn.

Cecily nodded.

'She's being followed.'

'We know this for a fact,' Tom told him. 'Captain Pinky's following her.'

Cecily pushed him.

'Ssh! He means Robert Wilson,' she told her father.

'What's that you say? Captain Pinky!'

Cecily thought her father sounded more interested now.

'We're not supposed to call him that, Mummy said, but he's been following Rose. So we wanted to warn her.'

Where's Rose gone?'

Cecily was silent. Should she tell him?

'Come on, C, where's your sister gone?'

Still Cecily hesitated. Her father's voice had changed and become the way it sometimes got when he spoke to Agnes.

'She's...'

'Why on earth should she want to go out at this hour?'

It was Tom who spilled the last of the beans.

'She's gone to the Ness,' he said.

Selwyn turned to look at him. To Cecily, her father seemed suddenly to have got taller. He towered above them both as he took Cecily by the shoulders and shook her.

'*Are you sure?*'

Dumbly Cecily nodded.

'Why? Answer me! It's important.'

'I don't know...'

'Because...' Tom said

'*What?* Because what? Tell me.'

'Because... she's meeting Captain Pinky... He's a spy, Daddy. And we think he's trying to capture her.'

Her voice fading, Cecily watched as her father turned and walked abruptly towards his bicycle leaning against the wall by the rambling rose.

'Go back inside the house,' he said softly over his shoulder, 'the scullery door is open. Go on. I'll talk to you later.'

They stood motionless but he stopped, waiting until they went reluctantly back. Only then did he cycle away.

Inside the scullery all they could see was Tom's jar of glow-worms.

'I think we should follow him,' Tom said.

Cecily was uneasy. She had no idea why it was, but her sense of foreboding had increased.

'I think your father might be in danger too,' Tom was saying. 'Come on, let's go.'

But they would never catch Selwyn up.

'It doesn't matter,' Tom said. 'Come on, we're wasting time. Your sister's out there too. I think Captain Pinky is a dangerous man. Spies usually are. He might have a gun.'

Somewhere in the back of her mind Cecily registered the fact that Tom was enjoying the excitement but her sense of dismay at having told on her sister sat like sour milk in her stomach. Perhaps though, Tom was right, and if they found Rose quickly then she could explain everything.

They ran over to the shed and collected the two bicycles. Then, with Tom balancing the jar of glowing worms on his handlebar, they cycled the half a mile in an unsteady line toward the river end of the Ness. In front of them a large black car on silent wheels moved with a soft purr. When they slowed down to take in the bend in the road, it gathered speed and disappeared. Chilled to the bone, Cecily cycled on.

At Bly fire station, those waiting for any disturbance, air-raid warnings, enemy sightings, unexpected army convoys passing through the high street, were not prepared for home-grown arson attacks. The firemen (both volunteers and professionals alike) had been tense for weeks, anticipating a possible invasion from Europe. War had been declared after all and, gas masks at the ready, they scanned the skies. But when the first glow of fire-light filled their horizon, they missed it. There hadn't been any sounds of exploding bombs, any anti-aircraft fire, any aircraft for that matter. So when the alarm was finally raised the firemen were startled. Having discounted the possibility of home fires, some precious minutes were lost.

At first there were all sorts of theories. Some thought it was a glow from a passing ship that had forgotten to black out its lights. Others thought the lighthouse had accidentally started turning. The firemen switched on the radio in case an important bulletin was being issued. The ARPs always contacted them by telephone but the telephone remained silent. So even the sight of Mr Selwyn Maudsley hurrying down the high street didn't alarm them. Everyone knew Mr Selwyn Maudsley was involved in costal defence of some kind. It took an ARP from Snape to come on the line before the Bly firemen were galvanised into action.

'Down by the pier, lads, no, no, the Last Pier, that place, you know. Let's go! Some idiot with nothing better to do, I expect. Wasting our time.'

'This will stop when they get the call-up, you'll see!'

And with a monstrous snort the fleet of engines burst from their building and set off down the empty coastal road. Ringing their bells hysterically, hiding their fireman's jolly laughter, joyous because they had never believed the inactivity would be over so soon.

Later, after the inquest, when responsibility had been established and blame apportioned, the Fire Chief visited Agnes to pay his respects and explain that they had done everything they could under the circumstances. But Agnes had been unavailable for comment. She had been lying down in her blacked-out room. Sedated. All the Chief had was Agnes' sister, Whatshername, the older one. Understandably, the woman had been in shock too. And, no, he hadn't liked her much. There was something cold and watchful about her. When the Chief had explained that they had done everything they could, she merely stood there eyeing him.

'Yes, we know that. We were present at the inquest, if you remember.'

The chief, feeling like a small boy caught out, explained that he had merely wanted to convey a word or two of sympathy to the mother.

'You feel guilty, I expect,' the woman had said.

The chief had said that no, this wasn't why he had come. The inquest had exonerated his men. They had set off as soon as the call came through.

Kitty Maudsley had lowered her eyes demurely but not before the Chief had seen the look in them. It was clear he wasn't welcome in the house. He left then. But as he reached the door he heard a small movement and, glancing back, he saw the younger sister. He stared at her for a moment, trying to remember her name. She stared back palely. He remembered noticing she had extraordinarily large eyes. Of a colour he had never seen before. Hesitating, wanting to say something, unable to think what comfort he might offer her, he smiled. But a voice called her and she vanished.

'My niece,' the woman Kitty Maudsley said in response to his enquiring glance.

He left then, but the story and the girl's expression would haunt the Chief for the rest of his life.

However, all of this was still in abeyance when Cecily and Tom (cycling, each with their jar of glow-worms on the handlebars) turned onto the coast road. Agnes' shock, the Fire Chief's guilt, the fire itself and what came in its wake, were still to come. The airborne Confetti War was still at the planning stage, Selwyn was still a free man. That night the children rode the dark road of innocence-about-to-be-lost. Innocence played a tune that night. It was a waltz they were all dancing but nobody realised it was the last waltz.

In the bedroom that Cecily had shared with her sister for the last time, a note lay under a pillow.

A note that was never delivered.

Darling Robert can we meet at the Last Pier instead of the Tower? (The bit that's boarded up.) I fear we have been overheard and I might be followed.

A billet-doux that he never got.

Robert Wilson, aka Captain Pinky, engaged in a clandestine arrangement with Rose, was in blissful ignorance of the change of the venue. He would stay where he was for almost an hour when the sudden sight of Selwyn seen through binoculars, followed by the flare of light in the sky, would worry him and send him hurrying towards the old, dangerous part of the pier.

A queer, shivery feeling in the pit of his stomach made him wish he had dealt with that loose cannon Maudsley sooner, caught him before he could do more damage.

The stench of Premonition filled his nose.

The taste of Terror was in his mouth.

The stain of Guilt began to appear on his body.

There were two courses of action left to Cecily and Tom. Which one should they take? Neither had ever played roulette so it was hardly surprising they got the rules mixed up.

'There he is!' Tom said.

Pinky's car was parked by the Martello tower, on the coast road, a little outside the town. And he was walking towards the Ness.

Perhaps he had a boat and he intended to sail to Germany like a pirate on the high seas?

Perhaps he wanted to capture Rose and take her hostage?

It was obvious to Cecily and Tom that they would have to rescue Rose. But where *was* Rose? And for that matter, Selwyn?

'Let's follow Pinky,' Tom commanded. 'He'll lead us to your sister. But let's stick to the road. He'll see us if we go the beach way.'

Cecily, who had begun to take off her socks, stopped and put them on again.

History began to unfold.

What are they up to now? Bellamy wondered with interest, tailing them from a distance.

A tail following a tail.

All behind like a cow's tail.

A cow, overreaching itself, in a universe where no jumpable moon would shine.

When the police, the *ordinary* beat-bobby, not someone from the army or the ARP or anyone connected with the War Effort, knocked on the front door of Palmyra House in the early hours of Monday morning, Agnes awoke to find a car was parked at an angle outside the house. Stumbling to the front door, she saw in fact there was more than one car.

Selwyn was led out of one. *Led* out?

Then when Agnes Maudsley heard her husband's voice uttering words no mother expects to hear, something of their meaning penetrated her sleep-destroyed brain. Understanding swelled in her throat and struggled to be let out. It overflowed in a stream of vomit through her mouth and nose. Its sound wasn't all that loud but the snuffle and choke of it was one that Cecily would remember. In Cecily's head (at least) the sound was more frightening *because* of its quietness. Standing beside Robert, never-again-to-be-Captain-Pinky-Wilson, Cecily remained silent, answering only those questions put to her.

Agnes did not remember the way Robert Wilson talked to her – softly and with something-more-than-concern in his voice. She did not remember how she had called him Captain Pinky in a voice that had Rose's jauntiness within it. Nor did she respond to Cecily's look of surprise as she tugged at her hand and tried to make her see that Pinky was a rude name. Agnes didn't seem to notice any of this.

Much later, after the Wake was over and the mess was outwardly beginning to be cleared up, Agnes fell into a drug-induced sleep and would wake to what Cecily would later privately call her After-Rose dreams. Agnes never remembered how, when she woke from these dreams, she beat people up. People like Pinky Wilson when he visited. And her sister Kitty. The only surprising thing in all of this was that she never thought of beating up Cecily.

Never.

The image of her daughter/stepdaughter, Cecily, seemed to have dropped off the edge of her horizon.

When she woke up from these drug-soaked dreams Agnes always seemed to be living in another time, neither before nor after the war, just another time entirely. The ARP wardens were constantly reminding Cook to pull down the blackout blinds that Agnes forgot. Mad Mrs Maudsley, was how the ARP referred to Agnes.

It would be possible to deduce from all of this that the war passed Agnes by and saved her from thinking of its horror by Rose's death. One unspeakable thing cancelling another. A silver lining in the otherwise black cloud her life had become.

On one occasion, Cecily later heard, Agnes answered the door to the vicar and in a split second of hideous rage she had attacked him, too, scratching his face, drawing blood, until thankfully, Cook had dragged her away and called the doctor. The vicar had fled as though the devil was on his tail but when the doctor questioned Agnes she had shaken her head, puzzled. All she knew was that she remembered the vicar from some funeral she had once attended. The doctor had given her a shot of morphine to take away the muddle in her head and, looking at her with genuine sadness, he too had left. Instructing Cook to call him immediately if anything like this happened again.

'Poor woman,' he murmured, shaking his head, picking up his hat and leaving on his bicycle.

The world, meanwhile, was involved in unspeakable events. Poland had lost the fight, Warsaw had surrendered, while here on the doorstep there seemed to have been a fifth column in the hatching. It was hard for a simple country doctor to explain that while mayhem raged all over Europe he could still feel an unbearable sorrow at having to write the death certificate for a young girl who, sixteen years before, he had delivered with his own hands.

Maybe the time had come to drop a million propaganda leaflets to the German people in a confetti war.

Neither the doctor, nor Agnes, nor Cook, nor Kitty, nor even Selwyn in his unopened letters from jail mentioned Lucio Molinello.

This was because:

The doctor had not heard The Story.

Agnes was too far inside a different world.

Selwyn had no knowledge of anything outside the prison walls.

Cook had forgotten all about it.

And Cecily, the Champion of Overheard Things, was too far away and too removed to question this aberration.

Suggesting that the only kind of significant Bliss was the one called Ignorance.

25

I WAS A FOOL to have come, thought Cecily, grief exploding again and again. What good is there in remembering? Pouring herself a glass of water, her clothes now dry, she went outside again. The pale after-rain sun slipped behind a cloud as the watcher who had observed her so patiently walked up to the house. In the dampness of the late afternoon he had an air of mourning. The day, having stolen his shadow, was now shaking him with its avalanche of memories. He hesitated, his hand hovering on the lock. Then, making up his mind, the watcher turned from the house and followed Cecily, instead.

Having found the spot where history lay in rotting boxes, Cecily did not know what came next. She had brought no flowers. What use were flowers to the dead? She'd never given them flowers in life, why start now? Nor was she the sort to clear the ground of weeds and rubbish. All around she noticed newer graves crowned by newer, garish offerings, resting on the mounds of freshly turned earth. At least two centuries lay sleeping in the churchyard.

In Loving Memory. What did you write if your memory wasn't loving? Or not even a proper memory?

In Confused Memory?

Or

In Small Fragments of Memory?

Perhaps.

Agnes had wanted her daughter buried in the grounds of St. Mary's Church. She had married Selwyn there and now she wanted God to witness what happened to the union he had blessed. In the graveyard, two yew trees of enormous height bent towards each other sharing gossip. They were well fed from the ground and watered by constant marshland rains. A few roses grew indifferently for the harsh winds had destroyed most of their flush.

Lying against the wall was a memorial plaque dedicated to all who had fallen in the war. Cecily saw Joe's name in gold letters.

Joe.

Representing the Maudsleys.

Joe, husband of Franca for only three weeks. Arriving on leave, blown to smithereens in Dunkirk afterwards.

There was no one about. Neglect flourished around the yews. Rain was threatening once again and summer seemed to have fled. She went inside the church. The watching stranger followed slowly behind. Once, a century before, a similar church had stood further up the coast. But bit by bit the sea had claimed it for its own and now all that was left were fifty-two bells beneath the waves. St Mary's of Bly had been built in a similar style, pebble by skilful pebble, in the hope that memory at least would not die. One day, many years hence, Britannia would again be forced to admit defeat and leave the sea to its own destructive devices. And this beautiful land, with its Martello towers and hidden underground bunkers built to look like pagodas, would lie in neglected sea-rot.

In the church the light stained by glass fell on the high altar, while fresh flowers left traces from another, more recent summer funeral. A box for offerings stood empty beside a few flickering candles. A font devoid of water waited to be blessed. There was no one sitting on the polished pews but Christ was ever present. In wood and gold if not in flesh. His mother, her blue sash represented by a flick of paint, carried an image of her son. Both mother and child stared at Cecily with mild curiosity in their eyes.

'At the heart of my life,' the Mother of God told Cecily, speaking directly to her 'is a murder. There's no getting away from it.'

Cecily noticed the statue spoke with an Italian accent.

'They tell the story, everywhere,' the voice confided. 'All over the world. Though not always from my perspective.'

She laughed. Cecily had never heard a statue laugh before. It was, in a sense, a cynical laugh. There was a pause during which the tide rolled away. Cecily saw there were painted pearls in the statue's eyes.

The candle flickered. Cecily sat on the second pew. Just as she once had. Other ghosts came and joined her, sitting quietly in twos and threes.

They were wearing old-fashioned clothes, smelling of camphor, their faces bathed in sepia light.

'We don't belong in this place any more,' they whispered. 'The lifespan of our story is over. Forget us!'

Cecily looked up at the wooden rafters where twenty-nine years ago voices had been raised in song.

'The first sorrow that has come to our land,' the vicar had said.

In spite of himself he had given Cecily a look. Pure evil, he had admitted to Aunt Kitty later. Cecily knew, she had overheard.

The rafters looked down at her, now. They reported that a shell fired immediately before the Blitz had just missed striking the spire. Something good happened, then.

The Mother of God, ignoring all the ghosts, told Cecily that repetition was the essence of storytelling. No matter how many retellings, it would never lose its power.

'Love,' she said, with certainty, 'has an eternal flame.'

Holding her son, watching him, powerless to change the narratives other people attributed to him, he remained, nevertheless, her story, she continued. Growing, leaving, going his own way, like an adolescent, misinterpreted, given speech bubbles to suit the whims of other men, still he had remained her son until the end. Entranced, Cecily listened.

From somewhere the scent of frankincense interrupted the smell of the sea.

Then, unexpectedly, sitting in the church now filled with light, Cecily became acutely aware of another presence behind her. Human, not celestial; flesh not spirit. She heard footsteps on tiles and the creaking of the pew behind her. She had a sudden clear insight but dared not turn round. Her face flushed delicately. My God, she thought, swallowing her fear, not knowing what she should do. She was frightened in case she had got it wrong. So she stared unblinkingly at the candle flame, its centre as blue as a pair of eyes from long ago.

Can love mutate, she asked herself? Was it wrong if it did? Was it wrong to look for love amongst the ashes? She was that dreadful thing, a rich woman unable to gather moss.

Sitting in the second pew in the church beside the sea these twenty-nine long years later, she remembered all of this as though it were unsteady footage shot with a hand-held camera.

A moving picture on old 35mm film. In vivid colour. Accidentally tinted in a piercing, acid blue.

Blue.

Blue like her sister's eyes.

Blue like the room in which her father had bedded her mother.

Blue like all the bluebirds Cecily had never seen.

The Mother of God watched Cecily as she sat on the second pew. She could not offer any comfort because she was stuck on her pedestal and could not move. She was a handicapped Mother, flawed like all mothers, everywhere.

Behind her, Cecily felt rather than saw the stranger move slightly. Her heart missed a beat and her hands began to shake. She was *certain* she knew who it was. But why was he here? Had he followed her across the beach? The heat that had started up on her face now increased. She was too petrified to move in case the sea had finally arrived to drown her.

There was nothing else for it.

Plucking up courage, Cecily turned and saw who it was that waited so patiently for her.

It was *Carlo!*

As still as a waterbird at rest.

Something caught in Cecily's throat, something else stole her voice.

She felt faint.

Why was he here? How had he found her?

And the sky outside turned a delicate blue like a curlew's egg in spring.

There were now two candles in the rack.

Dripping wax, like tears.

Cecily and Carlo stood staring at them. Anything was better than looking at each other.

The Curate walked in smiling bland words of welcome.

'Are you from this parish?' he asked and when they didn't answer, added, 'Welcome, anyway. The church is always open.'

The Curate knew the telltale signs of pain even when it was well hidden. He kept a slight smile on his face. Business as usual, it seemed to say.

Cecily and Carlo were silent. Then, without a word they turned as one and walked down the aisle. Towards the open door and the sea where a squadron of seagulls, white against the tender summer air, docked, all together, near a fishing boat. And where the remains of a tattered pier could still be seen faintly in the distance, still standing, though only just, on jauntily corroded legs.

26.

HISTORY HAD RETURNED when it was least expected, showing a gentler side. Mellowed over time, it was preparing to tell its tale. Cecily looked at Carlo and looked away, again. What she saw had the force to drown her.

Carlo was wearing dark glasses even though there was hardly any sun. Together they walked without a word towards Palmyra House. Cecily tall and willowy, wearing a violet cardigan that unintentionally matched the colour of her almond-shaped eyes, and a primrose yellow dress, a shade she had always loved. Her face was pale, her dimple deep even in repose, her mouth soft and vulnerable. Carlo saw all of this only dimly. She saw he carried the white stick of the partially sighted. But, perhaps because of the faintness of his vision, what little he did see struck him even more forcefully. Cecily had grown up.

It was soft weather with the quality of a hallucination. Cecily brought herself back across decades. When she smiled at him he was dazzled. Light and shadow raced across the land. Neither spoke but they walked side by side along the footpath towards the house. Cecily did not help him. Carlo seemed to know by touch every bump in the rough ground. Questions he had asked himself for years were surfacing and clamouring to be asked while conversely, she had become tongue-tied.

They were back, both of them; and the year was 1939, again.

All across Europe uniformed soldiers marched to the rhythm of an old terror. The dead piled high, naked, shoeless, armless. And one wantonly bombarded town was no different from another unless their individual stories were told.

What Lucio had wanted more than anything else was to take Agnes away with him to Bratto, to his old home, to the woods and valleys of his childhood. To show her his wife's grave in the little churchyard behind the church, the same one where Lucio had been christened. To show her his mother's *testaroli* oven and the fire made of chestnut wood. But history would decide what could and could not be done. History was the pulse that beat on the earth's surface. This is what he had told Carlo.

They had heard the rumours of what was being done to foreign nationals. Germans, Austrians, Jews, even. It was said that a camp was being set up to house them. In a few weeks, Lucio's contacts had warned, an exodus would begin. The men in the War Cabinet were panicking. Not knowing what to make of these rumours, Lucio trusted no one.

'You must be very careful,' he told Carlo. 'You are the one who will have to look after the others if anything were to happen to me.'

War had only just been declared, his uncle was a reckless man. Carlo feared he was walking into danger. And the look on Lucio's face as he hurried out was worrying.

Which was why Carlo had followed him that night.

Something moved in the trees. One small animal stalking another.

Lucio hadn't gone to Palmyra House. He changed his mind, decided to let Agnes sleep. It was late and the younger children were in the house with her. Tonight was her first night without her son. Only sleep would help. So Lucio decided to swim in the river instead. He had no idea that Carlo was following him.

There was an icy current in the river. All other sounds were obliterated beneath the water.

The sound of explosives.

The sound of police cars screeching.

And ambulances bringing stretchers for the dead.

Lucio swam, leaving no ripples. He felt as though a thousand ancient eyes watched him as he went across to the other bank. He held his clothes above his head to keep them dry, the coolness of the water and the river tiredness in his muscles made him unaccountably happy. In the darkness a smile drenched his face. It *will* be all right, he told himself. The war will pass, all that is needed is patience.

Breaking off his story, Carlo began to sing the words of an old song they used to sing as children. Listening, Cecily felt nailed to the spot.

> *Try to remember the kind of September*
> *When grass was green and corn was yellow*
> *Try to remember when life was so tender that*
> *Love was an ember about to billow.*

It was chance that made Carlo see Selwyn cycling towards the Ness but it was curiosity that made him leave his uncle swimming happily in the river and follow Selwyn instead. To Carlo, Selwyn had always been a slight enigma. Even when they had played against each other at the tennis match, Carlo had no sense of the man. In this time of danger, Carlo felt he should heed his uncle's words more urgently.

Investigate everything, trust no one.

There was something strange in the way Selwyn, throwing his bicycle in the grass, broke into a run.

'I was a little like you, in those days, Cecci,' Carlo said.

The old familiar name rocked gently between them.

The tide was going out. Neither Selwyn, nor Carlo following behind, needed a boat to cross to the Ness. There was a small underground alcove at the jetty used once as a storage place by local fisherman to keep their tackle. The council had had plans to clear it out but the war had made them forget. Selwyn waded to the island. From the sea end of the Ness it was possible to see the faint outline of the Martello tower in the distance and also the town's car park. But for that and the white foam of the sea, empty now of ships, there was nothing.

Carlo heard the piercing whistle of a curlew across the marshes.

It was the way, crouching in the shadows, he saw what happened next. He saw Selwyn open the door of the storage space as if there were no time to lose. He saw him search frantically until he had found what he wanted. Carlo was puzzled.

Selwyn turned his torch off and hurried out in the direction of the old wooden pier. Carlo waited. In the barely discernable gloom the structure was a sad sight. A dark, broken place next to a dark, abandoned place full of wind, bones and sighs. Selwyn crossed to the furthest end of what was grandly called the promenade. There was an old boat with oars beached behind the barbed wire. There were notices everywhere full of warnings.

Beware Of Rotting Boards,

Keep Out,

Exposed Wires.

Selwyn walked under the wire and stood looking at the boarded-up building.

Walking back towards Palmyra House, twenty-nine years later, this is what Carlo told Cecily.

'It's where Daddy kept his radio equipment,' Cecily said, interrupting. 'I know now. All his documents were inside. It came out in the papers at the time but I've only just read about it.'

Carlo nodded.

'He thought he was finished if Robert Wilson went there.'

Again Carlo nodded, letting her speak, knowing intuitively it was the first time she had voiced these things.

'And he panicked, I suppose,' Cecily said.

She sounded infinitely sad.

That night the roar of the North Sea had been deafening, Carlo told her, now. Then something had caught his attention, some slight movement.

'I hid in the shadows and watched. It was quite hard to see but I was sure that near the Martello tower, on the road across the marshes, was a tiny light.'

The hated Robert Wilson was looking through a pair of binoculars.

'He had gone there to meet Rose,' Cecily said.

Carlo hesitated.

'Rose was in love with him, you know,' Cecily continued.

She wanted to say more but the constriction in her throat stopped her.

'We thought Robert Wilson was a spy,' she said instead. 'We thought he might kidnap her and take her to Germany!'

'Oh Cecci,' Carlo said. 'You were such a little girl.'

They were both silent.

'Some years later,' Carlo continued, 'long after the war was over, my mother told me she had seen Rose that night.'

Rose on her bike, riding past her old school, passing the florist and the little café with its blacked out windows where the photograph of the King was displayed on the blind. Past the timbered meeting house, the bookshop, the butcher, the baker. Riding fast, past the ice-cream parlour.

'She must have been making for the pier,' Carlo said.

That final landmark of the town of Bly.

An object more absent than present.

And it was to this wretched place that beautiful, reckless Rose went. Determined to make her own future, change it from that of her mother's, but unaware that the future had plans of its own for her.

Fragile clouds had scudded across the inky sky. Assassins lurked in the shadows. Half an hour earlier Rose had set her shoulder to the job in hand and rowed steadily across to the Ness. The tide was in. When she'd reached the old pavilion with its witch's hat for a roof, she scrambled onto dry land, dragging the boat up to be hidden behind the shed. The door opened with a push.

Inside the pavilion a chill crept up through the floorboards. Selwyn thinking nothing of it, thinking his daughter was at the Martello tower, poured his kerosene around the base of the building.

Fear kept father and daughter silent.

Guilt flared its match.

Rose had stolen all the money in her father's study cupboard. It had been the last thing she had done.

At his trial (so Carlo heard years later) Selwyn Maudsley admitted to starting the fire. At his trial he took responsibility for her death.

The Molinellos were not present at his trial. Before it took place they had had trials of their own to deal with.

It was not the funeral, Carlo told Cecily, that he remembered, but the station platform. Men in uniform, knapsacks on the ground, women weeping through their goodbyes. Embroidered handkerchiefs fluttering in the fresh sea breeze.

Goodbye.

God bless.

Write when you can.

So long, cheerio.

All promises are made in order to be broken, he had thought, his mind numbed by lack of sleep.

Cecily hadn't seen him. Agnes, steering her by her elbow with one hand, a bag that looked as though it might break in the other, had been too busy crying to notice him. But Carlo had observed both her and an Agnes changed beyond all recognition. Was it possible she might have gone grey overnight?

And Cecily, Carlo had thought, bewildered by it all, where were they sending her? He remembered shock. Cecily was innocent.

Now as they reached Palmyra House, Cecily opened the door and memories rushed out with outstretched arms. The past exploding like firecrackers in their faces. Carlo saw peeling wallpaper. The patches of plaster showing underneath had combined with damp and rot to give the appearance of a gigantic bruise. Cook, long dead, waved at him from behind the old range.

Would you children like some apple turnover?

Carlo had loved her cooking. Rose used to laugh at the way he wolfed down everything Cook gave him.

'She loves you!' Rose used to say.

Cook had died many years before Agnes. Had she lived she would not have let the house get into the state it did. The walnut tree, struck by lightning four years before, still had a branch that gave a harvest large enough to fill a sack. The original one that Agnes had dragged towards the door before she died had rotted away and been eaten by mice but even now, each summer, walnuts fell to the ground. A smaller leaf shoot was growing up from one of the cracks in the earth. Carlo stared.

Inside the pantry he saw dimly a stack of empty ice-cream boxes with blurry labels. They had been brought over for the tennis match and never taken back. Moving closer, seeing his father's handwriting faintly on the box was very nearly Carlo's undoing. He placed his white stick against the door and sat on the chair Cecily found for him. Sea damp had laid siege to the house. The questions clamouring in his head were stilled by the things he darkly saw. Time travelled past him swiftly. Rose, was what he saw. All complete. Much quieter. A little older. But

Rose, nevertheless.

She handed him a mug of tea. He accepted, confused. The last time he had seen Cecily she hadn't been able to make tea. Then Cecily brought her face closer to his and he saw his mistake.

She was lovely to him. Her slender neck. Her hair. Her small-boned face. Her long fingers, the sadness of her smile.

It was Cecci, not Rose!

We had the experience, Cecily was thinking, wondering where she had read these words, *but we misunderstood the meaning*.

Carlo saw that the questions forming on her lips needed to be addressed.

Yes, he had lost the sight of one eye.

Yes, after the war. Back in Genova where he had gone to find out what had happened to his family. God knows his mother and sister had waited long enough for news.

He stared at Cecily. Had she forgotten, he asked, how all of a sudden, she had turned her head that day? Standing at the window, before the guard had closed the train door. No? She had glanced up from watching her mother's face, stopped her pleadings for a moment, and seen him. It had broken Carlo's heart.

He had wanted to come over and press his hand over hers on the glass. Palm to palm. But he had been told to keep away from the family. So he had watched instead.

A small mouth, crying. Lips that would some day be beautiful, already were. Eyes so violet that even passers-by would stop and stare.

She had been such a young girl, then. Now she had become a faultlessly elegant woman. Did she know?

Cecily shook her head, dumbstruck. *Faultless?*

Her sister's mouth. Only there was hurt there, too.

Goodbye Cecily, goodbye.

It had been the last time he had seen her.

Afterwards, when the train disappeared into the green tunnel on its coast-hugging journey, taking the army and the navy and

Cecily with it, the station went back to its sleepy emptiness.

He had walked back slowly, avoiding the main road, not wanting to see Agnes, not wanting to attract attention to himself. Everyone had known about Rose's death. The local newspaper had been so interested that for a while, a few weeks or so, Rose had become more important than the British Expeditionary Force. The death of a hundred and fifty-eight thousand men was easier to ignore than one young English girl killed by her own father. The court case was about to commence. The Allied Effort was not in the same sensational league.

Had he known what was waiting for him at home Carlo might have taken longer to get there.

27.

WHEN HE RETURNED home Carlo found the mayhem had already begun. Lucio had been arrested.

'Yes, Lucio!'

'What?' Cecily asked aghast. 'What had *he* done?'

The view back in 1939 was confused.

'He was an Italian, wasn't he?' Carlo said, his hands making a simple gesture. 'They took him away. I tried to get them to take me. I felt it was all my fault.'

Cecily stared. Never had she heard anyone else say such words.

Things far beneath the surface of the earth had begun to move.

Carlo waited. Giving her time to catch her breath, to speak if she wanted to. Then he told her.

'They took him away in a car like a thief. Oh the policeman was friendly enough. We all knew him, you see. He used to come to the ice-cream parlour with his two daughters.'

Cecily covered her mouth with her hand and Carlo nodded.

'Yes. The man told my father he was only doing his duty.'

Lucio didn't need to pack a bag. It was just a formality, they'd been told. Lucio had taken out a packet of cigarettes and stuck an unlit one between his lips. Then he grabbed his hat and put it on his head at an angle. Carlo remembered thinking his uncle looked like a gangster.

'In spite of ourselves, we smiled,' Carlo told Cecily. 'I remember him telling us *Torno presto!*, back soon. Then, two days later it was the turn of my father.'

The same policeman, but this time he'd brought along two others.

'We, my mother, Franca and I, were the only ones left in the shop.'

The police knocked on the door, politely.

'Again they told us it was just a routine. As if my father went to the police station every day.'

This time it was a different matter.

'My father asked about his brother but the policeman shook his head and said he had no information. But they asked my father to pack a small overnight bag. Just in case they were delayed. I remember my mother crying out, asking what my father had done.'

'What did the police say?' Cecily asked in a whisper.

'Nothing! He said my father hadn't done anything as far as he knew. Actually the man looked really upset. And he called my mother "madam". He'd never called her that before. He told her he was just obeying orders. And he wouldn't look at any of us. My father asked my mother for his passport. I saw her hand shaking as she gave it to him. But she kept a brave face. It was Franca who burst into tears.'

Carlo swallowed.

'My father turned to us all. I remember it so clearly. It was as though a piece of sky had fallen to the ground. It was like those old Italian fairy tales our mother used to tell us when we were small. I swear I heard a cock crowing. My father took my head in his hands and kissed me. Then he held my mother and my sister in his arms.

Non piangere! Non piangere! he told us. *Andrà tutto bene!* Don't cry, don't cry. Everything will be all right! He told me to help my brothers to look after the shop. He would be back very soon, he told us. We never saw him again.'

'And Lucio?'

'We never saw him again either.'

When the older boys came home they were outraged by what had happened and went to the police station to find out what was going on.

'My mother begged them to be careful. She sent clean shirts and a food parcel with them. She was worried they would be missing her cooking. So she packed some spaghetti and a little cheese and a *sugo*. She packed home-made biscotti and, fool-ishly, a small bottle of wine. For years we wondered if the wine was what did it.'

Cecily stared at Carlo, wordlessly. He shook his head. His brothers had vanished too.

'*Non piangere! Non piangere! Andrà tutto bene!*'

That night the moon was shaped like a scythe. The cock, Carlo remembered, crowed all night, delivering its tale of betrayal. Death was hiding everywhere. Behind closed doors, in the bushes, on other people's land.

'It was years before we found out what had actually hap-pened,' he told Cecily.

But by then their life had taken on the colours of a nightmare.

In the little sleepy town of Bly, not built for such matters, word went around as quickly as the fire that had cremated Rose. Soon everyone knew what had happened and there were some who tried to exorcise their fears by being supportive. For a few weeks the shop filled up. But that didn't last long. Fear and fire are equally panic-inducing. And the War was Here and Now.

The papers had nothing much to report. The war was a balloon that had been inflated to breaking point and now was deflating slowly. The ARPs yawned. Without Selwyn to lead them, they too were slacking.

Besides, no one knew what to think of Selwyn, Carlo told his daughter, speaking as gently as he could.

An empty box was what some said of the man.

Others thought there was plenty in the box but that it was hidden from view.

Maybe.

There wasn't any hard or fast opinion. The truth was Selwyn was neither liked nor disliked. He was the unknown.

A man uncertain of his patriotism, perhaps?

Made bitter against his own people because of the death of a brother?

Unstable, was possibly the best word for him. Or even an idealist who took the wrong fork in the road.

No one had known about his inner life.

So the town felt hit by a stun gun of unexplained events and the newspapers, seeing their chance, had a bit of a flutter on the subject. Speculation became a distraction for a time.

The town continued to black its nights out. The ARP's whistle was still heard, shrill as a quarrelsome bird, and the general opinion was that the war had to be endured if not cured. And although everyone knew about the *way* in which Rose had died and also *who* had killed her there wasn't anything anyone could do about it.

'It was years,' Carlo told Cecily, 'before any of us knew the UN-official story.'

'The one that *still* hasn't been written in any history book?'

'Yes. The one still talked about in secret.'

It had been separate from the main events, a story of a panic in high places.

A ship designed by fools, that involved a man with many names.

'Some of them forbidden by Agnes Maudsley,' said Cecily.

A clumsy judgment, a mistaken identity. A woman betrayed and an unlikely love, so strong it would last forever.

A carelessness that cost twenty thousand lives.

28.

NOW THE NIGHTMARE was back in force and Cecily was in the centre of it. Reliving it moment by moment.

'Why didn't we see Robert Wilson leaving Palmyra House?' she cried. 'Why? Why?'

Carlo shook his head.

'You didn't know what I did,' he said. 'You didn't know that Robert Wilson was working on War Office orders.'

On that fateful night, earlier on, after he had seen Agnes and before he was due to meet Rose, Robert Wilson parked his car near the Friends Meeting House. He needed to reach the towpath by eight. Darkness surrounded him, no headlights, no lamps, nothing. An earlier accident caused by the blackout made him drive with extra care. As a result everything took much longer.

He passed no one. In front of him the darkened sea moved with only a glint of foam. The tide was almost out. He stood for a moment longer waiting, thinking. Wanting badly to see her. When Rose had heard he was visiting the Italians she had wanted to go with him.

'I know them quite well,' she had said.

He had shaken his head and laughed, his mind filled with horror.

'Not a chance, it's business my darling. But I'll bring you some silk stockings tonight, I promise.'

Instantly she had been suspicious.

'Are you involved in the black market?' she asked, looking at him, consideringly.

He thought then how much she had grown since the beginning of this enchanted summer. And he had smiled because she looked very sweet in her blue dress.

'Robert?' she hesitated. 'It's… all right, isn't it?'

His heart was breaking.

'And why wouldn't it be?'

'You're only worried because I'm younger than you. That's it, isn't it?'

'I love you,' he said, kissing her briefly.

'You're not married, are you?'

He laughed.

'No, my darling thing, I'm not married. Believe me there is no one in the world I love except you. Let's wait until this war is over and I'll prove it to you.'

And he had left her.

'Oh you bastard,' he said to himself. 'You dirty, filthy bastard, Wilson. What the fuck are you doing?'

Within a few days her entire world was going to be turned upside down. That was absolutely inevitable and there was nothing he could do about it except leave her, as he must, to bear the hurt of it alone.

Until this summer he had been a clear-headed man, someone whose duty came before every other emotion. Now his mind was bludgeoned and confused. Did he not have a duty to *her*? Turning, he couldn't bear the thought of being late, of her waiting alone, he drove towards the town. There was still an hour left before he needed to be at the Martello tower.

Mario Molinello was at the back of the ice-cream parlour cleaning out the freezers. Lucio was unloading boxes from the car. A faint, sugary smell hung in the air. A wedding cake looking like a stranded iceberg waited on the counter for collection. There were letter-stencils kept neatly in an open drawer. One sectioned-out slot for each letter. Entering quietly, Robert Wilson peered at them. He noticed there was no 'K', no 'J' and no 'W'. He knew that they didn't exist in the Italian alphabet but surely these cakes were iced for English customers, too? He wondered what they used for the absent letters. Then he noticed the numbers. The number seven was moulded with an extra bar across it. He picked up one and stared at it, frowning.

Mario Molinello came in. He wasn't expecting any visitors. The element of surprise was what Robert Wilson had hoped for.

'Is it your lucky number?' Mario asked, his face breaking into a smile.

'No. I was just wondering about the different way we write the number seven.'

'Oh, yes!'

Mario put down the box of cutlery he had been carrying. He felt Robert Wilson was waiting for something else.

'They come from Italy, that's why,' he said.

'I noticed you have a few letters missing in the alphabet.'

'No, why?' Mario asked, not understanding.

'K, J, W.'

Had he come here to talk about the letters in the alphabet?

'No, no we have them, here. See? They are a different shape. They come from another alphabet! An English one!'

'Yes! I see.'

Robert Wilson looked around for somewhere to sit.

'I came here to ask you a few questions,' he said.

Mario led him further into the shop and drew up two chairs.

'*Vino?*'

'No thank you.'

'A coffee?'

Robert shook his head.

'Do you mind if I smoke?'

Mario went to fetch an ashtray. He hoped Anna and Franca were out of earshot.

'Now that we have declared war,' Robert began, tapping his cigarette on his case. There was a small silence.

'Like you, I was a listener in those days,' Carlo told Cecily.

The light in the room had seemed too bright.

'What does the Italian community feel about it?' Robert had asked.

Was this going to be another conversation about Fascism, Carlo wondered? His father was smiling timidly.

'That is exactly what Selwyn Maudsley asked me yesterday,' he said.

A war had intervened since yesterday.

Lucio, coming in with parts of the freezer, nodded at Robert and went through to the kitchen. Mario waited until he was out of earshot.

'There are some misunderstandings circulating,' he said, heavily.

He looked over nervously in the direction of the kitchen.

'These social clubs we belong to are really only a kind of worker's club. I don't think this is fully understood by some people. We aren't members of any Fascist party.'

Robert Wilson waited.

'For example I joined the club in order to facilitate many procedures.'

'What sort of procedures?'

Mario took a deep breath. He was beginning to get a pain in his chest.

'For example to renew our passports. Anna and I, and Lucio too, we still have Italian passports.'

'The children?'

'They were all born here. They are British!'

'I see. What other procedures does this... social club facilitate?'

Carlo sensed a slight change of tone in the conversation. This man had visited his family so often, was a friend of the Maudsleys, why was he asking these questions?

'The *rimess*,' Mario said, finally. 'The money transfers we send to our relatives. We all send money home to our elderly relatives. Anna still has a mother alive. I have both parents still living.'

Carlo heard his father's voice sounding agitated, guilty even. But he had nothing to be guilty of, Carlo thought. Why is he so timid? Lucio, hovering in the doorway, must have thought this too. Ignoring Robert Wilson, he stepped forward and spoke directly to his brother. Mario frowned.

'Tell him to get lost,' Lucio said in Italian, holding his anger like a gun in front of him. 'We pay our taxes. We aren't Fascists.'

Mario laughed, nervously. He made a gesture for Lucio to leave.

'My brother says the Italians in this country do not understand this business of Fascism. We have been out of Italy for so long that Mussolini and what the Fascists are up to is no concern of ours.'

'Really?'

'Yes. We are all anti-Fascists.'

There was a pause. Lucio continued to stand in the doorway, his hands parting the beaded curtain.

'Tell him to get lost,' he said in Italian. 'We've work to do.'

Robert Wilson turned slowly in his chair so he could look directly at Lucio.

'You know there is talk that the ice-cream parlours will be closed down because of the war,' he said.

Because of the war, thought Carlo. Only twenty-four hours, if that, and already this man talks about it as if it has been going on for years.

'I know,' Lucio said, in English.

Still he didn't move.

'Your government must not panic,' Lucio said. 'We are law-abiding people. We are not Fascists.'

'Of course!' Robert Wilson agreed.

He stood up and took another cigarette out of his case. Then he offered one to Lucio who shook his head slightly.

'You are good friends of the Maudsleys aren't you?'

'Yes,' Mario said. 'My daughter is engaged to Joe Maudsley.'

'So I heard. Congratulations. An Anglo-Italian union. I wish them every happiness!'

'Thank you.'

On the stairs, behind the slightly open door, Carlo continued to listen to his father's sweet, friendly voice and his uncle's anger.

'Goodbye,' Robert Wilson said, holding his hand out to Lucio who turned away at the same instant.

'Thank you for coming,' Mario said. 'And don't worry about the Italian community here. We are all loyal to Britain. Besides,' he added, beaming, 'we are neutral in this war.'

Another pause when a floorboard creaked.

'When exactly did your brother come over to England?'

'Lucio? In 1932. I invited him. We needed more help.'

Carlo felt a twinge in his chest.

As his father walked with the Wilson man to the door, Carlo was certain this was no ordinary visit. This man wasn't interested in Mario. This visit was about something else.

'Would you like a box of biscuits?' Mario asked, timidly.

'No thanks,' Robert said.

He slipped his cigarette case back into his pocket.

'I suppose you never thought of returning to your home?' he asked, casually. 'Just for the duration of the war I mean? You might find it safer in your own country.'

They had moved outside to the front entrance and Carlo crept further down the stairs. The two men stood for a moment in the doorway. The air was clean and fresh and faintly fishy. A low strain of music came drifting towards them from a blacked-out upstairs room. Richard Strauss' Horn Concerto, written for this dark hour. Both men paused and stared up at the sky, listening to the slow sadness of the French horn. Mario felt a jolt of fear.

'Beautiful,' Robert Wilson said. 'Strange how a German could produce such sublime music! You like Richard Strauss.'

It was a statement. Mario nodded. The music swelled and rushed towards its last bars and then there was silence.

'My home is here,' Mario said.

He sounded unutterably sad.

'We are entwined with you,' he said. 'Your history is ours too. We will stand by this country and resist this madman, together.'

He spoke humbly and seemed close to tears. Papi is growing old, Carlo thought, watching Robert Wilson's silhouette as he walked away. He remembered an odd comment Lucio had made recently. He had seen Robert Wilson several times giving Rose's Aunt Kitty flowers.

'He always buys that woman seven flowers,' Lucio had said. 'And I don't trust her either.'

But Robert Wilson was some sort of official. It was pointless to antagonise him.

Unease curdled in Carlo's stomach. A bell was ringing a warning in his head.

'The hunt,' his uncle had said, 'will soon be on. And Kitty McNulty is in the story somehow, you'll see!'

Mussolini was not finished with Germany yet. They were still in danger.

Looking out of the upstairs window, Carlo saw Lucio hurrying off somewhere. There was no sign of Mario. Uneasy without knowing quite why, he decided to follow his uncle, to make sure he was not in any danger. Which was why, when some time later the explosion occurred, it was Carlo who raised the alarm. Lucio, still swimming in the river, heard nothing. Both missed the two small figures, one of them holding up a jar of glow-worms, running towards Selwyn Maudsley. Moments before Scotland Yard arrived.

29.

IN THAT THEATRE of war, with all the world's stage in such chaos, the Lead Man played many parts and inevitably caused havoc.

'The war made fools of everyone,' Carlo told Cecily. 'Everything frightened the adults, they suspected everyone.'

It was hardly surprising the children had picked up on this fear.

The Leading Man, drinking claret and smoking strong cigars, delivered rousing speeches. He commissioned a splendid set of posters that would live in the hearts of the British people forever.

It wasn't his fault that he didn't get everything entirely right. It wasn't his fault if some people died unnecessarily. This was a war, dammit. People died in wars. Only the insane believed otherwise.

When the Leading Man said, 'Collar the lot!' he had meant it. In a manner of speaking.

The Stage Managers took their instructions from him and called for all hands on deck. The file (it was a new file that drew material from the old Black List files) had a new name. It was titled W.A.R. (Warning. Alien. Risk.)

A man was put in charge of Operation W.A.R. A man with several names.

Some called him Robert Wilson. Others Sweet William. Still others (now dead) had called him Captain Pinky.

He had an official code name, seldom heard until now: FINCH.

And a birth name that no one ever found out. Although afterwards he was called Dr Calvino, in memory of the work he had done to stamp out the fifth column, and in memory of a man who wrote Italian fairy tales.

It was considered an honour.

But during the conflict Finch had two important jobs. To find out about the fifth column and identify the man code-named 'Wotan'. In order to do this he had gone to Suffolk where there were groups of Italians clustered together near the Hokey-Pokey Ice-Cream Parlour. It wasn't Finch's fault that he should fall in love with Wotan's lovely daughter. That had not been part of any plan.

After the war Finch was ordered to leave the British Isles for a time. When he returned as 'Dr Calvino' he hunted out Agnes. Hunting was his speciality but he found, on this occasion, that in her presence all he had loved and lost came back to smite him. He reeled as from a physical blow, his face turning pale, his heart breaking all over again. He smiled a smile of infinite sadness.

'I loved her, you know,' he told Agnes, simply. 'She had my love then, she has it still.'

Agnes had nothing to say. Objects danced through the doors of her mind. She saw shoelaces of liquorice and jelly babies beside copies of *Schoolgirl's Own*. What did that mean? Dr Calvino let her ramble on. Better for the evening sun to fall full on her face as it sank for the last time. He understood how the rhythm of life for those who waited at home had been destroyed and he saw himself as a symbol of sorts. The cause of a million displaced people.

'I did not know then, how in only a few hours, she would be dead,' he told Agnes, following his own train of thought. 'I just knew that her face and the scent of the tobacco flowers nearby brought out all my feelings for her, in that last dusk.'

Dr Calvino looked at Agnes for her reaction but there was none. He felt he was speaking to an empty room.

'I shall never forget her,' he said, very softly, a prisoner of remorse. 'She is my life.'

And then he left.

Dr Calvino was put out to grass. Always after that, it was Rose's face he saw in his dreams. It was her unresolved look, the light draining away like a tide, that haunted him so terribly. These fluctuations of emotion drove him mad.

Some things, it seemed, flourished in a time of war. In his diary he wrote,

You win some, you lose some.

He wasn't an original man.

After the war, information, hard to come by during it, emerged from behind the bombed-out buildings. Like revellers after a drunken party, on unsteady feet, Information came sheepishly out of hiding. It was too late to change anything.

By now, the Molinello family, what was left of them, had flown to Italy. The story of Lucio and Mario, Giorgio and Luigi and Beppe and all the other prisoners travelled across the Atlantic Ocean on small rafts of rumour.

This was what Carlo found out.

The Molinello men had been taken to a camp.

Rumour suggested it was in Bury.

They were close enough to be visited, but Anna and Franca and Carlo hadn't known this at the time.

In the camp, living like rats, they sent home letters.

It took two months for the first letter from Mario, destination censored, to arrive. Reading it, horror-struck, Anna and Franca packed a parcel and sent it to the PO Box address.

The next letter to arrive came a month later.

My dear Anna and Franca and Carlo,
I don't know if you received my letter written on December 12...

Despairingly they packed another parcel.

Christmas came and went.

No one remembered it afterwards.

For Anna and Franca and Carlo, grief was the club foot they dragged around wherever they went. They had no idea where their menfolk were.

Joe came home and quietly married Franca in Our Lady of The Rosary. A week later he was gone, and some time after they heard he was missing in action. Franca had no more letters from him after that. Agnes, of course, was incapable of passing on information but many years later Carlo heard that letters from the forces to any foreign nationals in Britain were destroyed. Enquiries came to nothing, all their loved ones had vanished in a bunch; flowers cut in their prime.

In the New Year a few Italian women began contacting each other from different parts of the country. Very soon Anna heard talk of Italian men being rounded up and sent to prisoner-of-war camps around Britain.

The ice-cream parlour closed its doors and in order to make a little money Anna took in sewing when she could. Overnight the town put up a barricade of hostility towards them. It was as if they had never lived in England for all these years. Then in the spring of 1942, Cook and Partridge came to visit. They asked if Carlo might help with the enormous amount of work to be done at Palmyra Farm before the harvest.

Anna hadn't wanted him to go. Franca couldn't bear the name of the place mentioned. Carlo hadn't wanted to either but they needed the money and Partridge and Cook had a look of such sadness that he went.

They never spoke of what had happened. No one was mentioned but Cook made Carlo small sugarless apple turnovers to take home and Partridge gave him rabbit and vegetables whenever he could.

Once, just before the war ended, Cook kissed him and told him he was very brave. Just like Cecily. There had been tears in her eyes. Once too, Carlo saw Partridge mend the bicycle Cecily used to ride. He took it apart, oiled it and then he painted it a brilliant blue. Like the blue robin on the packet of starch Cook once used to wash the child's clothes.

When the war had been over for three months the Molinellos finally heard the rest of the story. They had moved to the village of Grondola, in Tuscany. Further down the valley the little town of Pontremoli was almost unrecognisable. The Germans while in retreat had attempted to blow up all that was beautiful. A medieval church, a Romanesque building that had withstood centuries of earthquakes. Other towns had been flattened too, as had the harbour area of La Spezia.

Only the sea, indestructible and salt blue, remained.

'You lived from one day to the next, Cecci,' Carlo said.

Cecily knew.

Weeks passed, months; years. Suddenly, two years had passed. The war remained in the near distance but you were still in it. It was there, decaying in your head.

The rest of the story came via a stranger passing through Grondola. The man brought Anna a basket of bright yellow *zucchini* flowers, picked and ready for frying. He remembered the ice-cream parlour in Bly. It was he who confirmed they had been in the camp in Bury.

There had been barbed wire,

broken windows,

filth everywhere.

The internees slept on bare boards.

The lavatories were disgusting.

The only water they had came from eighteen cold water taps.

There were 500 men. Each with their own prison number.

'Your husband Mario was there,' the man said. 'And your sons.'

And in amongst the medieval army of lice and dirt was Lucio. Almost unrecognisable.

'I was shocked,' the man said, speaking into an equally shocked silence. 'What were we doing in a place like this? There were Germans there with us!'

This had confused them further.

'What had we done except keep shops?'

The camp's commanding officer finally told them the real reason behind what was happening.

'You are a Fascist threat to the British people,' he had said, waving aside all protest, trampling on their hopes as if they were ants. At that Lucio became incandescent with rage.

'I told you all not to go near Mussolini's social club,' he'd screamed. 'Did you listen? I told you the administration was toxic.'

Laughter had escaped from Lucio like poison gas.

'I told you,' he'd screamed again. 'We are all on a black list of some sort.'

In the camp there was a Jewish refugee. He had been working for the BBC World Service but somehow he too had been rounded up.

Franca and Carlo had sat open-mouthed, holding their mother's hands. None of the internees had heard from their families since the day they had been captured. They were crazy with worry.

'Lucio talked about a woman all the time,' the man told Anna. 'He was crying a lot. And your husband... he was in a very bad way, too.'

And then, summer came at last. There were all kinds of rumours. At the end of June 1940 they were told they were going via Liverpool to the Isle of Man. The government wanted most of them deported in twenty-four hours.

From Liverpool this random harvest of men was taken to the city dock escorted by armed soldiers. All the Molinellos were in this first batch. Since they thought they were going to the Isle of Man by boat they had become more cheerful.

After three hours they were finally lined up and taken outside. But in front of them, instead of a little boat, was a 16,000-ton grey passenger liner called the *Arandora Star*. It was obvious to the prisoners they were being shipped somewhere far away.

Ahead of them and beyond the breakwater lay the sea, the mines, the U-boats, the torpedoes and the planes dropping bombs. The men were panicking badly. Who would tell their wives, their daughters, their sweethearts? When would they see them again?

Shortly before the internees boarded, barbed wire barricades were placed on the promenade deck and around all the exits. The Captain began complaining that evacuation in the event of an emergency would be difficult. But the wire remained.

Lucio was going crazy. He wanted to get a message to a woman called Agnes. He was making so much noise that towards midnight he was moved to another part of the ship.

Finally on July 1st 1940, the *Arandora Star* set sail from Liverpool. It was heading for St John's, Newfoundland, Canada.

The day was calm, the sea grey and grim. Huge seagulls glided in the wind as they left, their hearts crying out.

Leaving, a word so like grieving to them.

On their left was the coast of Ireland. On the right was Scotland. Some of the lifeboats had holes in them and worst of all, what none of them had known, was that the ship had left Liverpool unescorted, with no Red Cross flag and with its anti-aircraft guns visible from a distance. But all any of them could think of were their families left behind.

By now many of the men were crying uncontrollably as the ship zig-zagged its way across the water in an attempt to avoid enemy submarines. They did not know that the German officer who had sunk the *Royal Oak* in October was on his way back through these same waters to Germany. Or that his U-boat had one last torpedo left.

It was fired at 6.58 am and the ship was instantly plunged into darkness. Water poured into the gigantic hole in its side.

The ship was doomed, men were screaming and jumping overboard. The man recounting the story told the Molinellos that he saw Mario leap into the sea. He saw a large board being thrown immediately after him from above. It hit Mario on the head. It was the last the man saw of any of them before he too jumped ship.

'The sea was full of floating heads,' he said.

All waves behave like monsters, when they are out of sight of land. Forty minutes later the *Arandora Star* sank beneath the waters, forever.

'I will never forget how the sea looked immediately afterwards,' the man said. 'Deadly calm, silent; unreal.'

It was six hours before an RAF Sunderland flying boat picked up the SOS and rescued the few survivors.

In the silent room at Palmyra House so many decades later Carlo drained his tea.

'My father, my uncle and my brothers, enemies of the British people? Fascists, us?'

Twenty-eight years had passed away without a burial.

'Their bodies were never found,' Carlo spoke so softly Cecily had to lean forward to hear him.

'My sister had a dream one night,' he said. 'I remember waking up and my mother making us some warm milk.'

They had gone to their little shrine facing the sea and prayed until the dawn.

'*Guarda!*' Anna had said. 'Look, your father is in the sea. I feel it.'

Two days later a small notice appeared in *The Telegraph*.

Arandora Star sunk by U-boat. 1,500 Italians and Nazi internees in panic.

After that Home was the name of a place where he had not been born, Carlo told Cecily. It became a place of mountain streams and filial love.

It was a language learnt in his mother's arms.

A song sung in his father's voice.

A place where he might feel closer to his uncle and his brothers.

His brothers and Rose were all mixed up in his mind. Franca had been too traumatised to cope. She stopped speaking. Both Italian and English. Only their mother carried on, teaching her daughter how to have the will to live.

'My mother is incredible,' Carlo said. 'Her strength has carried us through these terrible years. She is the one who told me to look for you.'

'Why now?' Cecily found herself asking in almost a panic of tenderness.

The words came as a croak from her lips. She was unused to speaking. Carlo hesitated.

'She heard Kitty is dead. She wanted to know how you were. She... we... love you.'

'And Franca?' whispered Cecily. 'How is she these days?'

Again Carlo hesitated. Then he took Cecily's cold hands in both his.

'She had a son,' he said. 'I am an uncle. You are an aunt.'

Cecily was speechless.

Certain things were beyond words.

When Cecily had recovered, she wanted to know about Carlo's eye.

'An accident,' he said, wiping the tears from his face, too.

He took off the glasses and she saw his glass eye next to his one good one.

'I was on the beach in La Spezia with some boys. We were aimless, all of us. An ended war takes all aims along with it.'

They had found two metal rods and some round stones and decided to play golf. Carlo had stood behind one of the boys who swung the club. It had swung into Carlo's face and shattered his sunglasses. Some of the glass had embedded itself into his right eye.

Later, after he had been rushed screaming to the *pronto soccorso*, they had told him he would have to lose the eye. He was just twenty-one.

30.

HISTORY HAD ALWAYS behaved as though it were a flippable coin. You flicked one side over and you found Warfare. Then you flipped it again and you found Life. Neither side made any sense, although there had been plenty of questions asked on that terrible night. It was Cecily's turn to finish her own story.

'What were you doing out?' someone had asked Cecily, angrily.

'How did you know Rose had gone to the old pier?'

'What did you say to your father?'

'If you knew she was meeting someone, why didn't you tell me?' this last from Agnes.

There was no sign of Tom. He had vanished as soon as the police came.

'Daddy…' Cecily had whispered. 'I told him… she was being followed by…'

But then she had fallen silent for Robert Wilson was standing close by (before he drove off in his car to interview Cecily's father).

Two policemen were taking notes and the firemen were still at The Scene Of The Crime.

'You do realise what you've done, don't you?' someone, Cecily seemed to think it was Kitty, asked. '*You!*'

Questions and opinions whizzed backwards and forwards like tennis balls. One-love. Two-love. There weren't any words to describe what happened that night. Although there were those who tried to find some.

'A man constructs his own fate out of his sense of the world,' the philosopher amongst them said.

'What must it have been like for her?' those of little imagin-ation said.

'Our hearts go out to the whole family,' those who prided themselves on fairness said.

'The fault lies with the wife and mother,' those who played the blame card said.

And, 'It could have been avoided,' those with hindsight said.

Agnes was crying. She had to go to the hospital. Something about dental records. Did she have toothache then?

No one told Cecily *anything.*

'My life is ruined,' Agnes again, finally, her voice bloated by tears.

Who had she been talking to?

'You've killed your sister. You're going to have to live with this forever. *Forever.*'

Cecily's thoughts had floated above the cacophony of sounds. It was just her feet that were rooted to the ground.

He did it.

You did it.

He did it.

But where had Tom got to? How could he have vanished, leaving C to face the music?

'Where's Tom?' she asked, in a whisper.

No one heard her.

'We were trying to save her from Captain Pinky,' she said.

No one heard her.

'I heard Aunt Kitty telling Daddy that Pinky Wilson was a bad man,' she said, her whisper getting smaller with each word.

'I was feeding your father lines,' Aunty Kitty snarled, her face close up and distorted, angry tongue trailing spit. 'Oh how I wish you hadn't been born!'

Spit from Aunt Kitty had collected on Cecily's cheek but she dared not wipe it away. She decided in that moment she deserved spit on her face. It was a decision she would never share with anyone.

Things had changed with the flick of a flippable coin.

Some time after, when she had written her own conclusions in stone, Agnes had tried to hug Cecily. Tried and failed. Cecily was no longer a huggable girl. She would grow into an unhuggable person.

Then, at the police station Selwyn would be exposed like a peeled banana before being informed of a few things.

What had happened to his daughter was murder.

The penalty for espionage was death.

He could be hanged.

Sixteen agents had just been hanged in Wandsworth Prison.

There would be a trial to determine Selwyn's fate.

Being in love with your wife's sister was bad enough. Believing what she told you was worse.

Even the German double agents could do better than that.

Thanks to Kitty, Robert Wilson had known about Selwyn for a very long time.

Like Selwyn, Robert Wilson had loved the wrong person. Although Selwyn was given most of the pieces of the puzzle, no one thought to give any to Cecily. Later on she worked out some things for herself. She didn't always reach the correct conclusion. She apportioned blame in strange ways, taking most of it for herself.

She never visited her father, never saw him again after Rose's funeral when she had felt that small solidarity towards him as he tried not to cry. Now she told Carlo, 'My mother was obsessed with roses. Whenever she visited me she brought cushions and scraps of cloth, or cups and saucers. All with prints of roses on them.'

It was the first complete piece of information Cecily had given anyone. She gave it unasked, freely, and Carlo, understanding the effort it took, let her speak.

'She was afraid… she thought I had forgotten Rose.'

Carlo waited.

'She didn't know… the awful place I was living in, like a dark well… It was impossible to think of anything but Rose. If it hadn't been for that stupid game… I went along with Tom. Don't you see?' she asked, when Carlo said nothing, 'I felt… *responsible…*'

Carlo nodded. Yes, he understood how she felt. He saw the well she had been down, he smelt the dark, dankness of it. He too had been close to the ground. Buried alive with Guilt.

'How many times,' whispered Cecily, 'how many times do you think I re-ran that night…and Tom…'

What had happened to Tom?

Cecily shrugged.

'He was sent home, afterwards.'

'Agnes told my mother that Selwyn had been watched for a long time,' Carlo said. 'Kitty was the one,' Cecily said suddenly. 'She watched your family. She worked for Robert Wilson.'

The clouds in her head parted with force. She heard Kitty's voice clearly. Kitty, her birth mother. Talking about her own sister.

'That Italian is having an affair with my sister,' she had told Robert Wilson.

It had been long ago but the words were clear.

'*She* told him,' Cecily told Carlo with the certainty of her library-listening years.

Looking back was dangerous. Hadn't ancient myths advised against it? They were both stunned. The shock rocked them on their feet and threw them towards each other.

'I thought I loved your sister,' Carlo said, slowly. Carefully.

Cecily nodded. Careful too.

'I saw you together,' she said. 'By the lilac bush. At the tennis match.'

Carlo smiled. The smile was as Cecily remembered it, only now there was infinite sadness in the mix.

'You don't know how I regretted you seeing us like that,' he said, adding as she said nothing, 'I thought that was why you vomited!' And then he said, 'It was Bellamy who loved her more. Mine was just a fantasy to compete with him.'

Cecily was remembering.

But whom had Rose loved? Was it Robert Wilson? Or Bellamy? No one really knew. Rose was Rose. She wanted everyone's love.

'My mother knew,' Carlo said. 'She knew how you felt. Wait until she grows up, was what she said.'

Cecily blushed.

'I was jealous,' she admitted.

'Don't be,' Carlo was smiling again. 'You can't be, not looking as you do.'

She had become so used to expecting nothing sincere that a simple compliment pierced her.

Outside, in the disappointing summer light, the day was ending. Tomorrow would be a different sort of day. The flippable coin of history had disappeared for the moment.

There would be photographs published of the people who, once upon a time, had been called *aliens*. Soon someone would decide to build a wing in a museum to commemorate what had happened. People would put history behind glass. Objects like hair, and shoes and spectacles that would end up in museums. Thousands and thousands of them. Millions. Six million, in actual fact.

In a few decades, their stories would be part of all the classic stories about wicked witches and monsters. Stories for after dark. But what could be done about the aliens who had lost their suitcases out at sea? In the middle of the Atlantic?

'No one knows about that,' Carlo said.

Cecily looked at him. She felt she would never be able to stop looking at him.

She felt as if she had fallen through time and into the lives of others.

She felt as though she had been kept on ice and was only now being thawed.

Some things took years to understand. That was why childhood needed to be so long.

'Mine was cut short,' Cecily said.

Then slowly, while holding her breath, she took Carlo's dark glasses off. He didn't object. He had no need of them now that the light was dying. His good eye looked out at her brightly. His glass eye reflected the sunset.

'I never saw Daddy again,' Cecily whispered. 'There was no question of it while I was living with Kitty. And afterwards I couldn't face it. So I never understood what he was protecting me from.'

Carlo nodded.

It was a Suffolk day with only small particles of colour present.

A touch of blue.

A little rose-pink.

Watercolour skies that threatened rain.

A wind that swept the curlew's cry into the west.

Traces of sea-dissolved air.

The reproachful scent of honeysuckle.

A summer rose in a clear glass.

A day so lovely that it felt as though it could turn absence into something more solid.

What happened next had no connection with anything that had happened earlier or at any other time. It wasn't anything that could be easily explained. Words were useless under such circumstances. Carlo saw Cecily with his one good eye and she saw him with both of hers. Three eyes considered the situation and discovered that they wanted something that would have been impossible to have ownership of, before.

What happened then was neither expected nor un-expected, just completely right.

Like two spoons that fitted together.

Or a pod with two peas in it.

Or a ring slipped onto a slender finger.

The thing that happened next was not a fairy story. Neither Cecily nor Carlo believed in them any more.

And how could it be called love when they were both convinced there was no such thing?

But although there was no one in that sad old rose-strewn room in Palmyra House to disagree,

to Carlo, Cecily had grown into a beautiful, tender woman,

while to her, he was all those things she had once believed would last forever.

What happened did so only partly out of necessity.

And what they felt was not simply loss, unspeakable and terrible.

No.

So what harm was there in what happened next?

Twenty-nine years and some days after Cecily returned.

Acknowledgements

I would like to thank Maria Serena Balestracci for her book *Arandora Star, Dall'oblio alla memoria (From Oblivion to Memory)* (2008), which I used extensively in my research into the tragedy of the Arandora Star. During the writing of the novel I also used material from Mass Observation collected during the run up to the war.

Thanks are also due to Caterina Rapetti for her help in introducing me to some of the relatives of the Italian victims of this wartime accident and I owe a considerable debt to Gillian Stern who was the first to read the text of *The Last Pier* and offer suggestions. Right from the start Gillian cared passionately about the novel.

Support also came from other sources – Professor Rosy Colombo, with her wit and insight and John Martin for his delightfully unexpected help. No one has been more behind this project, however, than my editor at Hesperus, Sorcha McDonagh, without whom publication would never have been possible.